CULTIVATION IS A GAME

BOOK TWO

CULTIVATION IS A GAME

BOOK TWO

Kalzara

Podium

Published in 2026 by Podium Publishing
www.podiumentertainment.com

CULTIVATION IS A GAME

BOOK TWO

CHAPTER ONE

Kai and Shen Yu stood before the door to the Sect Master's quarters. They exchanged a brief glance before Kai raised his hand to knock.

A moment passed before a voice called out from inside.

"Enter."

The door swung open, revealing a spacious room adorned with elegant furnishings. At the far end, a figure stood facing the window with his hands clasped behind his back.

Dramatic pose: check, Kai thought wryly. *Now all we need is some ominous background music.*

As they approached, the Sect Master turned to face them. A smile spread across his face, but something about it made Kai's skin crawl.

That's . . . not a real smile. It looks forced. Creepy, even.

Pushing the thought aside, Kai bowed low. "Greetings, Master."

"Welcome, my new disciples," the Sect Master said. "I trust you're settling in well?"

"Yes, Master," Shen Yu replied. "The accommodations are more than satisfactory."

Kai nodded in agreement. "We're very grateful for your generosity, Master."

The Sect Master waved a hand dismissively. "Think nothing of it. You are my disciples now, after all. It's only right that you're treated accordingly."

He gestured for them to sit on the cushions arranged before a low table. As they settled themselves, the Sect Master took a seat opposite them.

"Now," he began, "I'm sure you're curious about your new status as my disciples. I currently have three other disciples. The youngest, Wang Lin, is twenty years old and is currently in the sect. You'll meet him soon enough."

Kai leaned forward slightly, his interest piqued. "And the others, Master?"

The Sect Master's smile turned slightly forced. "Ah, yes. Your senior brother and sister. I'm afraid you won't be meeting them for quite some time. They're . . . busy with important tasks."

Something in the Sect Master's tone made Kai wonder if there was more to that story, but he knew better than to pry.

"But enough about them," the Sect Master continued. "Today is about you two. We must complete the master–disciple tea ceremony to formalize our relationship."

He clapped his hands, and servants appeared carrying trays laden with a tea set and various implements. As they set up the ceremony, the Sect Master began to explain.

"The ceremony symbolizes the bond between master and disciple. The sharing of tea represents the sharing of knowledge and wisdom. The warmth of the tea signifies the warmth of the guidance and protection a master provides."

Interesting, Kai mused. *I wonder if this will have any effect on my System. New skill, maybe?*

The ceremony itself was surprisingly simple. Once the servants had left, the Sect Master brewed the tea using water infused with spiritual energy. He then poured it into three cups—one for himself and one for each of his new disciples.

"Drink," he instructed. "And as you do, focus on the connection forming between us."

Kai lifted the cup to his lips, inhaling the fragrant steam. As he sipped the tea, he felt a warmth spreading through his body. It was more than just the heat of the liquid—there was a spiritual component to it, a sense of connection forming.

A notification popped up in his vision:

Master–Disciple Bond Formed!
You are now officially recognized as a disciple of Sect Master Luo Qiang.
Effects:
Increased learning speed for techniques taught by your master
Ability to sense your master's general location and well-being
???

Huh. That's actually pretty useful. I wonder what that last effect is, though. Usually, when games hide effects like that, it's either something really good or really bad.

Once the ceremony was complete, the Sect Master had them sit down again. His expression turned serious as he regarded them.

"Now," he said, "I'd like to hear about your cultivation plans. What path do you intend to follow? Kai, let's start with you."

Kai paused, considering his answer carefully. *None of my plans are really a secret. Might as well be honest.*

"I'd like to focus on lightning techniques, Master," Kai said. "I feel a strong affinity for lightning, and I believe it suits my style."

The Sect Master nodded approvingly. "A good choice. Lightning techniques can be powerful indeed. But tell me, do you have any interest in particular fields of cultivation? Alchemy, perhaps? Or artifact refinement?"

Kai thought about this for a moment. He had put some thought into this before.

In most isekai stories, the protagonist would probably go for alchemy. It's a classic choice—create your own power-ups, sell them for resources, that kind of thing. But . . .

Kai realized that alchemy didn't really suit his style. He wasn't particularly interested in spending hours grinding ingredients and experimenting with formulas. It seemed too time-consuming and finicky for his tastes.

No, I need something that plays to my strengths. Something strategic, something that can give me an edge in various situations.

"Actually," Kai said, as an idea formed, "I'm quite interested in formations."

The Sect Master's eyebrows rose slightly. "Oh? That's an unusual choice. What draws you to formations?"

"From what I've read, they can be used for defense, offense, traps, even enhancing cultivation. It's like . . . like setting up the perfect strategy before a battle even begins."

As he spoke, Kai thought about the possibilities. *Trap formations to catch enemies off guard. Defensive formations to protect a base. Formations that can alter the environment or manipulate qi flow. The potential is incredible.*

"Plus," Kai added, "I've always been good at recognizing patterns and solving puzzles. I think that might translate well to understanding and creating formations."

From the corner of his eye, Kai noticed Shen Yu's eyes narrow imperceptibly at the mention of formations. The expression vanished as quickly as it had appeared.

Interesting. Does Shen Yu have some history with formations? Or maybe he sees it as a threat somehow?

The Sect Master nodded slowly, a thoughtful expression on his face. "A well-reasoned choice," he said. "We have a Nascent Soul Elder who is a master of formations. Elder Han. I'll arrange for you to meet with him soon."

Kai bowed his head slightly. "Thank you, Sect Master."

Luo Qiang then turned his attention to Shen Yu. "And what about you, Shen Yu? What are your cultivation plans?"

Shen Yu's face remained blank as he spoke. "I am interested in learning both the wind and lightning techniques of the Azure Sky Sect."

The Sect Master's eyebrows rose. "Both? That's quite ambitious. It would be better to focus on one element first. Mastering two simultaneously would be extremely difficult."

"I am confident in my ability to learn both," Shen Yu replied bluntly.

Luo Qiang paused for a moment, then let out a small sigh. It was clear he thought Shen Yu was overestimating himself. "Very well," he said. "Making your own mistakes now will teach you valuable lessons for the future."

Ouch, Kai thought. *That's a polite way of saying "You're going to fail, but at least you'll learn from it.*

"Is there anything else you're interested in studying?" the Sect Master asked Shen Yu.

Shen Yu shook his head. "No, Sect Master. I wish to focus solely on cultivation techniques for now."

The Sect Master nodded, though Kai thought he detected a hint of disappointment in the old man's eyes.

Shen Yu's really going all in on the stoic warrior trope, Kai thought.

"I see," Luo Qiang said. He reached into his robes and pulled out two scrolls, handing one to each of them. "These contain the first level of the sect's legacy lightning technique. The other eight levels will be given to you one at a time as you progress."

Kai unrolled his scroll, eager to see what it contained. As he began to read, a System notification appeared.

New technique available: Azure Sky Legacy Lightning (Level 1)
Would you like to learn this technique?
Yes/No

Not yet, Kai thought quickly. *If I absorb the scroll now, it'll disappear. That would be . . . awkward to explain.*

"Thank you, Master," Kai said, carefully tucking the scroll away.

The Sect Master nodded. "Study it well. Shen Yu, we'll see how you progress with this before I give you the wind technique."

The Sect Master then reached into his robes once more and pulled out two small rings. He tossed one to each of them. "These are storage rings," he explained. "They contain a pocket dimension where you can store items. These particular rings should be sufficient until you reach the Nascent Soul Realm."

Kai caught the ring and examined it curiously. *I already have an inventory system, but I guess this will help keep up appearances.*

"Thank you, Sect Master," Kai said, slipping the ring onto his finger.

"Now, then," Luo Qiang said, his gaze settling on Shen Yu. "You are dismissed, Shen Yu. Go to your quarters and begin studying the lightning technique. I'll send someone to fetch you later for our first lesson."

Shen Yu stood, bowed to the Sect Master, and left the room without a word.

What could the Sect Master want to talk about in private? Kai wondered. *I hope I haven't done anything to arouse suspicion.*

As the door closed behind Shen Yu, the Sect Master turned his full attention to Kai. His gaze seemed to intensify, making Kai feel as if he were being examined under a microscope.

"Kai," Luo Qiang said, his voice taking on a more serious tone, "there's something I'd like to discuss."

CHAPTER TWO

What did you want to talk about, Master?" Kai asked, keeping his voice level and his face neutral.

The Sect Master's gaze seemed to bore into Kai. "As part of our process for accepting new disciples, we conduct thorough background checks. It's standard procedure, you understand."

Kai nodded, his heart rate picking up slightly. He'd been expecting this, but it still made him nervous. "Of course, Master. That makes sense."

"However," the Sect Master continued, his brow furrowing slightly, "in your case, we encountered some . . . difficulties. Our investigations found nothing about your past except that you suddenly appeared in Misty Waterfall Village one day. No records, no family, no history. It's as if you simply materialized out of thin air."

Oh boy, here we go, Kai thought. *Time to play the amnesia card. It's cliché, but it's the best I've got, and quite effective . . . Probably why it's so common with isekai protagonists.*

He took a deep breath and put on a look of confusion. "I . . . I'm afraid I can't explain that, Master. The truth is, I have no memory of my life before I found myself in the forest near Misty Waterfall Village. It's all just . . . blank."

He watched the Sect Master's face carefully, looking for any sign that the cultivator could detect his lie. *Please don't have some kind of truth-sensing ability,* Kai silently pleaded. *That would be so unfair.*

The Sect Master's expression remained unreadable as he studied Kai. After a moment that felt like an eternity, he spoke. "I see. Amnesia is a rare condition, but not unheard of. Especially in our world, where cultivators sometimes encounter . . . unusual phenomena."

Kai nodded. "Yes, exactly! I've been trying to remember, but nothing comes back to me. It's very frustrating."

"I can imagine," the Sect Master murmured. "If you do happen to remember anything about your past, no matter how small or insignificant it might seem, I want you to come to me immediately. Understood?"

"Of course, Master," Kai replied, bowing his head slightly. "I'll tell you right away if I remember anything."

Fat chance of that. I'm not telling anyone in this world about my true origins. Not now, not ever. Trust is a luxury I can't afford here.

The Sect Master leaned back slightly. "Now, there's another matter I'd like to discuss. During the trials, I noticed you possess a rather . . . unique ability. The power to condense qi into physical forms. It's quite remarkable."

Kai shifted uncomfortably. He'd known this topic would come up eventually. It wasn't something he was trying to hide, but he still wasn't sure how to handle it. "Ah, yes. That ability. I've had it since I found myself in the forest. I'm not sure where it came from or why I have it."

"I see," the Sect Master said, his eyes narrowing slightly. "And it's related to a mark on your body, correct? Elder Feng mentioned something about it in his report."

Kai nodded, knowing there was no point in denying it. The Sect Master clearly already knew. "Yes, Master. There's a strange mark on my wrist. I don't know what it means or how I got it."

"May I see it?" the Sect Master asked, though his tone made it clear it wasn't really a request.

Not like I have much choice here, Kai thought. *Refusing would just make me look suspicious.*

"Of course, Master," he said aloud. He rolled up the sleeve of his robe, exposing his right wrist.

The Sect Master leaned forward, his eyes fixed on the mark. It resembled a stylized trident. What caught the Sect Master's attention, however, were the colors. Two of the prongs glowed blood red, while the third was a deep, inky black.

The old cultivator reached out, his fingers hovering just above Kai's skin. "May I?" he asked.

Kai nodded, knowing again that it wasn't a request.

"Fascinating," the Sect Master murmured as his fingers gently traced the mark. "I've never seen anything quite like this. The two red prongs and one black . . . Does this coloration have any significance that you're aware of?"

Kai shook his head. "No, Master. I don't know what it means or why it's colored that way."

"Has it changed at all?"

Kai hesitated for a moment, then decided to share a bit more information—it's not like it was something he could hide. "The colors do change sometimes. Occasionally, the prongs turn black or turn red, sometimes all of them or just one or two of them. But I've never seen any other colors."

The Sect Master's eyebrows rose slightly. "Interesting. And do these color changes correspond to anything? Any changes in your abilities or how you feel?"

Kai shook his head. "Not that I've noticed. The changes seem random."

The Sect Master's eyes flicked up to meet Kai's. "And you're certain there are no other techniques or abilities you've gained from this mark? Nothing at all beyond the qi condensation?"

Well, there's the whole respawning thing, Kai thought. *But I'm taking that secret to my grave. All of my graves, actually.*

"No, Master," he said aloud. "Just the qi condensation, as far as I know."

The Sect Master held Kai's gaze for a long moment, and Kai had the distinct impression that the old man didn't entirely believe him. But after a moment, the Sect Master nodded.

"Very well," he said. "I'm going to channel some of my qi into the mark. It may feel strange, but it shouldn't hurt. Let me know if you experience any unusual sensations."

Before Kai could respond, the Sect Master's fingers pressed more firmly against the mark, and Kai felt a surge of foreign qi entering his body. It was like a cool stream flowing into him, probing and searching.

The mark tingled more intensely but otherwise remained unchanged. After a minute or so, the Sect Master withdrew his hand. A look of disappointment flashed across his face before he schooled his features back to neutrality.

"Interesting," the Sect Master murmured. "It seems resistant to external qi. Another mystery to add to the list."

Kai let out a small sigh of relief. He hadn't been sure what would happen if the Sect Master probed the mark, but he was glad it hadn't revealed anything.

The Sect Master sat back, his eyes still fixed on Kai. "Now, I'd like you to demonstrate this qi condensation ability for me. Show me exactly what you can do."

"Certainly, Master," Kai said. He held out his hand, palm up, and concentrated. Qi flowed from his core, down his arm, and into his palm. As it gathered there, Kai shaped it with his mind, condensing it into a solid form.

A moment later, a hammer made of pure, condensed qi appeared in Kai's hand. It glowed with a soft blue light, looking both solid and ethereal at the same time.

The Sect Master leaned forward, his eyes wide with fascination. He reached out to touch the hammer.

"This is . . . extraordinary," the Sect Master said, turning the hammer over in his hands. "It's completely solid, with real weight to it. And you can create this at will?"

Kai nodded. "Yes, Master. Though, the constructs only last for a short time, but with practice it is slowly increasing."

As if on cue, the hammer flickered and then vanished after about six seconds. The Sect Master's hand closed on empty air, a look of fascination on his face.

"Remarkable," he murmured. "Truly remarkable. And you say you've always been able to do this?"

He's way too interested in this. I need to be careful not to reveal too much.

Kai nodded. "Yes, Master. Since I first became aware of my ability to manipulate qi."

The Sect Master nodded. "Excellent, excellent. Now, I'd like you to create another construct. This time, explain the process to me as you do it. I want to understand exactly how this ability works."

Kai considered the Sect Master's request for a moment. *I don't mind explaining it. It's a simple process, and without this mark, no one else could do it anyway. Might as well be straightforward.*

"Of course, Master," he replied. He held out his hand and focused on creating a simple dagger. "The process is actually quite straightforward," Kai began. "First, I gather qi from my core and direct it to my palm. As it gathers, I visualize the shape I want to create—in this case, a dagger."

The qi in Kai's palm began to glow and take shape.

"Next, I concentrate on condensing the qi," Kai continued. "I compress it, making it denser and more solid. It's similar to how water becomes ice under pressure. The more I compress it, the more solid and durable the construct becomes."

The glowing shape in Kai's hand solidified into a sleek dagger made of pure qi. It looked completely solid, with a sharp edge that caught the light.

"Finally, I maintain my focus to keep the construct intact," Kai finished. "The duration of the construct depends on how long I can maintain my concentration."

The Sect Master watched intently, his eyes never leaving the solid qi dagger. As Kai explained, the old man's expression shifted from curiosity to growing frustration.

"I see," the Sect Master said, his tone tight. "And this process . . . it truly comes naturally to you? No special techniques or methods?"

Kai shook his head. "No, Master. It's as simple as I've described. I think about what I want to create, and my qi responds."

The Sect Master's brow furrowed deeply, his frustration now plainly visible. He opened his mouth as if to ask another question, then closed it abruptly. Kai could almost see the wheels turning in the old man's head as he struggled to understand how such a simple process could be impossible for him to replicate.

After a long moment, the Sect Master spoke, his voice carefully controlled. "Very well. Thank you for the demonstration, Kai. You may go now. We'll begin your formal training soon."

"Thank you, Master," Kai bowed. "I look forward to learning from you."

As Kai turned to leave, he could feel the Sect Master's eyes boring into his back.

He's not satisfied with my explanations; he realizes it's a simple method. But that's fine. He understands that without the mark, it's impossible for him to replicate it.

Kai reached the door and paused, looking back at the Sect Master, who was still sitting there, his face a mask of deep thought.

"Is there anything else you need, Master?" Kai asked.

The Sect Master seemed to snap back to focus. "No, no. You're dismissed. Go and rest. You'll need your energy for the training to come."

Kai nodded and slipped out of the room, closing the door behind him. As soon as he was in the hallway, he let out a long quiet breath.

Well, that was intense. But I think I managed to get through it without revealing too much. Now I just need to keep my guard up and stay alert. In this world, you never know who might be a friend or an enemy. But I need to get stronger. Fast. The Sect Master is too interested in my abilities. If I'm not careful, I might end up as some kind of research subject rather than a disciple.

CHAPTER THREE

Liu Wei shifted uncomfortably in his chair, his eyes darting nervously around the room. Across from him sat Elder Jiang, his new master, whose face remained as impassive as a stone statue.

Should I say something? Liu Wei wondered, his palms growing sweaty. *No, that might be rude. I shouldn't speak first to an Elder. But how long are we going to sit here? Is this some kind of test?*

Just as Liu Wei felt he might crack under the pressure, Elder Jiang finally broke the silence.

"I am Elder Jiang," he stated simply. "Your new master."

Liu Wei blinked, caught off guard by the abrupt introduction. *That's it? But I . . . I already know that. This isn't how an introduction should go. You're supposed to tell me more about yourself!* But he kept his face carefully neutral, not wanting to offend the powerful cultivator before him. He opened his mouth, then closed it again, unsure how to respond. Elder Jiang's eyebrows drew together in a slight frown.

"Are you not going to introduce yourself?" the Elder asked, a hint of disapproval in his tone.

Liu Wei's eyes widened in panic. *Oh no! I was waiting for him to say more. I've already messed up!*

"I-I'm Liu Wei," he stammered, bowing his head quickly. "Your new disciple, Elder Jiang. It's an honor to meet you."

Elder Jiang nodded, apparently satisfied with this basic introduction. "Very well," he said. "Now, let me explain why I chose you as my disciple."

Liu Wei leaned forward slightly, eager to hear the reason. Had the Elder seen some hidden potential in him? Some spark of greatness?

"You seem to have a talent with the wind affinity," Elder Jiang stated matter-of-factly.

Liu Wei nodded, thinking back to the strange fruit he'd eaten from the ancient tree during the trip to the Whispering Woods. It had increased his elemental affinity for wind, though he hadn't fully understood what that meant at the time.

"I myself specialize in wind techniques," Elder Jiang continued. "It's a versatile element, capable of both graceful precision and devastating power when mastered properly."

He reached into his robes and pulled out a small multifaceted crystal.

"This is an Elemental Affinity Crystal," Elder Jiang explained, holding it up for Liu Wei to see. "It's a tool used to measure one's elemental affinities. When you channel qi into it, it will display colors corresponding to your elemental alignments."

Liu Wei leaned closer, fascinated by the object. This was his first time seeing such a crystal.

"The crystal tests for the major elements," Elder Jiang continued. "Fire, water, wind, earth, lightning, darkness, and light. Each has its own corresponding color." He held up the crystal, pointing to different facets as he spoke. "Red for fire, blue for water, green for wind, brown for earth, yellow for lightning, purple for darkness, and white for light."

Liu Wei nodded, committing the information to memory. *This is incredible*, he thought. *I never knew there was a way to actually see someone's elemental affinities.*

"Allow me to demonstrate," Elder Jiang said. He held the crystal in his palm and closed his eyes. A moment later, a soft glow emanated from his hand.

Liu Wei watched as the colors within the crystal shifted. The other hues faded away, leaving only a brilliant green that pulsed like a heartbeat.

"As you can see," Elder Jiang explained, opening his eyes, "my affinity is strongly aligned with wind. The brighter the color, the stronger the affinity." He held out the crystal to Liu Wei. "Now you try."

Liu Wei took the crystal carefully, marveling at how light it felt in his hand. He closed his eyes and focused, channeling his qi into the object as he'd been instructed. When he opened his eyes, he gasped. The crystal was glowing with a vibrant green, even brighter than it had been for Elder Jiang. But there was something else—a softer blue light pulsing alongside the dominant green.

Elder Jiang nodded approvingly. "Interesting. Your wind affinity is quite strong—even slightly stronger than my own. And you have a secondary water affinity as well, though it's much weaker."

Liu Wei stared at the crystal. *I knew I had a wind affinity from the fruit, but this water affinity . . . Was that my natural affinity?*

"It would be best to focus on developing your wind affinity," Elder Jiang advised. "But don't neglect your water affinity entirely. Used in conjunction, they can create powerful techniques."

Liu Wei nodded. "Yes, Master. I'll work hard to develop both!"

Elder Jiang's expression remained neutral, but Liu Wei thought he detected a hint of approval in the Elder's eyes.

"Now," Elder Jiang said, "what is your current cultivation method?"

Liu Wei felt his enthusiasm deflate slightly. "I . . . I only know the Basic Qi Gathering technique," he admitted, his voice small. "I haven't had the chance to learn any advanced cultivation methods yet."

To his surprise, Elder Jiang didn't seem disappointed. The Elder simply nodded, as if that was exactly what he'd expected.

"That's not unusual for new disciples," he said. "The Basic Qi Gathering technique is a good foundation, but it's insufficient for true advancement. It's also non-elemental, which means it's not taking advantage of your natural affinities."

Elder Jiang reached into his robes once more, this time producing a tightly bound scroll. "This," he said, "is the Wind Rider's Path. It's the cultivation method I personally use, and now, it will be yours to learn."

Liu Wei's eyes widened as he took in the scroll. Its case was made of polished wood inlaid with swirling patterns that seemed to move if he looked at them too long.

"The Wind Rider's Path has nine levels," Elder Jiang explained. "Each one will push your understanding of wind-natured qi to new heights. By the time you master the ninth level, you will breakthrough to the Immortal Ascension Realm and be able to ride the very currents of the air itself."

Liu Wei could barely contain his excitement as Elder Jiang handed him the scroll. He held it carefully, feeling the weight of knowledge and potential it contained.

"Let me explain the basics of the first level," Elder Jiang said. "Unlike the generic qi gathering method you've been using, this technique will teach you to attune yourself to the wind around you. You'll learn to draw in qi that's naturally aligned with your affinity, making your cultivation more efficient and powerful."

Liu Wei nodded eagerly, drinking in every word.

"The wind is ever present," Elder Jiang continued. "Even in stillness, there are currents and eddies of air. The first level will teach you to sense these subtle movements, to feel the breath of the world around you."

As Elder Jiang spoke, Liu Wei found himself becoming more aware of the air in the room. He could feel the faintest stirring against his skin, the gentle flow as he breathed in and out.

"Once you can sense the wind," Elder Jiang said, "you'll learn to draw it into yourself along with the qi. This will not only increase the speed of your qi absorption but also begin the process of refining your internal energy to match your wind affinity."

Liu Wei nodded, his fingers itching to unroll the scroll and begin studying immediately. He began to unfurl it, eager to see the technique described within.

But before he could open it fully, Elder Jiang's hand shot out to grasp the scroll firmly. Liu Wei looked up in surprise, worried he'd done something wrong.

"Wait," Elder Jiang said, his tone suddenly serious. "It seems we've forgotten something important."

Liu Wei blinked, his mind racing. What could they have overlooked? Had the Elder made a mistake in choosing him as a disciple?

"We haven't performed the master–disciple tea ceremony," Elder Jiang announced.

Liu Wei's brow furrowed in confusion. "The . . . what?"

Elder Jiang's expression remained impassive, but there was a glint in his eye that might have been amusement. "The master–disciple tea ceremony," he repeated. "It's an important tradition, one that formally establishes our relationship as master and disciple."

Liu Wei nodded slowly, trying to hide his embarrassment at not knowing about such an apparently crucial custom. "I see," he said, hoping he sounded more knowledgeable than he felt. "Of course, the tea ceremony. How could I forget?"

If Elder Jiang noticed his discomfort, he didn't comment on it. Instead, he rose from his seat and moved to a small cabinet in the corner of the room.

As Liu Wei watched his new master prepare for the ceremony, he couldn't help but compare Elder Jiang to Master Kai. The differences were striking.

Master Kai would have explained the tea ceremony to me first, Liu Wei thought. *He always made sure I understood things before we did them.*

He remembered how patient Kai had been, always ready with a joke or a story to make difficult concepts easier to grasp. Elder Jiang, in contrast, seemed to expect Liu Wei to already know these things.

But then again, Master Kai was new to being a teacher. Maybe this is how real masters are supposed to act.

Still, he couldn't shake a feeling of longing for his first master's more approachable style. Kai had felt like a friend as well as a teacher. Elder Jiang, despite his higher cultivation level and knowledge, seemed distant and hard to read.

I wonder what Master Kai is doing now. I hope he doesn't forget me. Maybe someday I'll be able to show him how much I've learned.

CHAPTER FOUR

H ey, what did I tell you about hiding?"

Zhi-Zhi froze inside his shell. The booming voice of his new master echoed through the massive cave. With a gulp, the tiny spirit tortoise poked his head out.

"H-hiding is for the weak!" Zhi-Zhi squeaked, his voice cracking. "And the reason tortoises have shells is not for protection but for attacking!"

Cang Long's enormous eye peered down at his new disciple. After a moment, he nodded, seemingly satisfied with the answer.

"Good, good," Cang Long rumbled. "You're learning. Now, let me tell you about the time I single-handedly saved the entire Azure Sky Sect from certain doom!"

As his master launched into yet another tale of his heroic exploits, Zhi-Zhi took the opportunity to look around. They were in an enormous cave, carved deep into the heart of a mountain. The rough stone walls stretched up so high that Zhi-Zhi could barely make out the ceiling.

But what truly caught his attention was the treasure. Piles upon piles of gold coins, glittering spirit stones, and all manner of precious artifacts littered the floor of the cave. It was like something out of tales the ancient tree spirit would read to him—a dragon's hoard come to life.

Of course he's a hoarder, Zhi-Zhi thought to himself. *He's a tortoise from a dragon bloodline. It's in his nature.*

Despite his desire to puff out his chest and feel proud of being a pure-blooded spirit tortoise, unlike his master, Zhi-Zhi couldn't help but quake in fear at the sheer size of the elder tortoise's shell.

Zhi-Zhi knew the significance of a tortoise's shell. A tortoise's shell was more than just protection—it was a symbol of status and power. The larger and more ornate the shell, the more respected the tortoise.

And right now, Zhi-Zhi was acutely aware of just how small and plain his own shell was compared to the magnificent azure-scaled fortress that protected Cang Long.

". . . and that's when I used my Shell Quake technique!" Cang Long was saying, his voice filled with pride. "The entire mountain range shook, and those upstart demons fled in terror!"

Zhi-Zhi nodded, trying to look impressed. But as his master continued to boast, he felt a growing sense of frustration. *Is this how Kai and Liu Wei feel when I talk?* he wondered. *No, no, my stories are more interesting, I can't be this bad. Can I?*

Remembering how Kai and Liu Wei often dealt with his own lengthy stories, Zhi-Zhi decided to try a similar tactic. Maybe if he poked some holes in Cang Long's tales, the massive tortoise would finally stop.

"But, Master," Zhi-Zhi piped up, trying to keep the nervousness out of his voice, "how could you shake an entire mountain range? Wouldn't that have damaged the sect as well?"

Instead of being annoyed, Cang Long's eyes lit up with excitement. "Ah, an excellent question, my young disciple! Allow me to show you the proof!"

With surprising agility for his size, Cang Long moved across the cave. He stopped at a particularly large pile of treasures and began rummaging through it with his massive claws.

"Aha!" he exclaimed, pulling out what looked like a chunk of rock. "This, my dear Zhi-Zhi, is a piece of the very mountain I shook that day. See how the layers are all twisted? That's from the force of my Shell Quake!"

Zhi-Zhi blinked in surprise. He hadn't expected actual evidence. "But . . . but what about the sect? Surely they would have been affected too?"

"Oh, they were." Cang Long chuckled. "But I had warned them beforehand, of course. The entire sect had evacuated to a safe distance. In fact . . ." He moved to another pile, this one filled with scrolls and books. After a moment of searching, he produced an ancient-looking document. "This is a letter of commendation from the Sect Master at the time, praising my quick thinking and decisive action," Cang Long said, his voice swelling with pride. "He even mentions how my warning saved countless lives!"

Zhi-Zhi's eyes widened. This was . . . actually impressive. But he wasn't ready to give up just yet.

"What about the demons?" he asked. "Surely they wouldn't have just run away from an earthquake. They must have had some sort of plan!"

"Ah, now we're getting to the good part!" Cang Long exclaimed. He waddled over to a weapon rack Zhi-Zhi hadn't noticed before. With great care, he lifted a wicked-looking spear from its stand.

"This," he said, holding the spear aloft, "is the weapon of the demon general who led the attack. When my Shell Quake disrupted their formations, I was able to engage him in single combat. It was a fierce battle, but in the end, I emerged victorious!"

Zhi-Zhi stared at the spear in awe. It was clearly a powerful artifact, its blade still gleaming with a demonic light even after all these years.

"But . . . but how did you wield a spear?" Zhi-Zhi asked. "We don't have hands like humans do."

Cang Long let out a booming laugh. "Ah, my young disciple, you have much to learn about the powers of high-level cultivation! When you reach my level, you can manipulate qi to form temporary limbs. Observe!"

With a short burst of qi, ghostly appendages appeared around Cang Long's massive form. One of them grasped the spear, wielding it with ease.

Zhi-Zhi's jaw dropped. This was far beyond anything he had imagined possible.

As Cang Long continued to show off various artifacts and documents, each one backing up another incredible story, Zhi-Zhi felt a strange mix of emotions bubbling up inside him.

On one hand, he was utterly amazed by his master's achievements. Each tale was more incredible than the last, and unlike Zhi-Zhi's own made-up stories, they all seemed to be true.

With each piece of evidence, Zhi-Zhi's skepticism faded, replaced by a growing sense of awe and . . . something else. Something that felt uncomfortably like shame.

"And this," Cang Long said, gesturing to a simple-looking rock with his massive head, "is a piece of the mountain I once carried on my back for a thousand years, just to win a bet with the Mountain Spirit!"

Zhi-Zhi stared at the rock, then at his master, then back at the rock. "But . . . but it's just a normal rock," he said.

Cang Long's eyes twinkled with amusement. "Is it? Pick it up, then."

Dubiously, Zhi-Zhi waddled over to the rock. It was about the size of his own shell, and he figured he could probably roll it if he tried hard enough. He pressed against it with his head, ready to push . . .

And nothing happened. The rock didn't budge an inch.

"What?" Zhi-Zhi exclaimed, pushing harder. Still, the rock remained immovable. "How is this possible?"

Cang Long let out another booming laugh. "That, my young disciple, is a fragment of the Unmoving Mountain, said to be the heaviest substance in all of creation. I carried the whole thing on my back for a millennium!"

As his master launched into yet another story, this one about how he once outswam a legendary water dragon, Zhi-Zhi felt tears welling up in his eyes.

What am I compared to him? he thought miserably. *I'm nothing but a fake, a liar who makes up stories because I have no real achievements of my own.*

But as he watched his master, a small spark of hope ignited in Zhi-Zhi's heart. Maybe, just maybe, Cang Long could help him become something more.

Perhaps under his tutelage, Zhi-Zhi could become a real tortoise worthy of pride, not the sham he currently was.

Then I could finally tell Kai real stories. I wouldn't have to make things up anymore.

"Master," Zhi-Zhi said, interrupting Cang Long mid-boast. "Do you . . . do you think you could teach me to be like you someday?"

Cang Long paused, looking down at his tiny disciple with an unreadable expression. For a moment, Zhi-Zhi feared he had overstepped.

But then, to his surprise, Cang Long's face split into a wide grin. "Like me? Oh no, little Zhi-Zhi. I'm going to teach you to be even better!"

Zhi-Zhi's eyes widened in shock. "B-better? But how? You're so amazing and I'm . . . I'm just . . ."

"You're just starting out," Cang Long finished for him. "But let me tell you a secret, little one. When I was your age, I was even smaller than you are now."

"Really?" Zhi-Zhi couldn't keep the disbelief out of his voice.

Cang Long nodded solemnly. "Oh yes. In fact, come with me. I want to show you something."

With that, the massive tortoise began to make his way deeper into the cave. Zhi-Zhi hurried after him, his tiny legs working overtime to keep up with his master's lumbering pace.

When they reached what appeared to be the back of the cave, the piles of treasure gave way to a more organized collection. Shelves carved directly into the rock held an assortment of items, each one carefully labeled.

Cang Long stopped in front of one particular shelf. With surprising gentleness, he used his qi-formed hands to lift a small object from its place.

"This," he said, lowering the item so Zhi-Zhi could see, "is my first shell."

Zhi-Zhi gasped. The shell in Cang Long's spectral grip was tiny, barely larger than Zhi-Zhi himself. It was a plain, unremarkable thing, with none of the luster or grandeur of Cang Long's current shell.

"But . . . but it's so small!" Zhi-Zhi exclaimed.

Cang Long chuckled. "Indeed it is. Hard to believe, isn't it? But we all start somewhere, my young disciple. The journey of a thousand li begins with a single step, as the saying goes."

Zhi-Zhi stared at the shell in wonder. "How . . . how did you grow so much?"

"Ah, now that's the real question, isn't it?" Cang Long said, carefully returning the shell to its place. "It took time, effort, and no small amount of hardship. But most importantly, it took belief. Belief in myself, and belief in the path I had chosen." He turned back to Zhi-Zhi. "Tell me, young one. Do you believe in yourself?"

Zhi-Zhi hesitated. Did he? For so long, he had hidden behind big words and made-up stories. But deep down, did he truly believe he could become something great?

"I . . . I don't know," he admitted finally, hanging his head in shame.

To his surprise, he felt a gentle touch on his shell. Looking up, he saw Cang Long smiling down at him.

"That's okay," the great tortoise said softly. "Belief can be learned, just like any other skill. And I'm going to teach you."

Zhi-Zhi felt a warmth spreading through him. For the first time, he felt hopeful.

"Now, then," Cang Long said, his voice taking on a more serious tone. "Let's begin your first lesson. Tell me, Zhi-Zhi, what do you think is the most important quality for a spirit tortoise to have?"

Zhi-Zhi thought hard. What would impress his master? What answer would a truly great tortoise give?

"Um . . . strength?"

Cang Long shook his massive head. "A good guess, but no. Try again."

"Wisdom?" Zhi-Zhi tried, remembering all the stories about wise old tortoises.

"Also important, but not the most crucial," Cang Long said. "One more try."

Zhi-Zhi racked his brain. What could be more important than strength or wisdom? Then, he remembered something Kai had once said during their journey. "Is it . . . perseverance?"

Cang Long's eyes lit up. "Excellent! Yes, perseverance is key. The ability to keep going, to never give up, even when things seem impossible. That is what separates true cultivators from the rest."

Zhi-Zhi nodded eagerly. "I understand, Master! I won't give up, no matter how hard it gets!"

"We'll see," Cang Long said, a hint of a challenge in his voice. "Now, for your first task. You see that spirit stone over there?" He gestured with his head toward a softly glowing crystal about the size of Zhi-Zhi's shell.

Zhi-Zhi nodded. "Yes, Master."

"I want you to move it," Cang Long said simply.

Zhi-Zhi blinked. "Move it? But . . . how? It's bigger than I am!"

Cang Long's expression remained impassive. "That's for you to figure out. You have until sunrise tomorrow. Remember, a true warrior uses everything at his disposal."

With that, the massive dragon-tortoise turned and began to lumber toward a darker part of the cave. "I'll return in the morning to see your progress. Good luck, my disciple."

As Cang Long disappeared into the shadows, Zhi-Zhi stared at the spirit stone.

How am I supposed to move something that big? I can barely move myself sometimes!

But then he remembered Cang Long's words about perseverance. This was his chance to prove himself, to start becoming the great spirit tortoise he wanted to be.

"All right," Zhi-Zhi said aloud, puffing out his tiny chest. "Time to get to work!"

CHAPTER FIVE

Kai sat cross-legged on his cultivation pillow, the scroll the Sect Master had handed him resting in his hands. His eyes flicked between the parchment and the glowing message floating before him.

> New technique available: Azure Sky Legacy Lightning (Level 1)
> Would you like to learn this technique?
> Yes/No

He tapped his fingers against the scroll, weighing his options.

If I accept, I'll master level one instantly. A few hours of practice and I could ask for the next level. But . . . His brow furrowed as he considered the downsides. *The scroll would vanish. How would I explain that to the Sect Master? He might think I sold it and leaked sect secrets.* A chill ran down Kai's spine as he imagined the consequences. *These cultivators are nuts. They guard their techniques like dragons hoarding gold. They might even kill me over it.*

He shook his head, cutting off that train of thought.

What am I thinking? I'd never risk my life over something so stupid.

With a sigh, Kai unfurled the scroll. His eyes widened as he saw the elegant Chinese characters covering the parchment. For a moment, the foreign script swam before his eyes. Then, as if by magic, the characters blurred and reshaped themselves into familiar English words.

Gotta love that System translation, Kai thought with a smirk. *I don't have to learn an entire language on top of everything else.*

His gaze fell on the title at the top of the scroll: "Heavenly Thunderstorm Cultivation Method."

Cultivators and their dramatic names. Everything has to be Heavenly this or Divine that.

He began to read the description, his eyebrows rising higher with each line.

"The Heavenly Thunderstorm Cultivation Method is a legendary technique passed down through generations of the Azure Sky Sect. This profound method

harnesses the raw power of lightning, allowing cultivators to channel the very essence of storms through their bodies.

"As practitioners advance through the nine levels of this technique, they will find themselves drawing ever closer to the fundamental truths of the universe. Those who reach the pinnacle of this cultivation path will transcend mortal limits, becoming one with the primal forces of nature.

"At the ninth and final level, the cultivator achieves a state of enlightenment where their qi becomes indistinguishable from lightning itself. They embody the unstoppable power of the tempest, their every action as swift and devastating as a thunderbolt."

Kai couldn't help but chuckle. *Sounds impressive, but cultivators always exaggerate. I wonder how much of this is actually true.*

As if in response to his thoughts, a new System message appeared.

> Name: Heavenly Thunderstorm Cultivation Method
> Rank: Legendary
> Description: A lightning-based cultivation technique. Masters of this method gain unparalleled control over lightning, eventually merging their essence with the primal forces of storms.

"Huh," Kai muttered, genuinely surprised. "Guess it wasn't exaggerating after all." He shook his head in amazement. *If it's really this powerful, I definitely need to learn it.*

Turning his attention back to the scroll, Kai focused on the first layer of the technique:

> Name: Lightning Meridian Awakening
> Description: This initial stage focuses on opening and reinforcing the meridians to handle the volatile nature of lightning qi. The cultivator must master special breathing techniques to circulate lightning qi through their body, gradually strengthening their spiritual pathways.
> Key Technique: Electric Meridian Flow—use controlled bursts of lightning qi to gradually open and fortify the meridians.

Kai nodded to himself.

Makes sense. I'll need to start from Qi Refining stage one, but at least I don't have to completely destroy my current cultivation. The transition in cultivation methods should be quite smooth. The Basic Qi Gathering technique is popular for a reason. It's like the tutorial level in a game—simple, effective, and doesn't lock you into any particular path.

He recalled what he'd learned about the technique. Unlike specialized methods that focused on specific elements or styles, the Basic Qi Gathering technique was universal. It taught cultivators how to sense, gather, and circulate qi without attuning it to any particular affinity.

This neutrality made it the perfect starting point for novice cultivators. They could build a solid foundation without committing to a specific path too early. When they were ready to specialize, they could easily transition to more advanced techniques without having to start from scratch.

If I'd picked a fire-based method or something similar right from the start, I'd be in trouble now. I'd have to break down my entire cultivation base and rebuild it from nothing to switch to a lightning path.

Kai continued reading, and his eyes fell on the description of the first meridian:

Meridian of the Tempest

Location: Crown of the Head

Method to Open: Thunder's Crown—the cultivator must meditate under an open sky during a storm while allowing raindrops and the natural energy of the tempest to strike the crown of their head, gradually awakening the meridian.

Kai's eyes widened slightly. *Meditate in a storm? With lightning striking my head? That sounds like a death sentence.* He took a deep breath, calming his nerves. *Relax. I'm at Qi Refining stage eight. If it's created for mortals, it won't kill me . . . probably.*

As he stared at the scroll, he thought of a new idea. *I wonder . . . If I copy out the technique myself, will the System let me learn it that way?*

It was worth a try. Kai glanced around his room and spotted a writing desk in the corner. He walked over and began rummaging through the drawers. *Come on, there's got to be something to write with in here.*

After a moment, his hand closed around a long feathered object. He pulled out a quill pen and turned it over in his hands with a look of curiosity. *A quill. Of course. No ballpoint pens in this world.*

For a brief moment, Kai entertained the thought of trying to invent modern writing implements. The image of himself leading an industrial revolution armed with nothing but half-remembered high school science flashed through his mind.

He snorted, shaking his head. *Yeah, right. I'm no super genius with the entire history of technology memorized. I'll leave the world-changing inventions to someone else.*

Settling himself at the desk, Kai dipped the quill in an inkwell and positioned it over a blank sheet of parchment.

Okay, how hard can this be? Just . . . write.

The moment the quill touched the parchment, Kai realized he had severely underestimated the difficulty of using such an archaic writing tool. The ink blob splattered across the page, creating a mess that looked more like a Rorschach test than writing.

"Damn it," Kai muttered, reaching for another sheet of parchment.

His second attempt wasn't much better. The quill scratched and caught on the paper, leaving a trail of uneven lines and ink splotches. Kai's handwriting, never particularly neat to begin with, now resembled the scrawl of a drunken chicken.

This is harder than it looks, he thought, gritting his teeth in frustration.

As he worked, memories of his old life flashed through his mind. Typing on a computer, tapping out messages on his phone—it all seemed so effortless compared to this struggle.

I never thought I'd miss homework, but right now I'd kill for a word processor.

After what felt like hours, but was probably only about twenty minutes, Kai finally managed to produce a somewhat legible copy of the first layer of the technique. He leaned back, massaging his cramped hand, and surveyed his handiwork.

Not exactly calligraphy, but it'll do.

He picked up the parchment, half expecting it to glow or trigger some kind of System response. But as the seconds ticked by, nothing happened. No messages appeared, no options to learn the technique materialized.

Kai sighed, setting the parchment back down. *Well, it was worth a shot.* He leaned back in his chair, pondering his next move. *Maybe it needs to be written in Chinese? Or, more likely, the person writing it might need to have mastered the technique first.*

As he mulled over his options, Kai realized he was at a crossroads. He could try to find someone else who knew the legacy technique and ask them to write it down—the Sect Master, his new senior brother Wang Lin, or even Shen Yu once he'd learned it. Alternatively, he could attempt the traditional method of learning through trial and error.

After a moment's consideration, Kai made his decision. *I'll try the traditional way first. It can't hurt to be less reliant on the System.*

He glanced at the glowing interface only he could see. While the System hadn't shown any signs of manipulating him so far, Kai knew better than to take anything for granted in this world.

What if I encounter another situation where the System doesn't work? Like with those immortal treasures . . .

The memory of his encounter with artifacts that could affect or bypass his System sent a shiver down his spine. It was a brutal reminder of how little he truly understood about his new reality.

Before I start training, I should learn more about this world. It's time I paid a visit to the library.

Decision made, Kai stood up and stretched. His stomach growled, reminding him that he hadn't eaten since before the Sect Master's tea ceremony. *Food can wait*, he thought. *First things first—I need more information.*

With that, Kai headed for the door and stepped out into the garden.

I need to approach this systematically, he thought. *Start with the basics—history, geography, common cultivation practices. Then I can move on to more advanced topics.* He couldn't help but chuckle at himself. *Listen to me, planning out a study schedule like I'm back in college. Some things never change, I guess.*

CHAPTER SIX

Just as Kai set off from his pagoda, a white-robed figure nearly collided with him. Kai instinctively sidestepped, narrowly avoiding the collision.

"Oh! I'm so sorry!" the young man exclaimed, stumbling back. His messy brown hair fell into his eyes as he bowed deeply. "Please forgive me, Senior Brother Kai! I didn't mean to get in your way."

Kai blinked, taking in the boy's appearance. *White robes . . . An Outer Disciple. Wait, I know this kid.*

"Chen Wei?"

The boy's eyes widened. "Y-yes! That's me. I'm honored you remember, Senior Brother." He bowed again. "And thank you so much for choosing me as your servant! I promise I won't let you down."

My servant? Oh right, I forgot about that whole thing. Kai had been so focused on his meeting with the Sect Master that he'd completely forgotten about selecting a personal servant. But as he looked at Chen Wei's eager face, an idea struck him. *Actually, this is perfect timing.*

Kai smiled. "No need to apologize, Chen Wei. In fact, your arrival is quite fortunate. I was just about to head to the library, but I'm not entirely sure where it is. Would you mind showing me the way?"

Chen Wei's face lit up. "Of course, Senior Brother! I'd be happy to guide you. Please, follow me."

As they set off down the path, Kai gestured for Chen Wei to walk beside him rather than behind. The boy seemed surprised but quickly fell into step.

As they walked, Kai noticed other disciples in white robes watching them. Many shot envious glances at Chen Wei.

To distract from the awkward atmosphere, Kai decided to probe for information. "Tell me about the library, Chen Wei."

Chen Wei's face lit up at the chance to be helpful. "Oh, the sect library is incredible, Senior Brother! It's one of the largest collections of knowledge in the entire kingdom. There are scrolls and books on every subject imaginable—history, geography, cultivation techniques, alchemy recipes, and so much more!"

"That sounds promising," Kai said. "What kind of access do disciples have?"

Chen Wei's excitement dimmed slightly. "Well, as an Outer Disciple, my access is quite limited. We're only allowed in certain sections, mostly basic cultivation manuals and general knowledge. But you're a Legacy Disciple! You should have access to almost everything, except perhaps some restricted areas for Elders only."

"What about you, Chen Wei?" Kai asked. "What do you like to study when you visit the library?"

Chen Wei's eyes lit up with excitement. "I love reading about sect history and famous cultivators! There are so many incredible stories. Did you know our sect once had a disciple named Yan who reached the Nascent Soul Realm in just three years?"

Kai's eyebrows shot up. "Three years? That's . . . incredible."

"Oh yes!" Chen Wei nodded enthusiastically. "Senior Brother Yan was a true prodigy. They say he mastered all of the sect's lightning techniques before he was twenty. Everyone believed he would become the next Sect Master."

Kai leaned in, intrigued. "So, what happened to this Yan? Did he become Sect Master?"

Chen Wei's expression turned somber. "That's the mystery. Senior Brother Yan disappeared a few hundred years ago. No one knows what happened to him. It was a huge loss for the sect."

Kai's eyes narrowed slightly. "Disappeared? Just like that?"

"Yes," Chen Wei replied. "One day he was here, amazing everyone with his talent. The next . . . gone. Some say he ascended early, others think he might have been killed by rival sects. But no one really knows."

Kai mulled this over. "Has anything like that happened since then?"

Chen Wei nodded slowly. "It has, actually. Every now and then, a promising disciple will vanish. Not as talented as Yan, but still . . . it's concerning."

Kai felt a chill run down his spine. *Multiple disappearances? That's not good.*

"How often does this happen?" Kai asked, trying to keep his voice casual.

Chen Wei furrowed his brow. "It's hard to say. Maybe once every few decades? It's not common, but it happens enough that people talk about it."

Great, Kai thought. *I show off my talent and become a Legacy Disciple, and now I find out my sect has a habit of losing its promising disciples. I need to be careful. Very careful. I can't let my guard down, not even for a moment. And I definitely need to investigate these disappearances further. My life might depend on it, especially if they went missing whilst in the sect . . .*

As they rounded a corner, a massive structure came into view. It was easily the largest building Kai had seen in the sect so far, its sweeping roof adorned with intricate carvings of dragons and phoenixes.

"Here we are!" Chen Wei announced proudly. "The Grand Library of the Azure Sky Sect!"

Kai let out a low whistle, genuinely impressed. "It's certainly . . . grand."

The library was a sprawling multistory building that seemed to blend seamlessly with the mountainside. Its walls were a pristine white, with large windows allowing natural light to flood the interior. The entrance was flanked by two massive statues of robed figures, their hands outstretched as if offering knowledge to all who entered.

As they approached the entrance, Kai noticed an old man in a white robe sweeping the steps.

Odd. You'd think they'd have younger disciples do the cleaning.

"Chen Wei," Kai said quietly, "who's that old man?"

Chen Wei glanced at the sweeping figure and shrugged. "Oh, him? That's just old Shan. He's an Outer Disciple who failed to reach Foundation Establishment. Now he just keeps the library clean."

Kai's eyes widened slightly at the description. *Wait a minute. Old man, seemingly insignificant job, guarding a place of great knowledge . . . This sounds suspiciously like a classic xianxia trope.*

Just as the thought crossed his mind, a System message appeared in Kai's vision:

Unknown Entity
Level: ???   Unable to identify.   Entity's level exceeds your perception ability by a significant margin.

Well, well, well, Kai thought, a small smile tugging at his lips. *Looks like my genre savviness is paying off. This "old man" is definitely more than he appears.*

Curious, Kai checked his map. Sure enough, the old man's position was marked by a large green dot. Comparing it to his memory of the Sect Master's marker, Kai estimated it was only slightly smaller. *So, probably in the same cultivation realm as the Sect Master, but a lower sub-stage. Interesting.*

Kai considered his options. In most stories, being kind to the undercover powerful character usually led to some benefit for the protagonist. And even if it didn't, what was the harm in being polite?

"Chen Wei," Kai said, "wait here for a moment. I'd like to say hello to Elder Shan."

Chen Wei's eyes widened in confusion. "Elder? But he's just a—"

Kai was already walking toward the old man, leaving a bewildered Chen Wei to scramble after him.

"Good morning," Kai said as he approached and bowed respectfully. "I'm Kai, a new disciple of the Azure Sky Sect. It's a pleasure to meet you."

The old man stopped sweeping and looked up, studying Kai intently. After a moment, he nodded. "Shan," he said simply.

Kai bowed again. "It's an honor to meet you, Elder Shan."

The old man's eyebrows rose slightly. "Elder? No, no. Just Shan. No Elder here, young man."

Playing the part well. But two can play at this game.

"My apologies, Shan," Kai said. "I shouldn't have presumed. I'm new here and still learning my way around."

An awkward silence fell. The old man stared at Kai expectantly, as if to say, "Well? What do you want?"

Not wanting to seem suspicious, Kai smiled. "I just wanted to say hello. It's my first time visiting the library."

Shan blinked, clearly not expecting such a simple reason. After a moment, he nodded again.

"Well, I won't keep you from your work," Kai said. "Have a good day, Shan."

As Kai turned to enter the library, he caught a glimpse of the old man's face. For just a moment, a flicker of . . . something . . . passed across his features. Interest? Amusement? It was gone too quickly for Kai to be sure.

Once inside, Chen Wei hurried to catch up with Kai. "Senior Brother," he whispered, "why did you speak to Old Shan?"

Kai smiled, knowing that if his hunch was correct, the old man could probably hear every word with his superior cultivation. "You know, Chen Wei, I come from a simple village. Just because I'm a Legacy Disciple now doesn't mean I've forgotten my humble beginnings. Everyone deserves respect, no matter their station."

Chen Wei's eyes widened, clearly impressed by Kai's words. "That's . . . that's very wise, Senior Brother."

And hopefully, that earns me some brownie points with our hidden powerhouse. If I'm going to be spending a lot of time in the library, it can't hurt to have him on my good side. Best case, it leads to some secret technique or hidden knowledge. Worst case, I've wasted a few minutes being polite. Low risk, potentially high reward.

As they stepped into the main hall of the library, Kai couldn't help but gasp. The main hallway of the library was impressive, to say the least. The ceiling soared high above, supported by tall pillars. Rows upon rows of shelves stretched out in every direction, filled with scrolls and bound volumes. Natural light filtered in through large windows, supplemented by glowing crystals placed strategically around the room.

Now this is more like it. If knowledge is power, then this place is a gold mine.

A middle-aged man in blue robes approached them, a gentle smile on his face. "Welcome to the Azure Sky Sect library," he said, bowing slightly. "I am Elder Jie, the head librarian. How may I assist you today?"

Kai returned the bow as he noted the System message that popped up:

Name: Elder Jie
Level: Nascent Soul Realm

"Greetings, Elder Jie," Kai replied. "I'm Kai, a new Legacy Disciple. I've come to do some research."

Elder Jie's eyebrows rose slightly. "Ah, yes. The Sect Master mentioned you might be paying a visit. Welcome, young Kai. What area of study interests you? Perhaps you'd like to see our technique scrolls? We have quite an impressive collection."

Kai shook his head. "Thank you, Elder, but not today. Since it's my first day here, I thought I'd start with some history and background information. There wasn't much of that available in my village, you see."

Elder Jie nodded approvingly. "A wise choice, young man. It's important to understand the foundations before delving into advanced techniques. Please, follow me. I'll show you to our history section."

As they walked, Elder Jie explained the library's organization system. "We use a color-coded system to denote different subjects. Blue for history, green for geography, red for combat techniques, and so on. As a Legacy Disciple, you have access to most sections, though some areas are restricted to Elders only."

Kai nodded, making mental notes. *This will save time later. No need to wander aimlessly when I can go straight to what I need.*

"Over there is our alchemy wing," Elder Jie said, indicating an area blocked by blue barriers. "And that staircase leads to the formation theory levels."

I'll definitely need to explore those areas later, especially the formation section.

They soon arrived at a section filled with blue-bound scrolls and books. Elder Jie gestured with a wave of his hands. "Here we are. This section contains our general histories. If you need anything more specific, please don't hesitate to ask. I or one of my assistants will be happy to guide you."

"Thank you, Elder." Kai bowed.

As the Elder departed, Kai turned to Chen Wei. "You're welcome to browse as well, Chen Wei. Just stay nearby in case I need anything."

Chen Wei's eyes lit up. "Really? Thank you, Senior Brother!"

As the boy scampered off to a nearby shelf, Kai began scanning the titles before him. *Let's see . . . "A Complete History of the Azure Sky Sect" . . . "Great Battles of the Eastern Continent" . . . "Legendary Cultivators Through the Ages" . . .*

His eyes suddenly locked onto a scroll near the bottom shelf. The title, written in elegant calligraphy, read: "The Era of the Gods."

Now that sounds promising, Kai thought, reaching for the scroll. *If I want to understand this world, might as well start at the beginning.*

As his fingers closed around the ancient parchment, Kai felt a slight tingle run through his hand. He glanced around, but nothing seemed amiss. Chen Wei was engrossed in a book a few shelves away, and the other disciples in the library went about their business as usual.

Probably just my imagination. Or maybe some kind of preservation technique on the scroll?

CHAPTER SEVEN

Kai settled into a chair in a quiet corner of the library with the ancient scroll cradled in his hands. As he unfurled it, a blue box appeared in his vision.

Item: The Era of the Gods Scroll
Rarity: Rare
Description: An ancient text detailing the mythical era before cultivation. Contains valuable historical information.

Kai's eyebrows rose. *Rare, huh? Looks like I stumbled onto something good.*

He began to read, the elegant script transforming into familiar English words before his eyes:

"In the time before cultivation, when the world was young and raw, the gods ruled supreme. These beings of immense power shaped the very fabric of reality, creating all that exists—including mortal life. But the gods were not content with their dominion. Each sought to be the supreme ruler, leading to endless conflicts that shook the heavens and earth.

"Among these warring deities was Anion, a god of wisdom and cunning. Seeing the potential in the mortal races, Anion chose a different path. He descended to the mortal realm and taught humans the first steps of cultivation, granting them the ability to harness the energy of the world—qi.

"At first, Anion used these cultivators as soldiers in his divine army, bolstering his strength against rival gods. But as millennia passed, the cultivators grew in power and knowledge. They pushed the boundaries of what was thought possible, eventually breaking through to the Immortal Ascension Realm itself.

"These new immortals looked upon their divine creators and no longer saw beings worthy of worship. They saw rivals. Having tasted divinity and found it within their grasp, the cultivators turned against their former masters.

"A great war erupted, shaking the very foundations of existence. The gods, immortal and eternal, could not be truly killed. But the cultivators found a way to seal them away. One by one, the gods were bound and banished, their power locked away from the world they once ruled.

"Thus ended the Era of the Gods, and the Age of Cultivation began . . ."

Kai leaned back, processing what he'd read. *Classic origin story. Feels like the setup for a major plot twist down the line.* He couldn't help but chuckle softly. *If this were a game, I'd bet my last coin that some "sealed god" is going to break free and cause havoc. Probably manipulating some power-hungry cultivator to release them.*

Kai rolled up the scroll. *Note to self: stay far, far away from any ancient-looking sealed artifacts. I'm not getting roped into a war against immortal beings, thank you very much.*

He turned to Chen Wei, who was engrossed in his own book nearby. "Hey, Chen Wei. Have you ever heard stories about the Era of the Gods?"

The young disciple looked up, eyes wide. "Oh yes, Senior Brother! Every child knows the tales. They say the Heavenly Pagoda of our sect was built on the ruins of a god's palace!"

"Interesting. And has anyone ever found . . . artifacts from that time?"

Chen Wei shrugged. "I've heard rumors of cultivators finding strange objects in ruins, but the Sect Master always confiscates them. Why do you ask, Senior Brother?"

"Just curious," Kai said casually. "History is fascinating, isn't it? Now, could you help me find a good map of the world? I'd like to study the geography a bit."

"Of course!" Chen Wei jumped up eagerly. "I know just the one. Follow me, Senior Brother!"

Chen Wei led him to a large table where a beautifully detailed map was spread out. Kai's eyes widened as he took in the vast expanse of the world before him.

"This is incredible," he murmured.

Chen Wei beamed. "Isn't it? This is the most up-to-date map of the known world. See how it's divided into four great regions?"

Kai nodded, studying the layout. The world was indeed split into four distinct areas: north, south, east, and west. Each region had its own unique geography and climate.

"We're here," Chen Wei said, pointing to a spot in the Eastern Region. "The Azure Sky Sect is located in the Misty Peaks, this mountainous area."

Kai leaned in, examining the Eastern Region more closely. It was a land of towering mountains, dense forests, and winding rivers. The Azure Sky Sect's location was marked by a small lightning bolt symbol.

"I see other sect symbols scattered around," Kai observed. "Are these all the cultivation sects in the east?"

Chen Wei nodded. "Yes, Senior Brother. But notice how some symbols are larger than others? Those represent the power and influence of each sect."

Kai's eyes narrowed as he spotted a massive symbol dominating the center of the Eastern Region. "And that one?"

"Ah," Chen Wei's voice took on a note of awe. "That's the Great Kirin Sect, the most powerful sect in the east. They're one of the four great sects that rule over the entire cultivation world."

Kai raised an eyebrow. "Only four? What about the Azure Sky Sect? Where do we rank?"

Chen Wei shifted uncomfortably. "Well . . . we're considered a medium-sized sect. The Azure Sky Sect is powerful, but not on the level of the four great sects or the Hidden Clans."

That's surprising. The Sect Master seemed incredibly strong, but the Azure Sky Sect is only medium sized. How powerful are these great sects?

"Tell me more about these four great sects," Kai said. "What makes them so special?"

Chen Wei's eyes lit up at the chance to share his knowledge. "The four great sects are each led by an Immortal Ascension cultivator—a true immortal who has transcended mortal limitations. In the east, we have the Great Kirin Sect. The north is ruled by the Great Roc Sect. The south belongs to the Great Leviathan Sect. And in the west, the Great Tiger Sect reigns supreme."

Kai nodded slowly, processing the information. "And the medium-sized sects like ours? Who leads them?"

"Medium sects are typically led by Enlightenment Realm cultivators," Chen Wei explained. "They're incredibly powerful but still a step below true immortals. Small sects are usually led by Astral Formation cultivators."

Enlightenment Realm . . . That must be where our Sect Master is, Kai realized. *And probably that old man Shan too.*

"What's the relationship between the great sects and medium sects like ours?" Kai asked.

Chen Wei's expression grew serious. "It's . . . complicated, Senior Brother. Medium sects like ours have to pay tribute to the great sects in our region. In exchange, we receive a measure of protection and access to some of their resources."

Kai frowned. "Tribute? What kind of tribute?"

"Spirit stones, rare materials, sometimes promising disciples," Chen Wei said quietly. "It's a heavy burden, but the alternative is . . . worse."

Ah, politics, Kai thought grimly. *Some things never change, no matter what world you're in.*

"I see," he said aloud, tapping his chin thoughtfully. "Could you find me some information on the different cultivation realms? I'd like to understand the path ahead of me better."

"Of course!" Chen Wei hurried off, then returned moments later with a stack of scrolls. "These should cover the basic information from Qi Refining to Immortal Ascension."

"Thank you, Chen Wei. And could you ask Elder Jie for a scroll that has detailed information about the Qi Refining Realm specifically? I'd like an in-depth explanation of the theory behind cultivation in this realm."

"An in-depth explanation?" Chen Wei's eyes widened slightly. "Of course, Senior Brother. I'll do my best to get that scroll for you."

A few moments later, Chen Wei hurried back to Kai's table, slightly out of breath but with a smile on his face. In his hands, he carefully cradled a jade-green scroll case. "Senior Brother, I have it!"

Why is a Qi Refining cultivator out of breath? Kai wondered, slightly shaking his head at his servant's enthusiasm.

"That was quick. Did you have any trouble?"

Chen Wei shook his head. "Not at all! When I mentioned your name, Elder Jie smiled and said it had already been recorded that you would be borrowing this scroll. He seemed pleased that you were taking your studies so seriously."

"Thank you, Chen Wei," Kai said as he took the scroll case. He examined it closely, turning it over in his hands. "This looks valuable. I should keep it safe."

He made a show of reaching toward his ring finger, as if to place the scroll in a storage ring. However, what Chen Wei couldn't see was the blue box that appeared in Kai's vision:

Store item in inventory?
Yes/No

Kai mentally selected "Yes," and the scroll case vanished from his hands, safely tucked away in his inventory.

To Chen Wei, it appeared as though Kai had simply slipped the scroll into his storage ring.

"I'll study this in detail later," Kai said. "For now, let's go through these other scrolls you brought. I want to get a general overview of all the cultivation realms."

CHAPTER EIGHT

Kai settled back into his chair and unrolled the first scroll. As he read, he found himself nodding along. The early stages were familiar territory:

Qi Refining: The foundation of cultivation. Cultivators learn to sense and manipulate qi, strengthening their bodies and spirits.

Foundation Establishment: Cultivators form a stable qi foundation in their dantian.

Core Formation: The qi foundation is compressed into a dense core, allowing for more advanced techniques and the beginning of true immortality.

Nascent Soul: A cultivator forms a miniature version of themselves from pure qi, giving them the ability to fly and extending their lifespan.

Standard progression, Kai thought. *But what comes next?*
He unrolled the next scroll, and his eyes widened.

Astral Formation: Cultivators learn to project their consciousness into the stars, forming connections with celestial bodies. This grants them immense power and the ability to draw on starlight to power their techniques.

Now that's interesting, Kai mused. *I wonder if it's literal star connection or more metaphorical.*

Enlightenment: At this stage, cultivators gain profound insights into the nature of reality. They can manipulate fundamental forces and even create small pocket dimensions.

Creating dimensions? That's some high-level stuff. It's probably the Enlightenment cultivator who created the pocket dimension for the Trial of Endurance.

Finally, Kai reached the last scroll.

> Immortal Ascension: The pinnacle of cultivation. Those who reach this realm truly transcend mortality, gaining eternal life and godlike powers. Cultivators at this stage are considered living embodiments of natural laws.

Kai let out a low whistle. "Well, that explains a lot."

Chen Wei, who had been hovering nearby, looked at him curiously. "What do you mean, Senior Brother?"

Kai gestured to the scrolls. "This progression. It puts everything into perspective. The gap between a medium sect and a great sect isn't just political or numbers based—it's a fundamental difference in power."

Chen Wei nodded solemnly. "That's right. They say when an Immortal Ascension cultivator fights seriously, they have to fight in the heavens to prevent the world from being reduced to rubble."

Note to self: do not *anger any Immortal Ascension cultivators,* Kai thought wryly.

"Chen Wei," Kai said, "you've been incredibly helpful. Thank you."

The young disciple beamed. "It's my honor to serve you, Senior Brother! Is there anything else you need?"

Kai shook his head. "Not right now. I think I need some time to process all this information."

As Chen Wei bowed and retreated, Kai leaned back in his chair, his mind whirling with everything he'd learned.

So, I'm in a world with sealed gods, immortal cultivators, and sects paying tribute like feudal vassals. This is . . . a lot.

He glanced at his status window, focusing on his current level: Qi Refining stage eight.

I've got a long way to go before I can even think about challenging the big players. For now, I need to focus on survival and cultivation. Kai's eyes drifted back to the map, lingering on the symbol of the Great Kirin Sect. *Know your enemy,* he thought. *Or in this case, know the power players who could squash you like a bug if you're not careful.*

He stood up to stretch after his hours of reading. As he did, he glanced at the stack of books and scrolls they had accumulated. "Chen Wei, I think we've done enough reading for one day. How about we take a break and grab some food?"

Chen Wei looked up from his book as his stomach growled in response, causing both of them to laugh. As they stood to leave, Kai cast one last look at the library around them.

So much knowledge, so many secrets, he thought. *I'll definitely be coming back here often.*

As they walked out, Kai nodded respectfully to Old Shan, who was still sweeping near the entrance. The old man gave him a slow nod in return.

Outside, the sun was starting to set, painting the sky in brilliant shades of orange and purple. Kai took a deep breath, enjoying the clean mountain air.

"So, Chen Wei," he said as they walked, "what's good to eat around here?"

Chen Wei's face lit up. "Oh, Senior Brother, you have to try the spirit-fruit dumplings! They're amazing!"

As Chen Wei launched into an enthusiastic description of the sect's cuisine, they made their way to the dining hall. Unlike the dining hall in the trial area, this was a large open-air pavilion. Disciples of all ranks milled about, chatting and eating.

As they entered, Kai noticed several people turning to look at him, whispering amongst themselves. He caught snatches of conversation:

"Black robes . . . Is that the new Legacy Disciple?"

"I heard he impressed the Sect Master . . ."

"Do you think he'll reach Nascent Soul before he's thirty?"

"How will Senior Brother Wang Lin react to this?"

Chen Wei tugged on Kai's sleeve. "Senior Brother, over here! I'll show you where to get the best dishes."

After they loaded their trays with an assortment of colorful and fragrant foods, they found a quiet table in a corner, away from most of the curious stares. As they sat down, Chen Wei looked at Kai with admiration.

"Senior Brother, may I ask you something?"

Kai nodded, taking a bite of a dumpling. It was delicious, bursting with flavors he couldn't quite identify. "Go ahead."

"How do you stay so calm?" Chen Wei asked. "If it were me, I'd be overwhelmed by everything—being chosen as a Legacy Disciple, meeting the Sect Master, all the attention . . ."

Kai considered the question carefully. He couldn't exactly tell Chen Wei that he was treating this whole experience like a complex strategy game. Instead, he said, "I try to take things one step at a time. Focus on what I can control and learn as much as I can about what I can't."

Chen Wei nodded thoughtfully. "That's very wise, Senior Brother."

Kai shrugged. "It's just common sense. In cultivation, as in life, knowledge is power. The more you understand about your situation, the better equipped you are to handle it."

As they continued to eat, a commotion across the dining hall caught Kai's attention.

To his surprise, he spotted Liu Wei surrounded by three larger Inner

Disciples. Two loomed over Liu Wei, while the third hung back, looking uncomfortable.

"Come on, street rat," one of the disciples sneered, shoving Liu Wei. "Hand over your spirit stones. A former bandit like you doesn't deserve them anyway."

Liu Wei raised his hands. "Please, I don't have any to give. I just got here and—"

The second disciple cut him off with a laugh. "Liar! We know all disciples get a starting allowance. Fork it over, or we'll take it by force."

Kai's eyes flicked to the bullies' statuses.

Name: ???
Level: Qi Refining Stage 7 Qi: 200 Strength: 52 Agility: 51 Durability: 54
Name: ???
Level: Qi Refining Stage 6 Qi: 150 Strength: 40 Agility: 41 Durability: 43
Name: ???
Level: Qi Refining Stage 5 Qi: 100 Strength: 30 Agility: 29 Durability: 32

They're stronger than Liu Wei. Kai's eyes narrowed. *But he needs to learn to stand up for himself. Let's see how he handles this.*

Chen Wei tugged at Kai's sleeve. "Senior Brother, isn't that your friend? Shouldn't we help him?"

"Wait," Kai held up a hand. "Let's see what happens."

Liu Wei glanced around nervously, clearly looking for an escape route. "I really don't have any spirit stones. Please, just let me go."

The leader grabbed Liu Wei's collar. "Wrong answer, trash. Looks like we'll have to teach you a lesson."

As the disciple raised his fist, Kai sighed and tensed, ready to intervene. But before he could move, a high-pitched voice rang out across the dining hall.

"Hey! Don't you bully my disciple!"

Everyone froze, looking around in confusion. Suddenly, a tiny green shape zipped through the air and landed on Liu Wei's shoulder.

CHAPTER NINE

The dining hall fell silent as all eyes turned to the tiny green shape perched on Liu Wei's shoulder.

The tortoise's high-pitched voice rang out again.

"I said, don't bully my disciple!"

For a moment, nobody moved. Then laughter erupted across the hall.

"Did that little turtle just call the new guy his disciple?" one disciple said, snickering.

"Maybe it's a new pet trick," another chimed in. "Next it'll do a backflip!"

The leader sneered at Zhi-Zhi. "Beat it, pipsqueak. This is between us and the street rat."

Kai watched closely, noticing something odd about Zhi-Zhi's demeanor. The little tortoise wasn't puffing out his chest or hiding in his shell like usual. Instead, his eyes were narrowed, and he seemed . . . serious.

Well, this is new, Kai thought. *Looks like our little friend grew a backbone.*

Liu Wei shifted uncomfortably, trying to whisper to the tortoise. "Zhi-Zhi, please, it's not worth getting involved. I can handle this. We don't need to fight."

Zhi-Zhi raised a tiny claw, gently shushing Liu Wei. Then he turned to face the bullies, his small form radiating an unexpected intensity. Suddenly, the air around them grew heavy. An invisible pressure descended on the group, making it hard to breathe. The bullies' eyes widened in shock as they felt the weight of Zhi-Zhi's aura.

One of them stumbled backward, his face pale. "N-ninth stage," he muttered, his voice trembling. "How is this possible?"

The leader's sneer faltered, replaced by a look of disbelief. "You're lying," he said, but his voice lacked conviction. His eyes darted between Liu Wei and the tiny tortoise on his shoulder.

"You're bullying Liu Wei because of his low cultivation realm, aren't you? Why don't you try bullying me instead?"

The leader's face contorted with anger and embarrassment. "Don't mock me, you stupid turtle!" he shouted, then lashed out with a qi-infused palm strike aimed at Zhi-Zhi.

In a flash, Zhi-Zhi retreated into his shell. The Inner Disciple's attack struck the green surface and rebounded with shocking force. There was a sickening crack as the bully's own qi-enhanced strike smashed into his chest, sending him flying backward into his companions.

The dining hall fell silent as the lead bully crumpled to the ground, gasping for air. His friends stared in horror, looking between their fallen leader and the small tortoise that had emerged unscathed from its shell.

The bullies exchanged nervous glances, their earlier bravado evaporating as they realized that Zhi-Zhi was in fact a ninth-stage Qi Refining spirit beast.

"We . . . we didn't know he was your disciple," the leader stammered as he tried to get back on his feet. "It was just a misunderstanding."

"A misunderstanding?" Zhi-Zhi's eyes narrowed, and he gave a slow, deliberate blink. "Why did you attack me, then?"

The leader took a step back, sweat beading on his forehead. "I . . . I just wanted to be sure you're at the ninth stage . . ."

"I see," he said, his tiny beak clicking softly. "Then I'm sure you won't mind handing over your spirit stones to make amends."

The bullies' jaws dropped. "Our spirit stones?" one of them squeaked.

"You heard me," Zhi-Zhi said. "Hand them over. Now."

Is this really happening? Kai's eyes widened as he watched the scene unfold. *The little guy is robbing them!*

With shaking hands, the bullies reached into their storage rings and pulled out small pouches. They hesitantly offered them to Liu Wei, who seemed just as shocked as everyone else.

Zhi-Zhi nodded in satisfaction. "Good. Now leave. And if I hear about you bothering my friend again . . ." He let the threat hang in the air, somehow managing to look menacing despite his small size.

The bullies scrambled away, nearly tripping over each other in their haste to exit the dining hall. As they disappeared, excited chatter broke out among the remaining disciples.

"Did you see that?"

"I can't believe they got robbed by a turtle!"

"It's not a turtle; it looks more like a tortoise!"

"And it's at the ninth stage of Qi Refining!"

Zhi-Zhi turned to Liu Wei, his expression softening slightly. "You can keep the spirit stones," he said, his voice gentler now. "Use them for cultivation. Your, um . . . your current level could use a boost. Not that there's anything wrong with where you are now! It's just . . . well, there's always room for improvement, right?"

Zhi-Zhi's claws fidgeted slightly on Liu Wei's shoulder, betraying his discomfort at trying to phrase things delicately. "What I mean is, these spirit stones could really help you catch up to . . . I mean, advance your cultivation more quickly. Yes, that's it."

Liu Wei stared at Zhi-Zhi, his mouth hanging open. He looked the tortoise up and down as if trying to spot what had changed. "I . . . Thank you," he managed to stammer out. "But . . . what happened to you? You're so . . . different."

Kai watched the exchange with interest, noting the shift in Zhi-Zhi's demeanor. *Looks like his new master did more than just train him*, he thought. *He's actually starting to act like a proper cultivator. Even though he's uncomfortable being . . . nicer, that's still a lot of progress in a few days . . . What did his master have him do?*

Deciding it was time to leave, Kai caught Chen Wei's eye and gestured toward the exit. As they stood to leave, Chen Wei looked surprised.

"Senior Brother, aren't we going to talk to your friends?" he asked as they walked out of the dining hall.

Kai shook his head. "Not now. They're having a moment, and it looks like they're growing well by themselves. Sometimes the best thing you can do for your friends is to let them stand on their own."

As they stepped out into the cool evening air, Kai's mind wandered back to his first encounter with Zhi-Zhi in the Whispering Forest, when he'd found the little tortoise hiding in his shell, terrified as rogue cultivators tried to kidnap him.

It wasn't long ago that Zhi-Zhi was cowering from low-level cultivators, Kai mused. *Sure, he was facing weak opponents just now, but that confidence . . . It's genuine. His master must be quite something.*

He couldn't help but feel a small surge of pride. While he hadn't been directly responsible for Zhi-Zhi's growth, he had played a part in connecting the spirit beast with his new master.

Maybe I should check in on them soon, Kai thought. *It'd be interesting to see how their training is going.*

As they walked back toward Kai's quarters, Chen Wei's curiosity got the better of him. "Senior Brother, if you don't mind me asking . . . how did you become friends with a spirit beast? And such a powerful one, at that?"

Kai chuckled at Zhi-Zhi being called powerful. "It's a long story, Chen Wei. Let's just say we ran into each other at the right time and place."

Chen Wei nodded, clearly bursting with more questions but too polite to press further. As they reached Kai's pagoda, Kai paused at the entrance.

"Chen Wei, I have a task for you," he said. "Could you go to the sect's treasury and collect my stipend? I believe as a Legacy Disciple I'm entitled to a monthly allowance of spirit stones."

Chen Wei's eyes widened. "Of course, Senior Brother! I'll go right away." He hesitated for a moment before adding, "Um, would you like me to explain the different allowances for disciples when I'm back?"

"That would be helpful." Kai nodded.

As Chen Wei hurried off, Kai entered his room and settled onto his cultivation pillow. He closed his eyes and focused on his breathing as he waited for Chen Wei to return.

About fifteen minutes later, a knock at the door interrupted Kai's meditation. "Enter," he called out.

Chen Wei stepped in, carrying a small but clearly heavy pouch. He set it down carefully on a nearby table before turning to Kai with an excited expression. "I have your stipend, Senior Brother."

Kai nodded, gesturing for Chen Wei to continue.

"Well," Chen Wei began, "as an Outer Disciple, I receive ten low-quality spirit stones each month. It's not much, but it helps with basic cultivation resources."

Kai raised an eyebrow. *Ten stones a month? That's practically nothing.*

Chen Wei continued, "Inner Disciples get fifty low-quality spirit stones monthly. It's a significant increase, which is why many Outer Disciples work so hard to advance."

"And Core Disciples?" Kai prompted.

"They receive one hundred low-quality spirit stones each month," Chen Wei said, his voice filled with awe. "It's enough to purchase some truly valuable resources."

Kai nodded, processing the information. "And Legacy Disciples like myself?"

Chen Wei's eyes widened. "Legacy Disciples receive one thousand low-quality spirit stones every month, Senior Brother. It's . . . it's an incredible amount."

A hundred times what an Outer Disciple gets, Kai thought. *The sect really values its Legacy Disciples.*

"Tell me about the different qualities of spirit stones," Kai said. "How do they compare?"

Chen Wei's face lit up at the chance to share his knowledge. "Well, Senior Brother, it's quite interesting. One mid-quality spirit stone is equivalent to one hundred low-quality stones. And one high-quality stone is worth one hundred medium-quality stones."

Kai's eyebrows shot up. "So, one high-quality stone is worth ten thousand low-quality stones?"

Chen Wei nodded enthusiastically. "Exactly, Senior Brother! As for anything higher than that . . ." He trailed off, looking a bit embarrassed. "Well, I'm afraid I don't know. Such high-grade spirit stones are beyond my knowledge."

Interesting, Kai thought. *So there are even more powerful spirit stones out there. I wonder what they're capable of.*

"Thank you, Chen Wei," Kai said. "You've been very helpful. You can leave the spirit stones here and take the rest of the evening off."

Chen Wei bowed deeply. "Thank you, Senior Brother. Is there anything else you need before I go?"

Kai shook his head. "No, that will be all. Good night, Chen Wei."

As the door closed behind his servant, Kai reached for the pouch of spirit stones. He opened it carefully and poured the contents onto the table. A pile of glowing, crystalline stones tumbled out, each about the size of a large marble.

A thousand low-quality spirit stones, Kai mused. *In game terms, this would be like starting cash. But it would be good to pay a visit to the treasury myself and make sure Chen Wei isn't swindling me. I don't think he is, but it doesn't hurt to be sure.*

He picked up one of the stones, feeling the gentle pulse of energy within it. It was tempting to start using them right away, either to boost his cultivation and see how it compared to the spirit stones he had retrieved from the bandit leader's corpse, or to purchase resources. But Kai knew better than to rush into things blindly.

First, I need to understand exactly what I'm working with. It's time to dive deeper into this cultivation system.

He set the spirit stone down and retrieved the jade-green scroll case he'd gotten from the library earlier from his inventory. As he unrolled the scroll of detailed information about the Qi Refining Realm, Kai settled in for a long night of study.

This reminds me of cramming for finals back in college, Kai thought with a wry smile. *Except now, instead of worrying about grades, I'm studying to avoid getting killed by cultivation mishaps.*

CHAPTER TEN

As Kai unrolled the scroll, he half expected a System prompt to appear and ask if he wanted to learn its contents instantly. But no such message came.

Not that it matters. I couldn't exactly explain a vanishing scroll to the librarian. The parchment crackled softly as Kai began to read:

"The Qi Refining Realm: Foundation of Immortality. To step onto the path of immortality, one must first master the Qi Refining Realm. This initial stage of cultivation is divided into nine levels, each representing a significant milestone in a cultivator's journey.

"The first and most crucial step is to awaken one's ability to sense and absorb qi. This marks the transition from mortal to cultivator, opening a world of possibility previously hidden from view.

"As the cultivator progresses through the nine stages of Qi Refining, they must activate nine key meridians within their body: Crown of the Head, Third Eye, Throat, Heart Center, Solar Plexus, Lower Dantian, Sacral Region, Legs, and Soles.

"Each meridian serves as a conduit for qi, allowing the cultivator to channel and manipulate this vital energy with increasing skill and power. The order in which these meridians are awakened can vary, though many choose to focus on the Third Eye early to develop their spiritual sense . . ."

Kai paused in his reading, a soft smile playing on his lips. *Looks like I got lucky,* he mused. *Waking up in this world with the first stage of Qi Refining already unlocked saved me a lot of trouble.*

His eyes drifted to the strange trident mark on his wrist. Was this the source of his head start? Or was it just a side effect of whatever or whoever it was that had brought him to this world? Kai shook his head, pushing the questions aside for now. He had more pressing matters to focus on.

Returning to the scroll, Kai continued reading about the nine meridians. He'd already unlocked eight of them through his System-assisted leveling, leaving only one—the Heart Center—still dormant.

But that's not my priority right now, Kai reminded himself. *I need to follow the Azure Sky Legacy Lightning technique, which means starting with the Crown of the Head.*

He continued reading, his eyes widening as he came across a section on spiritual sense:

"Spiritual sense, awakened through the opening of the Third Eye meridian, allows a cultivator to perceive qi and spiritual energies beyond their physical senses. This extrasensory ability is crucial for advanced techniques such as Qi Detection, enabling cultivators to sense the presence and strength of others from a distance."

Kai's brow furrowed as he considered this. *So that's what Qi Detection is based on. Interesting . . . But my map function seems way more powerful. Even if immortals can hide from it, it's still better than spiritual sense, which Foundation Establishment cultivators can fool.*

Still, Kai knew better than to rely solely on his System abilities. He'd need to develop his spiritual sense eventually, even if it wasn't his immediate focus.

The next section of the scroll detailed the process of closing meridians.

Closing a Meridian: Temporary Regression for Greater Growth

While it may seem counterintuitive, there are times when a cultivator must close an awakened meridian. This process temporarily limits one's cultivation, reducing it by one stage for each closed meridian. However, this regression allows for the reawakening of meridians using specialized techniques, potentially leading to greater power and deeper understanding of one's chosen cultivation path.

To close a meridian, follow these steps:
Enter a deep meditative state, focusing your awareness on the chosen meridian.
Visualize the flow of qi through the meridian as a stream of light.
Gradually narrow this stream, constricting the flow of qi.
When the stream has become a thin trickle, imagine a barrier forming, blocking the flow entirely.
Hold this visualization until you feel a subtle "click" within your body, signaling the meridian's closure.

Caution: closing multiple meridians simultaneously can leave a cultivator vulnerable. It is advisable to close and reopen meridians one at a time, maintaining a stable level of power throughout the process.

Kai nodded to himself as he finished reading. *Smart advice. I'm definitely not leaving myself defenseless in a sect full of cultivators who might decide I'm more valuable as a cultivation resource than as a disciple.*

He set the scroll aside and straightened his posture, preparing to attempt the meridian closure technique. He closed his eyes and tried to focus on the Crown of the Head meridian.

All right, let's do this step by step.

But as Kai tried to sense the meridian, he realized he had no idea what he was looking for. His brow furrowed in concentration. *Come on, it should be right there at the top of my head. Why can't I feel anything?*

He took a deep breath, attempting to sink into meditation. He tried to visualize the flow of qi through his body, but all he saw in his mind's eye was a vague, indistinct blur.

This is ridiculous. I'm at Qi Refining stage eight. I should be able to do this easily. But Kai had never had to actually *feel* his meridians before. The System had always just . . . handled it. He'd level up and suddenly he'd have a new meridian open. No effort required.

Maybe I'm overthinking this. Let's try again.

He focused all his attention on the top of his head, straining to sense even the slightest tingle of energy. For several long minutes, he sat there, trying over and over again.

Just as he was about to give up, Kai felt . . . something. A faint whisper of energy, so subtle he almost missed it.

Is that it? It has to be.

Latching onto that faint sensation, Kai tried to follow the scroll's instructions.

Narrow the stream . . . constrict the flow . . .

But how do you narrow something you can barely feel? Kai gritted his teeth, pushing his concentration to its limits. In his mind, he imagined squeezing that whisper of energy, trying to force it into a trickle.

For a moment, nothing seemed to happen. Kai was about to let out a frustrated sigh when suddenly, he felt a subtle shift within him. It was like a door quietly clicking shut, but so faint he almost thought he'd imagined it.

Kai's eyes snapped open. "Did it work?" he muttered, unsure if he'd actually accomplished anything or just given himself a headache.

To his relief, a message appeared.

Meridian Closed: Crown of the Head
Cultivation reduced to Qi Refining Stage 7

"Well, that was a little harder than I expected," Kai murmured as he stood up, stretching to work out the stiffness from sitting so long. Now came the real test—reawakening the meridian using the Azure Sky Legacy Lightning technique.

"Time to find myself a storm," he muttered, heading for the door.

As Kai stepped outside, he was startled to see Chen Wei hurrying toward him. His eyes narrowed slightly in suspicion.

"Chen Wei? I thought I dismissed you earlier. What are you doing here?"

The young disciple fidgeted nervously, his eyes darting around. "I . . . I'm sorry, Senior Brother. It's just . . . my friends said . . ."

Kai raised an eyebrow, waiting for Chen Wei to continue.

Chen Wei took a deep breath and blurted out, "They said I might lose my position as your servant if I wasn't here to help you when you needed it! I didn't want to risk disappointing you, so I came back to check if you needed anything."

Kai's expression softened slightly as realization dawned on him. *Oh right, he should be staying in the servant's quarters. I completely forgot about that.*

He'd been so focused on his own cultivation that he'd neglected to properly settle his new servant.

"Chen Wei," Kai said, his voice gentler now. "You don't need to worry about losing your position. But . . . I realize I forgot to offer you proper accommodations. There's a servant's room in my pagoda. You're welcome to stay there if you'd like."

Chen Wei's eyes widened in surprise and relief. "R-really? You'd let me stay in your pagoda, Senior Brother?"

Kai nodded, feeling slightly awkward about the whole situation. "Of course. It's meant for my personal servant, after all. You should have a place to rest nearby."

"Thank you, Senior Brother!" Chen Wei exclaimed, bowing deeply. "I . . . I accept your kind offer."

As Chen Wei straightened up, Kai decided to change the subject. "Now that you're here, I actually could use your help. I need to find a place with constant storms for my cultivation. Any ideas?"

"Of course!" Chen Wei beamed. "Follow me, Senior Brother, I'll take you to the Thunderpeak Plateau."

As they walked, Kai decided to probe for more information. "Tell me, Chen Wei, have you ever trained at Thunderpeak Plateau?"

The young disciple's enthusiasm dimmed slightly. "Ah, no, Senior Brother. As an Outer Disciple, I'm not allowed there without special permission. It's mainly for Core Disciples and above."

Kai raised an eyebrow. "But you're my servant now. Surely that grants you some privileges?"

Chen Wei's eyes widened. "I . . . I hadn't thought of that! Do you think it would be okay for me to accompany you?"

"We'll soon find out," Kai said with a slight smile. *No harm in bringing the kid along. He might prove useful, and if nothing else, it'll build some loyalty. Even though he is my servant, the System hasn't added him to my Follower list . . .*

As they neared the edge of the sect grounds, the air began to crackle with charged energy. In the distance, Kai could see dark clouds swirling around a towering plateau.

"There it is," Chen Wei said, his voice filled with awe. "Thunderpeak Plateau."

Jagged bolts of lightning danced between the clouds, occasionally striking the plateau's peak. The constant rumble of thunder filled the air.

"Impressive," Kai murmured. *If this doesn't open the meridian, nothing will.*

As they approached the base of the plateau, a disciple in purple robes stepped forward to block their path.

"Stop right there," he commanded. "This area is restricted to—" The disciple's eyes widened as he noticed Kai's black robes. "Forgive me, Legacy Disciple. I didn't realize . . . Please, go right ahead."

Kai nodded, then gestured to Chen Wei. "My servant will be accompanying me."

The guard hesitated for a moment, then bowed. "As you wish."

As they passed, Kai could hear Chen Wei's excited whisper. "Did you see that, Senior Brother? He just let us through!"

Kai simply nodded, not surprised.

They began climbing the path up the plateau. With each step, the air grew thicker and thicker with electrical energy. Kai could feel his hair starting to stand on end.

"Senior Brother," Chen Wei called out, his voice slightly strained. "How long do you plan to stay up here?"

Kai glanced back at his servant. The boy's face was pale, his eyes darting nervously at each flash of lightning.

"Not too long," Kai assured him. "Just long enough to complete a cultivation session. You don't have to come all the way up if you're uncomfortable."

Chen Wei shook his head firmly. "No, I want to help however I can!"

Brave kid, Kai thought approvingly. *Or maybe just desperate to prove himself. Either way, it could be useful.*

As they neared the summit, the storm intensified. Lightning bolts struck closer and more frequently, the thunder now a constant, deafening roar.

Kai spotted a flat area near the peak that was partially sheltered by an overhanging rock. "There," he shouted over the storm. "That looks like a good spot."

They hurried to the shelter, Chen Wei visibly relieved to be out of the direct path of the lightning.

"All right," Kai said, settling into a cross-legged position. "I'm going to meditate now. Keep watch and make sure no one disturbs me."

Chen Wei nodded eagerly. "Yes, Senior Brother! I won't let you down."

As the young disciple took up a vigilant stance at the edge of their shelter, Kai closed his eyes and focused on his breathing.

Now, let's see what this Heavenly Thunderstorm cultivation method can do.

Kai recalled instructions from the legacy lightning scroll. *"The cultivator must meditate under an open sky during a storm while allowing raindrops and the natural energy of the tempest to strike the crown of their head, gradually awakening the meridian."*

Taking a deep breath, Kai extended his senses outward.

Come on, he thought. *I'm right here. Hit me with your best shot.*

CHAPTER ELEVEN

Kai took a deep breath, trying to focus on the faint trickle of energy he'd felt earlier when closing the meridian. He tilted his head back, exposing the crown of his head to the rain. Cold droplets pelted his skin, making him flinch.

This better not give me pneumonia . . . Kai shook his head wryly. Pneumonia was the least of his concerns.

"Um, Senior Brother?" Chen Wei's nervous voice cut through the sound of rain. "Are you sure this is safe?"

Kai cracked one eye open. "Probably not. But that's cultivation for you."

Chen Wei gulped but nodded, clearly trying to look brave.

Closing his eyes again, Kai attempted to open himself to the storm's energy, whatever that meant. He pictured his body as an empty vessel waiting to be filled with lightning.

At first, nothing seemed to happen. Kai frowned and concentrated harder. He pictured himself as a lightning rod, trying to draw the storm's energy toward him.

Come on, where's the lightning?

As if in response to his thoughts, a bolt of lightning struck nearby, causing Chen Wei to yelp in surprise. Kai's eyes snapped open.

"Senior Brother! Are you all right?" Chen Wei called out, his voice shaky.

Kai nodded. "I'm fine. That was just a warm-up. But it looks like we need to get closer to the action."

He stood up and scanned the area. A jagged rock formation jutted out from the plateau's peak, offering the perfect vantage point.

"There," Kai said, pointing. "That's where we need to be."

Chen Wei's eyes widened in alarm. "But, Senior Brother, that's right in the middle of the storm!"

Kai grinned, a glint of excitement in his eyes. "Exactly."

As they made their way toward the rock formation, the wind picked up, howling around them.

This is more like it.

As he reached the base of the rock formation, Kai turned to Chen Wei. "You can stay here if you want. It might get a bit intense up there."

Chen Wei hesitated for a moment, then squared his shoulders. "No, Senior Brother. I'll come with you. It's my duty to assist you, no matter the danger."

Kai nodded approvingly. "All right, then. Let's climb."

They scrambled up the slick rocks, the storm intensifying with each foot of elevation gained. By the time they reached the top, they were both soaked to the bone, their robes clinging to their bodies.

Kai positioned himself at the highest point, the wind whipping his hair into a frenzy. Chen Wei crouched nearby, looking both terrified and exhilarated.

"Now what, Senior Brother?" Chen Wei shouted over the howling wind.

Kai closed his eyes, raising his face to the sky. "Now, we wait for lightning to strike." He thought back to the scroll's instructions. "Become a conduit for the storm's power," he muttered. "Like a living lightning rod . . ."

With that, he raised his arms, palms up, as if welcoming the storm. He imagined tendrils of electricity reaching down from the clouds, searching for a target.

Here I am, he thought. *Nice, juicy lightning rod right here.*

For a long moment, nothing changed. Then Kai felt a tingling sensation on his skin, like static electricity but stronger.

Is it working? he wondered, hardly daring to hope.

The tingling intensified, spreading across his body. It wasn't painful, exactly, but it wasn't comfortable either. Kai gritted his teeth, forcing himself to remain still.

"Senior Brother!" Chen Wei cried out in alarm. "You're . . . you're glowing!"

Kai's eyes snapped open. Sure enough, faint blue sparks danced across his skin, growing brighter by the second.

Well, that's new and surprisingly not painful, Kai thought, torn between fascination and concern. *But is it actually doing anything?*

He closed his eyes again, focusing inward. The energy coursing over his skin felt wild, untamed. It wasn't entering his body, just skittering across the surface.

I need to guide it in somehow, Kai realized. *But how?*

He pictured the closed meridian at the crown of his head, imagining it as a locked door. The lightning was the key, but he needed to insert it into the lock.

Kai concentrated, trying to direct the electricity to that specific point. It was like herding cats made of lightning—every time he thought he had it, the energy would slip away.

"Come on," he muttered through clenched teeth. "Work with me here."

Minutes ticked by as Kai grew increasingly frustrated. The tingling sensation was starting to become uncomfortable, bordering on painful.

This isn't working, he thought grimly. *I need a different approach.*

Kai took a deep breath, forcing himself to relax. He'd been trying to control the lightning, to bend it to his will. But maybe that was the wrong tactic. *What if I sync up with the element's natural rhythm?*

Instead of fighting the erratic dance of electricity across his skin, Kai tried to match it. He let his thoughts flow in jagged, unpredictable patterns, mirroring the lightning's path. To his surprise, the discomfort began to fade. The energy no longer felt like it was trying to escape. Instead, it seemed to pulse in time with his heartbeat.

That's more like it, Kai thought, a smile tugging at his lips. *Now, let's try this again.*

With his mind and the lightning in sync, Kai once more attempted to guide the energy to the crown of his head. This time, instead of trying to force it, he simply . . . invited it.

The effect was immediate. Kai gasped as he felt a surge of power rush to the top of his skull. It was like someone had poured liquid fire directly into his brain.

"Senior Brother!" Chen Wei's voice seemed to come from very far away. "Are you all right? Should I get help?"

Kai wanted to reassure his servant, but he couldn't spare the concentration. Every ounce of his focus was on the incredible sensation at the crown of his head.

The locked door of his meridian was vibrating now. Kai could almost see it in his mind's eye—a glowing, pulsing gateway.

Just a little more, he thought, gritting his teeth against the increasing pressure. *Come on, open up!*

The energy built and built until Kai felt like his skull might crack open from the strain. Just when he thought he couldn't take anymore, something . . . shifted.

With a sensation like a cork popping from a bottle, the meridian burst open. Lightning flooded in, racing through pathways Kai hadn't even known existed in his body. Kai's eyes flew open, and he let out a cry that was equal parts pain and exhilaration. Blue-white light blazed from his skin, illuminating the surroundings.

Chen Wei yelped and stumbled backward, shielding his eyes. "S-Senior Brother? What's happening?"

Kai couldn't answer. He was too busy trying to contain the incredible rush of power flowing through him. As the initial surge began to subside, he became aware of changes in his perception. The storm around him seemed different now. He could feel the electricity in the air, sense the patterns of energy in the clouds above.

Slowly, carefully, Kai got to his feet. His body felt charged, almost weightless. Static electricity crackled between his fingers as he flexed them.

"That," he said, a grin spreading across his face, "was absolutely wild."

Chen Wei approached cautiously, eyes wide with a mixture of fear and admiration. "Senior Brother, are you . . . okay? You look different."

Kai glanced down at himself. Faint lines of blue light traced patterns under his skin, following what he assumed were his meridians. As he watched, they began to fade, leaving only a slight residual glow.

"I'm better than okay," Kai said, still grinning.

As if on cue, a familiar notification appeared in his vision:

Congratulations!

You have successfully converted your Crown of the Head Meridian to Thunder's Crown!

Lightning Affinity increased to 22%

New Skill Unlocked: Static Charge (Level 1)

You have gained 100 XP!

Now we're talking. I wonder what else this new meridian can do.

Kai began stretching his muscles, which were stiff from hours of meditation. "How long was I meditating?"

Chen Wei looked up at the sky. "Most of the night, Senior Brother. The sun is starting to rise."

Time really seems to fly when cultivating . . .

"Come on," Kai said, clapping his servant on the shoulder. "Let's head back. I've got to get some sleep, and then I have some experimenting to do."

As they neared the base of Thunderpeak Plateau, Kai noticed the guard who had let them pass earlier was still on duty. The man's eyes widened as they approached.

"Legacy Disciple," the guard said, bowing. "I hope your cultivation was successful?"

Kai nodded, keeping his expression neutral. "It was . . . enlightening," he said carefully.

The guard seemed to want to ask more questions, but a look from Kai silenced him. They passed by without further conversation.

I'll need to be careful. People will be watching me closely now. There's no need to brag about every little success I have—not when there might be a kidnapper on the loose . . .

CHAPTER TWELVE

Rays of afternoon sunlight peeked through the windows of Kai's pavilion, gently rousing him from his sleep. He blinked a few times, adjusting to the light. As he sat up, stretching his arms above his head and yawning, he heard a voice from outside.

"Senior Brother Kai? Are you awake?" Chen Wei called softly. "I've left a warm basin of water outside for your morning wash."

Kai smiled to himself. *Chen Wei is certainly taking his duties seriously.*

"Thank you, Chen Wei," Kai called back. "I'll bring it in now."

He stood up, his muscles still a bit stiff from the previous night's cultivation. The events came flooding back—the storm, the lightning, the awakening of his crown meridian. Kai's fingers tingled at the memory.

I wonder if I'll ever get used to this cultivation stuff, he mused as he made his way to the door. Opening it, Kai found a steaming basin of water waiting for him. He carefully lifted it, appreciating the warmth seeping through the ceramic.

"Is there anything else you need, Senior Brother?" Chen Wei asked, hovering nearby.

Kai shook his head. "This is perfect. Thank you."

After carrying the basin back into his room, Kai set it down and dipped his hands into the warm water, then splashed some on his face. The sensation was familiar yet strange. Back on Earth, he'd have stumbled to the bathroom, turned on the tap, and had instant hot water. Here, someone had to heat the water over a fire and carry it to his room.

It's like camping, except the camping never ends.

He continued his morning ablutions, using a soft cloth to wash himself. As he did, he couldn't help but compare it to his time in Misty Waterfall Village.

At least I'm not jumping into a freezing lake anymore, Kai thought with a chuckle. *Though, I bet some cultivators would say that's good training.*

Once he finished bathing, Kai dried himself off and donned a fresh set of black robes.

As he stepped out of his sleeping area, a delightful aroma wafted through the air. Kai's stomach growled in response, reminding him that he hadn't eaten since before his cultivation session at Thunderpeak Plateau.

In the main room of the pavilion, Kai found a low table set with various dishes. Steam rose from bowls of rice and soup, while plates of vegetables and meat dishes waited invitingly. Standing nearby, looking nervous, was Chen Wei.

"Good morning, Senior Brother," Chen Wei said, bowing slightly. "I . . . I prepared breakfast for you."

Kai nodded, taking in the spread before him. "It looks great, Chen Wei. Thank you."

Despite his words, Kai didn't immediately sit down to eat. Instead, he stood there, eyes slightly unfocused as he examined each dish.

Name: Rice Porridge
Description: A nutritious dish made from rice cooked in water until soft and creamy.
Effects: None detected

Name: Steamed Vegetables
Description: A mix of local vegetables lightly seasoned and steamed to perfection.
Effects: None detected

Name: Grilled Fish
Description: Freshwater fish grilled with herbs and spices.
Effects: None detected

Kai nodded to himself, satisfied with the results. *No poison detected. Not that I really expected Chen Wei to try anything, but better safe than sorry.*

This was a precaution he had decided to take after hearing about the mysterious disappearances of genius disciples over the years. It might seem paranoid, but Kai preferred caution to ending up as another statistic.

"Senior Brother?" Chen Wei's worried voice broke through Kai's thoughts. "I . . . I'm sorry if the food doesn't look good. I can try to make something else if you prefer."

Kai blinked, realizing how his behavior must appear. "No, no, it's not that at all. Everything looks delicious. I was just . . . taking it all in. It's been a while since I've had such a nice breakfast."

Relief washed over Chen Wei's face. "Oh, I see. I'm glad you think it looks good, Senior Brother."

Kai sat down at the table, gesturing for Chen Wei to join him. "Come on, let's eat. You must be hungry too after last night's adventure."

Chen Wei hesitated for a moment before sitting across from Kai. "Thank you, Senior Brother. But . . . are you sure it's appropriate for me to eat with you?"

Kai waved off his concern. "Of course it is. You're my servant, but we're both cultivators here."

As they began to eat, Kai couldn't help but savor each bite. The rice porridge was creamy and comforting, the vegetables crisp and flavorful, and the fish perfectly cooked.

This beats instant ramen any day.

He had never given much thought to cooking back on Earth, living mostly on takeout and microwave meals. But he could appreciate the skill that went into preparing a meal like this from scratch.

"This is really good, Chen Wei," Kai said between bites. "Where did you learn to cook like this?"

Chen Wei's cheeks reddened slightly at the praise. "My family runs an inn back home. I grew up helping in the kitchen and tending to guests."

"How'd you end up joining the sect, then?" he asked.

"A cultivator stayed at our inn," Chen Wei explained. "He sensed I had some aptitude and recommended I apply to join the Azure Sky Sect. My parents were overjoyed—they saw it as a chance for me to have a better life."

Kai nodded thoughtfully. It was a common story in this world—talented youths plucked from obscurity and given a chance to pursue immortality through cultivation.

Kind of like getting a scholarship to a prestigious university back on Earth. Except with more lightning bolts and qi . . .

"And how are you finding sect life so far?" Kai asked.

Chen Wei's eyes lit up. "It's amazing, Senior Brother! There's so much to learn. Though . . ." he hesitated.

"Go on," Kai encouraged.

"Well, it can be a bit overwhelming at times," Chen Wei admitted. "Some of the other disciples look down on those of us from common backgrounds. And the cultivation techniques are so complex . . ."

Kai nodded. He could relate to feeling out of his depth in this new world.

"You'll get the hang of it," Kai assured him. "Just take it one step at a time. And don't let anyone make you feel inferior. Talent and hard work are what matter in cultivation, not your background."

Chen Wei smiled gratefully. "Thank you, Senior Brother."

They continued eating in comfortable silence for a while. Kai found himself relaxing, enjoying the simple pleasure of a good meal shared with someone else.

It's nice, almost like having a roommate. Except this roommate can shoot fireballs and probably bench press a car.

As he ate, Kai's mind wandered to his cultivation plans for the day. He needed to further refine his newly opened Thunder Crown meridian. And then there was the matter of opening the next lightning meridian . . .

One step at a time, he reminded himself. *No point rushing and making mistakes.* Kai's thoughts then turned toward Chen Wei. *And I need to sort out this whole servant situation. Having him cook every meal is a waste of his potential as a cultivator.*

Once they finished their meal, Kai leaned back, patting his stomach contentedly. "That was excellent. Thank you."

Chen Wei beamed, clearly relieved and pleased. "I'm glad you enjoyed it, Senior Brother. Shall I prepare lunch and dinner as well?"

Kai shook his head. "Actually, Chen Wei, I don't think you need to cook for me all the time."

The young servant's face fell, his earlier joy evaporating in an instant. "Oh . . . I see. Was the food not to your liking after all? I promise I can improve—"

"No, no," Kai quickly interjected, realizing his mistake. He let out a small laugh. "The food was delicious. That's not the issue at all."

Chen Wei's brow furrowed in confusion. "Then . . . why, Senior Brother?"

Kai leaned back, considering how to explain. "Chen Wei, you're a cultivator first and foremost. Yes, you're my servant, but that doesn't mean you should neglect your own cultivation. Cooking takes time—time you could be using to train and grow stronger."

"But serving you is my duty," Chen Wei protested weakly.

"And you're doing an excellent job," Kai assured him. "But think about it this way: the stronger you become, the more useful you'll be to me. A powerful servant is far more valuable than a good cook, wouldn't you agree?"

Chen Wei's eyes widened as understanding dawned. "I . . . I hadn't thought of it that way, Senior Brother."

Kai nodded. "Besides, I don't mind going to the dining hall for meals. There's no need for you to spend hours cooking when we have that option available."

"Are you sure, Senior Brother?" Chen Wei asked, still seeming uncertain.

"Absolutely," Kai confirmed. "Your cultivation should be your priority. Of course, I still appreciate your help with other tasks, but let's focus on what's truly important for both of us—getting stronger. That's an order from your senior brother."

A determined look came over Chen Wei's face. "I understand, Senior Brother. I'll do my best to become stronger!"

"Good," Kai said, standing up. "Now, I'm going to be doing some cultivation of my own. Don't disturb me unless it's an emergency, all right? Use this time to cultivate yourself."

Chen Wei nodded eagerly. "Yes, Senior Brother!"

As Chen Wei began clearing the table, Kai retreated to his private cultivation area. He settled down on a comfortable cushion and pulled out the Heavenly Thunderstorm cultivation manual.

All right, time to get back on the grind!

CHAPTER THIRTEEN

Kai unrolled the Heavenly Thunderstorm scroll, his eyes finding the section on the crown meridian he had opened the night before.

Key Technique: Electric Meridian Flow—use controlled bursts of lightning qi to gradually open and fortify the meridians.

He took a deep breath, centering himself. *Okay, I've opened the meridian. Now I need to fortify it. Sounds simple enough . . . right?*

He closed his eyes and focused on the sensation of qi flowing through his body. After his experience on Thunderpeak Plateau, it was easier to identify the unique feeling of lightning qi. *It's like . . . a tingling current, always wanting to move.*

Following the manual's instructions, Kai began to direct small bursts of lightning qi toward his crown meridian. The first attempt was . . . less than successful.

A jolt of electricity shot through Kai's skull, making him wince. *Ouch. Okay, maybe a little less power next time.*

He tried again, this time using a gentler touch. The lightning qi flowed more smoothly, creating a pleasant buzzing sensation at the top of his head.

That's more like it, Kai thought, a small smile playing on his lips.

As he continued the exercise, Kai felt the meridian slowly expanding, becoming more receptive to the flow of lightning qi. It was a strange sensation, like his skull was becoming a lightning rod.

I wonder if this is how Benjamin Franklin felt, Kai mused, then chuckled at the absurdity of the thought.

Time seemed to slip away as he focused on the technique. The world around him faded, his awareness narrowing to the flow of qi through his body. It was almost meditative, in an electrifying sort of way.

Suddenly, Kai felt something . . . shift. The crown meridian seemed to pulse, and for a brief moment, he could have sworn he saw a flash of light even with his eyes closed.

A series of System notifications popped up.

> Congratulations!
> You have successfully fortified the Thunder's Crown Meridian!
> New Skill Unlocked: Crown of Lightning (Level 1) (Passive)
> Description: A temporary visible aura of lightning can form around the cultivator's head during meditation, which boosts the cultivator's qi regeneration by 5%.
>
> New Skill Unlocked: Sky's Favor (Level 1) (Passive)
> Description: The cultivator's absorption rate increases by 5% whenever they are under an open sky. This increases to 10% during stormy weather.
>
> New Skill Unlocked: Electric Resistance (Level 1) (Passive)
> Description: The cultivator gains 5% resistance to lightning-based attacks, reducing the damage taken from electric or lightning-based techniques.
>
> You have gained 300 XP!

Kai's eyes widened as he read through the notifications. *Now we're talking! This is way better than just Static Charge.*

Initially, he had been somewhat disappointed when opening the meridian had only granted him the Static Charge skill and a two percent increase in lightning affinity. These new skills, while still offering relatively small percentage boosts, were much more promising.

And they'll likely improve as I open more lightning meridians. The Electric Resistance, in particular, could be incredibly useful in a lightning-focused sect like this.

Kai nodded, pleased with himself. He couldn't help but feel a sense of accomplishment. It was one thing to gain skills through the System, but actively cultivating and unlocking new abilities felt . . . different. More rewarding, somehow.

Eager to continue his progress, Kai turned his attention back to the cultivation manual. His eyes fell on the next section.

> Meridian of the Storm Eye
> Location: Third Eye (Forehead)
> Method to Open: Lightning Insight—the cultivator focuses on the space between their eyebrows while visualizing a storm cloud gathering. A special herb, Thundergrass, is placed on the forehead to stimulate the meridian's opening.

Kai let out a small sigh of relief. *At least this one doesn't involve standing on a mountain peak during a thunderstorm.*

He read through the instructions carefully, committing them to memory. The use of Thundergrass intrigued him. *I wonder what other mystical herbs exist in this world. Maybe I should start a garden . . .*

Shaking off the momentary distraction, Kai focused on the task at hand. He knew he'd need to close his Third Eye meridian before attempting to reopen it with the lightning technique. But first things first—he needed to get his hands on some Thundergrass.

I'll get the herb before I close the meridian.

Decision made, Kai stood up and stretched to work out the stiffness from sitting so long. He made his way out of the pavilion, looking for Chen Wei.

He found the young disciple in the garden, seated in a meditation pose. A faint glow surrounded Chen Wei, indicating he was in the middle of cultivation.

Good, Kai thought approvingly. *He took my advice seriously.*

Not wanting to disturb Chen Wei's cultivation, Kai waited patiently. He took the opportunity to observe the garden and note the various plants and flowers. Some looked familiar, while others were completely alien to him.

I wonder if any of these have special properties for cultivation, Kai mused. *Even though I don't want to specialize in alchemy, it wouldn't hurt to learn more about magical plants.*

After a few minutes, the glow around Chen Wei began to fade. The young disciple's eyes fluttered open, a look of contentment on his face.

"Ah, Senior Brother!" Chen Wei said, quickly scrambling to his feet and bowing. "I'm sorry, I didn't notice you there. Do you need something?"

Kai waved off the apology. "No need to apologize. I'm glad to see you taking your cultivation seriously."

Chen Wei beamed at the praise. "Thank you, Senior Brother. I was just practicing the breathing techniques you showed me."

"Good, good." Kai nodded. "I need your help with something. Do you know where I can get an herb called Thundergrass?"

Chen Wei's brow furrowed in thought. "Thundergrass? I believe I've heard of it. It's used in some lightning-based cultivation techniques, right?"

"That's right," Kai confirmed. "I need some for my next stage of cultivation."

"I see," Chen Wei said, nodding. "Well, the sect should have some in the Celestial Herb Pavilion. That's where they keep all the special cultivation resources."

Kai raised an eyebrow. "Celestial Herb Pavilion? Fancy name."

Chen Wei chuckled. "Everything in the sect has a fancy name, Senior Brother. You should see what they call the latrines in the Outer Sect."

Kai couldn't help but laugh at that. "I'm almost afraid to ask. All right, then, can you show me the way to this Celestial Herb Pavilion?"

"Of course, Senior Brother," Chen Wei said eagerly. "It's not far from here. Follow me!"

CHAPTER FOURTEEN

Kai and Chen Wei made their way through the Azure Sky Sect as they headed toward the Celestial Herb Pavilion.

"So," Kai said, breaking the silence. "What can you tell me about this Celestial Herb Pavilion?"

Chen Wei's face lit up at the question. "Oh, it's a marvelous place, Senior Brother! It's where the sect keeps all its rare and valuable herbs. They say some of the plants there are over a thousand years old!"

Kai raised an eyebrow. "A thousand years? That's impressive."

Wonder if they have any Earth plants that have gone extinct. Could be valuable if I ever decide to head back—well, that's if there even is a way to head back . . .

As they walked, Kai noticed other disciples hurrying about their daily routines. Some carried scrolls or practice weapons, while others seemed lost in meditation even as they moved.

"Is it open to all disciples?"

Chen Wei shook his head. "Not exactly, Senior Brother. Outer Disciples like me need special permission to enter. But as a Legacy Disciple, you should have unrestricted access."

They rounded a corner, and Kai's eyes widened slightly. Before them stood a massive structure that looked more like a greenhouse than a traditional building. Its walls were made of what appeared to be crystal, allowing sunlight to stream through freely.

"Wow," Kai muttered, impressed despite himself. "That's . . . not what I expected."

Chen Wei nodded enthusiastically. "It's beautiful, isn't it? The crystal walls are specially designed to filter and enhance spiritual energy. They say it helps the herbs grow stronger and faster."

As they approached the entrance, they found a pair of disciples in white robes standing guard. The disciples bowed deeply as Kai approached.

"Welcome, Senior Brother," one of them said. "How may we assist you today?"

Kai nodded in acknowledgment. "I'm here to acquire some Thundergrass for my cultivation."

The guards exchanged a quick glance before the second one spoke. "Of course, Senior Brother. Please enter. One of our herbalists will assist you shortly."

As Kai and Chen Wei stepped inside, they were hit by a wave of fragrant air. The interior was even more impressive than the outside. Rows upon rows of plants stretched as far as the eye could see, each section carefully labeled and maintained.

It's like a magical Costco for plants.

A figure approached them. The man wore robes of deep purple embroidered with golden symbols that seemed to shift and change as he moved.

"Greetings, young Legacy Disciple," the man said, his voice carrying a hint of amusement. "I am Alchemist Zhang, overseer of the Celestial Herb Pavilion. I didn't expect our humble abode of botanical wonders to be so popular today."

So popular? What does he mean by that?

Kai bowed slightly. "I'm Kai. I'm looking for Thundergrass herb."

Zhang's eyebrows rose. "Ah, another one looking into lightning techniques? One of our herbalists will assist you." He turned and called out, "Li Jing! Come here, please."

Another one? Kai's eyes narrowed.

A young woman in green robes hurried over, her long black hair tied back in a braid. She bowed to Zhang and Kai. "Yes, Alchemist Zhang?"

"Please show young Kai to the Thundergrass section," Zhang instructed. "And answer any questions he might have."

"Of course," Li Jing replied, turning to Kai with a bright smile. "Please, follow me."

As they walked through the pavilion, Kai couldn't help but notice the other disciples browsing the shelves. Some wore the white robes of Outer Disciples, but most sported the red of Inner Disciples. They all gave Kai a wide berth, eyeing his black robes with a mixture of awe and wariness.

It's like being a high-level player in a starting zone, Kai mused. *Everyone's afraid I might one-shot them if they look at me wrong.*

As they passed by a section of particularly colorful flowers, Kai noticed a familiar figure examining the plants. Shen Yu stood with his back to them, seemingly absorbed in his study of a bright-blue flower.

What's he doing here? And what's he looking at?

Kai slowed his pace, trying to get a better look without being obvious. Shen Yu's hand hovered over the flower, a faint glow emanating from his palm.

As if sensing Kai's gaze, Shen Yu suddenly looked up. Their eyes met, and for a moment, Kai saw a flash of . . . something in the other boy's expression. Surprise? Wariness? It was gone too quickly to tell.

Shen Yu's face settled into its usual calm mask as he abandoned the herb and began walking toward Kai. As he passed by, he leaned in close, his voice barely a whisper.

"You should have listened to my advice."

Before Kai could react, Shen Yu had disappeared into the crowd of disciples and herbalists.

"Senior Brother?" Chen Wei's voice snapped Kai out of his thoughts. "Is everything all right?"

Kai blinked, realizing he had stopped walking. "Yes, everything's fine. Let's keep going."

As they continued following Li Jing, Kai's mind raced with possibilities. Was Shen Yu trying to help him? Or was this some kind of trap?

Why can't he be straightforward? No need to be so cryptic . . . I need more information. But how to get it without revealing what I know . . . or don't know?

They finally reached a section near the back of the pavilion.

Li Jing gestured to a row of plants that looked like miniature lightning bolts frozen in time. "Here we are, Legacy Disciple. The finest Thundergrass in the Azure Sky Sect."

Kai leaned in for a closer look, careful not to touch the volatile-looking plants.

A translucent window appeared in Kai's vision.

Thundergrass (High Quality)
Description: A rare herb that grows in areas frequently struck by lightning. Contains concentrated lightning essence.
Uses: Cultivation aid for lightning-based techniques; ingredient in high-level lightning pills and elixirs.
Warning: Highly volatile. Handle with care.

"Impressive," Kai murmured. "How much for a portion suitable for one cultivation session?"

Li Jing hesitated for a moment. "For a portion of this quality, it would be eighty low-grade spirit stones, Legacy Disciple."

Kai managed to keep his expression neutral, but internally he winced. *Eighty spirit stones? Even though I have over a thousand spirit stones, I have a lot of other things I want to look into buying.*

He glanced at Chen Wei, who was trying not to look shocked at the price. An idea formed in Kai's mind.

"Chen Wei," he said casually. "You come from a merchant family, don't you? Perhaps you could handle this transaction for me."

Chen Wei's eyes widened in surprise. "M-me, Senior Brother? But . . . I'm just an Outer Disciple. Surely you don't want me to—"

Kai placed a hand on Chen Wei's shoulder, giving him an encouraging smile. "I trust your judgment, Chen Wei. Show me what you can do."

Li Jing looked between them, clearly confused by this turn of events. "Legacy Disciple, I . . . I'm not sure if—"

Kai held up a hand, silencing her protest. "It's all right. Chen Wei speaks with my authority in this matter."

Let's see how he handles this. It'll be a good test of his skills.

Chen Wei took a deep breath and squared his shoulders. When he spoke, his voice was steadier than Kai had ever heard it.

"Miss Li," he began, "while we certainly appreciate the quality of your Thundergrass, eighty spirit stones seems a bit steep. Perhaps we could discuss a more . . . reasonable price?"

Li Jing blinked, clearly thrown off balance by this turn of events. "I . . . Well, our prices are set by the head alchemist. I'm not sure if I have the authority to negotiate."

Chen Wei nodded sympathetically. "Of course, I understand. But surely as a representative of the Celestial Herb Pavilion, you have some discretion? After all, we're not just talking about any customer here, but a Legacy Disciple of the Azure Sky Sect."

Kai watched as Chen Wei continued to negotiate. The young disciple's demeanor had completely changed. Gone was the nervous, eager-to-please servant. In his place stood a confident, articulate negotiator.

He's got talent. With the right training, he could be incredibly useful.

After several minutes of back-and-forth, Li Jing finally relented. "Very well. For the Legacy Disciple, we can offer the Thundergrass for fifty spirit stones. But please understand, this is a one-time courtesy."

Chen Wei bowed deeply. "Thank you for your generosity, Miss Li. The Azure Sky Sect appreciates your flexibility in this matter."

As Li Jing went to prepare the Thundergrass for transport, Kai turned to Chen Wei with a smile. "Well done. You've got quite a talent for negotiation."

Chen Wei's face flushed with pride, but Kai noticed a hint of discomfort in his eyes. "Thank you, Senior Brother. I . . . I hope I didn't overstep my bounds."

Kai shook his head. "Not at all. You did exactly what I asked. Now, let's get that Thundergrass and head back. I've got some cultivation to do."

As they left the Celestial Herb Pavilion, Thundergrass safely stored in a special container and in his inventory, Kai noticed Chen Wei fidgeting nervously.

"Something on your mind?" Kai asked casually.

Chen Wei hesitated before speaking. "Senior Brother, I . . . I hope you don't think less of me for haggling like that. I know as cultivators we're supposed to be above such worldly concerns, but . . ."

Kai held up a hand, stopping Chen Wei mid-sentence. "Chen Wei, let me ask you something. In a battle between two equally skilled cultivators, what do you think gives one the edge?"

Chen Wei furrowed his brow in thought. "Well . . . better techniques? Or maybe stronger spiritual energy?"

Kai nodded. "Those are certainly factors. But often it comes down to who has better resources. More spirit stones for cultivation, rarer herbs for breakthroughs, higher quality weapons and artifacts. And how do you get those things?"

"By . . . by having more spirit stones?"

"Exactly," Kai said with a smile. "In this world, spirit stones aren't just currency. They're power. Every stone you save through skillful negotiation is a stone that can be used for cultivation, for acquiring knowledge, for gaining an edge over your competitors." He paused, letting his words sink in. "Never be ashamed of your merchant background, Chen Wei. Those skills you learned? They're just as valuable as any cultivation technique. And in the right hands, maybe even more so."

Chen Wei's eyes widened as he processed Kai's words. "I . . . I never thought of it that way, Senior Brother. Thank you for your wisdom."

Kai chuckled. "Don't thank me yet. Now that I know what you can do, I think I'll put you in charge of all my resource acquisitions from now on. If you're willing, of course."

Chen Wei's eyes widened in shock. "M-me? But, Senior Brother, I'm just an Outer Disciple. Surely someone of your status should have a more . . . qualified assistant."

Kai placed a hand on Chen Wei's shoulder, his voice firm but kind. "Chen Wei, in the short time I've known you, you've shown intelligence, loyalty, and now, impressive negotiation skills. Those qualities are far more valuable to me than status or cultivation level."

Though, I have to admit, nothing can beat a loyal high-leveled cultivator . . .

"But," he continued, "I understand if you're not comfortable with the responsibility. It's your choice."

Chen Wei stood silent for a moment, his expression a mix of emotions. Finally, he took a deep breath and bowed deeply.

"Senior Brother, I would be honored to serve you in this capacity. I promise I won't let you down."

Follower Gained: Chen Wei
Loyalty: 50

Kai nodded, satisfied. *Finally, the System recognizes him as my follower. Now I can work on building up his loyalty.*

As they walked back toward Kai's residence, his mind turned to the encounter with Shen Yu. *What was he doing in the herb pavilion?*

Kai recalled the herbs Shen Yu had been examining. He pulled up his System interface, searching his memory for details.

Azure Lightning Flower
Description: A rare herb that grows in areas with high concentrations of lightning essence. Known for its ability to enhance lightning-based cultivation techniques.
Rank: Uncommon

Wind Whisper Grass
Description: A delicate herb that thrives in areas with strong wind currents. Often used in techniques involving speed and agility.
Rank: Uncommon

Interesting combination. Lightning and wind . . . I know he is planning on mastering both legacy cultivation methods. Could he be using some secret recipe that has yet to be discovered to help him?

And then there is the warning about the Sect Master. Is the Sect Master linked to the mysterious disappearances? It wouldn't surprise me; he does seem a little creepy . . .

Regardless, I need more information. I guess I have to pay Shen Yu's pavilion a visit.

CHAPTER FIFTEEN

The sun had begun to set as Kai stood outside Shen Yu's pavilion, the evening breeze rustling his black robes. He had just returned to the Legacy Disciple quarters after dismissing Chen Wei, who was now cultivating in the servant's quarters.

"Shen Yu?" Kai called out, his voice carrying across the quiet courtyard. "Are you there?"

Silence greeted him. Kai waited a moment, then took a step forward. Instantly, a shimmer of energy rippled across the air in front of him as glowing lines of blue light appeared around the pavilion's perimeter.

Protection formations, Kai thought, stepping back quickly. *Of course. Every Legacy Disciple's pavilion would have basic defenses against intruders.* He sighed, running a hand through his hair. *Looks like Shen Yu doesn't want to talk. Or he's not here. Either way, I'm not getting in.*

Kai turned away from the pavilion. *Next time I see him alone, I'll have to confront him. But not somewhere too isolated. If he really is what I suspect . . .* A chill ran down Kai's spine as he considered the possibilities. *Reincarnator or regressor—both are dangerous. But a regressor? That's on a whole other level.*

He had played enough games and read enough stories to know the terrifying implications of someone who had lived through these events before. *If Shen Yu is a regressor, how much does he know about me? Was I even in the previous timeline? And what's his deal with the Sect Master? There's clearly some history there.*

Kai's eyes narrowed as he walked. Whatever was going on between Shen Yu and the Sect Master, he wanted no part of it. He had enough on his plate just trying to survive and advance in this world without getting caught up in ancient grudges or time-traveling schemes.

Best to focus on my own cultivation for now. I can worry about Shen Yu's secrets later.

As Kai approached his own pavilion, he forced his mind to clear. He had important work to do tonight, and he couldn't afford to be distracted by speculation about his fellow disciple's true nature.

Entering his private quarters, Kai made his way to the cultivation room. He settled onto a cushion in the center of the floor, crossing his legs and straightening his back.

All right, time to get to work. First step: closing the Third Eye meridian.

Kai took a deep breath, then let it out slowly as he closed his eyes. He focused his attention on the space between his eyebrows, searching for the telltale tingle of energy that would indicate the meridian's location.

At first, he felt nothing. Kai frowned and concentrated harder.

Come on, I know you're there. I've done this before.

Minutes ticked by as Kai struggled to sense the elusive meridian. Just as frustration began to set in, he felt it—a faint buzz of energy.

There you are.

Now that he'd found it, Kai focused on the sensation. He visualized the flow of qi through the meridian as a stream of light. Slowly, carefully, he began to narrow that stream. The process was much easier this time. The meridian seemed to respond readily to his will, the flow of energy slowing to a trickle.

Practice really does make perfect.

With a final push of concentration, Kai felt the meridian close completely. A subtle *click* resonated through his body.

Meridian Closed: Third Eye
Cultivation reduced to Qi Refining Stage 7

Kai allowed himself a small smile of satisfaction. *One down, one to go. Now for the tricky part.*

He reached into his inventory and withdrew the container of Thundergrass he'd purchased earlier. The crystalline box glowed faintly.

All right, let's see what this Lightning Insight method can do.

Kai carefully opened the container, the scent of ozone filling the air. He plucked a single blade of Thundergrass and placed the herb on his forehead, right between his eyebrows. A jolt of energy surged through him the moment the Thundergrass made contact with his skin. Kai gasped, his back straightening involuntarily.

Whoa. That's . . . intense.

Kai closed his eyes once more and focused on the space between his eyebrows. Following the manual's instructions, he began to visualize a storm cloud gathering in that spot.

At first, nothing happened. The mental image kept slipping away to be replaced by random thoughts and distractions. Kai took a deep breath and refocused his efforts.

Come on, picture the storm. Dark clouds, swirling winds, flashes of lightning . . .

Slowly, the image began to solidify in Kai's mind. He could almost hear the rumble of thunder, feel the electric charge in the air. The Thundergrass on his forehead began to tingle, a faint warmth spreading from the herb.

That's it. Build the storm . . .

In his mind's eye, Kai saw lightning flashing within the cloud. Each bolt sent a jolt through his body, making his fingers twitch. The warmth on his forehead intensified, spreading outward.

Almost there . . .

Kai pushed harder, imagining the storm growing stronger and stronger. The mental lightning increased in frequency, each flash brighter than the last. The tingling sensation spread from his forehead down his spine, making his whole body feel charged.

Just when Kai thought he couldn't take any more, something . . . shifted. It felt like a door bursting open in his mind, releasing a flood of energy. Kai gasped as lightning seemed to course through his entire being.

His eyes flew open, and for a moment, the world looked . . . different. Sharper, somehow.

The sensation faded quickly, but Kai knew something fundamental had changed. He reached up to touch the spot where he'd placed the Thundergrass. The herb had disintegrated, leaving only a faint residue on his skin.

A series of System notifications appeared.

Meridian Opened: Third Eye
Cultivation returned to Qi Refining Stage 8

Congratulations!
You have successfully converted your Third Eye Meridian to Storm Eye!
Lightning Affinity increased to 25%

Skill Leveled Up!
Crown of Lightning (Level 2)
Effect: A temporary visible aura of lightning can form around the cultivator's head during meditation, which boosts the cultivator's qi regeneration by 10%.

Skill Leveled Up!
Sky's Favor (Level 2)
Effect: The cultivator's qi-absorption rate increases by 10% whenever they are under an open sky. This increases to 15% during stormy weather.

Skill Leveled Up!

Electric Immunity (Level 2)
Effect: The cultivator gains 10% resistance to lightning-based attacks, reducing the damage taken from electric or lightning-based techniques.

New Skill Unlocked: Storm Eye (Level 1)
Description: The cultivator can create a small eye made of lightning energy. This eye can be detached and sent to scout nearby areas, allowing the user to see through it.
Range: 100 meters

You have gained 400 XP!

Kai's eyebrows rose as he read through the notifications. *Now we're talking. This is more like it.*

He focused on the new skill, Storm Eye. Following his instincts, Kai channeled a small amount of lightning qi to his forehead, which caused a tiny blue orb of energy to form and hover just in front of him.

Whoa. It's like a magical drone.

Kai concentrated on willing the lightning construct to move. The orb drifted across the room and stopped near a bookshelf. Suddenly, Kai's vision split. He could still see normally through his own eyes, but he also had a second perspective—a view of himself from the bookshelf.

"That's . . . incredibly weird," Kai said aloud, watching his own mouth move from the other angle.

He experimented for a few minutes, guiding the lightning eye around the room. The dual vision was disorienting at first, but Kai could see the potential usefulness of such an ability.

Remote scouting, seeing around corners, maybe even spying if I can make it small enough . . . Yeah, this could be really handy.

As the novelty wore off, Kai allowed the construct to dissipate. He sat back down on his cultivation cushion.

No wonder this is the Azure Sky Sect's prized skill. The enhanced perception alone is a huge advantage, never mind the other benefits.

Kai closed his eyes and focused on his newly opened Storm Eye meridian. *Two down, seven to go. I wonder what other surprises this method has in store.* He glanced out the window and was surprised to see the first hints of dawn peeking over the horizon. *Wow, I really lost track of time there. I should probably get some rest.*

As he prepared to turn in, a thought struck him. *Maybe I could use the Storm Eye to check on Shen Yu, see what he's up to . . .*

But almost immediately, Kai shook his head, dismissing the idea. *No, that's *too risky. The Storm Eye is an Azure Sky Sect skill. It would be shocking if the barrier formations didn't have precautions against it—especially a level-one skill like mine.*

With a sigh, Kai settled onto his bed. *Better to play it safe for now. I'll find another way to get information.*

CHAPTER SIXTEEN

Kai sat cross-legged in his room, frustration etched across his face. For the past three days, he'd been attempting to open the third meridian, the Meridian of Rolling Thunder. Despite his efforts, he had yet to make any real progress.

He unrolled the cultivation scroll once more, eyes scanning the text that he had already memorized.

> Meridian of the Rolling Thunder
> Location: Throat
> Method to Open: Voice of the Storm—the cultivator chants an incantation that mimics the sound of rolling thunder. The vibrations of the chant gradually open the Throat Meridian.

Kai sighed, running a hand through his hair. *This is like trying to unlock a new skill tree without meeting the prerequisites. There must be something I'm missing.*

He took a deep breath and prepared to attempt the incantation again. The strange syllables rolled off his tongue, a rhythmic chant that was supposed to mimic rolling thunder.

"Grum-bul-lum-bum, kra-ka-thoom . . ."

As he chanted, Kai focused on his throat, trying to direct his qi to that area. He imagined storm clouds gathering, electricity crackling in the air. But no matter how hard he concentrated, he couldn't feel the telltale signs of a meridian opening.

After several minutes, Kai stopped, letting out a frustrated groan. *This is going nowhere. Maybe I need to grind some more basic skills before tackling this advanced technique.*

"Senior Brother?" Chen Wei's voice called from outside the room. "The Sect Master has summoned you for your first lesson."

Kai stood up, stretching his stiff muscles. *Perfect timing. Maybe I can get some answers from the Sect Master.*

He opened the door to find Chen Wei waiting patiently. "Thanks, Chen Wei. Has Shen Yu been informed as well?"

Chen Wei nodded. "Yes, Senior Brother. One of the elders went to his pavilion to inform him."

"I see," Kai mused. "Does Shen Yu have a servant?"

Chen Wei shook his head. "No, Senior Brother. It's only me and Senior Brother Wang Lin's disciple in the servants' quarters for the Legacy Disciples."

Interesting. Shen Yu with all his secrets probably can't afford to have any servants around.

As they made their way to the Sect Master's quarters, Kai's mind raced. *I need to pay attention to everything, especially how Shen Yu interacts with the Sect Master. There might be clues about his true nature.*

They arrived at the building, and Chen Wei bowed and stepped back, leaving Kai to enter alone. Inside, Kai found the Sect Master sitting on a raised platform, his expression unreadable. To Kai's right, Shen Yu knelt on a cushion, his posture perfect and his face calm.

It's like facing the final boss with an NPC whose allegiance is unclear, Kai thought as he took his place opposite Shen Yu.

The Sect Master's gaze swept over them both, a slight nod the only acknowledgment of their presence. Then, to Kai's surprise, he turned to Shen Yu with a smile.

"Congratulations, Shen Yu, on awakening the seventh meridian using the Heavenly Thunderstorm cultivation method. Your progress is truly remarkable."

Kai's eyes widened slightly. *Seventh meridian? In just one week? Here I am, stuck on the third, and this guy's already more than doubled my progress.*

Shen Yu merely inclined his head slightly, his expression unchanged.

The Sect Master then turned to Kai, his smile a bit less enthusiastic. "You've made good progress as well, Kai. Two meridians isn't too bad for a beginner."

Isn't too bad? Kai repeated in his head, trying to keep his face neutral. *I thought I was making decent progress with natural cultivation. Guess I need to step up my game.*

He forced himself to nod respectfully. "Thank you, Master. I'll continue to work hard."

I need to stop comparing myself to Shen Yu, Kai reminded himself. *For all I know, he could have been close to the Immortal Ascension Realm in his previous life. This is like competing against a max-level player who's started a new character.*

The Sect Master clasped his hands together. "Now, before we begin your lesson, I'd like to test your elemental affinities. This will help guide your future cultivation."

Probably would have been a good idea to do this before we started cultivating using the new method, Kai thought.

The Sect Master produced a multifaceted crystal and held it up for them to see. "This is an Elemental Affinity Crystal. When you channel qi into it, it displays colors that correspond to your elemental alignments."

He proceeded to explain what each color indicated. To demonstrate, he channeled his own qi into the crystal. It glowed with a mixture of yellow and green light.

"As you can see, I have strong affinities for both lightning and wind," the Sect Master explained. He then handed the crystal to Shen Yu. "Your turn, young disciple."

Shen Yu took the crystal without a word and channeled his qi into it. The crystal glowed a bright, pure red.

The Sect Master's eyebrows rose fractionally before his expression smoothed out. "Interesting. You have a strong fire affinity, Shen Yu, but no others. Most cultivators struggle with techniques outside their elemental alignment. It's quite . . . unusual for someone with no lightning affinity to progress so quickly in the Heavenly Thunderstorm method."

Shen Yu remained silent, his face betraying nothing.

No lightning affinity? Kai thought, his mind racing. *Then how . . .* Suddenly, he remembered seeing Shen Yu examining some basic lightning and wind herbs at the Celestial Herb Pavilion. *Could those have something to do with his rapid progress?*

The Sect Master shook his head slightly, then turned to Kai with a wry smile. "Well, Kai, it's your turn. Perhaps you'll surprise us as well."

Kai took the crystal from Shen Yu, their eyes meeting briefly. He thought he saw a flicker of . . . something in Shen Yu's gaze, but it was gone too quickly to interpret.

As he channeled qi into the crystal, Kai wondered what his results would show. *I know I have a twenty-five percent lightning affinity from my stats, but do I have any others?*

The crystal in his hands began to glow. Yellow light suffused most of it, confirming his lightning affinity. But to Kai's surprise, portions of the crystal turned completely black.

The Sect Master's eyes widened, a mix of shock and perhaps a hint of fear crossing his face before he regained his composure. Kai glanced at Shen Yu expecting to see surprise, but instead, he found what looked like recognition or even anticipation in the other disciple's eyes.

"What . . . what does black mean?" Kai asked.

The Sect Master cleared his throat. "Black indicates a rare element—the chaos element."

Kai's eyes widened. *No wind element but instead a chaos element? Could this have something to do with my isekai situation? In most stories, the world is surrounded by chaos qi. Maybe being transported here gave me this affinity?*

"I've never heard of a chaos affinity," Kai said carefully. "Do we have any techniques in the sect that could help me develop it?"

The Sect Master laughed, but it sounded forced. "Only the largest sects would have such techniques, and even they might only possess one or two. It's an exceedingly rare and difficult element to cultivate. For now, I suggest we focus on your lightning affinity."

Kai nodded but filed the information away for later. *There has to be a way to develop this. If it's tied to my arrival in this world, it could be key to understanding why I'm here . . . and if there were others like me.*

"Sect Master," Kai ventured, "what determines a person's elemental affinities? Is it something we're born with, or can it change?"

"That's a matter of much debate among cultivators," the Sect Master replied. "We believe affinities are influenced by a range of factors: personality, life experiences, bloodline, and even the circumstances of one's birth or significant life events. Some say that profound spiritual experiences can awaken new affinities."

Like being transported to another world? Kai thought wryly.

The Sect Master's expression grew serious. "Kai, you need to keep your chaos affinity a secret for now. Such rare abilities can attract . . . unwanted attention."

Kai nodded, understanding the implication. *In game terms, I've just discovered I have a super rare class. Best not to advertise it until I level up enough to defend myself. Though, I would feel better if the Sect Master didn't know . . .*

"Now," the Sect Master continued, "let's begin our lesson. Shen Yu, what aspect of your cultivation do you need guidance with?"

Shen Yu spoke for the first time, his voice calm. "I don't require assistance with the Heavenly Thunderstorm method at present. However, I would like to begin learning the Azure Sky Legacy Wind technique."

The Sect Master's brow furrowed as he considered this request. After a moment, he shook his head. "Not yet, Shen Yu. Complete the first layer of the Heavenly Thunderstorm method and open the final two meridians. That will be the optimal time to introduce the wind cultivation method."

Shen Yu nodded once, accepting the decision without argument.

"If that's all, you're dismissed," the Sect Master said to Shen Yu. "I'll work with young Kai on his cultivation now."

As Shen Yu stood to leave, Kai caught another brief, unreadable glance from the other disciple. Then Shen Yu was gone, leaving Kai alone with the Sect Master.

CHAPTER SEVENTEEN

The Sect Master turned his full attention to Kai. "Now, Kai, let's discuss your progress. You seem to be having trouble with the third meridian?"

Kai took a deep breath. "Master, I've been struggling with the Meridian of Rolling Thunder for three days now. I haven't made any real progress."

The Sect Master's eyebrows rose slightly. "I see. Can you describe what happens when you attempt to open it?"

Kai nodded, thinking back to his many failed attempts. "I chant the incantation as instructed. I can feel my qi moving toward my throat, but . . . nothing happens. The meridian doesn't open."

The Sect Master tapped his chin, his eyes narrowing in thought. "Interesting. Tell me, Kai. How do you perceive thunder?"

The question caught Kai off guard. He blinked, trying to understand its relevance. "Thunder? It's . . . loud and rumbling, I suppose."

The Sect Master shook his head. "Think deeper, young disciple. What is the true nature of thunder?"

Kai furrowed his brow as he recalled thunderstorms from both his old world and this new one. "Well . . . it's not just one sound, is it? There's the initial crack followed by the rumble. And sometimes it's a low growl, other times a sharp boom."

A smile tugged at the corners of the Sect Master's lips. "Exactly. Thunder is complex, with layers and interplay between different tones and vibrations. It's not simply a single continuous sound."

Of course, Kai thought. *It's like sound design in a game. You don't just use one audio file for thunder—you layer multiple sounds to create a realistic effect.*

The Sect Master stood up, his robes rustling softly. "Perhaps a demonstration will help clarify things. Watch closely."

Kai leaned forward, eager to see what the Sect Master would do. The older cultivator closed his eyes, took a deep breath, and began to chant.

"Grum-bul-lum-bum, kra-ka-thoom . . ."

At first, the chant sounded similar to what Kai had been doing. But then, the Sect Master's voice changed. It cracked like lightning, then rumbled low like distant thunder. The sound rose and fell, sometimes a whisper, sometimes a roar.

Kai watched as the Sect Master's throat vibrated visibly. The air around them seemed to thrum with energy.

When the Sect Master finished, he opened his eyes and looked at Kai. "Do you understand now?"

Kai nodded slowly. "I think so. It's not about making a continuous sound. It's about building and releasing energy, like real thunder does."

"Precisely," the Sect Master said, looking pleased. "The Meridian of Rolling Thunder isn't about constant power. It's about the ability to build, release, and resonate."

Just like combo moves in a fighting game, Kai thought. *It's not about mashing one button, but about stringing together different actions.*

The Sect Master gestured for Kai to stand. "Now, try it again. Let your voice crack and rumble. Feel the vibrations shift in your throat."

Kai got to his feet, feeling a mix of nervousness and excitement. He took a deep breath, centering himself. *Okay, let's do this. Think of it like adjusting audio settings, finding the right balance.*

He began the incantation, this time focusing on varying his tone. He let his voice fluctuate, sometimes high and sharp, sometimes low and rumbling. As he chanted, he paid close attention to the sensations in his throat.

At first, nothing seemed different. But then, Kai felt a tingling sensation deep in his throat. It grew stronger and spread outward. Energy built within him, rising and falling like waves.

Kai's voice grew stronger, more resonant. The air around him began to vibrate, just as it had for the Sect Master. The tingling in his throat intensified, becoming almost uncomfortable.

And then, with a sensation like a dam breaking, Kai felt something shift inside him. His voice boomed out in perfect mimicry of rolling thunder. The sound filled the room, making the walls tremble slightly.

As the last echoes faded, Kai stood there, breathing heavily. He looked at the Sect Master, who nodded with satisfaction.

"Well done, Kai. You've opened the Meridian of Rolling Thunder."

A familiar notification popped up in Kai's vision:

Congratulations!
You have successfully opened the Meridian of Rolling Thunder!
Cultivation returned to Qi Refining Stage 8
Lightning Affinity increased to 27%

Skill Leveled Up!
Crown of Lightning (Level 3)
Effect: A temporary visible aura of lightning can form around the cultivator's head during meditation, which boosts the cultivator's qi regeneration by 15%.

Skill Leveled Up!
Sky's Favor (Level 3)
Effect: The cultivator's qi-absorption rate increases by 15% whenever they are under an open sky. This increases to 20% during stormy weather.

Skill Leveled Up!
Electric Immunity (Level 3)
Effect: The cultivator gains 15% resistance to lightning-based attacks, reducing the damage taken from electric or lightning-based techniques.

New Skill Unlocked: Thunder Voice (Level 1)
Description: Your voice can now mimic the sound and power of thunder, potentially stunning or intimidating opponents.

You have gained 400 XP!

"Thank you, Sect Master," Kai said, bowing deeply. "Your demonstration was incredibly helpful. I don't think I would have figured it out on my own."

The Sect Master waved off the thanks. "You did the work, Kai. I merely pointed you in the right direction. Remember this lesson: in cultivation, understanding the deeper mechanics is often crucial."

Kai nodded, filing away the advice. *Makes sense. It's like knowing the underlying game mechanics instead of just button-mashing.*

"Now," the Sect Master continued, "I want you to work on the next three meridians. Try to complete the sixth meridian by our next lesson. If you encounter any difficulties, don't hesitate to come to me."

"Yes, Sect Master," Kai replied. "I'll do my best."

As Kai turned to leave, the Sect Master spoke once more. "And Kai? Well done today. You show promise."

Kai bowed again and left the room. As he walked back to his quarters, he couldn't help but reflect on the lesson. *Despite his ulterior motives, I have to admit, he's a damn good teacher.*

Kai shook his head, pushing those thoughts aside for now. He had work to do. Three more meridians to open.

As he entered his pavilion, Chen Wei jumped to his feet. "Senior Brother! How did your lesson go?"

Kai smiled at his eager servant. "It went well, Chen Wei. I opened the third meridian."

Chen Wei's eyes widened. "That's amazing, Senior Brother! You're progressing so quickly!"

If only he knew, Kai thought wryly, *I'm actually behind Shen Yu.*

"Thank you, Chen Wei," Kai said aloud. "But I still have a lot of work to do. I need to open three more meridians before my next lesson with the Sect Master."

Chen Wei nodded enthusiastically. "Is there anything I can do to help, Senior Brother?"

Kai thought for a moment. "Actually, yes. Could you bring me some food and water? I'll need to keep up my strength while cultivating."

"Of course!" Chen Wei exclaimed, practically bouncing with excitement. "I'll be right back!"

As Chen Wei hurried off, Kai sat down on his meditation mat. He pulled out the Heavenly Thunderstorm scroll and unrolled it to the section on the fourth meridian.

Meridian of the Thunderous Heart

Location: Heart Center

Method to Open: Electric Pulse—the cultivator places their hands over their heart, focusing on the rhythmic pulse. They must visualize bolts of lightning striking their heart and align their heartbeat with the rhythm of thunder.

Kai's eyes widened as he read the instructions. He let out a low whistle, shaking his head in disbelief. "Well, that's certainly one way to stop my heart," he muttered dryly. "Nothing says 'cultivation' quite like self-induced cardiac arrest."

This world's cultivation methods are insane, Kai thought. *This should definitely come with a warning label. "Caution: may cause death or severe electrocution. Attempt at your own risk."*

He reread the instructions, trying to wrap his head around the concept. The idea of deliberately visualizing lightning strikes to his heart made him more than a little uneasy.

"I wonder if there's a cultivation insurance policy." Kai sighed, a wry smile on his face. "Or maybe a 'lightning strike survivor' achievement?"

CHAPTER EIGHTEEN

Kai placed his hands over his chest, feeling the steady rhythm of his heartbeat beneath his palms. Kai began to visualize bolts of lightning striking his heart in time with each pulse.

At first, nothing seemed to happen. Kai furrowed his brow, concentrating harder. He imagined the lightning growing stronger, more frequent, as he tried to sync it perfectly with his heartbeat.

Come on, it's like timing a combo move. Just got to get the rhythm right . . .

A tingling sensation began to spread through his chest. Kai's hopes rose. Was it working? The tingling intensified, becoming almost uncomfortable. His heart rate increased, thumping harder against his ribs.

Steady now. Don't want to overclock the System.

He tried to maintain the visualization, keeping the lightning strikes in sync with his accelerating pulse. The energy built, and for a moment, Kai thought he had it.

Then, without warning, the energy dissipated. The tingling faded, leaving Kai feeling slightly out of breath and more than a little disappointed.

He opened his eyes and sighed as he looked down at the scroll. "Well, that was anticlimactic," he muttered.

Kai glanced out the window, noting the position of the sun. He'd been at this for hours. *I should probably take a break. No use burning myself out.*

As he stood up, Kai couldn't help feeling a twinge of frustration. Part of him had hoped he'd be able to master this technique quickly, like a protagonist unlocking a new skill with ease. But reality, it seemed, had other plans.

It's fine. Real cultivation takes time and effort. But I do wish I could use the System to learn it instantaneously.

Kai walked over to his desk and picked up a cup of now-cold tea. He sipped it anyway, grimacing slightly at the bitter taste.

"Senior Brother?" Chen Wei's voice called from outside the room. "Are you finished with your cultivation for now?"

"Come in, Chen Wei," Kai replied, setting down the cup.

The young servant entered, bowing respectfully. "I brought some fresh fruit and water, in case you needed refreshment."

Kai smiled. "Thank you. That's exactly what I need right now."

As Chen Wei set down the tray, he glanced curiously at the open scroll. "How is your cultivation progressing, Senior Brother?"

Kai shrugged and picked up an apple from the tray. "Slowly. This new meridian is proving . . . challenging."

Chen Wei's eyes widened. "But you're a Legacy Disciple! Surely it can't be that difficult for someone of your talent?"

Kai chuckled, shaking his head. "Talent isn't everything, Chen Wei. Even the most gifted cultivators have to put in the work." *And I'm not exactly working with a cultivator's background or a prodigy's talent here.*

"Of course, Senior Brother," Chen Wei said quickly, looking slightly embarrassed. "I didn't mean to imply . . . It's just, well, you've progressed so quickly already."

Kai took a bite of the apple, considering his words carefully. "Progress isn't always linear. Sometimes you hit roadblocks. The key is to keep pushing forward."

As Kai finished the apple, his mind was already turning back to the problem at hand. *There has to be something I'm missing. Maybe I need to approach this from a different angle . . .*

He spent the rest of the day alternating between meditation attempts and studying the scroll, searching for any clue he might have overlooked. By nightfall, Kai was no closer to opening the meridian, but he refused to let it discourage him.

Rome wasn't built in a day, and I'm not going to become an immortal overnight. Just got to keep grinding.

The next few days fell into a similar pattern. Kai would wake early, attempt to open the meridian, study the scroll, then try again. Each failure only strengthened his resolve.

The Sect Master's offer of help lingered in the back of his mind, but he pushed it aside. He knew how cultivation worked in this world. Masters didn't hold their disciples' hands through every little challenge. They expected you to struggle, to push your limits before you came to them.

Besides, Kai mused as he prepared for yet another attempt, *I've only been at this for a few days.*

On the fourth day, as the sun was setting, Kai sat back on his heels, rubbing his temples. Another unsuccessful attempt. He could feel the energy, could almost grasp it, but something was still . . . off.

A knock at the door interrupted his thoughts. "Enter," Kai called out.

Chen Wei stepped in carrying a tray laden with steaming dishes. The aroma of spiced meat and vegetables filled the room, making Kai's stomach growl.

"I thought you might be hungry, Senior Brother," Chen Wei said, setting the tray down on a low table. "You've been working so hard, I worried you might forget to eat."

Kai's expression softened. "Thank you, Chen Wei. You're right, I did lose track of time." He moved to sit at the table and noticed Chen Wei hesitating. "Well, don't just stand there. Take a seat and dig in."

Chen Wei smiled, visibly relaxing. "Of course, Senior Brother. Thank you." He sat down across from Kai without further prompting.

As they ate, Kai found his mind wandering to practical matters. *I've been so focused on cultivation that I haven't given much thought to my financial situation.*

"Chen Wei," Kai said between bites, "I've been meaning to ask you something."

The young servant looked up attentively. "Yes, Senior Brother?"

"You mentioned before that your family owns an inn. What other ways does your family earn money?"

Chen Wei's eyes lit up at the question. "Oh, we have several ventures! Besides the inn, we have a small trading caravan that travels between towns. My older sister manages a textile shop, and my uncle runs a vineyard just outside the city."

Kai nodded, impressed by the family's entrepreneurial spirit. "That's quite diverse. Smart to have multiple income streams."

"Father always says not to put all your eggs in one basket," Chen Wei said proudly. Then he looked at Kai curiously. "If you don't mind me asking, Senior Brother, why are you interested in earning money?"

Kai leaned back, considering how to answer. "Well, as a Legacy Disciple, I receive a monthly allowance of spirit stones. It's generous, but not limitless. And in my experience, you can never have too many resources."

Chen Wei nodded. "Father says the same thing about money. But . . . what ways can a cultivator earn spirit stones? I mean, aside from sect missions and tournaments."

Kai grinned. "That's exactly what I was going to ask you. Any ideas?"

Chen Wei's brow furrowed in thought. "Well . . . I've heard some cultivators take on disciples or offer tutoring services. Others sell talismans or pills they've crafted. And some even act as mercenaries or guards for merchant caravans."

"Interesting options," Kai mused. *Tutoring could work, but it might take time away from my own cultivation. Talisman crafting sounds promising, but I'd need to learn the skill first. And mercenary work . . . Probably not the best idea while I'm still in the Qi Refining Realm. Also, leaving the sect would just put me in unnecessary danger.*

"What about trading?" Kai asked. "I remember you mentioning your family has some experience with that."

Chen Wei nodded enthusiastically. "Oh yes! Trading can be very profitable. Some cultivators specialize in finding rare herbs or minerals and selling them to sects or other cultivators. Others buy goods in one town and sell them for a profit in another."

Kai's eyes lit up. *Now that sounds promising. Buy low, sell high, and take advantage of market inefficiencies.*

"Chen Wei," Kai said, leaning forward, "I think I've found my side business. How would you like to help me start a small trading operation?"

Chen Wei's eyes widened. "Me? But . . . I don't know much about trading, Senior Brother. I've only heard stories from my family."

"That's more experience than I have. And you've got good instincts. I think your perspective could be valuable in this."

Chen Wei fidgeted nervously. "I . . . I'd be honored to help, Senior Brother."

Kai nodded, pleased. "Excellent. Now, let's start brainstorming. What goods do you think would be in high demand among cultivators?"

As they discussed potential products and markets, Kai found himself impressed by Chen Wei's knowledge. The young servant might not have direct experience, but he'd clearly been paying attention to his family's business discussions.

"You know," Kai said after a particularly insightful suggestion from Chen Wei, "you deserve more than just a servant's wage for this kind of work. How about I give you a percentage of the profits?"

"Oh no, Senior Brother! I couldn't possibly. This is my job as your servant. I already receive ten low-grade spirit stones a week, which is more than generous."

Kai shook his head firmly. "Chen Wei, you're a stage-seven Qi Refining cultivator. You'll need more resources than that if you want to break through to the next level and enter the Inner Sect someday."

Chen Wei hesitated, clearly torn between his sense of duty and the opportunity being offered. "Well, if you insist, Senior Brother. But really, even five percent would be more than enough."

"Ten percent," Kai countered.

Chen Wei's jaw dropped. "Ten percent? But that's . . . that's too much, Senior Brother!"

Kai smiled. *I would have gone up to twenty-five or even thirty-three percent, but if he's happy with ten, who am I to argue?*

"It's settled, then," Kai said. "Ten percent of the profits will go to you. Consider it an investment in your future, Chen Wei. The stronger you become, the more you can help me in return."

Chen Wei bowed deeply. "Thank you, Senior Brother. I . . . I don't know what to say."

"You don't need to say anything," Kai replied. "Just keep up the good work.

Now, let's start planning our first venture. I'm thinking we should start small, maybe with some common cultivation resources that are always in demand . . ."

As they delved into the details of their new business plan, Kai felt a sense of satisfaction. *This is a good start. Extra income, a loyal helper, and a chance to learn more about this world's economy. It's like setting up a gold-farming operation.*

The rest of the evening flew by as they refined their plans. By the time they finished, Kai had a clear idea of their first steps.

"All right, Chen Wei," Kai said as they wrapped up. "Tomorrow, I want you to start gathering information. Find out what cultivation resources are in highest demand right now and who the main suppliers are. Don't make any purchases yet—just scout the market."

Chen Wei nodded eagerly. "Yes, Senior Brother! I'll visit the sect's trading area and ask around discreetly."

"Good," Kai said. "And remember, we're starting small. We don't want to draw too much attention right away."

CHAPTER NINETEEN

The morning sun filtered through the window as Kai sat cross-legged on the floor, his eyes closed in deep meditation. A faint crackling sound filled the air, and anyone who entered the room would have seen an unusual sight: a crown of lightning dancing above Kai's head.

As he focused on his cultivation, Kai could feel the electric energy coursing through his body. With each breath, the lightning grew stronger, more controlled.

After an hour of meditation, Kai opened his eyes and stretched. The crown of lightning faded away, leaving behind a slight tingling sensation on his scalp.

Another day, another meditation session, and still no progress on opening the next meridian.

He glanced at the door, expecting Chen Wei to return any moment with information about trading opportunities in the sect. While he waited, Kai's mind turned to his plans for the future.

Once we have enough capital from trading, I should think about forming a guild. It's not typical in this world, but it could give us a real advantage.

Kai knew that in most xianxia stories, cultivators preferred to work alone. Cultivation was often portrayed as a solitary journey, with practitioners seeking enlightenment through isolation and personal trials.

But in other fantasy worlds, people group together in guilds all the time. Mage guilds, warrior guilds . . . Why not a cultivator guild? He began to list the potential benefits in his mind. *We could earn spirit stones without leaving the sect, reduce personal danger, pool resources and knowledge, all while creating a support network. And as we grow stronger, we could become a real powerhouse within the sect. Right now, we're just Qi Refining cultivators—no threat to the current power structure. But once we reach higher realms like Nascent Soul . . . We'd have some serious weight to throw around.*

Kai already had a small group forming around him—Liu Wei, Zhi-Zhi, and Chen Wei—but he knew it wasn't enough to form a proper guild yet.

I wonder if the System will even let me form a guild. It's worth checking. System, is it possible to form a guild with my followers?

A translucent blue window appeared before him.

> Guild Creation available.
> Would you like to proceed?

Kai's eyes lit up. "Yes!"

> Congratulations!
> You have initiated guild creation.
> Please choose a name for your guild.

Kai paused, considering. His first instinct was to call it the Gamer Guild, but he quickly dismissed that idea.

That would be way too obvious, he chided himself. *If there are other isekai protagonists in this world, I'd be painting a target on my back. Gotta be smarter than that.*

He pondered for a few moments, running through various cool-sounding names in his head. Then his eyes fell on the strange trident-shaped mark on his wrist.

The Trident Guild. That could work. It's mysterious enough to sound cool but doesn't give away any of my secrets.

> Guild Name Confirmed: Trident Guild
> Guild Leader: Kai Thorn
> Guild Members: 0

Kai frowned at the last line. *Zero members? But what about Liu Wei, Zhi-Zhi, and Chen Wei?*

As if sensing his confusion, another message appeared:

> To add members to your guild, you must formally invite them, and they must accept. Current relationships do not automatically translate to guild membership.

"Ah," Kai murmured. "That makes sense." *Can't have people joining without their knowledge. I'll be the leader, obviously. Chen Wei and Liu Wei can compete for the second-in-command spot—a little friendly rivalry never hurt anyone. And Zhi-Zhi . . . Well, every respectable guild needs a mascot, right?*

He made a mental note to speak with his followers as soon as possible. The sooner he could get them officially on board, the better.

> Would you like to view the Guild Management interface?
> Y/N

"Yes," Kai replied, eager to learn more about this new feature.

A complex diagram appeared before him, filled with various tabs and options. Kai's eyes darted from one section to another, taking in as much information as he could.

There were sections for member management, resource allocation, mission assignments, and even an internal ranking system. One particular feature caught Kai's attention: a loyalty meter for each member.

Interesting, Kai thought. *This could be useful for keeping track of potential problems.*

As he delved deeper into the interface, Kai found options for setting guild rules, establishing a headquarters, and even creating specialized roles for members.

This is perfect. With this system, I can run the guild like a well-oiled machine. Everyone will have their place, their purpose.

He spent the next hour exploring the guild interface, making mental notes of the most important features. By the time he finished, Kai felt confident that he had a solid grasp of how to manage his fledgling organization.

Now I just need to convince the others to join. Liu Wei should be easy enough. Chen Wei too, given our new business arrangement. Zhi-Zhi might be trickier, but I'm sure I can find a way to appeal to that little troublemaker.

As Kai closed the guild interface, he heard footsteps approaching his door. He quickly composed himself, adopting a casual pose as he waited for the knock.

That must be Chen Wei. Time to see what he's learned about the market.

"Enter."

The door opened, and Chen Wei stepped in, looking slightly out of breath but excited.

"Senior Brother," Chen Wei said with a bow. "I've returned with the information you requested."

Kai nodded, gesturing for Chen Wei to sit. "Excellent. Tell me what you've learned about the trading opportunities in the sect."

Chen Wei sat down across from Kai and pulled out a small notebook. "I visited the sect's trading area and spoke with several merchants and fellow disciples. I tried to be discreet, as you instructed."

"Good," Kai said. "What did you find out?"

Chen Wei flipped open his notebook. "The most in-demand cultivation resources right now are spirit herbs, particularly those used for breakthrough pills. There's also a high demand for low-grade spirit stones and basic talismans."

"Any specific herbs that stand out?"

"Yes." Chen Wei nodded enthusiastically. "Cloud Grass and Starfire Root are especially sought after. They're key ingredients in pills that help cultivators break through to the Foundation Establishment Realm."

That makes sense. Lots of disciples are probably stuck at the bottleneck between Qi Refining and Foundation Establishment. Hmm, should I go the typical protagonist route and become an alchemist? With the System, it shouldn't be too hard to learn . . .

"What about the suppliers?" Kai asked. "Who are the main players in the market?"

Chen Wei consulted his notes again. "There are three major suppliers of spirit herbs within the sect. The largest is run by Elder Bao of the Alchemist Division. The other two are smaller operations run by Core Disciples."

"And the spirit stones and talismans?"

"Spirit stones are mainly supplied by the sect itself," Chen Wei explained. "But there's always a demand for more, especially among Outer Disciples. As for talismans, there are several small-scale producers but no dominant supplier."

Interesting. There might be an opportunity there. Especially since I'm interested in formations and talismans.

"Good work, Chen Wei," Kai said, genuinely impressed by the young man's thoroughness. "This is exactly the kind of information we needed."

"Thank you, Senior Brother. I'm glad I could help. What's our next move?"

Kai leaned back, considering their options. "We need to start small, as we discussed. I don't know enough about talismans, so I think our best bet is to focus on spirit herbs for now. We can buy them from outside suppliers and sell them within the sect at a markup."

And once we earn enough spirit stones, I can buy some alchemy skill scrolls. Then we won't need external suppliers anymore.

"But won't we be competing with Elder Bao and the other suppliers?" Chen Wei asked, looking worried.

Kai grinned. "That's the beauty of it. We're not going to compete directly. We're going to find a niche."

Chen Wei looked confused. "A niche?"

"A specific market segment that isn't being served well by the current suppliers," Kai explained. "For example, we could focus on providing small quantities of herbs to Outer Disciples who can't afford to buy in bulk from the bigger suppliers."

Understanding dawned on Chen Wei's face. "Oh! Like how my family's inn caters to travelers who can't afford the fancy inns in the city center?"

"Exactly." Kai nodded. "We'll start small, build a reputation for reliability and fair prices, and then expand from there."

"That's brilliant, Senior Brother! When do we start?"

Kai held up a hand. "Not so fast. We need to do more research first. I want you to go back to the trading area tomorrow and gather more specific information. Find out exact prices for Cloud Grass and Starfire Root from different suppliers. Also, talk to some Outer Disciples and see how much they typically spend on cultivation resources each month."

Once we have that information, we can start sourcing from external suppliers. And when we've built up enough capital, I'll invest in those alchemy skills. It's a long-term strategy, but it should pay off big time.

Chen Wei nodded eagerly, jotting down notes. "I'll do that first thing in the morning, Senior Brother."

"Good," Kai said. Then he paused, considering his next words carefully. "Chen Wei, there's something else I wanted to discuss with you."

The young servant looked up, curious. "Yes, Senior Brother?"

Kai took a deep breath. *Time to recruit my first guild member . . .*

CHAPTER TWENTY

Kai leaned back, considering how to explain the concept of a guild to Chen Wei. He didn't know if they used that word in this world, so he decided to use a term more familiar in this setting.

"Chen Wei," Kai began, "I'm starting my own faction within the sect."

Chen Wei's eyes widened. "A faction, Senior Brother? But you're already a Legacy Disciple. Why would you need a faction?"

Kai smiled. "Being a Legacy Disciple is great, but it's also isolating. I think we can accomplish more if we work together as a team."

"I see." Chen Wei nodded slowly. "And what would this faction do, exactly?"

"Well," Kai said, "we'd support each other in our cultivation, share resources, and take on missions together. It's about pooling our strengths and covering each other's weaknesses."

Chen Wei looked intrigued. "That does sound beneficial. But won't the sect Elders disapprove?"

Kai shook his head. "Not if we do it right. We're not going against the sect; we're just organizing ourselves to be more effective within it. Think of it as . . . a study group, but for cultivation."

"I understand," Chen Wei said. "And you . . . you want me to be part of this faction?"

"Exactly." Kai nodded. "You'd be one of the founding members. But before you decide, let me explain the rules I've come up with."

As Kai spoke, he noticed blue text appearing in his vision.

Guild Rules Added:
Loyalty to the guild and its members.
Share information beneficial to the guild.
Assist other members when possible.
Keep guild matters confidential.
Contribute a portion of personal gains to guild resources.

Do not harm other guild members.
Betrayal of guild rules will result in the Guild Leader being notified.

Kai blinked, surprised at how the System was integrating his impromptu rules. *Well, that's convenient. I guess I'm on the right track.*

"Those sound like reasonable rules, Senior Brother," Chen Wei said. "But what will you call this faction?"

Kai grinned. "I'm calling it the Trident Guild."

Chen Wei's eyes lit up with recognition. "Guild? Ah, like the Merchant's Guild in the city or the Alchemist's Guild in the sect? That's a clever choice, Senior Brother."

It's a common term here after all. I definitely would have known that if I wasn't so obsessed with just cultivating. Well, anyway, that makes things much easier.

"Exactly. I thought it would be fitting for our group. It has a certain . . . professional ring to it, don't you think?"

Chen Wei nodded. "Indeed, Senior Brother. It sounds very official and respectable."

Using a familiar term will make our guild seem more legitimate to others in the sect. And it reduces the risk of standing out to any potential isekai protagonists who might be around.

"I'm glad you approve, Chen Wei," Kai said with a smile. "So . . . would you like to join the Trident Guild?"

Chen Wei stood up and bowed deeply. "It would be my honor, Senior Brother."

Chen Wei has accepted the guild invitation.
Where would you like to place the Trident Mark on his body to show allegiance?

Kai blinked, taken aback by the sudden message. *A mark? I didn't expect this. Is it just to show allegiance, or does it have special abilities like my own?*

"Chen Wei," Kai said, trying to keep his excitement in check, "as a member of the Trident Guild, you'll receive a special mark. Where would you like it placed?"

Chen Wei looked startled. "A mark? Like . . . a tattoo?"

"Not exactly," Kai said, though he wasn't entirely sure. "It's more of a spiritual imprint, I believe. It won't be visible to others unless you choose to reveal it."

At least, I hope that's how it works. I should probably check the details before we proceed. System, can you give me more information about this mark?

The Trident Mark serves multiple purposes:

> It identifies guild members to each other.
> Guild members can communicate with each other from a distance.
> Members can use credits earned through missions to activate the mark's powers to a limited degree.
> The mark will be visible to non-guild members when its abilities are in use.

Kai's eyes widened. *This . . . this is huge. My guild members could potentially condense qi, like me, or even . . . respawn after death?*

"Chen Wei," Kai said, trying to keep his voice calm, "the mark is more significant than I initially realized. It will grant you access to special abilities as you complete tasks for the guild. Think of it as . . . a cultivation aid."

Chen Wei's eyes lit up. "Really? That's amazing! In that case, I'd be honored to bear the mark. But where do you think it should go, Senior Brother?"

Kai considered for a moment. "How about on your right shoulder blade? It's easy to conceal but also accessible if needed."

Chen Wei nodded. "That sounds perfect."

Kai stood up and placed his hand on Chen Wei's right shoulder blade. He felt a brief surge of energy, and Chen Wei gasped.

"Did you feel that?" Kai asked.

Chen Wei nodded, his eyes wide. "Yes, it was . . . warm. And it felt like . . . like a surge of power."

Kai smiled. "Good. That means it worked. Now, Chen Wei, I need you to do something for me. Can you go find Liu Wei and Zhi-Zhi and bring them here? It's time to invite them into the guild as well."

Chen Wei bowed. "Of course, Senior Brother. I'll find them right away." He turned and left the room.

As the door closed behind Chen Wei, Kai let out a long breath. *That went better than I expected. Now, let's see what else this guild system can do.*

> Guild members who die and have enough credits to respawn will reappear at the location of the Guild Leader.

Kai nodded to himself. *That's incredibly convenient, especially if someone gets killed in a place where they're stuck. It's like having a mobile respawn point.*

He opened his map function and noticed a new feature. Chen Wei's location was now visible as a small blue dot.

Interesting. So, I can always see where my guild members are. And—wait, is that . . . ?

Kai noticed another dot on the map, this one gold in color. He zoomed in and saw it was labeled "Sect Master."

Oh yeah, since the tea ceremony, I guess I can now see the Sect Master's location too. With how strange he's been acting, at least I'll know if he's nearby or following me. But then again, if he's spying from far away with some Enlightenment-level technique, I won't know, so I still need to keep my guard up.

Kai sat down, then began to plan out potential missions and ways to earn credits for his guild members.

We'll need to start small. Maybe some gathering missions in the nearby forest? Or we could offer our services to other disciples for a fee. As we build up our reputation and resources, we can take on bigger challenges.

He thought about the trading operation he and Chen Wei had discussed earlier. *That could be our first big guild project. We'll use our combined knowledge and resources to corner the market on certain cultivation supplies. It's like setting up a player-run economy in an MMO. Find the most in-demand items, control the supply, and watch the profits roll in.*

He began jotting down ideas in a notebook, occasionally glancing at the map to check Chen Wei's progress. The blue dot representing his first guild member was moving quickly through the sect compound.

Kai paused in his writing, a new thought occurring to him. *I should probably come up with some sort of initiation ceremony. Nothing too elaborate, but something to make new members feel like they're part of something special.*

He began sketching out ideas for a simple ritual. *Maybe a recitation of the guild rules, followed by a symbolic gesture . . . like clasping hands over the Trident Mark? That might be a little difficult for Chen Wei . . . And we could have special robes or accessories for guild members to wear during meetings.*

Kai chuckled to himself. *Look at me, getting all caught up in the details. But that's what makes a good guild leader, right? Attention to detail and planning for every contingency. Not only that but humans love to feel part of a group, even if these humans could collapse a mountain with a thought.*

He turned his attention back to the guild interface, exploring the various menus and options available to him as the guild leader.

Guild Management Options:
Member Rankings
Mission Assignment
Resource Allocation

Kai was so engrossed in his planning that he almost missed the sound of footsteps approaching his door. He quickly closed the guild interface and composed himself, trying to look casual as he waited for the knock.

Here we go. Time to expand the Trident Guild.

The door opened, and Chen Wei stepped in, followed by Liu Wei and Zhi-Zhi. Liu Wei looked curious, and Zhi-Zhi was perched on Liu Wei's shoulder.

"Senior Brother," Chen Wei said with a bow, "I've brought Liu Wei and Zhi-Zhi as you requested."

Kai nodded, a smile spreading across his face. "Excellent work, Chen Wei. Please, everyone, come in and make yourselves comfortable. We have much to discuss."

This is it. The real beginning of the Trident Guild. Time to see if I can turn this ragtag group into a force to be reckoned with. Let the recruitment begin!

CHAPTER TWENTY-ONE

As they settled into their seats, Kai took a moment to observe them. Liu Wei seemed more confident than before, his posture straighter and his eyes clearer. Zhi-Zhi, on the other hand, appeared less boastful than even the last time Kai had seen him in the canteen.

Interesting character development. Time to gather some intel.

"So," Kai began, his tone casual, "how have you both been? It's been a while since we last spoke."

Liu Wei bowed his head slightly. "It's been . . . an adjustment, Master. My new master, Elder Jiang, is strict but fair. The training has been difficult, but . . ." He paused, a proud smile tugging at his lips. "I've managed to break through to the fifth stage of Qi Refining."

Kai's eyebrows rose slightly. "That's impressive, Liu Wei. Congratulations."

Name: Liu Wei
Level: Qi Refining Stage 5
Qi: 100/100
Strength: 33
Agility: 34
Endurance: 32
Intelligence: 15
Wisdom: 12
Loyalty: 80/100
Elemental Affinities:
Wind: 20%
Water: 15%
Skills:
Basic Qi Gathering (Level 1)
Wind Rider's Path (Level 2)
Wind Step (Level 2)

Stealth (Level 2)
Lockpicking (Level 2)
Dagger Proficiency (Level 2)

The System's information confirmed Liu Wei's words. Kai's eyes lingered on the Wind Rider's Path.

I'm glad Liu Wei now has a real cultivation method.

"Your new master seems to be teaching you well," Kai said, nodding approvingly. "The Wind Rider's Path is a respected cultivation method."

"How did you know . . ." Liu Wei's eyes widened slightly. "Are you familiar with it, Master?"

Kai smiled enigmatically. "Something like that."

Turning his attention to Zhi-Zhi, Kai asked, "And what about you, little one? How have you been faring with your new master?"

To Kai's surprise, Zhi-Zhi didn't immediately launch into a boastful tirade. Instead, the spirit beast's eyes shone with admiration as he spoke.

"Master Cang Long is amazing!" Zhi-Zhi exclaimed. "He's so wise and powerful. Did you know he can create entire islands with his qi? And he's teaching me all sorts of techniques. Like how to reinforce my shell with spiritual energy, and how to . . ."

As Zhi-Zhi continued to share his master's virtues, Kai found himself smiling. The little tortoise's character seemed to have undergone quite a transformation.

Looks like Zhi-Zhi found a role model. That's good. A mentor figure will help temper that ego of his.

After letting Zhi-Zhi ramble for a few more moments, Kai gently cut in. "I'm glad to hear you're both progressing well. Actually, that's part of why I asked Chen Wei to bring you here today."

Liu Wei and Zhi-Zhi fell silent, their attention fully on Kai.

Kai quickly summarized his plan to form a guild within the sect, explaining the benefits of working together and supporting each other. He emphasized how it would allow them to share resources, take on missions as a team, and combine their strengths.

"What kind of benefits are we talking about?" Zhi-Zhi asked.

Always looking out for number one, eh? Kai thought, amused. *Some things never change.*

"Well," Kai said, "for starters, members of the guild would have access to a unique form of communication. It's similar to spiritual transmission, but distance isn't an issue. You'd be able to contact any guild member, anywhere, at any time."

Liu Wei's eyes widened. "That's . . . impressive. How is that possible?"

Kai smiled mysteriously. "Let's just say it's a special technique I've developed. But that's not all. You've all seen my qi-condensing ability, right?"

They nodded, and Kai held out his hand. With a thought, he condensed his qi into a small glowing hammer. The others leaned in, fascinated.

"If you complete enough missions for the guild," Kai continued, "you'll gain the ability to use this technique as well."

Liu Wei gasped softly. "Really? But . . . how?"

Kai dispelled the qi construct. "It's part of the guild's—let's call it a cultivation secret. The more you contribute to the guild, the more you'll be able to tap into this power."

The room fell silent for a moment as Liu Wei and Zhi-Zhi processed this information. Then, chaos erupted.

"What? Really?" Liu Wei exclaimed, leaping to his feet. "Master, that's . . . that's incredible! With an ability like that, I could—"

"I could create an impenetrable fortress!" Zhi-Zhi interrupted, his eyes gleaming. "No, a floating island! No, wait, a—"

"Calm down, both of you," Kai said, holding up his hands. "Remember, you'll need to earn this ability through hard work and dedication to the guild."

As Liu Wei and Zhi-Zhi continued to chatter excitedly about the possibilities, Kai noticed Chen Wei's more subdued reaction. *Right, he hasn't seen me use this ability much. I'll need to make sure he understands its value too.*

Kai cleared his throat, regaining everyone's attention. "So, would you like to join?"

Liu Wei was quiet for a moment, his expression thoughtful. Then he nodded, a small smile on his face. "I'd be honored. To be honest, I've . . . missed having you as my master. This feels right."

Kai felt a warmth in his chest at Liu Wei's words. *Loyalty is a rare and valuable thing in this world*, he thought. *I'm glad I chose to bring Liu Wei with me.*

"Thank you, Liu Wei. I'm glad to have you on board." He turned to Zhi-Zhi. "And what's your decision?"

Zhi-Zhi puffed up his chest, trying to look important. "Well, I'll have to think about it. After all, I'm quite busy with my own training, and Master Cang Long might not approve of—"

Kai raised an eyebrow. "I see. Well, if you're not interested, that's fine. This is a limited-time offer, after all. I'm sure we can find another spirit beast to join in your place."

"Wait!" Zhi-Zhi exclaimed, his facade crumbling. "I . . . I accept! I want to join the guild!"

Kai struggled to keep a straight face. *Zhi-Zhi is still as predictable as ever.*

"Excellent," Kai said, smiling. "Welcome to the Trident Guild, both of you."

Liu Wei tilted his head. "The Trident Guild?"

"Yes, that's the name I've chosen for our faction," Kai answered as he looked at the mark on his right wrist. "Now, there's one more thing we need to do to make your membership official. Each guild member receives a special mark. It's what allows for the long-distance communication I mentioned and what will eventually grant you access to the qi-condensing ability." He held up a hand to forestall any questions. "Don't worry. It's not visible unless you choose to reveal it. But I do need to know where you'd like the mark placed."

Liu Wei considered for a moment. "Could I have it on my right forearm?"

Kai nodded. "Of course. Zhi-Zhi?"

The spirit tortoise hesitated. "Um . . . can it go on my shell? Or would that not work?"

"Your shell is fine," Kai assured him. "The mark is spiritual in nature, so it will work regardless of where it's placed."

With their choices made, Kai approached Liu Wei first. He placed his hand on the former bandit's right forearm and channeled a small amount of qi. Liu Wei gasped as a faint trident-shaped mark appeared briefly before fading from view.

> New guild member added: Liu Wei

Kai smiled at the System message, then moved to Zhi-Zhi. He placed his hand on the spirit tortoise's shell and repeated the process.

> New guild member added: Zhi-Zhi

"There," Kai said, stepping back. "It's done. You're now officially members of the Trident Guild."

Liu Wei rubbed his forearm, a look of wonder on his face. "I can feel it. It's like . . . a warm presence."

Zhi-Zhi was twisting his neck, trying to see the mark on his shell. "Does this mean I can talk to you whenever I want now?"

Kai nodded. "That's right. Just focus on the mark and think of who you want to communicate with. It might take some practice at first, but you'll get the hang of it."

As the others experimented with their new ability, Kai's mind turned to the more serious matters at hand. *Now comes the tricky part. How much should I tell them about the guild's true capabilities?*

He thought about the respawn ability, the ace up his sleeve that had saved his life more than once. It was tempting to share this information with his guild members, to assure them that they had a safety net.

But I can't tell them about the respawn ability. If the sect found out, they'd never let me leave. They'd probably lock me up and use me as some kind of resurrection machine.

Kai made his decision. *Better to keep that ability hidden for now. I can always reveal it later if absolutely necessary.*

Your request to hide the respawn ability from guild members has been granted. You will have the option to respawn fallen members if they have sufficient credits.

Perfect. That gives me some flexibility without revealing too much.

"There's one more thing you should know about the guild marks," Kai said, his tone serious. "They have . . . a protective quality. If you're ever in mortal danger, the mark will activate and try to save you. I can't say more than that right now, but know that being part of this guild means you have an extra layer of security."

The others nodded, looking both intrigued and slightly confused.

That should be enough to hint at the respawn ability without giving too much away. If the worst happens and I need to use it, I can come up with an explanation then.

"Now," Kai said, clapping his hands together, "let's talk about our first guild activity."

The others leaned in, eager to hear more.

"We're going to start a trading operation," Kai explained. "Nothing too big at first, but with the potential to grow into something significant."

He outlined the plan he and Chen Wei had discussed earlier, explaining how they would focus on supplying cultivation resources to Outer Disciples who couldn't afford to buy in bulk from the larger suppliers.

"Each of you will have a role to play," Kai continued. "Chen Wei has been gathering information on the current market. Tomorrow, he'll share what he's learned, and we'll start putting our plan into action."

Liu Wei nodded thoughtfully. "This could work well, Master. My time with the bandits taught me a lot about supply and demand. I could help identify potential customers and negotiate deals."

"Excellent idea, Liu Wei. You can help Chen Wei with that."

Zhi-Zhi puffed up his chest. "And what about me? What's my role in this grand plan?"

Kai smiled. "You, Zhi-Zhi, have perhaps the most important role of all. You'll be our scout and our secret weapon."

The spirit tortoise's eyes widened. "Secret weapon?"

Kai nodded. "That's right. Your small size and ability to hide in your shell make you perfect for gathering information unnoticed. And if anyone tries to cheat us or cause trouble, well . . . they certainly won't be expecting a spirit beast at Qi Refining stage nine to pop out and teach them a lesson, will they?"

Zhi-Zhi's chest swelled with pride. "No, they certainly won't! I'll show them the might of a spirit tortoise!"

And there's the Zhi-Zhi we know and love, Kai thought, amused. *At least now his boasting might actually be useful.*

"Remember," Kai cautioned, "this operation needs to start small and grow naturally. We don't want to draw too much attention too quickly. The goal is to build a stable, profitable enterprise that will benefit all of us in the long run."

The others nodded their understanding.

"Good," Kai said. "Now, let's go over the specifics of what we'll be trading and how we'll structure our operation . . ."

An hour later, the meeting began to wind down, and Kai could see the wheels turning in each of his guild members' heads. Liu Wei was already muttering to himself about potential information sources, while Zhi-Zhi was listing off offensive techniques under his breath. Chen Wei was scribbling notes in a small book, probably planning out tomorrow's market research.

This is a good start. We've got a solid core group, each with their own strengths. Now we just need to execute our plan.

"All right," Kai said, drawing everyone's attention once more. "We'll meet again tomorrow evening to discuss Chen Wei's findings and plan our first trades."

The others nodded as they filed out of the room.

Once he was alone, Kai pulled up his guild management interface.

Trident Guild Status:

Members: 4

Guild Level: 1

Available Missions: 0

Guild Funds: 0 spirit stones

Not much to look at yet. But every guild has to start somewhere. We'll build this up, step by step.

CHAPTER TWENTY-TWO

Kai sat cross-legged on his cultivation pillow, eyes closed in deep concentration. A crown of lightning danced above his head. As he focused, a charge of lightning began to surround his chest, pulsing in rhythm with his heartbeat.

Almost there, Kai thought, maintaining his focus. *Just need to sync the lightning with my pulse.*

He visualized bolts of lightning striking his heart, aligning each strike with the steady *thump-thump* of his heartbeat. The energy built, growing more intense with each passing moment.

Suddenly, Kai felt a shift within his body. His eyes snapped open. It had worked. A smile spread across his face as he looked down at the scroll beside him.

Meridian of the Thunderous Heart

Location: Heart Center

Method to Open: Electric Pulse—the cultivator places their hands over their heart, focusing on the rhythmic pulse. They must visualize bolts of lightning striking their heart and align their heartbeat with the rhythm of thunder.

I did it. Another meridian opened.

As if on cue, a series of blue windows appeared before him.

Congratulations!

You have successfully opened the Meridian of the Thunderous Heart!

Cultivation returned to Qi Refining Stage 8

Lightning Affinity increased to 30%

Skill Leveled Up!

Crown of Lightning (Level 4)

Effect: A temporary visible aura of lightning can form around the cultivator's head during meditation, which boosts the cultivator's qi regeneration by 20%.

Skill Leveled Up!
Sky's Favor (Level 4)
Effect: The cultivator's qi-absorption rate increases by 20% whenever they are under an open sky. This increases by 25% during stormy weather.

Skill Leveled Up!
Electric Immunity (Level 4)
Effect: The cultivator gains 20% resistance to lightning-based attacks, reducing the damage taken from electric or lightning-based techniques.

New Skill Unlocked: Heart of Thunder (Level 1)
Description: Unleash a powerful thunderous shockwave from your heart that stuns and damages nearby enemies while providing a surge of protective energy for 10 seconds to allies within the radius.

You have gained 400 XP!

Not bad. The Heart of Thunder skill seems pretty useful. It's like an AOE stun with a party buff. Could come in handy if I ever need to protect the others during a group battle.

As he put the scroll away, Kai felt a sense of satisfaction. Opening meridians was never easy; he knew the difficulty would only increase as he continued, but he was getting better at it.

Just glad I finally cracked this one. The lightning cultivation method is working well for me. He stood up, stretching his arms above his head. *Now, time to check on the others and see what info Chen Wei managed to gather.*

As if on cue, a knock sounded at the door.

"Come in," Kai called out.

The door opened to reveal Chen Wei, Liu Wei, and Zhi-Zhi. They filed into the room, taking seats around Kai.

"Senior Brother," Chen Wei said with a bow. "I've gathered the information you requested."

Kai nodded. "Excellent. Let's hear it."

Chen Wei pulled out his small notebook and began to read. "I've collected data on the exact prices for Cloud Grass and Starfire Root from various suppliers outside the sect. Each bundle contains thirty pieces of either material. The prices range from fifty to eighty spirit stones per bundle, depending on quality and quantity."

"Good start," Kai said. "What about the Outer Disciples? How much do they typically spend on cultivation resources?"

"On average, Outer Disciples spend between ten and fifty spirit stones per month on cultivation resources," Chen Wei replied. "This varies based on their cultivation level and personal wealth, of course."

Interesting, Outer Disciples get a stipend of ten spirit stones a month, but they need more than that just to continue cultivating. Kai nodded as he remembered seeing the Outer Disciples always busy with one manual job or another.

Liu Wei leaned forward. "That's quite a range. Did you notice any patterns in their spending habits?"

Chen Wei nodded. "Yes, actually. Those closer to breaking through to the next stage tend to spend more, often pushing their budgets to the limit."

That's a potential market we could tap into, but that might not be enough. Hmm, I think I have a better idea . . .

"What about qi-gathering pills?" Kai asked. "What's the current market price for those?"

Chen Wei consulted his notes. "Low grade qi-gathering pills sell for about thirty spirit stones each in the sect's market. However, I also looked into the materials needed to make them."

Kai raised an eyebrow. "Oh? And what did you find?"

"The main ingredients are Spirit Grass, Yin Berries, and Qi Crystals," Chen Wei explained. "If bought separately, these materials cost about fifteen spirit stones per pill."

Half the price . . . If we could make our own, we'd double our profit margin.

"Did you look into alchemy at all?" Kai asked.

Chen Wei nodded enthusiastically. "Yes, Senior Brother. I gathered information on the different levels of alchemy and alchemists. There are five main levels: novice, apprentice, journeyman, master, and grandmaster."

"And the cost of basic alchemy skill scrolls?" Kai pressed.

"A basic novice-level alchemy guide scroll costs about five hundred spirit stones," Chen Wei replied.

That's half of my current funds. But it could be a worthwhile investment.

"What do you all think?" Kai asked, looking around at his guild members. "Should we stick with trading Cloud Grass and Starfire Root, or should we consider making our own qi-gathering pills?"

Liu Wei spoke up first. "Making our own pills could be more profitable in the long run, but it would require a larger initial investment. Plus, we'd need to ensure our quality matches or exceeds what's currently on the market."

"I say we make the pills!" Zhi-Zhi grinned.

"Chen Wei, what's your opinion?" Kai asked.

Chen Wei hesitated for a moment before speaking. "I believe making our own pills could be very profitable, Senior Brother. However, it would require more time and effort than simply trading existing goods. We'd need to factor in the time spent on learning to produce pills."

He's right. Time is a resource too, especially in cultivation. However, since the scroll would belong to me, it wouldn't matter if it disappeared, so I could learn it instantaneously.

After a moment of consideration, Kai made his decision. "All right, here's what we're going to do. We're going to start by making our own qi-gathering pills."

"Really?" Liu Wei asked, looking surprised. "Are you sure, Master?"

Kai nodded. "Yes. It's a bigger risk but also a bigger potential reward. Plus, it gives us more control over our product."

"Excellent choice!" Zhi-Zhi exclaimed. "I knew you'd see the wisdom in it!"

More like I saw the profit margin, Kai thought wryly.

"Chen Wei," Kai continued, "I need you to go outside the sect and purchase the materials we need for the pills. Take Zhi-Zhi with you."

Chen Wei bowed. "Of course, Senior Brother. How many spirit stones should I take for the purchases?"

Kai did some quick mental math and brought out some spirit stones from his inventory. "Take three hundred spirit stones. That should be enough for a good initial stock of materials."

"Understood," Chen Wei said, taking the pouch from Kai and making a note in his book.

Kai turned to Zhi-Zhi. "Zhi-Zhi, you're going as protection. Stay hidden and don't get involved in the negotiations. Your job is to watch for any signs of trouble and protect Chen Wei if necessary."

Zhi-Zhi puffed up his chest. "I shall be as silent as a shadow and as vigilant as a mountain eagle!"

As long as you're as silent as a shadow, we should be fine, Kai thought, amused.

"Liu Wei," Kai said, turning to the former bandit. "I want you to start scouting potential customers within the sect. Focus on Outer Disciples who are close to breaking through. They're likely to be our best market."

Liu Wei nodded, a determined look in his eyes. "I understand, Master."

"Good," Kai said. "Remember, we're not making any sales yet. Just gather information on who might be interested. A list of customers will be useful once we start selling, so start on that. Let's get some preorders."

"What will you be doing, Senior Brother?" Chen Wei asked.

Kai stood up, straightening his robes. "I'm going to the Alchemist Pavilion to buy some skill scrolls. We can't make pills without the knowledge, after all. We'll meet back here in four days. I should have some pills ready by then."

The others exchanged surprised glances.

Liu Wei spoke up. "Master, forgive me, but . . . learning to make pills takes years of study. Even the most talented alchemists spend months mastering the basics."

Kai smiled confidently. "I appreciate your concern. But trust me. I have my ways. Plus, we're just talking about basic qi-gathering pills to start with, not some high-level elixir."

Chen Wei bit his lip, clearly torn between respect for Kai and disbelief at the timeline.

Zhi-Zhi puffed up. "Now see here! Even my master couldn't—"

Kai held up a hand, cutting off the spirit tortoise's protest. "Four days. Trust me."

As they filed out of the room, Kai could hear them whispering among themselves, their doubt palpable. He couldn't help but smile.

It's the best long-term decision. If we can establish ourselves as reliable pill makers, we could corner a significant portion of the market. I did want to avoid competing with the big boys from the get-go, but hopefully, my title as Legacy Disciple should give me enough protection. Especially since no one will expect me to become an alchemist so suddenly.

He looked into his inventory and began to manage his finances.

Five hundred for the skill scroll, three hundred for materials, which I've already handed to Chen Wei. That leaves me with two hundred as an emergency fund. It's cutting it close, but it should work. In another week, the month will end, and I'll get another one thousand spirit stones anyway.

CHAPTER TWENTY-THREE

Kai stood in the hallway of the Alchemist Pavilion, his eyes darting from one corner to another. Unlike the Celestial Herb Pavilion, this place buzzed with activity. Everywhere he looked, he saw alchemists hurrying about.

Wow, this place is like an anthill, Kai thought, observing the organized chaos around him. *Reminds me of crafting districts. Always busy, always productive.*

The air was thick with the scent of herbs and minerals, a complex mix that tickled Kai's nose. He could hear the distant clanging of mortar and pestles, the bubbling of concoctions, and the occasional hiss of steam.

As Kai stood there, taking in the sights and sounds, a young man in blue robes approached him. The man's eyes widened slightly as he noticed Kai's black robes.

The blue-robed man bowed deeply. "Greetings, Legacy Disciple. This humble one is Ye Tao, a novice alchemist. How may I be of service?"

"Hello, Ye Tao," Kai replied, his voice calm and measured. "I'm Kai. I'm looking to learn some alchemy. I heard you have some beginner guides available?"

Ye Tao's eyes widened, surprise evident on his face. He quickly schooled his expression, but not before Kai caught the reaction.

Interesting. Looks like none of the other Legacy Disciples have shown any interest in alchemy.

"Of course, Senior Brother Kai," Ye Tao said. "We have several excellent guides for beginners. May I ask what sparked your interest in the art of alchemy?"

Kai considered his response carefully. *No need to reveal too much. A vague answer should suffice.*

"I've always been fascinated by the process of transformation," Kai said, his tone nonchalant. "Turning simple ingredients into powerful elixirs . . . It's quite remarkable, don't you think?"

Ye Tao nodded vigorously. "Indeed, Senior Brother! Alchemy is truly a wondrous art. The ability to refine and transmute, to create something greater than the sum of its parts . . . It's nothing short of magical."

He's certainly passionate about it.

"Well said, Ye Tao," Kai replied with a small smile. "Now, about that guide . . ."

"Ah, yes!" Ye Tao exclaimed. "Please, follow me. I'll show you to our collection of beginner texts."

As they walked through the bustling hallways, Kai took mental notes of everything he saw. Alchemists of various ranks hurried past, some carrying stacks of scrolls, others balancing trays of bubbling vials.

This place is a gold mine of information. I'll need to come back here when I have more time to explore.

Ye Tao led Kai to a quieter section of the pavilion. The walls here were lined with shelves, each filled with scrolls and books of various sizes.

"Here we are," Ye Tao said, gesturing to the shelves. "These are our beginner texts. Is there any particular aspect of alchemy you're interested in? Herbal remedies? Qi-enhancing elixirs? Poison crafting?"

"I think it's best to start with the fundamentals," Kai replied. "Do you have a comprehensive guide that covers the basic principles of alchemy?"

Ye Tao's face lit up. "We do have just the thing. Please, wait here a moment."

The young alchemist hurried off, leaving Kai alone in the quiet section. Kai took the opportunity to examine the shelves more closely.

Interesting titles, he thought, reading the labels on the scrolls. *"A Beginner's Guide to Herbal Infusions," "Fundamentals of Mineral Refinement," "Qi Circulation in Alchemical Processes." I could spend weeks just reading through these.*

A few minutes later, Ye Tao returned carrying a thick scroll. He presented it to Kai with both hands, a look of reverence on his face.

"This is our finest guide for beginners," Ye Tao said, his voice filled with pride. "It contains the most important basic five techniques needed for alchemy. If one were to master these techniques to their peak, it would be enough to become a journeyman alchemist."

Kai took the scroll, feeling its weight in his hands. *This is the one Chen Wei was referring to.*

"What are these five techniques?"

Ye Tao's eyes sparkled as he began to explain.

"The first technique is Essence Extraction. This is the foundation of all alchemy and teaches you how to draw out the purest essence from herbs, minerals, and other materials. The second is Elemental Fusion. This technique allows you to combine different elemental properties in your concoctions and create more potent and complex effects. Third is Qi Infusion. This technique teaches you how to imbue your creations with qi, which enhances their potency and allows for the creation of cultivation aids."

Now we're getting to the good stuff, Kai mused. *This is probably crucial for making those qi-gathering pills.*

"The fourth technique is Stability Control. This is vital for preventing your concoctions from becoming unstable or explosive during the creation process."

Ah, the safety measures. Definitely important.

"And finally," Ye Tao said, his voice filled with awe, "there's Spiritual Resonance. This advanced technique allows you to attune your creations to specific spiritual frequencies and create pills and elixirs tailored to individual cultivators or cultivation methods."

Interesting. That sounds like it could be incredibly useful for customizing pills for the guild members. I could focus on that later down the line.

"These five techniques form the core of alchemy," Ye Tao concluded. "Master them, and you'll have a solid foundation for any pill."

Kai nodded, impressed. "That does sound comprehensive. How much does this scroll cost?"

Ye Tao hesitated for a moment before answering. "This particular scroll is quite valuable. It's priced at five hundred low-quality spirit stones."

That's exactly what Chen Wei said, but I should probably negotiate a bit.

"That's quite expensive for a beginner's guide," Kai said, his tone casual. "Are you sure there isn't a more . . . economical option?"

"I assure you, Senior Brother, this scroll is worth every spirit stone," Ye Tao replied. "The techniques contained within are distilled from centuries of alchemical wisdom. Many have used this very scroll as the foundation for illustrious careers in alchemy."

"Is there any way we could make it more affordable?" Kai asked.

Ye Tao shook his head firmly. "The prices are set by the Head Alchemist; it would be a violation of the rules to manipulate the prices, even for a Legacy Disciple."

Kai sighed for a moment then nodded. "Very well. I'll take it."

"An excellent decision, Senior Brother! You won't regret it."

Kai reached into his inventory and retrieved the five hundred low-quality spirit stones. He handed them over to Ye Tao, who accepted them with a deep bow.

"Thank you, Senior Brother," Ye Tao said. "Is there anything else you need?"

Kai was about to decline when a thought struck him. *Wait a second. There's usually some kind of certification process for crafting professions. I should probably check if that applies here too.*

"Actually, Ye Tao," Kai said, "I have a question. Once I've learned these techniques, would I be able to start creating and selling pills immediately?"

Ye Tao's eyes widened in surprise. "Ah, I see you're thinking ahead! You're right, there is one more step before you can officially sell pills."

Kai raised an eyebrow, encouraging Ye Tao to continue.

"Before anyone can start selling pills," Ye Tao explained, "they must pass an alchemy exam and become a certified novice alchemist."

I knew it. There's always a quest or a test to unlock new professions.

"I see," Kai said aloud. "Can you tell me more about this exam? What does it entail?"

Ye Tao nodded eagerly. "Of course. The exam to become a novice alchemist consists of three parts."

Kai nodded as he listened intently.

"The first part is a written test," Ye Tao began. "It covers basic alchemical theory, herb identification, and safety procedures. You'll need to demonstrate a solid understanding of the fundamental principles of alchemy."

That shouldn't be too hard. With the System, I can probably learn all that information quickly if they're skill scrolls.

"The second part," Ye Tao continued, "is a practical test. You'll be required to create a basic pill under observation. Usually, it's something simple like a minor healing pill or a low-grade qi-replenishment pill."

"And the final part?"

Ye Tao smiled. "The final part is an oral examination. A senior alchemist will ask you questions about your creation process, your understanding of alchemical principles, and how you would handle various scenarios that might arise during alchemy."

Ah, the classic "defend your work" part of any exam. I'll need to be prepared to explain my methods clearly.

"I see," Kai said aloud. "And how often are these exams held?"

"The exams are held monthly," Ye Tao replied. "The next one is in three days, but I'd suggest you practice for a few months at least."

Kai considered for a moment. *Three days . . . That's cutting it close. But with the System's help, it might be possible.*

"I'll see how it goes," Kai said with a confident smile. "One more question, Ye Tao. What are the benefits of becoming a certified novice alchemist?"

"Oh, there are many benefits!" Ye Tao's eyes lit up. "First and foremost, you gain the legal right to sell your alchemical creations within the sect. You also gain access to the Alchemist Pavilion's resources—our libraries, our ingredient stores, and our practice rooms. You'll be able to take on alchemy-related missions from the sect. These can be quite lucrative and often involve creating specific pills or researching new alchemical formulas."

Missions that can be completed within the sect is one of the main reasons I was interested in becoming an alchemist or a Formation user, but with the System, it shouldn't take me too long to become both, at least to the novice level.

"And of course," Ye Tao added, "there's the prestige. Alchemists are highly respected. Even a novice alchemist commands a certain level of respect."

Respect is good, but the access to resources and missions is the real prize here.

"Thank you, Ye Tao," Kai said. "You've been incredibly helpful. I think I have everything I need for now."

"It's my pleasure, Senior Brother. If you have any more questions as you begin your alchemical journey, please don't hesitate to ask. We're always happy to assist a budding alchemist, especially one of your status."

Kai nodded, then paused as a thought struck him. "Actually, Ye Tao, there is one more thing. Do you have any recommendations for practice materials? Things I could use to experiment with as I learn these techniques?"

"For beginners, I would recommend starting with some common herbs and minerals. Things like Spirit Grass, Yin Berries, and basic Qi Crystals are perfect for practicing Essence Extraction and Qi Infusion," Ye Tao answered.

Those are the exact ingredients for low-grade qi-gathering pills, Kai thought, pleased. *This works out perfectly.*

"For Elemental Fusion," Ye Tao continued, "you might want to try working with elemental essences. We have starter kits available that contain small amounts of various elemental materials. They're quite safe for beginners."

"And what about equipment? What sort of tools would I need to start practicing?" Kai asked.

"For basic practice, you don't need anything too elaborate," Ye Tao explained. "A good quality mortar and pestle, a set of measuring tools, and a few heat-resistant containers should be sufficient to start. Oh, and a small furnace for pill refinement, of course."

"I see. Is it possible to purchase the equipment here at the Alchemist Pavilion?"

Ye Tao's face brightened. "Of course! We have complete beginners' sets available. They include everything you'd need to start your alchemical journey."

"And the cost?" Kai asked, raising an eyebrow.

"A full set, including the small furnace, would cost one thousand low-grade spirit stones," Ye Tao replied. "It's a bit of an investment, but the quality is excellent, and it will serve you well as you learn."

One thousand spirit stones . . . That's more than I can afford right now. But maybe there's another option . . .

"What about practice space?" Kai inquired. "You mentioned practice rooms. Is it possible to rent a room here to use the equipment?"

"Absolutely!" Ye Tao clapped his hands. "We have practice rooms available for rent. They're fully equipped with all the necessary tools and safety measures."

"And the cost for that?"

"The rooms can be rented for five spirit stones per hour," Ye Tao explained. "It's quite reasonable, especially for beginners who aren't ready to invest in their own equipment yet."

Perfect. Kai smiled. *I can practice the techniques at home, then come here to actually create pills when I'm ready.*

CHAPTER TWENTY-FOUR

The small village of Greenleaf was nestled among three hills, a patchwork of fields stretching out around it. Thatched roofs and wooden buildings huddled together. In the distance, workers toiled under the hot sun as they tended to the crops.

In one of the larger fields, a group of farmers worked diligently, their backs bent as they moved through rows of plants. A middle-aged man stood at the edge of the field, his arms crossed as he observed their efforts with a critical eye. This was Yu Fen, a former disciple of the Azure Sky Sect.

Yu Fen's graying hair was tied back in a simple ponytail, and his clothes, while of decent quality, showed signs of wear. As he watched the workers, his lips pressed into a thin line.

"You there!" he called out to a young man struggling with a hoe. "Put your back into it! You're barely scratching the surface."

The worker nodded quickly, redoubling his efforts. Yu Fen shook his head, muttering under his breath. "Useless, the lot of them."

If only I had broken through to Foundation Establishment, he thought bitterly. *I wouldn't be stuck here managing these peasants.*

Behind Yu Fen stood two men, both in their early twenties. They were his followers, cultivators who had attached themselves to the former disciple in hopes of learning from him. Both were at Qi Refining stage seven, a respectable level for those outside a major sect.

"Master Yu," one of them spoke up. "Should we demonstrate the proper technique to the workers?"

Yu Fen waved a dismissive hand. "Don't waste your energy, Liang. These fools barely have the capacity to understand basic farming, let alone the intricacies of qi-enhanced labor."

The other follower, a stocky man named Mu, nodded in agreement. "You're right, Master. It's best to save our strength for more important tasks."

As they stood there, a commotion began to stir in the village. People were gathering, pointing and whispering. Yu Fen's eyes narrowed as he spotted the cause of the excitement—a young man in white robes walking purposefully through the village.

"An Azure Sky Sect disciple?" Mu muttered.

Yu Fen's jaw clenched. "Outer Disciple, by the look of his robes. What business does he have here?"

They watched as the newcomer made his way toward their field. As he drew closer, Yu Fen could see that he was quite young, probably no more than sixteen or seventeen. The boy's eyes scanned the area, finally settling on Yu Fen and his followers.

"Greetings," the young man said as he approached, bowing politely. "My name is Chen Wei. I'm looking for Yu Fen. Might that be you, sir?"

Yu Fen raised an eyebrow, studying the boy. "I am Yu Fen. What brings an Outer Disciple of the Azure Sky Sect to our humble village?"

Chen Wei straightened, a polite smile on his face. "I've heard about some of the materials you're selling, sir. My master is interested in making a purchase."

His master? Yu Fen thought, intrigued. *An Inner Disciple, perhaps?*

Out loud, he said, "Is that so? And who might your master be?"

Chen Wei hesitated for a moment before responding. "I'm afraid I'm currently not at liberty to say, sir. But I can assure you, he's very interested in doing business."

Yu Fen nodded slowly, his mind working. He gestured to Liang and Mu, who immediately moved to stand behind him. The subtle show of force wasn't lost on Chen Wei, whose eyes flickered briefly to the two men.

"Well, Chen Wei," Yu Fen said, his tone casual, "I'm afraid you may have wasted a trip. You see, I already have plenty of customers for my goods. In fact, demand has been so high that I'm not sure I see the point in selling at my old prices anymore."

Chen Wei's brow furrowed slightly. "I see. Well, perhaps we could discuss a new price that would be beneficial for both parties?"

Yu Fen smiled, but there was no warmth in it. "Of course, of course. Why don't we step into my office and talk numbers?"

As they walked toward a small building at the edge of the field, Yu Fen's mind raced. *This could be an opportunity. If this boy's master is truly influential, a favorable deal could open new doors. But if not . . .*

Inside the cramped office, Yu Fen settled behind a desk while Chen Wei took a seat across from him. Liang and Mu remained standing, flanking the door.

"Now, then," Yu Fen began, leaning forward. "Let's talk business. What exactly are you looking to purchase, and in what quantities?"

Chen Wei pulled out a small notebook, consulting it briefly. "We're interested in Spirit Grass, Yin Berries, and Qi Crystals. Ideally, enough to produce around twenty low-quality qi-gathering pills."

Yu Fen's eyebrows shot up. "Twenty? That's quite an order for an Outer Disciple's master. Are you sure you have the spirit stones to cover such a purchase?"

Chen Wei nodded confidently. "My master has provided me with sufficient funds, sir. Now, about the price . . ."

What followed was a back-and-forth negotiation that lasted nearly half an hour. Chen Wei proved to be surprisingly adept for his age, countering Yu Fen's inflated prices with well-reasoned arguments and alternative offers.

This boy is no fool, Yu Fen thought grudgingly. *He's been well trained.*

As their discussion wore on, Yu Fen found himself growing increasingly frustrated. Chen Wei refused to budge beyond a certain point, and the price he was offering, while fair, wasn't the windfall Yu Fen had hoped for.

Finally, Yu Fen slammed his hand on the desk. "Enough! I've entertained this long enough. My final offer is five hundred spirit stones for the lot. Take it or leave it."

Chen Wei frowned. "I'm sorry, sir, but that's simply too high. My master was very clear about the maximum we could spend. The price should be around three hundred spirit stones. Perhaps we cou—"

"Perhaps," Liang cut in, "you should consider your position more carefully, little Outer Disciple."

Chen Wei turned to look at him. "Excuse me?"

Mu stepped forward, cracking his knuckles. "What my friend means is that you're awfully far from the safety of your sect, boy. It might be wise to show some . . . flexibility in your negotiations."

Yu Fen watched Chen Wei carefully, noting the flicker of fear that passed across the young man's face. *Good. Let him sweat a little.*

"Now, now," Yu Fen said, his tone deceptively mild. "There's no need for threats. I'm sure Chen Wei understands the delicate nature of his situation. After all, we have some very powerful backers in this region as well as in the sect. It would be a shame if an accident were to befall such a promising young cultivator."

Chen Wei's eyes darted between the three men, his earlier confidence evaporating. "I . . . I don't understand. Are you threatening me?"

Yu Fen spread his hands in a gesture of mock innocence. "Threatening? Not at all. Simply explaining how things work out here in the real world. The sect won't care if a single Outer Disciple goes missing, you know. It happens all the time."

Chen Wei swallowed hard, then seemed to steel himself. "My master is a Legacy Disciple of the Azure Sky Sect. If anything happens to me—"

The laughter that erupted from Yu Fen and his followers cut Chen Wei off mid-sentence. Yu Fen wiped a tear from his eye, shaking his head.

"Oh, you poor naive boy," he said. "Do you think I don't know how it is? I was an Outer Disciple once, long ago. I know all about the lies and exaggerations you tell to make yourselves feel important."

Chen Wei's face reddened. "It's not a lie! My master really is—"

"Enough!" Yu Fen roared, all pretense of friendliness gone. His aura flared, the oppressive weight of a stage-nine Qi Refining cultivator filling the small room. Chen Wei gasped, visibly struggling under the pressure.

"Let me explain how this is going to work," Yu Fen said, his voice dangerously soft. "You're going to hand over all the spirit stones you brought with you. In exchange, I might consider letting you leave here in one piece. Understand?"

Chen Wei's eyes widened in panic. "But . . . but I can't! The spirit stones aren't mine. They belong to my master! Please, you don't understand—"

Yu Fen stood abruptly, his chair scraping against the floor. "I understand perfectly. You came here thinking you could play with the big boys, and now you're in over your head. It's time you learned a harsh lesson about the cultivation world, boy."

With a burst of qi-enhanced speed, Yu Fen vanished from behind the desk and reappeared directly in front of Chen Wei, who had no idea how things had escalated so far.

The young disciple's eyes barely had time to widen before Yu Fen's fist came hurtling toward his face.

But the blow never landed.

CHAPTER TWENTY-FIVE

A small, round object suddenly materialized between Yu Fen and Chen Wei. Yu Fen's fist connected with it, and he stumbled backward, pain shooting through his hand.

"What in the—" he began but was cut off by a high-pitched voice.

"Chen Wei didn't come alone, you big bully! He's under my protection!"

The round object unfurled, revealing itself to be a small tortoise. It glared up at Yu Fen with surprising ferocity for such a tiny creature.

Yu Fen's eyes narrowed as he studied the newcomer. "A spirit beast? Here?"

The tortoise puffed out its chest, trying to look intimidating despite its small size. "That's right! I am Zhi-Zhi, and you'd better back off if you know what's good for you!"

Despite his bravado, Zhi-Zhi felt a tremor of fear run through him as he met Yu Fen's intense gaze. *Stay calm*, he told himself. *Remember your training. Master Cang Long wouldn't be scared of this bully!*

Yu Fen's lips curled into a sneer. "How amusing. The little Outer Disciple brought his pet along for protection. I'm quaking in my boots."

"I'm the disciple of the great Cang Long!"

Yu Fen's eyebrows rose at the mention of Cang Long. Even he, years removed from the sect, knew that name. Cang Long was a legend, the guardian beast of the Azure Sky Sect. If this little spirit beast was truly his disciple . . .

But no. Yu Fen shook his head, dispelling the momentary doubt. This had to be another bluff, another desperate attempt by these Outer Disciples to save themselves.

"Cang Long's disciple?" Yu Fen scoffed. "Do you take me for a fool? Cang Long wouldn't waste his time on a pipsqueak like you."

Zhi-Zhi's face fell for a moment, hurt flashing in his eyes. But then his expression hardened, determination replacing the fear. "Think what you will," he said, his voice steadier now. "But know this: I won't let you harm Chen Wei!"

Yu Fen's followers exchanged uneasy glances. This was not how they had expected things to go. A spirit beast, even a young one, was not to be trifled with lightly.

But Yu Fen was not so easily deterred. With lightning speed, he lashed out at Zhi-Zhi, but the spirit tortoise was faster than he looked. Zhi-Zhi retreated into his shell just as Yu Fen's fist connected, and the blow glanced off the impenetrable surface.

"Ow!" Yu Fen yelped, shaking his hand. "What is that shell made of?"

Zhi-Zhi poked his head out, a smug expression on his face. "Back off before I start attacking!"

Yu Fen's face contorted with rage. "Liang! Mu! Deal with the Outer Disciple. I'll handle this impudent creature."

As his followers moved toward Chen Wei, Yu Fen focused his attention on Zhi-Zhi.

"Wind Blade Strike!" Yu Fen shouted, slashing his hand through the air. A crescent of compressed air shot toward Zhi-Zhi.

The spirit tortoise's eyes widened. *Oh no, that looks dangerous!* He quickly retreated into his shell once more. The wind blade struck the shell, creating a loud ringing sound but leaving no visible damage.

Meanwhile, Chen Wei found himself facing off against Liang and Mu. Despite being outnumbered, the young disciple held his ground.

"Flowing Wind Palm!" Chen Wei called out, his hand glowing with a soft blue light. He struck out at Liang, who barely managed to dodge the attack.

Mu attempted to flank Chen Wei, but the Outer Disciple was ready. "Whirlwind Kick!" Chen Wei spun, lashed his leg out in a qi-enhanced roundhouse, and caught Mu in the chest, sending him stumbling backward.

I can do this, Chen Wei thought, his confidence growing. *They're not at the level of the disciples I've fought.*

Back with Yu Fen and Zhi-Zhi, the battle had turned into a strange game of cat and mouse. Yu Fen unleashed attack after attack, but Zhi-Zhi's shell proved impervious to them all.

"Stand still and fight like a real cultivator!" Yu Fen roared in frustration.

Zhi-Zhi poked his head out just long enough to retort, "I am fighting like a real cultivator! A smart one who uses his strengths!"

As the battles raged on, Yu Fen found himself growing increasingly annoyed. *This is taking too long. That spirit beast's defense is too strong, and the Outer Disciple is holding his own against Liang and Mu. Time to end this.*

With a burst of speed, Yu Fen disengaged from Zhi-Zhi and turned his attention to Chen Wei. The young disciple was preoccupied with fending off Liang and Mu, leaving him vulnerable.

The tortoise is too slow to protect him now. One clean hit and this farce will be over.

Just as Yu Fen prepared a sneak attack, a voice cut through the chaos of the room.

"What exactly is going on here?"

Everyone froze. Standing in the doorway was a young man dressed in the red robes of an Inner Disciple of the Azure Sky Sect. His aura was clearly beyond the Qi Refining Realm. He was, without a doubt, a Foundation Establishment cultivator.

Yu Fen's eyes widened. "B-Boss!" he stuttered, immediately bowing low. "I . . . We were just—"

The newcomer raised a hand, silencing Yu Fen's fumbling explanation. His gaze swept the room, taking in the scene before him.

"I see," he said, his voice cold. "And would someone care to explain why my subordinates are attacking an Outer Disciple of my sect?"

Yu Fen swallowed hard. "There . . . there must have been some misunderstanding, Boss. We were simply negotiating a business deal, and things got a bit . . . heated."

The Inner Disciple's eyes narrowed dangerously. "Is that so?"

He turned his attention to Chen Wei and Zhi-Zhi, his expression softening slightly. "You two. I recognize you. You're friends of the new Legacy Disciple, aren't you?"

Chen Wei nodded, still catching his breath. "Yes, sir. My name is Chen Wei, and this is Zhi-Zhi. We're here on behalf of Senior Brother Kai."

The Inner Disciple nodded thoughtfully. "I see. Well, allow me to introduce myself. I am Lin Yue, an Inner Disciple of the Azure Sky Sect. And it seems I owe you an apology for the behavior of my . . . associates."

He shot a dark look at Yu Fen, who seemed to shrink under his gaze.

"Now, then," Lin Yue continued, "perhaps we can discuss this business deal in a more civilized manner? I'm sure we can come to an arrangement that satisfies everyone."

After an hour of discussion, Lin Yue and Chen Wei finally came to an agreement. Chen Wei had brought three hundred spirit stones with him, as per Kai's instructions. Initially, this would have been enough for materials to make twenty qi-gathering pills, as each set of materials cost fifteen spirit stones.

However, due to Lin Yue's intervention and as compensation for the earlier "misunderstanding," Yu Fen agreed to a substantial discount. The final deal was struck at three hundred spirit stones for materials sufficient to produce twenty-five qi-gathering pills.

As Chen Wei and Zhi-Zhi prepared to leave with their hard-won goods, Lin Yue pulled them aside.

"Please convey my apologies to your master for this incident," he said. "And let him know that if he ever needs assistance with matters outside the sect, he's welcome to contact me directly."

Chen Wei bowed deeply. "Thank you, Senior Brother Lin. I'll be sure to pass along your message."

As they walked away, Zhi-Zhi perched on Chen Wei's shoulder, the young disciple couldn't help but feel a mix of relief and pride. *We did it*, he thought. *We completed the mission, even if it didn't go exactly as planned. Wait until Senior Brother Kai hears about this!*

Back in his office, Lin Yue stood by the window watching Chen Wei and Zhi-Zhi disappear down the road. His eyes narrowed in thought.

Lin Yue turned back to face Yu Fen and his followers, who were standing nervously in the corner of the room.

"Now, then," Lin Yue said. "Let's discuss your recent . . . indiscretions."

Yu Fen swallowed hard, sweat beading on his forehead. "Boss, I swear, we didn't know they were connected to a Legacy Disciple. We were just trying to—"

Lin Yue held up a hand, silencing him. "Save your excuses, Yu Fen. You were willing to kill a sect member over petty spirit stones. Not only that but that disciple has a scarier backing than my own. Your actions today have jeopardized our operations and potentially created an enemy out of someone who could have been a powerful ally. Do you understand the gravity of your mistake?"

Yu Fen nodded quickly, his face pale. "Yes, Boss. It won't happen again. I promise."

Lin Yue's eyes narrowed. "See that it doesn't. For now, you'll continue your work here, but know that you're on thin ice. One more misstep, and you'll find yourself wishing you were merely expelled from the sect."

As Yu Fen and his followers scurried out of the office, Lin Yue sat down at the desk, his mind working furiously. *This new Legacy Disciple, Kai . . . He's not what I expected. Sending his subordinates out on errands like this—and with a spirit beast for protection, no less—means he's either very confident or very foolish.*

Lin Yue pulled out a small communication talisman and activated it with a pulse of qi. "Mo Fe, I need you to gather all the information you can on the new Legacy Disciple, Kai. Be discreet but thorough. I want to know everything—his background, his abilities, his connections within the sect. Take a look at both the Celestial Herb Pavilion and the Alchemy Pavilion in particular. Our friend is interested in herbs. Oh, and report back to me as soon as possible."

As he ended the transmission, Lin Yue leaned back in his chair, a small smile playing on his lips. *Things are about to get very interesting in the Azure Sky Sect. I'd better make sure I'm prepared for whatever comes next. Allying myself with a Legacy Disciple wouldn't hurt . . .*

CHAPTER TWENTY-SIX

Kai sat cross-legged on his meditation cushion, his eyes fixed on the glowing blue window floating before him. The scroll he'd purchased from the Alchemist Pavilion lay unfurled on the table nearby.

Basic Novice Alchemy Guide acquired.
Would you like to learn the skills?
Y/N

Kai's lips curved into a small smile. *This is it. The first step toward becoming an alchemist. With this, I can start producing pills for the guild and generate some much-needed income.*

"Yes."

The moment the word left his lips, Kai felt a rush of information flood his mind. It was like drinking from a firehose of knowledge—theories, techniques, and practices all poured into his consciousness at once. He closed his eyes and let the information settle.

When he opened them again, five new notifications had appeared before him:

New Skill Unlocked: Essence Extraction (Level 1)
Description: The foundational technique for drawing out the purest essence from herbs, minerals, and other materials.

New Skill Unlocked: Elemental Fusion (Level 1)
Description: A technique for combining different elemental properties in concoctions to create more potent and complex effects.

New Skill Unlocked: Qi Infusion (Level 1)
Description: The art of imbuing creations with qi, which enhances their potency and allows for the creation of cultivation aids.

New Skill Unlocked: Stability Control (Level 1)
Description: A vital technique for preventing concoctions from becoming unstable or explosive during the creation process.

New Skill Unlocked: Spiritual Resonance (Level 1)
Description: An advanced technique for attuning creations to specific spiritual frequencies to create pills and elixirs tailored to individual cultivators or cultivation methods.

Kai's eyes scanned over each skill, his mind already working to process and categorize the information. *Five skills, each essential for alchemy. I'll need to practice them all if I want to pass that exam in three days.* He stood up, stretching his arms above his head. *Let's start with the basics. Essence Extraction seems like the logical first step.*

Kai held out his hand, focusing on the newly acquired knowledge of Essence Extraction. He closed his eyes and visualized the process as described in the skill's information.

Okay, so the first step is to gather qi in my palm, he thought, concentrating on drawing his spiritual energy to his hand. A faint blue glow appeared around his fingers. *Good. Now, I need to shape it into a sort of . . . spiritual sieve.*

He focused on molding the qi, trying to form it into a netlike structure. The blue energy flickered and wavered as it struggled to hold its shape.

This is harder than I thought, Kai mused, his brow furrowing in concentration. *It's like trying to weave with electricity.*

After several minutes of intense focus, Kai managed to form a crude, unstable net of qi in his palm. He opened his eyes, studying his handiwork.

"Not perfect," he muttered, "but it's a start."

He reached for a nearby cup of water, deciding to practice on something simple. Holding the qi net over the cup, Kai attempted to extract the essence of the water. To his surprise, a few droplets of water actually rose from the cup, suspended in his qi net. They seemed . . . different somehow. Clearer, more vibrant.

Is this . . . pure water essence? Kai wondered, studying the droplets closely. *It looks more concentrated, somehow.*

The effort of maintaining the qi net was starting to strain him, and after a few more seconds, his concentration slipped. The net dissipated, and the water droplets fell back into the cup with a small splash.

Kai let out a breath he hadn't realized he'd been holding. "Well, that was . . . interesting."

He glanced at the cup of water, then around his room. *I should probably practice this more, but without proper materials, there's only so much I can do. Let's move on to the next skill.*

Kai turned his attention to Elemental Fusion. This skill seemed more complex, requiring the manipulation of different elemental energies.

Okay, so for this one, I need to gather two different types of elemental qi and combine them, Kai thought, recalling the information from the skill description. *I have no idea how to even sense chaos qi, so I can forget about that for now. I can already manipulate lightning and wind to some degree, so let's start with those.*

He held out both hands and concentrated on gathering lightning qi in his right hand and wind qi in his left. It took several minutes of intense focus, but eventually, small sparks danced in his right palm while a tiny whirlwind formed in his left.

Now for the tricky part, Kai thought, slowly bringing his hands together. *I need to merge these without letting them cancel each other out.*

As his hands drew closer, Kai could feel the energies resisting each other. The sparks crackled and the wind swirled more violently, both threatening to dissipate.

Come on, Kai urged, gritting his teeth. *Mix, damn it!*

For a brief moment, the lightning and wind energies touched, creating a swirling vortex of electrified air between his palms. Then, with a small *pop*, both energies vanished, leaving Kai's hands empty.

"Damn," Kai muttered, shaking out his hands. "That's harder than it looks."

He took a deep breath, centering himself. *Okay, let's try again. Maybe if I start with smaller amounts of each element . . .*

Kai spent the next hour practicing Elemental Fusion, gradually making progress. By the end, he could maintain a small orb of swirling lightning and wind for a few seconds before it destabilized.

"Two down, three to go," Kai said to himself, wiping a bead of sweat from his brow. The constant manipulation of qi was starting to tire him out, but he pressed on. He had already realized that these skills could be used for more than just alchemy. Perhaps in the future he could create his own techniques, especially if he involved his Qi Condensation skill.

Shaking his head, Kai turned to the next skill on the list, Qi Infusion. This one seemed more straightforward, at least in theory.

So, I need to imbue an object with my qi, enhancing its properties, Kai mused, looking around his room for a suitable target. His eyes fell on a small rock sitting on his windowsill.

Kai picked up the rock, turning it over in his hand. *This should work. Now, how do I go about infusing it with qi?*

He closed his eyes and focused on the flow of energy within his body. Slowly, carefully, he directed a stream of qi toward his hand, willing it to seep into the rock.

At first, nothing seemed to happen. The rock remained cool and inert in his palm. But as Kai continued to pour qi into it, he felt a subtle change. The stone grew warmer, and he could sense a faint vibration emanating from it.

Kai opened his eyes and studied the rock closely. To his amazement, it was glowing faintly with a blue light—the color of his qi.

"It worked," he breathed, a smile spreading across his face. "I actually did it!"

The glow faded after a few moments, but Kai could still feel a residual energy in the stone. *I wonder how long the infusion lasts. And what exactly did it do to the rock? Something to experiment with later, I suppose.*

Setting the rock aside, Kai turned his attention to the next skill: Stability Control. This one seemed particularly important, especially given the volatile nature of alchemical concoctions.

Okay, so this is about maintaining balance in a mixture of energies or elements, Kai thought, recalling the skill description. *But how do I practice that without actual ingredients?*

After a moment's consideration, Kai decided to improvise. He gathered his lightning and wind qi, holding them separately in his mind. *Now I need to bring these together without letting either element overpower the other,* he thought as he slowly began to merge the energies.

It was like trying to balance on a tightrope while juggling. Each element seemed to have a mind of its own, constantly trying to expand and consume the other. Kai's brow furrowed in concentration as he struggled to keep them in check.

For a brief moment, he managed to achieve a perfect balance—a swirling sphere of lightning and wind, each element distinct yet harmonious. Then, with a soft *whoosh*, the sphere collapsed, and the energies dissipated into the air.

Kai let out a long breath, feeling drained. "That . . . was intense."

Despite his fatigue, Kai felt a sense of accomplishment. *Four out of five. Just one more to go.*

The final skill, Spiritual Resonance, seemed to be the most advanced of the set. Kai read over the description again, trying to wrap his head around the concept.

"Attuning creations to specific spiritual frequencies . . ." How am I supposed to practice that? he wondered, scratching his head.

After some thought, Kai decided to try a meditation exercise. He sat back down on his cushion, closing his eyes and focusing on his own spiritual energy. *If I can attune something to my own frequency, that would be a start.*

Kai began by observing the flow of qi through his body, paying close attention to its rhythm and vibration. It was like listening to a song only he could hear, a unique melody that defined his spiritual essence.

Once he felt he had a good grasp on his own frequency, Kai reached for the qi-infused rock he had created earlier. Holding it in his hand, he tried to align its energy with his own.

At first, nothing seemed to happen. The rock's energy remained distinct, out of sync with Kai's own qi. But as he continued to focus, pouring his concentration into the task, he felt a subtle shift. The rock's energy began to pulse in time with his own, its frequency gradually aligning with Kai's spiritual essence. It was a strange sensation, like finding perfect harmony in a duet.

Kai opened his eyes and looked down at the rock in wonder. It wasn't glowing this time, but he could feel a deep connection to it, as if it had become an extension of himself.

"Incredible," Kai murmured, turning the rock over in his hand. "If this works with actual pills . . ." He trailed off, his mind racing with potential applications. *Custom-tailored pills, elixirs attuned to specific cultivation methods, maybe even—*

Kai's thoughts were interrupted by a knock at the door. He quickly set the rock aside and stood up.

"Come in," he called out.

The door opened, revealing Chen Wei. The young disciple bowed deeply.

"Senior Brother," Chen Wei said, "I've returned from the mission. We . . . encountered some difficulties, but we were successful."

Kai raised an eyebrow. "Difficulties? What happened?"

Chen Wei hesitated for a moment, then launched into a detailed account of the encounter with Yu Fen and his group, as well as the timely intervention of Lin Yue.

As Chen Wei spoke, Kai's expression remained calm, but his mind was working overtime. *So, there's an Inner Disciple running some kind of operation outside the sect. And he's interested in me. This could either be a problem or an opportunity.*

When Chen Wei finished his report, Kai nodded slowly. "You both did well, Chen Wei. Especially in a difficult situation. Did you manage to secure the materials?"

Chen Wei's face brightened. "Yes, Senior Brother! In fact, thanks to Lin Yue's intervention, we got an even better deal. We have enough materials to make twenty-five qi-gathering pills."

"Excellent work," Kai said, allowing a small smile to cross his face. "Both you and Zhi-Zhi."

Chen Wei beamed at the praise. "Thank you, Senior Brother. What would you like us to do next?"

Kai considered for a moment. "For now, hand me the materials. I'll need to rent a practice room at the Alchemist Pavilion to actually create the pills. In the meantime, I want you to gather more information on this Lin Yue. Be discreet about it."

"Of course, Senior Brother," Chen Wei said with a bow.

As he turned to leave, Kai called out, "Oh, and Chen Wei?"

The young disciple paused at the door. "Yes, Senior Brother?"

"Good job handling yourself in that fight. Keep up with your training."

Chen Wei's face lit up with pride. "Thank you, Senior Brother! I will!"

As the door closed behind Chen Wei, Kai let out a long breath. *Things are moving faster than I anticipated. I need to master these alchemy skills quickly if I'm going to keep up.* He picked up the qi-infused rock again, turning it over in his hand. *I wonder . . .*

Kai focused on the rock as he tried to combine several of the skills he had just learned. He began by extracting the essence of the stone, then attempted to infuse it with a fusion of lightning and wind qi. As he worked, he kept tight control of the stability of the energies, all while trying to attune the whole process to his own spiritual frequency.

It was like trying to solve five complex puzzles simultaneously while juggling electrified torches. Sweat beaded on Kai's brow as he poured all his concentration into the task.

For a brief, shining moment, it all came together. The rock in his hand began to crackle with inner lightning, its very essence seeming to resonate with Kai's own energy. He could feel the perfect balance of elements within it.

Then, as quickly as it had come, the moment passed. The crackling faded, and Kai was left holding what appeared to be an ordinary rock once more.

He let out a long, slow breath. "Well . . . that was something."

Skill Leveled Up!
Essence Extraction (Level 2)

Skill Leveled Up!
Elemental Fusion (Level 2)

Skill Leveled up!
Qi Infusion (Level 2)

Skill Leveled Up!
Stability Control (Level 2)

Skill Leveled Up!
Spiritual Resonance (Level 2)

You have gained 500 XP!

Kai's eyebrows shot up in surprise. "All at once? I guess combining the techniques paid off."

CHAPTER TWENTY-SEVEN

Kai stood in the practice room of the Alchemist Pavilion, taking in his surroundings. The room was smaller than he expected but well equipped. Shelves filled with various jars, vials, and tools lined the walls. A large stone table dominated the center of the room, its surface scarred and stained from countless alchemical experiments.

In one corner, a small furnace glowed with a steady heat. Next to it, a set of scales and measuring tools sat neatly arranged on a side table.

Kai sighed, running his hand over the smooth surface of the worktable. *I can't wait to have my own setup*, he thought. *But for now, this will have to do.*

From his inventory, he withdrew the materials he'd need for his first attempts at pill-making: Spirit Grass, Yin Berries, and Qi Crystals.

The Spirit Grass was green, and its blades were long and slender with a faintly sweet aroma that filled the air as Kai set it on the table. Next came the Yin Berries. They were small dark-purple fruits that looked almost black in the room's lighting. These berries were prized for their ability to balance and stabilize qi. Finally, he picked up one of the Qi Crystals, turning it over in his hand. Unlike spirit stones, which cultivators could use directly to boost their cultivation, Qi Crystals were primarily used in pill-making and weapon formation. Their energy was too raw and unstable for direct absorption.

The thought of weapon forging sparked another train of thought. *Once I've got enough spirit stones saved up, I could try my hand at creating a weapon. The System crafting menu should make that interesting.*

Kai shook his head, pushing the thought aside for now. He had more immediate concerns. From his inventory, he produced a small scroll—the recipe for the qi-gathering pill. It had cost him 150 spirit stones. A significant investment, but he knew it would be worth it.

He unrolled the scroll and read over the instructions once more:

Qi-Gathering Pill (Low Grade)
Ingredients:

1 blade of Spirit Grass
3 Yin Berries
1 Qi Crystal (crushed)

Method:
1. Use Stability Control throughout the process to prevent volatile reactions.
2. Extract the essence from the Spirit Grass using the Essence Extraction technique.
3. Crush the Yin Berries and mix with the Spirit Grass essence.
4. Pulverize the Qi Crystal and add to the mixture.
5. Use Elemental Fusion to combine the ingredients.
6. Apply Qi Infusion to stabilize the mixture.
7. Finally, use Spiritual Resonance to attune the pill to general qi frequencies.
8. Form into a pill and heat in the furnace for precisely 49 seconds.

Kai looked at his pile of ingredients. He had enough for twenty-five attempts, but he knew better than to expect success on every try. *If I can make twelve successful pills, I'll be able to make sufficient profit. That'll be a win.*

Taking a deep breath, Kai began his first attempt. He picked up a blade of Spirit Grass, holding it gently between his fingers. He closed his eyes and focused on the Essence Extraction technique he'd learned. Kai extended his qi as he felt for the essence within the grass. It was there, pulsing just beneath the surface. He began to draw it out, visualizing his qi as a sieve, filtering the pure essence from the physical matter.

For a moment, it seemed to be working. A faint green mist began to form above the grass. But then Kai felt his control slip. The essence scattered, dissipating into the air.

"Damn," Kai muttered, opening his eyes. The Spirit Grass in his hand had withered, its vibrant green faded to a dull brown. He'd failed to extract its essence properly, rendering it useless.

Okay, that was too forceful. I need to be gentler, need to coax the essence out rather than trying to pull it.

He picked up another blade of Spirit Grass, determined to do better this time. Again, he closed his eyes and extended his qi. This time, he imagined his qi as a gentle stream and encouraged the essence to flow out naturally.

Slowly, a green mist began to form above the grass. Kai carefully guided it into a small glass vial, feeling a surge of satisfaction as the essence collected at the bottom.

"That's more like it," he said with a small smile.

Next, Kai turned his attention to the Yin Berries. He placed three in a mortar and began to crush them with the pestle. As he worked, he focused on maintaining a steady rhythm, infusing each stroke with a touch of qi to help break down the berries more thoroughly.

Once the berries were reduced to a fine paste, Kai added them to the vial containing the Spirit Grass essence. He swirled the vial gently, watching as the two substances began to mix.

Now came the tricky part. Kai took the Qi Crystal and placed it in a separate mortar. He began to grind it down, applying steady pressure. The crystal resisted at first but gradually began to give way under Kai's persistent efforts.

This is harder than I expected, Kai thought, wiping a bead of sweat from his brow. *No wonder alchemists are so respected. This takes real skill and patience.*

Finally, the crystal was reduced to a fine glittering powder. Kai carefully added it to the vial with the other ingredients. Now it was time for the real test—combining everything using Elemental Fusion.

Kai held the vial in both hands, closing his eyes to focus. He began to channel his qi into the mixture, visualizing the different elements within each ingredient—the vital energy of the Spirit Grass, the balancing force of the Yin Berries, the pure qi of the crystal—all swirling together in a complex dance.

He tried to guide them, encouraging them to merge and combine. For a moment, it seemed to be working. The mixture in the vial began to glow softly, the different components starting to blur together.

But then Kai felt something go wrong. The energies began to clash, repelling each other instead of combining. The glow in the vial intensified, becoming uncomfortably bright.

"No, no, no," Kai muttered, trying to regain control. But it was too late. With a small *pop*, the mixture in the vial suddenly evaporated, leaving behind nothing but a faint acrid smell.

Kai opened his eyes and stared at the empty vial in frustration. "Well, that didn't work," he said to the empty room.

He set the vial aside and took a deep breath, calming himself. *Okay, what went wrong there?* he thought, analyzing his failure. *I was too aggressive with the fusion. I need to be more subtle—guide the energies rather than force them.*

Determined to do better, Kai began his second attempt. This time, he took extra care with each step, moving slowly and deliberately.

The Essence Extraction went smoother this time, the green mist of Spirit Grass essence collecting easily in a new vial. Kai crushed the Yin Berries with careful precision, ensuring they were reduced to a perfectly smooth paste before adding them to the essence.

When it came time to grind the Qi Crystal, Kai took his time, applying steady, even pressure until the crystal was a fine, uniform powder. He added it to the vial with the other ingredients, then paused to take a moment to center himself before attempting the Elemental Fusion again.

This time, Kai approached the fusion more gently. He extended his qi into the mixture, but instead of trying to force the components together, he simply encouraged them to mingle. He visualized the energies dancing around each other, gradually coming closer and closer together.

For a while, it seemed to be working. The mixture in the vial began to shimmer, the different components starting to blur at the edges. But as Kai continued to guide the fusion, he realized something was off. The energies weren't fully combining—instead, they were forming distinct layers in the vial.

Something's not right, Kai thought, frowning. He tried to adjust his technique, encouraging the layers to mix. But as he did so, he felt the delicate balance he'd achieved start to slip.

Suddenly, the mixture in the vial began to bubble violently. Kai's eyes widened in alarm. He quickly set the vial down on the table and took a step back, just in time. With a loud *pop*, the contents of the vial exploded outward, splattering the table and nearby tools with a sticky residue.

Kai stared at the mess, a mix of frustration and determination on his face. "Well," he said aloud, "at least it didn't evaporate this time. Progress, I suppose."

He began to clean up the failed attempt as he tried to figure out what went wrong.

The fusion was better, but still not quite right. I managed to get the energies to interact, but they weren't truly combining. And I completely forgot about Stability Control—that's probably why it exploded at the end.

As he wiped down the table, Kai found himself chuckling softly. *You know,* he thought, *if someone had told me a few months ago that I'd be this invested in magical pill-making, I'd have thought they were crazy. But here I am, getting frustrated over exploding potions like some kind of fantasy alchemist.*

With the mess cleaned up, Kai took a moment to review the recipe again. He realized he'd been so focused on the Essence Extraction and Elemental Fusion that he'd neglected some of the other techniques. *Qi Infusion, Stability Control, Spiritual Resonance—I need to incorporate all of these if I want to succeed.*

Determined to get it right this time, Kai began his third attempt. He started with the Essence Extraction, once again coaxing the green mist from a blade of Spirit Grass. This time, as he guided the essence into the vial, he also began to infuse it gently with his own qi.

Qi Infusion from the very beginning, Kai thought. *This should help stabilize the essence and make it more receptive to combining with the other ingredients.*

Next, he crushed the Yin Berries, again taking care to maintain a steady rhythm and infuse each stroke with qi. As he added the berry paste to the vial, he focused on maintaining the stability of the mixture, using the Stability Control technique he'd learned.

Steady now, Kai thought, watching the mixture carefully. *Keep everything balanced.*

When it came time to add the powdered Qi Crystal, Kai took extra care. He sprinkled the powder in slowly, bit by bit, using Stability Control to ensure each addition was properly incorporated before adding more.

Finally, it was time for the Elemental Fusion. Kai took a deep breath and centered himself. He extended his qi into the mixture and gently encouraged the different components to mingle. This time, instead of trying to force them together, he visualized them as dancers, each with their own rhythm, gradually coming into sync with each other.

As he worked, Kai made sure to maintain his Stability Control, keeping a close eye on the energies to ensure nothing became too volatile. Slowly, ever so slowly, he felt the components beginning to merge.

It's working, Kai thought, a spark of excitement in his chest. But he didn't let it distract him. He knew he wasn't done yet.

As the fusion progressed, Kai began to apply the Spiritual Resonance technique. He focused on attuning the merging energies to a general qi frequency, one that would be compatible with most cultivators. It was like fine-tuning an instrument, adjusting each component until they all sang in harmony.

After what felt like hours but was probably only minutes, Kai felt the mixture stabilize. He opened his eyes and looked down at the vial. The liquid inside was a soft pearlescent white, gently pulsing with qi.

"I think . . . I think I did it," Kai murmured, hardly daring to believe it.

But he knew he wasn't finished yet. Carefully, Kai poured the liquid onto a small flat stone designed for pill formation. Using his qi, he began to shape the liquid, condensing it into a perfect small sphere.

Once the pill was formed, Kai picked it up carefully and placed it in the furnace. He set the timer for exactly forty-nine seconds, as the recipe specified, and waited.

The seconds ticked by slowly. Kai found himself counting along in his head, his eyes fixed on the furnace. *What if it dissolves? What if it explodes? What if I did everything right except this last step?*

Finally, after what felt like an eternity, the timer chimed. Kai quickly opened the furnace and, using a pair of tongs, carefully removed the pill.

It was perfect. A small round pill, slightly larger than a pea, with a soft pearlescent sheen. Kai could feel the qi emanating from it.

"I did it," Kai breathed, a wide smile spreading across his face. "I actually did it!"

He held the pill up to the light, admiring his handiwork. Then, curious to see how the System would classify his creation, Kai focused on the pill and willed its information to appear.

A blue window materialized before him:

Item Created: Qi-Gathering Pill
Quality: Poor
Effects: Increases qi-absorption rate by 10% for 1 hour
Warning: Toxic, may lead to Qi Deviation

Kai's smile faded and was replaced by a frown as he read the last line. "Toxic?" he murmured, staring at the warning. "That's . . . not good."

CHAPTER TWENTY-EIGHT

Three hours later, Kai held a small pill between his thumb and forefinger, a sense of accomplishment washing over him.

Item Created: Qi-Gathering Pill
Quality: Low
Effects: Increases qi-absorption rate by 20% for 3 hours.

A smile spread across Kai's face. It had taken two more attempts after his initial success, but he'd finally managed to create a low-grade qi-gathering pill. The improvement from his earlier efforts was significant—better potency, longer duration, and, most importantly, no toxicity warning.

Not bad, Kai thought, turning the pill over in his hand. *It's not perfect, but it's a solid start.*

He knew he couldn't consistently produce pills of this quality yet. Sometimes he'd still fail entirely, ending up with a useless lump of ingredients. Other times, he'd produce a poor-quality pill, which were potentially toxic if used improperly. But this . . . this was progress.

This should be enough to pass the exams, Kai mused as he carefully placed the pill in a small jade box he'd brought for storage, then put it in his inventory. *If I can replicate this during the practical test, I should be in good shape.*

The thought of the upcoming alchemy exam sent a mix of excitement and nervousness through him. He'd come a long way in a short time, but he knew he'd be competing against disciples who'd been studying alchemy for years.

Still, I've got a few advantages they don't. The System, for one.

Shaking his head, he glanced around the practice room, noting the scattered tools and the lingering scent of herbs in the air. It had been a long, intense session, but Kai felt it was time well spent. Not only had he improved his pill-making skills, but he'd also gained a deeper understanding of the alchemical process.

Now, Kai thought, stretching his arms above his head, *I just need to get some rest, and I should be ready for the exam in two days.*

* * *

On the day of the exam, the sun had barely risen over the Azure Sky Sect when a steady stream of disciples began making their way toward a large circular building near the center of the compound. This wasn't the usual combat arena where disciples tested their martial prowess: the building's exterior remained unchanged—a grand structure of white stone with blue markings etched into its surface—but inside, the usual training equipment and weapon racks had been cleared away. It had been transformed into a venue for a different kind of challenge: the alchemy exam.

As the participants approached, their nervous chatter filled the air.

"I barely slept last night," a young woman with long black hair confessed to her friend. "I kept dreaming about mixing the wrong ingredients and blowing up the exam room."

Her companion, a young man, laughed. "At least in your dreams you made it to the practical part. I'm worried I'll fail the written test again before I even get to touch a cauldron."

"Come on, Fu, you've been studying for months," the woman reassured him. "You won't fail again. You know this stuff better than anyone."

Fu shook his head. "Maybe. But, Hui, have you seen the competition? I heard even some of the Core Disciples are taking the exam this year."

The young woman's eyes widened. "Really? Why would they bother? They're already . . ."

Her words trailed off as a hush fell over the crowd. Heads turned to watch a figure approaching in black robes, which set him apart from the sea of white-clad Outer Disciples.

Kai walked toward the arena. His face held a blank expression as he felt the weight of dozens of stares on him; he could almost hear the thoughts behind them.

Who does he think he is?

Just because he is a Legacy Disciple, does he think he can pass the exam in three days?

He must be so confident. Or maybe just arrogant.

Kai wouldn't blame them for these assumptions. If he were in their shoes, he'd probably think the same. But they didn't know about the System, about how he'd managed to cram months of learning into just three intense days of study and practice.

As he passed by a group of whispering disciples, he caught fragments of their conversation, which confirmed his thoughts.

". . . heard he's only been practicing for a few days . . ."

". . . probably thinks he's too good for us . . ."

". . . bet he fails spectacularly . . ."

Kai kept his expression neutral as he made his way to the entrance of the arena, joining the line of nervous disciples waiting to be let in.

As he walked past, he noticed a group of young men huddled together, furiously comparing notes.

"Quick, quiz me on the properties of Spirit Grass!" one of them demanded.

His friend obliged, rapid firing questions. "What's the optimal harvesting time for Spirit Grass?"

"Uh . . . during the full moon?"

"Wrong! It's at dawn on the day after the full moon. Come on, you need to know this!"

Looks like I'm not the only one feeling the pressure, Kai thought.

As they waited, he overheard more snippets of conversation around him.

"I heard the written test is brutal," a thin pale-faced boy was saying. "My senior brother took it last year and said there were questions about herbs he'd never even heard of."

"That's nothing," replied a girl with short spiky hair. "I'm more worried about the practical. What if they ask us to make something we've never practiced before?"

"They wouldn't do that," a third voice chimed in, though he sounded far from certain. "Would they?"

They're so focused on what might go wrong, Kai thought. *They're forgetting that this is just the first step. Pass or fail, it's all part of the journey.*

The doors to the arena swung open, and the crowd of disciples began to file in. Kai followed, taking in the transformed interior. The usual sand-covered floor had been replaced with smooth stone tiles. Rows of desks filled most of the space, each equipped with brushes, ink, and blank scrolls.

At the far end of the arena, Kai could see a raised platform where several older disciples in green robes stood watching the incoming examinees. Their faces were stoic, betraying no emotion as they observed the nervous crowd.

As the last of the participants entered, a hush fell over the arena. A middle-aged man in green robes with gold embroidery stepped forward on the platform, raising his hands for silence.

"Welcome, disciples of the Azure Sky Sect," he said, his voice carrying easily across the arena. "I am Elder Bin, and I will be overseeing your alchemy exam today." He paused, his gaze sweeping across the assembled disciples. For a moment, his eyes seemed to linger on Kai, a flicker of curiosity passing across his face before he continued, "This exam will test not just your knowledge, but your practical skills and your ability to think on your feet. It is divided into three parts: a written test, a practical demonstration, and an oral examination."

A murmur ran through the crowd at this, and Elder Bin waited for it to subside before continuing.

"The written test will cover basic alchemical theory, herb identification, and safety procedures. You will need to demonstrate a solid understanding of fundamental alchemical principles."

Kai nodded to himself. *Thanks to the System, I should be able to handle that.*

"The practical test will require you to create a basic pill under observation. You may be asked to make a minor healing pill or a low-grade qi-replenishment pill, among other possibilities."

This elicited another round of whispers from the crowd. Kai could see several disciples looking nervous, while others seemed excited at the prospect.

"Finally," Elder Bin continued, "the oral examination will be conducted by a senior alchemist, like myself. You will be asked questions about the creation process, tested on your understanding of alchemical principles, and presented with scenarios that might arise during alchemy. You will need to explain how you would handle these situations." He paused, letting the information sink in. "Remember, this exam is not just about memorization. We are looking for disciples who can think critically and apply their knowledge in practical situations. Alchemy is as much an art as it is a science." Elder Bin's stern expression softened slightly. "I know many of you are nervous. But remember, every master alchemist started exactly where you are now. Trust in your training, stay calm, and do your best. That is all we ask. You are not competing against anyone but yourself. No sect can ever have enough alchemists." He gestured to the rows of desks. "We will begin with the written portion of the exam. Please take your seats. You will find everything you need at your desk. You have two hours to complete this portion. Begin when you are ready."

As the disciples began to move toward the desks, Kai could hear the nervous chatter starting up again.

"Two hours? Is that enough time?"

"I hope I can remember everything . . ."

"Good luck, everyone!"

CHAPTER TWENTY-NINE

K ai made his way to an empty desk near the back of the arena. As he sat down, he could feel the eyes of nearby disciples on him, curiosity and suspicion mingling in their gazes. He ignored them, focusing instead on the materials before him.

A stack of blank scrolls sat neatly at one corner of the desk. Beside them were several brushes of varying sizes and a pot of ink. At the center of the desk lay a sealed scroll—the exam questions.

Kai took a deep breath, centering himself. *All right, System,* he thought. *Let's see if the Basic Novice Alchemy Guide was enough.*

He broke the seal on the scroll and unrolled it, revealing the first question:

> 1. Describe the process of Essence Extraction and explain its importance in pill creation.

Kai allowed himself a small smile. *Starting off with the basics, I see.* He dipped his brush in ink and began to write, answering question after question.

> 30. List five common mistakes in herb preparation and their potential consequences.

Kai's brush moved swiftly across the paper. *Improper drying leading to loss of potency . . . Incorrect cutting techniques causing uneven distribution of active compounds . . .*

Around him, he could hear the scratching of brushes and the occasional frustrated sigh from his fellow examinees. But Kai remained focused, barely aware of the passage of time as he focused on his own exam.

> 56. Explain the difference between Yin and Yang herbs and provide three examples of each.

"Yin herbs are those that cool and calm the body's energies, while Yang herbs warm and invigorate. Examples of Yin herbs include Moon Lotus, Frost Grass, and Tranquil Root. Yang herbs include Fire Ginseng, Sun Pepper, and Dragon Scale Leaf."

Satisfied with his answer, Kai moved on.

---

89. Describe the proper method for harvesting Spirit Grass to maximize its potency.

Ah, this was what those guys were arguing about earlier, Kai thought with a smile. He put brush to paper once more.

"Spirit Grass should be harvested at dawn on the day following a full moon. The harvester must use a silver sickle and cut the grass at a forty-five-degree angle, being careful not to damage the roots. The grass should be immediately placed in a jade container to preserve its spiritual essence."

---

98. Explain the principle of Elemental Harmony and its application in creating balanced elixirs.

This question gave Kai pause. He remembered struggling with this concept during his practice sessions. He wrote carefully, explaining how different elemental energies could be balanced within a pill to create more stable and effective results.

As he neared the end of the exam, Kai found himself facing a particularly challenging question:

---

118. Describe a scenario where a typically stable alchemical reaction might become volatile, and explain how you would prevent or mitigate such an occurrence.

Kai tapped his brush against his chin, considering. *This is where real-world experience would come in handy*, he thought. *But I can work with what I know.*

He began to describe a scenario where impurities in the ingredients could lead to an unexpected reaction. He detailed the warning signs an alchemist should watch for and the steps they could take to stabilize the mixture.

As he wrote, a memory surfaced of one of his failed attempts at pill creation. The mixture had become unstable, nearly exploding in his face.

That's it. I can use that experience here.

Kai added to his answer by describing the techniques he had used to prevent a full-blown explosion. He explained how careful application of qi and quick thinking could save not just the concoction but potentially the alchemist's life as well.

As he finished his answer, Kai heard Elder Bin's voice ring out across the arena. "You have thirty minutes remaining."

A ripple of panic seemed to pass through the room. Kai could hear the increased scratching of brushes and muffled exclamations of surprise. He glanced around, noting the furrowed brows and tense postures of his fellow examinees.

Thirty minutes, Kai thought. *Plenty of time to review my answers.*

As Kai was reviewing his answers, he became aware of a faint whispering nearby. At first, he tried to ignore it, focusing on his own exam. But the whispers grew more insistent, impossible to tune out completely.

"Psst, Li, what did you put for question seven?" a hushed voice asked.

"I think it was about the Yin–Yang balance in pill cores," came the barely audible reply. "I wrote that—"

Suddenly, a sharp voice cut through the whispers. "Disciples Li and Fei!"

Kai looked up to see Elder Bin standing over two pale-faced young men a few desks away. The elder's face was a mask of disappointment and anger.

"You were explicitly told that there was to be no communication during the exam," Elder Bin said. "Your actions show a blatant disregard for the rules and a lack of integrity befitting an alchemist of the Azure Sky Sect."

The two disciples looked terrified, their faces drained of color. "Elder Bin, please—" one of them started to say, but the elder held up a hand, silencing him.

"There will be no excuses," Elder Bin said firmly. "You have violated the trust placed in you and the sanctity of this examination. You are both hereby expelled from this exam. Leave the arena immediately."

A gasp went through the room as the two disciples, heads bowed in shame, gathered their things and shuffled toward the exit. The other examinees watched in stunned silence, the reality of the situation sinking in.

As the door closed behind the expelled disciples, Elder Bin addressed the room. "Let this serve as a reminder to you all. Alchemy is a discipline that requires not just knowledge and skill but also integrity and respect for the craft. Any further attempts at cheating will be met with the same consequence. Return to your exams."

Kai watched as Elder Bin returned to his position at the front of the room. The arena was now eerily quiet, the scratching of brushes on scrolls the only sound to be heard.

Even in the world of cultivation, some things never change. Exams are exams, but no matter where you are, you can expect cheaters.

"Time's up! Please put down your brushes and remain seated. We will collect your exam papers shortly," Elder Bin announced.

Kai set down his brush and leaned back in his chair, letting out a long, slow breath.

As the exam scrolls were collected, he could hear the buzz of conversation growing around him. Disciples were comparing answers, lamenting over questions they had struggled with, and speculating about what the practical exam might entail.

"I completely blanked on the question about rare herb substitutions," one disciple groaned.

"Really? I thought that was one of the easier ones," another replied. "It was the theoretical question on advanced purification techniques that got me."

"I just hope I wrote enough," a third voice chimed in. "I felt like I was running out of things to say for some of those questions."

Kai remained silent, listening to the chatter around him. He was curious to hear how others had found the exam, but he was also aware that his presence seemed to make many of the other disciples uneasy, so he remained silent.

As the last of the scrolls were collected, Elder Bin stepped forward once again. "Well done, all of you," he said, his voice carrying a hint of warmth that hadn't been there before. "Completing this exam is an achievement in itself. Take a moment to breathe and center yourselves."

He paused, allowing the disciples to do just that. Kai closed his eyes and took a deep breath, then let it out slowly. He could feel the tension in the room starting to dissipate, replaced by a sense of nervous anticipation.

"When you are ready," Elder Bin continued, "please make your way to the preparation area for the practical portion of the exam. You will be called in one by one to demonstrate your pill-making skills. While you wait, you may review your notes or meditate, but please do not discuss the exam or attempt any last-minute practice."

As the disciples began to stand and move toward the designated area, Kai remained seated for a moment longer. He took another deep breath, centering himself.

One down, two to go, he thought. *The real test is yet to come.*

CHAPTER THIRTY

The participants waited in silence in the practical area of the arena. Tension filled the air as they stood, lost in their own thoughts.

A young woman to Kai's left was repeatedly clenching and unclenching her fists, her eyes closed in concentration. To his right, a thin pale-faced boy muttered ingredient lists under his breath, as if trying to burn them into his memory at the last minute.

They're so nervous. It's just an exam. This is not a demonic sect: even if they fail, it's not the end of the world. I'm pretty sure there's some here that have done the exams three or four times already. Just pay the fifty spirit stones for the exam fee, and they let you do it as many times as you want.

A few minutes later, Elder Bin arrived, accompanied by an old man in gold robes. The newcomer's presence caused several disciples to straighten their posture.

Elder Bin cleared his throat. "Disciples, your attention please. We have a special guest with us today for the practical portion of the exam."

He gestured to the old man beside him. "This is Elder Xiao, the Alchemy Master of the Azure Sky Sect. It is a rare honor for him to attend these examinations, so I trust you will all do your utmost to impress."

Kai raised an eyebrow. *The Alchemy Master, huh? This just got interesting.*

Elder Xiao stepped forward, his eyes sweeping over the assembled disciples. "I look forward to seeing what the next generation of Azure Sky alchemists can do. Remember, true alchemy is not just about following recipes. It's about understanding the essence of the materials and the flow of qi. Show me your insight, not just your memorization."

Elder Bin nodded, then addressed the disciples once more. "Now, for the practical component of the exam. Your task is to craft one low-grade qi-replenishing pill within three hours."

Kai's eyes narrowed slightly. *Low-grade qi-replenishing pill? I've been practicing qi-gathering pills, but I've never made this one before.*

He quickly ran through what he knew about the two types of pills. *Qi replenishing only restores qi, while qi gathering not only replenishes, albeit at a slower rate, but also increases qi absorption and capacity. Logically, qi gathering should be more complex. This might not be as hard as I thought.*

Around him, other disciples were having similar thoughts.

"Qi replenishing? That's not too bad," one disciple whispered.

"Speak for yourself," another hissed back. "I've never made one before!"

Elder Bin's voice cut through the chatter. "You will find all necessary materials at your assigned stations. Remember, you have three hours. Begin when you're ready. May the heavens favor your efforts."

As the disciples moved to their stations, Kai approached his own. He found three ingredients laid out before him, different from what he'd used for qi-gathering pills.

All right, let's see what we're working with here. He activated the System to get a detailed view of the ingredients.

Item: Qi Root
Description: A common herb with moderate qi-enhancing properties. Often used as a base in qi-related pills.

Item: Azure Petal
Description: Flower petals with a calming effect. Helps stabilize qi and promote smooth circulation.

Item: Spirit Crystal Powder
Description: Finely ground crystals that amplify the effects of other ingredients. Adds potency to pills.

Kai raised an eyebrow. *Interesting. These are different from the qi-gathering pill ingredients I've been practicing with. This should be . . . enlightening.*

As the other disciples scrambled to start, Kai took a moment to read over the provided recipe. *Even if I fail, at least I'll have another recipe memorized.*

Low-Grade Qi-Replenishing Pill:
1. Prepare Qi Root by slicing thinly and extracting essence.
2. Grind Azure Petals into a fine powder.
3. Mix extracted Qi Root essence with Azure Petal powder.
4. Add Spirit Crystal Powder gradually while infusing mixture with qi.
5. Form mixture into a pill shape and stabilize with controlled heat.
6. Infuse completed pill with purified qi to enhance potency.

Kai nodded to himself. *Seems straightforward enough.*

He began by focusing on the Qi Root, using the Essence Extraction technique. As he sliced the root thinly, he concentrated on drawing out its pure essence.

This is different from the qi-gathering ingredients. The essence feels . . . calmer, somehow. Less potent but more stable.

Next, he turned his attention to the Azure Petals. Using a mortar and pestle, he ground them into a fine bluish powder. The sweet scent wafted up, and Kai could feel a subtle calming effect.

Interesting. These petals must help balance and stabilize the qi. Clever combination with the more energetic Qi Root.

As he worked, Kai glanced around at the other disciples. Many were furrowing their brows in concentration, some muttering instructions to themselves. A few looked on the verge of panic.

"Oh no, oh no," a young disciple nearby moaned. "I think I added too much Spirit Crystal Powder!"

"Shh!" his neighbor hissed. "Focus on your own work!"

Kai shook his head. *Keep calm and carry on, as they say.*

He returned his attention to his own concoction and carefully mixed the extracted Qi Root essence with the Azure Petal powder. The two substances seemed to swirl together, creating a pale blue mixture.

Now came the tricky part. Kai began to add the Spirit Crystal Powder, bit by bit, while simultaneously infusing the mixture with his qi. This required careful concentration and control.

Steady now. Too much qi could destabilize the mixture. Too little and it won't bind properly.

As he worked, Kai could feel the mixture growing more potent. The Elemental Fusion technique came into play, helping him balance the various properties of the ingredients.

Sweat beaded on his forehead as he carefully molded the mixture into a pill shape. Now for the final step: stabilizing the pill with controlled heat.

Kai closed his eyes, focusing intently. He channeled his qi to create a gentle warmth around the pill. Slowly, carefully, he increased the heat, watching for any signs of instability.

Almost there . . .

Finally, with a small sigh of relief, Kai completed the heating process. The pill before him looked . . . well, like a pill. It was roughly spherical, with a pale blue color and a slightly glossy sheen.

Now for the moment of truth, Kai thought as he picked up the pill to examine it more closely.

Item Created: Qi-Replenishing Pill
Quality: Poor

Effects: Restores 10 qi
Warning: Toxic, may lead to Qi Deviation

Kai sighed, setting the pill aside. *Well, that's disappointing. But not entirely unexpected for a first attempt.*

He glanced around the room, assessing the progress of the other disciples. To his surprise, he noticed a few purple-robed Core Disciples who had already finished their pills. They sat calmly at their stations, looking rather pleased with themselves.

Most of the red-robed Inner Disciples seemed to be nearing completion as well. As for the white-robed Outer Disciples, Kai saw many frustrated expressions and failed attempts.

A nearby disciple let out a groan of despair. "It's hopeless! I'll never get this right!"

"Calm down," his friend whispered. "You still have time for another attempt."

Kai nodded to himself. *They're right. I've got time for one more try. Let's figure out where I went wrong.* He closed his eyes and mentally reviewed each step of the process. *The Essence Extraction seemed fine, as did the initial mixing. But something went off during the Qi Infusion and heating process . . .* His eyes snapped open. *Of course! I treated it too much like a qi-gathering pill. This one needs a gentler touch, one that's more focused on stability than raw power.*

Kai prepared for his second attempt. He carefully measured out fresh ingredients, his movements more precise this time.

"One hour remaining, disciples," Elder Bin called out, causing a ripple of panic through the arena.

Cutting it close. But I can do this.

Kai began again, this time paying careful attention to the unique properties of each ingredient. As he extracted the essence from the Qi Root, he focused on its calming nature rather than on trying to draw out maximum potency. When mixing the Azure Petal powder, he took extra care to achieve a perfectly smooth consistency. *The stability of the mixture is key*, he reminded himself.

As he added the Spirit Crystal Powder, Kai used his Qi Infusion technique with a lighter touch. Instead of pushing raw power into the mixture, he focused on creating a harmonious blend of energies.

It's like a cultivation technique, he realized. *Finding the right balance, the perfect flow of qi.*

The mixture began to take on a soft glow. Kai allowed himself a small smile. *That looks more promising.*

Forming the pill shape came easier this time, the mixture more pliable and responsive to his touch. As he began the heating process, Kai closed his eyes and focused intently on maintaining the delicate balance he'd achieved.

Gentle now. Like coaxing a flame, not forcing it.

Time seemed to slow as Kai poured his concentration into the final steps. He could feel the pill stabilizing, its energy settling into a steady, soothing rhythm.

Finally, with a deep breath, Kai opened his eyes. The pill before him was a perfect sphere, its surface smooth and unblemished. It glowed with a soft blue-white light.

Kai picked up the pill, a smile spreading across his face as he examined it. It felt . . . right. Balanced. Harmonious.

The blue message before him confirmed his success:

Item Created: Qi-Replenishing Pill
Quality: Low
Effects: Restores 30 qi

Kai's smile widened. *Now that's more like it. It's not spectacular, but it's a solid low-grade pill. That should be enough to pass.*

As he carefully placed the pill in a jade box for preservation, he heard Elder Bin's voice ring out across the room. "Time's up! Please step away from your stations. We will now begin the evaluation process."

CHAPTER THIRTY-ONE

Kai looked around, curious to see how his fellow examinees had fared. The Core Disciples seemed relaxed, quietly chatting among themselves. Most of the Inner Disciples also appeared confident, though a few looked worried. Among the Outer Disciples, the mood was mixed. Some looked pleased with their efforts, while others seemed on the verge of tears.

As the evaluation began, Kai found himself standing next to a nervous-looking Outer Disciple. The young man, probably no more than eighteen, was fidgeting with the sleeves of his white robe.

"H-how do you think you did?" the disciple asked Kai, his voice trembling slightly.

"I think I managed to create a passable pill. How about you?"

The disciple's shoulders slumped. "I'm not sure. My first attempt was a complete failure. The second one looked better, but . . . I don't know if it's good enough."

Kai nodded. "The first time is always the hardest. But remember, even attempting this exam is an achievement. Many disciples never even make it this far."

The young man's eyes widened slightly. "You're right. I hadn't thought of it that way. Thank you, um . . ."

"Kai."

"Thank you, Senior Brother Kai," the disciple said, bowing slightly. "I'm Wu Gang."

Their conversation was interrupted as Elder Bin approached their section with Elder Xiao following close behind. The two elders moved from station to station, examining the results of each disciple's efforts.

When they reached Wu Gang, the young disciple presented his pill with shaking hands. Elder Bin took it and turned it over in his palm before passing it to Elder Xiao. The old alchemist held it up to the light, his eyes narrowing as he studied it.

"Barely passable," Elder Xiao pronounced. "But passable, nonetheless. You have much to learn, young one."

Wu Gang's face lit up. "Thank you, Elder Xiao! I will work hard to improve!"

As the elders moved on, Wu Gang turned to Kai, his eyes shining. "I passed! I can't believe it!"

Kai smiled. "Congratulations. You earned it."

Then it was Kai's turn. He presented his pill to Elder Bin, who raised an eyebrow as he took it. "Interesting," the elder murmured before handing it to Elder Xiao.

Elder Xiao held up the pill to examine it closely. His eyes narrowed as he studied the small sphere, turning it this way and that.

A blue box appeared before Kai:

Name: Elder Xiao
You are not of a sufficient level to see this being's stats.

From the size of the blue dot on the map, he seems to be at the level of Zhi-Zhi's master, so I'm assuming he's at the Astral Formation stage.

After a long moment, the Elder looked at Kai with an expression of disbelief.

"Is it truly the case that you only began practicing alchemy three days ago?"

Kai nodded, keeping his expression neutral. "Yes, Elder. That's correct."

The Elder shook his head, a small smile playing at the corners of his mouth. "In all my years, I have never seen talent quite like this. You must be an alchemy genius, young man."

As Elder Xiao spoke, another blue message appeared in Kai's vision:

Congratulations! Your talent has impressed a Master Alchemist. You have gained the title: Alchemy Prodigy Description: Your innate talent for alchemy has been recognized by a true master of the craft. This title increases your learning speed for alchemy-related skills by 2x and improves your success rate in pill formation by 20%.

Well, that's certainly useful, Kai thought, careful not to let his satisfaction show on his face. *This should make advancing my alchemy skills much easier.*

Elder Xiao sighed, his gaze distant. "Luo Qiang has stolen quite a talent," he muttered, almost to himself. He began to mumble, seemingly lost in thought. "Perhaps if I were to . . . No, that wouldn't work. Maybe if . . ."

Kai stood silently, waiting for the Elder to finish his musings. After a moment, Elder Xiao shook his head and focused on Kai once more.

"Young man, I will need to have a conversation with your master," he said firmly. "Such talent cannot be allowed to go to waste. We must ensure you receive the best possible training."

Kai smiled awkwardly, unsure how to respond. *Getting the backing of another top figure in the sect wouldn't be a bad thing. Especially one as respected as Elder Xiao. I just don't want to get caught up in Elder politics . . .*

"Thank you for your kind words, Elder," Kai said, bowing slightly. "I'm honored by your praise."

Elder Xiao reached out and patted Kai's shoulder, his eyes twinkling. "I look forward to testing your comprehension in the next round, young Kai. I have a feeling you'll surprise us all once again."

With that, the elder leaned in close to one of the nearby alchemists and whispered something Kai couldn't quite catch. Then, with a final nod to Kai, Elder Xiao moved on with Elder Bin to the next station.

As they walked away, Kai let out a small breath. *That went better than expected.*

Wu Gang turned to him with wide eyes. "Congratulations, Senior Brother Kai!" he exclaimed. "Elder Xiao seemed really impressed with your pill."

Kai shrugged, trying to downplay the Elder's praise. "Thank you, Wu Gang. You did well too."

As Wu Gang began to respond, another blue message appeared before Kai's eyes:

Name: Wu Gang

Qi: 25/100
Level: Qi Refining Stage 5
Strength: 30
Agility: 32
Durability: 30

For a moment, Kai considered recruiting Wu Gang to his guild. The young disciple's earnest personality could be an asset. However, a nagging doubt made him pause.

System, can I have an unlimited number of members in my guild? Kai asked silently.

A Level 1 guild can only have 10 members, including the Guild Leader.

Kai sighed internally. *I'll need to be more selective, then. It would be smart to recruit a novice alchemist, someone who could focus on the trade while I work on other aspects of cultivation. But Wu Gang might not be the best choice for that.*

He looked around the room, assessing the other disciples. The purple-robed Core Disciples caught his eye first, but Kai quickly dismissed them. *They'd be too arrogant to follow a new Legacy Disciple like me. Maybe Wang Lin has some under him, but they wouldn't give me the time of day.*

Instead, Kai focused his attention on the red-robed Inner Disciples. He began checking their stats, looking for anyone who stood out.

Name: ???
Qi: 89/150 Level: Qi Refining Stage 6 Strength: 42 Agility: 41 Durability: 40

Not bad, Kai thought, *but nothing special either.*

Name: ???
Qi: 140/200 Level: Qi Refining Stage 7 Strength: 55 Agility: 51 Durability: 49

Qi Refining stage seven and pretty strong, but not really what I'm looking for in an alchemist.

Just as Kai was about to give up, his eyes fell on a red-robed girl standing near the front of the room. As he focused on her, her stats appeared:

Name: ???
Title: Alchemy Talent Qi: 140/200 Level: Qi Refining Stage 7 Strength: 50 Agility: 55 Durability: 51

Kai's eyes widened. *A title! And an alchemy-related one at that.*

He quickly read the description of the Alchemy Talent title: *"You possess a natural affinity for the alchemical arts. This title increases your success rate in pill formation by ten percent and reduces the qi cost of alchemical techniques by ten percent."*

Not as impressive as my new title, but still quite good. She could be exactly what I'm looking for.

As if on cue, Elder Xiao approached the girl's station. Kai watched as the elder examined her pill, a look of approval spreading across his face.

"Well done, Disciple Xie Li," Elder Xiao said. "Your control over the pill's stability is impressive. Keep refining your technique, and you'll go far in the alchemical arts."

Xie Li bowed deeply, her face flushed with pride. "Thank you, Elder Xiao. I will continue to work hard."

Talented and modest, Kai thought. *Definitely someone to keep an eye on.*

As the last of the pills were evaluated, Elder Bin stepped forward to address the group. "Disciples, you have all done well today. The practical portion of the exam is now complete. Please proceed to the waiting room outside. We will call you in one by one for the final part of the examination."

The disciples began to file out of the room, a mix of relief and nervousness on their faces. Kai timed his exit carefully, making sure to end up walking beside Xie Li as they headed to the waiting area.

As they entered the corridor, Kai turned to her with a friendly smile. "Congratulations on your performance," he said. "You did quite well in there."

Xie Li looked up at him, surprise evident in her eyes. It was clear she hadn't expected the new Legacy Disciple to speak to her.

"Oh! Thank you," she replied, a slight blush coloring her cheeks. "But you did much better. Elder Xiao seemed really impressed by your pill."

Kai shrugged. "We all have our strengths. I was particularly impressed by your control over the Spirit Crystal Powder. That's usually the trickiest part."

Xie Li's eyes lit up at the mention of alchemy techniques. "Oh, yes! I find that if you add it in three stages instead of all at once, it's easier to maintain stability."

As they entered the waiting room, Kai nodded thoughtfully. "That's clever. I hadn't thought of that approach. Do you mind if I ask how you came up with it?"

Xie Li smiled, clearly pleased to be discussing her passion. "Well, it was actually an accident at first. I was nervous during a practice session and added the powder too slowly. But then I noticed the mixture was more stable than usual."

They found a quiet corner of the waiting room and continued their conversation. Kai listened intently as Xie Li explained her technique in more detail, asking questions and offering his own insights.

I can't just ask her to join my guild out of nowhere, Kai thought as they talked. *Better to build some rapport first. Besides, this is actually quite interesting.*

Around them, some of the disciples were frantically flipping through notes, while others sat in tense silence, eyes closed in concentration.

"Disciple Jin Hui," a voice called out. Kai turned to see a young woman in white robes stand up, her face pale with nervousness.

"Good luck," someone whispered as Jin Hui made her way to the examination room.

As the minutes ticked by, more names were called. But Kai and Xie Li remained engrossed in their discussion of alchemy theory.

"What about the Azure Petals?" Kai asked. "I noticed they seemed to have a calming effect on the mixture. Do you think that property could be enhanced somehow?"

Xie Li's eyes widened with excitement. "Oh, absolutely! I've been experimenting with different grinding techniques. If you grind them under moonlight, it seems to enhance their Yin properties."

"Have you tried combining that with—"

"Xie Li!" a voice called out, interrupting their conversation. "You're next for the oral assessment."

Xie Li stood up, smoothing her robes nervously. "Well, I guess it's my turn," she said, offering Kai a small smile. "Thank you for the conversation, Senior Brother Kai. It was . . . really nice."

Kai nodded, returning her smile. "The pleasure was mine. Good luck with your assessment, though I doubt you'll need it."

As Xie Li walked away, Kai leaned back in his seat.

That went well. She seems intelligent and passionate about alchemy. And she's not arrogant like some talents tend to be. She's definitely a good candidate for the guild. Now I just need to figure out the best way to approach her about it.

CHAPTER THIRTY-TWO

Kai sat in the waiting room as the other disciples around him fidgeted nervously or frantically reviewed notes, but Kai remained outwardly calm. He'd learned long ago that panicking never helped in high-pressure situations.

An hour ticked by slowly. Kai observed as more and more disciples were called in for their oral exams until, finally, the door opened and Xie Li emerged. Her cheeks were flushed, and her eyes sparkled with excitement. As she passed by Kai, she flashed him a quick smile before being led away by one of the proctors. Kai noticed her exam had taken significantly longer than the others.

Interesting. They must have recognized her talent and wanted to test her further.

He watched as Xie Li disappeared through the door, feeling a twinge of disappointment that he couldn't speak with her again. *I'll have to find her later. She could be a valuable ally . . .*

"Kai Thorn," a voice called out, breaking through his thoughts.

Kai stood and smoothed out his black robes. He took a deep breath, centering himself. *Show time.*

As he approached the examination room, he could feel the eyes of the remaining disciples on him. Kai ignored them all as he pushed open the heavy wooden door and stepped inside.

The room was smaller than he expected, with dark wood paneling and shelves lined with ancient-looking tomes and alchemical equipment. A large window let in the afternoon sunlight.

At the center of the room sat a long table. Behind it were three figures: Elder Bin, Elder Xiao, and another Kai didn't recognize. Their faces were impassive as they gestured for him to take the seat across from them.

Kai sat down, his posture straight but relaxed. He met each Elder's gaze in turn, careful to show respect without appearing intimidated.

Elder Bin cleared his throat. "As you know, this oral examination will test your understanding of alchemical principles, creation processes, and your ability to handle unexpected situations. Elder Po, Elder Xiao, and I will be conducting the examination."

Stay calm. You've prepared for this, Kai reminded himself as he nodded.

Elder Bin began. "Let's start with the basics. Can you explain the principle of Essence Extraction and its importance in pill creation?"

Kai took a moment to gather his thoughts before responding. "Essence Extraction is the foundation of alchemy. It's the process of drawing out the purest, most potent aspects of an ingredient. This is crucial because the quality of the extracted essence directly impacts the potency and stability of the final product." He paused, considering how to elaborate. "For example, when extracting essence from Spirit Grass, the timing and technique used can greatly affect the result. Extracting at dawn after a full moon using a silver blade will yield a more potent essence than harvesting at noon with a regular knife."

Elder Po nodded. "Good. Now, can you describe the relationship between Essence Extraction and Qi Infusion?"

Kai's brow furrowed slightly as he considered the question. *This is a bit trickier. They're testing how well I understand the interactions between techniques.*

"Essence Extraction and Qi Infusion are complementary techniques," Kai began. "The purity and potency of the extracted essence determine how effectively it can be infused with qi. A poorly extracted essence might resist Qi Infusion or become unstable when infused. On the other hand, a well-extracted essence can accept and amplify the infused qi, resulting in a more powerful final product." He paused, then added, "Additionally, the type of qi used in the infusion should be compatible with the nature of the extracted essence. For instance, using Yang qi to infuse an essence with strong Yin properties could lead to instability or even a negation of effects."

Elder Po's eyebrows rose slightly. "You seem to have a good grasp of the interplay between techniques."

Elder Bin leaned forward. "Let's move on to Elemental Fusion. Can you explain its importance in creating complex pills?"

Kai nodded. "Elemental Fusion is crucial for creating pills with multiple effects or for balancing opposing forces within a single pill. It allows an alchemist to combine ingredients with different elemental properties harmoniously." He thought for a moment, then continued, "For example, creating a pill that both invigorates and calms would require fusing Yang and Yin elements. Without proper Elemental Fusion, these opposing forces might negate each other or cause the pill to become unstable."

"And how would you go about achieving this fusion?" Elder Po interjected.

"The key is to find a balance point between the elements. This often involves introducing a neutral element as a bridge or using techniques to gradually blend the opposing forces. The exact method would depend on the specific elements involved and the desired outcome of the pill." Kai paused, then added, "It's also important to consider the order of fusion. Sometimes, fusing the weaker elements first before introducing the stronger ones can lead to a more stable result."

Elder Xiao, who had been silent, suddenly spoke. "Interesting approach. Now, let's consider a more complex scenario."

Kai straightened in his seat, his full attention on Elder Xiao. *This is unexpected. What's he planning?*

Elder Xiao's eyes gleamed as he presented the scenario. "Imagine you're tasked with creating a pill that enhances a cultivator's affinity with both fire and water elements simultaneously. This pill must not only boost these opposing elements but also ensure they don't conflict within the cultivator's body. How would you approach this challenge?"

Kai blinked, momentarily taken aback. *This is far beyond novice level, possibly journeyman or even master-level theory. He's testing my limits . . .*

The other two Elders exchanged surprised glances but remained silent.

Kai took a deep breath before beginning, "This is a complex problem that would require careful application of multiple techniques," he began slowly. "The first challenge would be selecting appropriate ingredients that embody fire and water essences without being mutually destructive." He paused, thinking through the process step by step. "I would start by using Essence Extraction on fire-attributed and water-attributed ingredients separately. The key would be to extract essences that are pure but not overly potent, to avoid immediate conflict.

"Next, I would use Elemental Fusion to create a neutral bridge element, perhaps using earth-attributed ingredients. This bridge would serve as a buffer between the fire and water essences. The fusion process would be delicate. I'd gradually introduce the fire and water essences into the neutral base, using Stability Control techniques to prevent any violent reactions. The goal would be to create a harmonious blend where fire and water coexist without neutralizing each other.

"Once the fusion is stable, I'd use Qi Infusion to imbue the mixture with balanced qi and reinforce the harmony between the elements. This step would be crucial in ensuring the pill doesn't cause internal conflict when consumed.

"Finally, I would use Spiritual Resonance techniques to attune the pill to the general spiritual frequency of human cultivators. This would help the body accept and utilize the dual-nature pill without rejection. But this whole process is easier said than done."

Elder Xiao listened intently, his expression unreadable. When Kai finished, the elder nodded. "An interesting approach," he mused. "Not precisely what I would do and likely unrealistic, but for a novice, it's a remarkably insightful attempt."

Elder Bin cleared his throat. "I agree. That was certainly a thorough explanation. Now, let's move back on to—"

"If I may," Elder Xiao interrupted again, leaning forward with a glint in his eye. Elder Bin slightly frowned but nodded, gesturing for Elder Xiao to continue.

"Let me pose another scenario to you. Imagine you're in the field, far from your usual supplies. A fellow cultivator has been gravely injured and needs a powerful healing pill immediately. You have access to local herbs, but they're not the standard ingredients you're used to working with. How would you approach this situation?"

Real-world problem-solving, not just regurgitating facts . . .

Kai took a deep breath, centering himself before responding. "That's certainly a challenging scenario, Elder Xiao. The first step would be to quickly assess the available herbs and the nature of the cultivator's injury. I'd focus on identifying herbs with strong healing properties, even if they're not the standard ingredients for healing pills. Plants with high vitality or regenerative properties would be key." Kai leaned forward. "Given the time constraint, I'd have to simplify the pill-making process. Instead of a fully formed pill, I might opt for a potent elixir or even a raw paste that could be applied directly to the wound."

He then paused, considering the potential complications. "The main challenge would be ensuring the stability and safety of the concoction without access to my usual tools and stabilizing agents. I'd likely use a combination of qi manipulation and natural balancing ingredients to prevent adverse reactions." Kai looked directly at Elder Xiao. "It wouldn't be as refined or potent as a properly prepared healing pill, but in an emergency situation, the goal would be to create something effective enough to stabilize the injured cultivator until proper medical attention could be obtained."

Elder Xiao nodded slowly, a small smile playing at the corners of his mouth. "And how would you test the safety of this improvised remedy? You wouldn't want to further endanger your injured comrade."

Kai's brow furrowed slightly as he considered the question. *This is the real test,* he thought. *Balancing urgency with caution whilst also being an ethical dilemma.*

"Testing would indeed be crucial, Elder," Kai began carefully. "Given the emergency nature of the situation, we couldn't afford a lengthy testing process, but we also couldn't risk making the situation worse." He paused, organizing his thoughts. "I would start by using my qi sense to analyze the energy of the concoction, looking for any obvious signs of instability or harmful interactions." Kai's voice took on a more decisive tone as he continued. "Then, I would test a small amount on myself. As the creator of the remedy, I would have the best chance of recognizing and counteracting any negative effects quickly."

He saw Elder Bin's eyebrows raise at this but pressed on. "I would apply a tiny amount to a small cut or scrape on my own body. This would allow me to observe both topical reactions and any internal effects from absorption." Kai leaned back slightly, his expression serious. "It's not a perfect solution, and it does carry some personal risk. But in an emergency situation where a fellow cultivator's life is at stake, I believe it's a necessary precaution."

Elder Xiao's smile widened slightly. "A bold approach, young Kai. Many would hesitate to put themselves at risk in such a manner."

"In critical situations, hesitation can be more dangerous than calculated risk, Elder." Kai met the Elder's gaze steadily as he prayed he didn't have some technique that could detect lies. "As alchemists, I believe it's our responsibility to ensure the safety of our creations, even in less-than-ideal circumstances."

Elder Xiao turned to the other Elders. "I believe we've seen enough. Disciple Kai, you may proceed to the room where successful examinees are receiving their novice alchemist tokens."

Elder Bin and Elder Po looked surprised by the quick decision but didn't object.

"Thank you, Elders," Kai said, bowing. "I'm honored by your guidance and assessment."

As Kai left, he heard Elder Xiao address the other Elders. "Continue with the remaining examinations. I need to speak with the Sect Master immediately."

CHAPTER THIRTY-THREE

Sect Master Luo Qiang sat in his private quarters, a frown creasing his brow. He drummed his fingers on the armrest of his chair, lost in thought. His drumming was shortly interrupted by a sharp knock at the door.

Luo Qiang's brow furrowed slightly. He wasn't expecting any visitors at this hour.

"Come in."

The door swung open to reveal Elder Xiao. The Alchemist Master's eyes were bright with excitement.

"Luo Qiang," Elder Xiao began as he strode into the room. "I'm glad I was able to get a hold of you. I have urgent news that just couldn't wait."

Luo Qiang raised an eyebrow. "What is it, old friend?"

Elder Xiao's lips curved into a smile. "It's about your disciple. He's a prodigy."

The Sect Master's eyebrows rose slightly. He had expected great things from Shen Yu, but for Elder Xiao to be this excited . . . "Shen Yu has shown promise in alchemy as well?"

Elder Xiao shook his head, his excitement growing. "No, not Shen Yu. I'm talking about Kai Thorn."

Luo Qiang's eyes widened slightly, a flicker of surprise crossing his face. "Kai Thorn? The one with the strange mark? Explain, Xiao."

Elder Xiao took a deep breath, as if trying to contain his enthusiasm. "I just finished overseeing the novice alchemy examination. Kai's performance was . . . extraordinary."

The Sect Master leaned forward in his chair, his interest fully captured. "Go on."

"First, his pill creation was flawless. For someone who claims to have only started learning alchemy three days ago, it was unheard of. Not even my master learned pill making that fast." Elder Xiao's eyes gleamed as he spoke. "But it was his performance during the oral examination that made me certain."

Luo Qiang listened intently as Elder Xiao recounted the events of the examination. With each passing moment, his eyebrows rose higher.

"I posed theoretical scenarios far beyond novice level," Elder Xiao continued. "Questions that brute memorization couldn't answer, questions that would challenge even some of our intermediary alchemists. And Kai . . . He answered them all. His answers weren't correct, of course, but he provided insights that I've rarely seen in cultivators four times his age."

The Sect Master's eyes narrowed. *A prodigy in alchemy. This boy could be even more valuable than I first thought.*

"His understanding of alchemical principles, his ability to think on his feet, his willingness to take calculated risks—it's all there, Luo Qiang," Elder Xiao said, his voice filled with a mixture of awe and excitement. "This boy has the potential to become a master alchemist. Perhaps even . . ."

Elder Xiao paused, as if hesitant to voice his next thought.

"Perhaps even what?"

"Perhaps even surpass me one day," Elder Xiao finished, his voice barely above a whisper.

The weight of those words hung in the air between them. For Elder Xiao, widely regarded as one of the greatest alchemists of their generation, to make such a statement was no small thing.

Luo Qiang sat back in his chair, processing this new information. *An Immortal-Rank talent, and now this. The heavens truly are smiling on this boy . . .*

"I see," the Sect Master said slowly. "And what do you propose we do with this information, old friend?"

Elder Xiao's eyes lit up. "I want to take him as my disciple."

The words hung in the air for a moment. Luo Qiang's eyes narrowed, a flicker of something dark passing behind them.

"No," he said, his voice firm. "The boy is my disciple."

Elder Xiao's excitement faltered, replaced by confusion. "But Luo Qiang, surely you see the potential here? With my guidance, he could become one of the greatest alchemists our sect has ever produced."

The Sect Master shook his head again. "I understand your enthusiasm, Xiao, but my decision stands. Kai Thorn will remain under my tutelage."

Elder Xiao's brow furrowed, his earlier excitement giving way to suspicion. "Why are you so adamant about this, Luo Qiang? I know you're not usually this invested in disciples. Your focus has been on your own breakthrough for centuries now. It's not like you have time to dedicate to training them. You barely give that boy Wang Lin any time at all!"

The Sect Master opened his mouth to respond but found himself struggling to articulate a reason. His hesitation didn't go unnoticed by Elder Xiao.

Seeing the Sect Master's hesitation, Elder Xiao's eyes widened in realization. "I hope you're not thinking of using the boy for . . . *that.*"

The Sect Master's silence was all the answer the Elder needed.

"Luo Qiang," Elder Xiao sighed. "That method won't work. We've tried it before, remember? The cost is too high, and the chances of success are negligible."

"But if we use the boy, it might work this time!" Luo Qiang burst out, his carefully maintained facade cracking for a moment. "You've seen his talent, his unique abilities. He could be the key, Xiao!"

Elder Xiao shook his head sadly. "Listen to yourself, old friend. This isn't the way. Think about what you're suggesting."

The two old friends stared at each other, the weight of unspoken words hanging between them. Elder Xiao saw the desperation in Luo Qiang's eyes, the hunger for advancement that had consumed him for centuries.

"Luo Qiang," Elder Xiao said softly. "It would be better to nurture the boy. Guide him, teach him. One day, he might help you break through with his own achievements and discoveries. Isn't that a better path than . . . the alternative?"

The Sect Master's shoulders sagged slightly, the weight of centuries seeming to press down on him. For a long moment, he was silent, lost in thought.

Finally, Luo Qiang looked up, meeting Elder Xiao's gaze. "Perhaps . . . perhaps you're right."

A hint of a smile tugged at Elder Xiao's lips. "Of course I'm right. I usually am, you know."

Luo Qiang snorted. "Don't push your luck, old man." He sighed, running a hand through his hair. "Very well. The boy will remain my disciple, but . . . you can teach him whatever you'd like. His alchemy training will be in your hands."

A wide smile spread across Elder Xiao's face. He gave a small bow to the Sect Master. "Thank you, old friend. You won't regret this decision."

As Elder Xiao turned to leave, Luo Qiang called out, "And Xiao?"

The Elder paused at the door, looking back.

"Keep me informed of the boy's progress," Luo Qiang said. "I'm . . . curious to see how he develops."

Elder Xiao nodded, a sad look briefly passing in his eyes. As he walked out of the room, Luo Qiang could hear him muttering excitedly about potential successors and breakthrough theories.

As the door closed behind Elder Xiao, Luo Qiang leaned back in his chair.

Patience. The path to immortality is a long one. What's a few more centuries of careful planning and preparation?

CHAPTER THIRTY-FOUR

Kai followed the group of successful examinees into a small chamber adjacent to the examination room. At the front of the room, an elderly disciple sat behind a table, meticulously recording names and handing out small tokens.

As Kai approached, he noticed the token's intricate design—a mortar and pestle surrounded by swirling Chinese symbols. The elderly disciple looked up at him with a tired smile.

"Name?" he asked, his voice slightly hoarse from repeating the same question countless times.

"Kai Thorn," Kai replied, keeping his voice steady despite the excitement bubbling within him.

The disciple's eyes widened slightly at the name, his gaze flickering to Kai's black robes. "Ah, the new Legacy Disciple. Congratulations on passing the exam."

He scribbled Kai's name in a large ledger before handing over one of the bronze tokens. "This marks you as a novice alchemist of the Azure Sky Sect. Wear it with pride."

Kai accepted the token, feeling its weight in his palm. He turned it over, studying the craftsmanship.

Not bad, he thought. *Wonder if it has any special properties beyond just being a fancy ID.*

New Item Acquired: Novice Alchemist Token
Description: Proof of your status as a novice alchemist in the Azure Sky Sect.
Grants access to basic alchemy resources and facilities within the sect.

Ah, there we go. Useful, but nothing too exciting.

New Title Acquired: Novice Alchemist
Description: Increases your chances of success by 5% when crafting novice-level recipes.
You have gained 100 XP!

Now that is exciting.

As he turned away from the table, Kai's eyes scanned the room, searching for a familiar face. He spotted Xie Li near the back, her red Inner Disciple robes standing out among the sea of white-robed Outer Disciples. She was speaking with another young woman, her expression animated as she gestured with her hands.

Kai made his way through the crowd, politely excusing himself as he navigated around excited disciples. As he approached, Xie Li glanced up, and her eyes lit up as she saw him.

"Senior Brother Kai," she greeted him with a small bow. "Congratulations on passing the exam."

Kai returned the gesture. "Thank you, and congratulations to you as well. Your performance was impressive."

Xie Li's cheeks flushed slightly at the compliment. "You're too kind. I still have much to learn."

The young woman beside Xie Li cleared her throat softly, looking between them with curiosity. Xie Li started, as if suddenly remembering her companion.

"Oh! My apologies," she said quickly. "Senior Brother Kai, this is my friend Li Ting. Li Ting, this is Senior Brother Kai, the new Legacy Disciple."

Li Ting's eyes widened as she hurriedly bowed. "It's an honor to meet you, Senior Brother Kai. We've heard so much about you."

"Oh? And what have you heard?" Kai raised an eyebrow.

Li Ting hesitated, suddenly looking unsure. "Well . . . that you're incredibly talented, and that you impressed the Elders and even the Sect Master during the entrance exam."

"I see. Well, I wouldn't put too much stock in rumors. I'm just here to learn and improve, like everyone else."

Li Ting nodded, a look of understanding crossing her face. "That's admirable, Senior Brother. It's easy to get caught up in competition and forget why we're really here."

Kai turned his attention back to Xie Li, seeing an opportunity. "Speaking of learning and improving, I was wondering if you'd be interested in practicing alchemy together sometime? Your insights during our earlier conversation were fascinating, and I think we could both benefit from collaboration."

Xie Li's eyes widened in surprise, a mix of excitement and hesitation crossing her face. "I . . . I would be honored, Senior Brother Kai. But are you sure? Surely there are more advanced alchemists you could practice with."

Kai shook his head, offering a small smile. "Advanced doesn't always mean better for learning. Sometimes it's more beneficial to work with someone closer to your own level. Besides, your approach to alchemy is intriguing. I think we could learn a lot from each other."

Li Ting watched the exchange. "Xie Li, you should definitely accept! This is an amazing opportunity!"

Xie Li bit her lip, considering for a moment before nodding. "You're right. Thank you, Senior Brother Kai. I would love to practice alchemy with you."

"Excellent," Kai said, his smile widening slightly. "We can discuss the details later and find a time that works for both of us."

This is perfect. Not only will I have a chance to recruit her for my guild, but I can also gauge her skills more thoroughly.

As Kai opened his mouth to suggest a time, a hush fell over the room. He turned to see Elder Xiao striding through the crowd, his gaze fixed directly on Kai. The disciples parted before the Elder as whispers of excitement and curiosity rippled through the room. Elder Xiao came to a stop in front of Kai, his expression unreadable.

"Disciple Kai," he said. "Come with me. There are matters we must discuss."

Kai blinked in surprise. "Of course, Elder. But . . ." he glanced at Xie Li.

Elder Xiao chuckled. "Don't worry. You'll have plenty of time to find a dual cultivation partner later. This is important."

Kai held back a sigh, realizing the Elder had completely misunderstood the situation. "I'm sorry, we'll have to continue this conversation another time," he said to Xie Li.

Xie Li bowed again. "Of course, Senior Brother. Thank you for the offer. I look forward to our future practice sessions."

"Practice sessions, eh?" Elder Xiao laughed, winking at Kai. "Is that what they're calling it these days?"

Kai felt his face heat up as he gave Xie Li a small apologetic nod before following Elder Xiao out of the room, acutely aware of the curious stares and barely suppressed giggles boring into his back.

They walked in silence through the corridors of the sect, their footsteps echoing off the stone walls. Kai noticed they were heading toward a part of the complex he hadn't visited before, the architecture becoming more ornate as they progressed.

Finally, Elder Xiao came to a stop before a plain wooden door. He pressed his palm against it, and Kai felt a pulse of qi as the door swung open silently.

"Enter," Elder Xiao said, gesturing for Kai to go first.

Kai stepped into the room, his eyes widening slightly as he took in his surroundings. It was a spacious chamber, filled with shelves upon shelves of bottles, jars, and strange implements. The air was thick with the scent of herbs and minerals, and in the center of the room stood a massive stone table, its surface covered in complex alchemical arrays.

This must be Elder Xiao's personal alchemy workshop.

Elder Xiao closed the door behind them and moved to stand across from Kai, his eyes studying the young disciple.

"I'm sure you're wondering why I've brought you here," the Elder began, his tone now serious.

"Yes, Elder. I admit I'm curious about the reason for this meeting."

Elder Xiao's lips quirked into a small smile. "Direct and honest. Good. I appreciate disciples who don't waste time with unnecessary flattery." He walked around the stone table, running his fingers along its edge as he spoke. "As you may have guessed, this is about your performance in the alchemy exam. Your theoretical knowledge is . . . surprisingly advanced for someone who claims to have only started learning alchemy a few days ago."

Kai tensed slightly, wondering if he had somehow given himself away. Elder Xiao continued, seemingly oblivious to Kai's discomfort.

"Normally, I would have taken such a promising student as my personal disciple immediately. However"—a note of frustration entered his voice—"Luo Qiang has . . . other plans for your training."

Ah, of course. The old "you're too valuable to be given away" routine.

The Elder Xiao then sighed, shaking his head. "Politics and cultivation should not mix, but alas, that's the reality we live in. However, the Sect Master has agreed to allow you to learn alchemy under my guidance, even if I cannot formally take you as my disciple."

Learning from the sect's top alchemist would be an incredible opportunity. I can't let it pass.

"Thank you, Elder Xiao. I'm honored." Kai bowed.

The Elder waved a hand dismissively. "Save your thanks for when you've actually learned something. Your theoretical knowledge may be impressive for a novice alchemist, but theory alone does not make a great alchemist. You need practice—a lot of it." He fixed Kai with a stern gaze. "I've brought you here to assess your practical skills and begin your true training. Are you prepared for that, Disciple Kai?"

Kai straightened his posture, meeting the Elder's eyes. "Yes, Elder. I'm ready to learn."

Elder Xiao nodded approvingly. "Good. Now, before we begin, I have some critiques based on your exam performance." He began pacing slowly around the table, his voice taking on a lecturing tone. "Your understanding of elemental interactions is solid, but you tend to overcomplicate things. In alchemy, simplicity often yields the best results. Remember, we're guiding natural processes, not forcing them."

Kai listened intently, absorbing every word.

"Additionally," Elder Xiao continued, "your ideas about improvisation in the field were creative but somewhat reckless. While quick thinking is admirable, an alchemist must always prioritize stability and safety. A hastily made remedy can often be worse than no remedy at all." He stopped pacing and turned to face Kai directly. "That being said, your willingness to take calculated risks shows promise. With proper training, you could become a truly exceptional alchemist."

Kai bowed slightly. "Thank you for your insights, Elder. I'll work hard to improve in these areas."

Elder Xiao nodded, a ghost of a smile playing at his lips. "See that you do. Now, let's put your skills to the test. Which pill would you like to attempt making?"

Kai considered for a moment. He knew he needed to craft the qi-gathering pills to sell soon. "I'd like to try making a qi-gathering pill, if that's acceptable, Elder."

Elder Xiao raised an eyebrow. "An interesting choice. So, why have you selected that particular pill?"

"Well, to be honest, Elder, the qi-gathering pill and the qi-replenishing pill are the only recipes I'm familiar with at the moment."

The Elder's eyes narrowed slightly, a knowing look crossing his face. "I see. And I suppose you learned the qi-gathering pill recipe to sell its pills for some profit, didn't you?"

Kai's silence and awkward expression were answer enough. Elder Xiao burst into laughter, the sound echoing off the workshop walls.

"Ah, youth," he said, shaking his head in amusement. "Always so focused on immediate gains. A qi-gathering pill is always a novice alchemist's first venture. But in a few years, you'll realize such profit is nothing compared to the wealth of knowledge and skill you can accumulate. You need to focus on your alchemy skills, young Kai. That's your true future."

That's easy for you to say, Kai thought, careful to keep his face neutral. *You've already got wealth and power in the sect. For me, it's a long-term investment.*

Aloud, he said, "You're right, Elder. I'll dedicate myself to improving my skills. That's why I'd like to practice making more qi-gathering pills. My success rate is only about sixty to seventy percent for low-grade pills at the moment."

Elder Xiao's eyebrows shot up. "Only sixty to seventy percent? My boy, that's an excellent success rate for a novice alchemist. Most struggle to achieve even fifty percent consistency at your level."

Kai blinked in surprise. The Elder was right: Kai was comparing himself to those protagonists he had only read about.

"Now," Elder Xiao continued, "you can do whatever you'd like with the pills you successfully create. Just make sure not to sell any poor-grade ones. They can be toxic if consumed."

Kai nodded solemnly. "I understand, Elder. My instincts warned me about that as well."

Elder Xiao clapped his hands together. "Excellent. Then let's begin. I'll guide you through the process step by step, offering advice along the way."

Kai moved toward the central table, then paused. "Uh, Elder Xiao? I'm afraid I don't have any materials with me."

The Elder chuckled. "Of course you don't. What kind of master would I be if I didn't provide materials for my student?"

With a wave of his sleeve, three bundles appeared on the table: Spirit Grass, Yin Berries, and Qi Crystals. Kai's eyes widened as he realized there were enough materials for at least twenty-five attempts.

This is great. I can use my own materials for more pills later when I'm alone.

Elder Xiao gestured toward the materials. "Now, then, Disciple Kai. Shall we begin?"

Kai felt a smile spread across his face as he stepped up to the table. "Yes, Elder. I'm ready."

Elder Xiao watched closely as Kai began to sort through the materials. "Very good," he said. "Now, start by preparing the Spirit Grass. Remember, the key is in how you cut it . . ."

CHAPTER THIRTY-FIVE

K ai trudged back to his quarters, his body heavy with exhaustion. Elder Xiao had pushed him to his limits, making him craft pills until his qi reserves were completely drained. Despite the fatigue, a sense of accomplishment filled him. The old man's guidance had been invaluable for improving Kai's success rate and boosting his confidence in pill-making.

Twenty low-grade qi-gathering pills. Not bad for a day's work.

As he walked, he glanced down at his hand, where five poor-grade qi-gathering pills rested. His brow furrowed as he contemplated what to do with them. Throwing them away seemed wasteful, but selling them would go against alchemist ethics. Whilst he wasn't concerned with the ethical issue, the last thing he wanted was to lose his newly acquired alchemy token by breaking the rules.

Maybe I could use them for experiments. Or find a way to recycle the ingredients—

His thoughts were abruptly interrupted as someone collided with him, nearly knocking him off balance. Kai looked up to see a young man in white robes—an Outer Disciple—stumbling backward.

"I-I'm so sorry, Senior Brother!" the youth stammered, his eyes wide with panic. "Please forgive my clumsiness!"

Before Kai could respond, a System message flashed before his eyes:

Name: ???
Title: Fast Hands Level: Qi Refining Stage 6 Qi: 150/150 Strength: 48 Agility: 50 Endurance: 49

"Hold on," Kai called out, but the young disciple was already backing away, bowing repeatedly.

"It won't happen again, Senior Brother. I promise!" With that, the young man turned and dashed off, disappearing into the crowd of disciples milling about the courtyard.

Kai's focus turned to the new title.

Title: Fast Hands
Description: Your dexterity and sleight of hand are exceptional. Your movements are twice as fast for acts requiring quick, subtle hand movements.

Fast Hands? Wait a minute . . .

He glanced down at his hand again and froze. Where there had been five poor-grade pills now only three remained.

That little thief!

Su Jie's heart pounded as he wove through the crowded streets of the Outer Sect, putting as much distance as possible between himself and the Legacy Disciple he'd just robbed. It was a risky move, he knew, but desperation had driven him to it.

It's not like he'll come looking for me, Su Jie reassured himself. *To someone like that, we're all just faceless nobodies.*

He ducked into a narrow alley, finally slowing his pace as he caught his breath. Leaning against the cool stone wall, Su Jie closed his eyes and tried to calm his racing thoughts.

Five years. That's how long he'd been stuck at the peak of Qi Refining stage six. When he'd first joined the Outer Sect, Su Jie had been filled with dreams of rapid advancement. He'd imagined himself rising to the Inner Sect within a year, impressing the Elders with his talent and determination.

What a joke, he thought bitterly. *Seven years later, and I'm still here, scraping by on the lowest rung of the sect.*

Su Jie's mind drifted back to his childhood, to the grimy streets of the capital where he'd grown up. An orphan with no name and no future, he'd learned to survive by his wits and quick hands. Petty theft and picking pockets had kept him fed, but it was a precarious existence.

Then, like a miracle, an Azure Sky Sect Elder had visited the city. Su Jie, desperate for a way out, had tried to pickpocket the imposing cultivator. Instead of punishment, he'd received an opportunity. The Elder, amused by the boy's daring, had offered him a place in the sect.

I thought I'd found my ticket to a better life, Su Jie mused, a wry smile twisting his lips. *Instead, I just traded one form of poverty for another.*

Pushing off from the wall, Su Jie made his way deeper into the alleys of the Outer Sect. He couldn't risk returning to the communal cultivation areas. The so-called "senior brothers" who ruled over the lower ranks would demand their cut as a "protection fee."

Su Jie had learned that lesson the hard way too. His first year in the sect, he had managed to win a low-grade spirit stone in a disciples' competition. His joy had been short-lived. That very night, a group of older disciples had cornered him and "asked" for a contribution to the "Outer Sect welfare fund."

When Su Jie had refused, they beat him so badly he couldn't train for a week. Since then, he had learned to keep any gains a secret.

After what felt like an eternity of twists and turns, Su Jie arrived at his destination: a tiny half-collapsed shrine tucked away in a forgotten corner of the sect. He'd discovered it months ago and had been using it as a private cultivation spot ever since.

After slipping inside, Su Jie settled into a cross-legged position on the dusty floor. He pulled out the two pills he'd swiped from the Legacy Disciple and examined them closely in the dim light filtering through the cracks in the walls.

They look like standard qi-gathering pills, he thought, turning one over in his palm. *Low-grade, but that's still better than anything I could afford on my own.*

Without further hesitation, Su Jie popped one of the pills into his mouth. He grimaced at the bitter taste but forced himself to swallow. Closing his eyes, he began to circulate his qi, waiting for the pill's effects to kick in.

At first, everything seemed normal. Su Jie felt the familiar warmth of qi spreading through his meridians, gradually intensifying as the pill's power took hold. But then something changed. The warmth became uncomfortable heat, then searing pain.

Su Jie's eyes snapped open as panic set in. This wasn't right. Qi-gathering pills were supposed to be gentle, just helping to accumulate and refine qi. This felt like his very blood was boiling.

What's happening? he thought frantically, struggling to control the chaotic energy surging through his body. *Did I take too much? Or is this . . .*

With dawning horror, Su Jie realized the truth. The pill he'd stolen wasn't a low-grade qi-gathering pill at all. It was a poor-grade imitation, unstable and dangerous.

He tried to disperse the qi, to push it out of his body, but it was too late. The corrupt energy had taken hold and sent him spiraling into Qi Deviation. Su Jie's muscles seized, his back arching as waves of agony crashed over him.

As darkness began to creep in at the edges of his vision, Su Jie heard a voice. Cool, calm, and terrifyingly familiar.

"Stealing from me," the Legacy Disciple said, stepping out of the shadows, "was a bad idea."

CHAPTER THIRTY-SIX

Kai stood over the convulsing form of Su Jie, his expression a mixture of pity and disappointment. He'd followed the young thief at a distance, curious to see what he'd do with the stolen pills. This outcome, while not entirely unexpected, was far from what he'd hoped for.

I could have stopped him sooner, Kai thought, kneeling beside Su Jie. *But I wanted to see if he'd notice the difference between a real pill and a poor imitation. There goes any hope of selling off poor-grade qi-gathering pills as low-grade.*

Su Jie's body arched in pain, and a strangled gasp escaped his lips. Kai's hand hovered over the boy's chest, sensing the chaotic qi roiling beneath the surface.

Qi Deviation at stage six isn't too difficult to rectify, especially since it was caused by a pill. I just have to let out the toxic qi.

"Listen to me," Kai said firmly. "I'm going to help you, but you need to focus. Can you hear me?"

The disciple's eyes flew open, and he managed a weak nod, his face contorted in agony.

"Good. Now, I want you to picture a calm lake. The surface is smooth, undisturbed. Focus on that image."

As Kai spoke, he placed one hand on Su Jie's forehead and the other over his heart. "This is going to hurt, but it's better than the alternative."

Closing his eyes, Kai began to channel his qi into Su Jie's body. He could feel the chaotic energy raging through the young disciple's meridians, threatening to tear him apart from the inside. Carefully, methodically, Kai began to guide the corrupt qi out of Su Jie's system.

"That's it," Kai encouraged. "Keep focusing. Let my qi guide yours. Don't fight it."

It was a delicate process, one that required all of Kai's concentration and control. Sweat beaded on his forehead as he worked to draw out the poisonous energy bit by bit. Su Jie's body jerked and spasmed, but Kai held him steady, refusing to let go until the last traces of the poor-grade pill's effects were purged.

Finally, after what felt like hours, Kai sat back, exhausted but satisfied. Su Jie lay still, his breathing ragged but steady. The immediate danger had passed.

Now comes the hard part, Kai thought, watching as Su Jie's eyes fluttered open. *Dealing with this.*

"W-what happened?" Su Jie croaked, his voice hoarse and weak. "Am I . . . am I dead?"

Kai couldn't help but chuckle. "Not yet, though you came pretty close. How are you feeling?"

Su Jie blinked, focusing on Kai's face. Recognition dawned in his eyes, quickly followed by fear. "You! But how . . . Why . . ."

"Why did I save you, you mean?" Kai asked, raising an eyebrow. "Or why did I follow you in the first place?"

Su Jie struggled to sit up, wincing at the lingering pain in his muscles. "Both, I guess. I don't understand any of this."

Kai sighed, leaning back against the crumbling wall of the shrine. "Let's start with the basics, then. Do you know what Qi Deviation is?"

Su Jie nodded hesitantly. "It's when your qi goes out of control, right? When you try to cultivate beyond your limits or use techniques you're not ready for."

"Close enough," Kai said. "It can also happen when you introduce corrupt or unstable qi into your system. Like, say, by taking a poor-grade pill thinking it's a proper cultivation aid."

Su Jie's eyes widened in understanding. "The pills I took . . . They weren't real qi-gathering pills?"

"Oh, they were real, all right," Kai replied. "Real failures, that is. Alchemy isn't an exact science, especially for beginners. Sometimes the process goes wrong, and you end up with pills that are more poison than medicine."

"But why would you have pills like that?" Su Jie asked, a tinge of anger creeping into his voice. "And why didn't you stop me from taking them?"

Kai's expression turned serious. "I was going to dispose of them properly. As for why I didn't stop you . . . Well, I was curious. I wanted to see what you'd do with them. It was a gamble, I'll admit. One that nearly cost you your life. But you should never have stolen them."

Su Jie looked down, shame coloring his cheeks. "I'm sorry," he mumbled. "You're right. I . . . I shouldn't have stolen from you. I was just . . . desperate."

"I gathered that much," Kai said, his tone softening slightly. "Want to tell me why? It might help me decide what to do with you."

For a moment, Su Jie remained silent, apparently weighing his options. Then, with a deep breath, he began to speak. He told Kai everything—his childhood on the streets, his recruitment into the sect, and his years of struggle and stagnation in the Outer Sect.

As Su Jie's story unfolded, Kai listened intently, his mind working to process the information. When the young disciple finally fell silent, Kai nodded slowly.

"I see," he said. "You're not the first to feel trapped in the Outer Sect, and you won't be the last. But stealing and taking unknown pills isn't the answer. You could have died today, Su Jie."

"I know," Su Jie replied, his voice barely above a whisper. "I just . . . I didn't know what else to do. I can't afford proper cultivation resources, and without them, I'll never advance. It feels like I'm running in place while everyone else moves forward."

Kai sighed, rubbing his temples. Part of him wanted to turn Su Jie in, to let the sect deal with the thief and rule breaker. But another part . . . another part saw potential.

He's resourceful, if misguided. That Fast Hands title could be useful . . .

"All right, Su Jie," Kai said at last. "I'm going to give you a choice."

Su Jie looked up, hope and fear warring in his eyes.

"Option one: I turn you in to the sect Elders. The sect takes stealing pills very seriously. You'll be punished for theft and unauthorized use of alchemy products. Best case scenario, you'll be demoted or expelled from the sect."

Su Jie paled but nodded.

"Option two," Kai continued, "you work for me. In secret. I'll help you train, provide you with safe resources to advance your cultivation. In return, you'll run errands for me, gather information, and yes, occasionally use those 'fast hands' of yours for my benefit."

Su Jie's eyes widened in disbelief. "You . . . you'd do that for me? Even after I stole from you?"

Kai shrugged. "Consider it an investment. You have potential, Su Jie. It'd be a shame to waste it. But make no mistake—this isn't charity. I'll work you hard, and I'll expect results. Cross me, and you'll wish I had turned you in instead. Understood?"

Su Jie nodded vigorously. "Yes! Yes, I understand. I won't let you down, I swear it!"

"Good," Kai said, standing up. "Then let's get you back to the dormitories. You need rest after that Qi Deviation. We'll talk more tomorrow about your new . . . duties."

As they made their way back through the sect grounds, Kai's mind raced with possibilities. Chen Wei stayed mostly at the Legacy Disciple quarters; having a set of eyes and ears in the Outer Sect could prove invaluable. And if Su Jie's talents could be properly honed . . .

This could be the start of something interesting. I don't trust him enough to recruit him yet, but if he proves useful and loyal, then I may have just found another guild member.

Su Jie walked beside him in silence, still processing the night's events. His near-death experience, the unexpected mercy from the Legacy Disciple he had wronged, the sudden change in his fortunes . . . It was almost too much to take in.

As they reached the Outer Disciple dormitories, Kai turned to Su Jie. "Remember, not a word of this to anyone. As far as the sect is concerned, nothing happened tonight. Got it?"

"Of course. I won't say anything." Su Jie nodded.

"Good," Kai said. "Get some rest. I'll contact you soon with your first assignment."

CHAPTER THIRTY-SEVEN

Kai sat cross-legged in his pavilion, his gaze sweeping over the three figures seated before him. He reached into his robes and produced a small pouch. He opened it carefully to reveal twenty small round pills.

"Here are the low-grade qi-gathering pills."

Chen Wei's eyes widened slightly as he looked at the pills. He nodded, a hint of familiarity in his expression. "Thank you, Senior Brother Kai. I've had the opportunity to use one before."

Kai then noticed a flicker of hesitation cross Chen Wei's face. The young disciple seemed to be wrestling with something, his fingers tapping nervously on the table's surface.

"What is it, Chen Wei?" Kai asked, raising an eyebrow. "You look like you have something on your mind."

Chen Wei took a deep breath before speaking. "It's about the deal we made, Senior Brother. Regarding how the profits are split."

Kai's eyes narrowed slightly. "Are you not happy with the ten percent?" He couldn't help but notice the confused looks that passed between Liu Wei and Zhi-Zhi at this mention of profit sharing.

Chen Wei quickly shook his head. "No, no, it's not that. It's just . . . Now that we're part of the guild, I don't think it's fair for me to have a share of the profits while the other guild members don't."

Is he asking for the others to get a split too? Or is he saying he doesn't want a share at all? Kai fell silent as he tried to decipher Chen Wei's intentions.

As if reading Kai's thoughts, Chen Wei continued, "Since we're all in this together now, I . . . I don't want a share anymore. I think it would be better if the profits went to the guild as a whole."

Kai blinked, genuinely surprised. He knew the Azure Sky Sect was considered a righteous sect, but he hadn't expected such . . . selflessness. *I certainly wouldn't do the same in his shoes, or in this case, sandals. Well, this only benefits me, so why not?*

After a moment of consideration, Kai nodded slowly. "You're right, Chen

Wei. Since we're no longer just business partners but a guild, this makes sense. Sometimes we need to do things for the better of the guild as a whole."

Chen Wei's face lit up with a smile, clearly relieved that Kai understood and agreed with his suggestion.

Kai turned his attention to the group as a whole. "Now, let me explain how this is going to work. Each of you will receive a low-grade qi-gathering pill for your own cultivation after you complete this job."

Liu Wei and Zhi-Zhi perked up at this news while Chen Wei nodded.

"But more importantly," Kai continued, his voice taking on a serious tone, "your work will contribute to your trident mark. As you know, this mark is crucial. Once your contribution is high enough, it will allow you to condense qi."

All three of them nodded eagerly.

Turning his attention back to the task at hand, Kai addressed Liu Wei. "Now, Liu Wei, do you have the list of potential buyers?"

Liu Wei nodded and produced a small notebook from his robes. He flipped it open and began to read. "Yes, Senior Brother Kai. I've compiled a list of thirty potential buyers, all of whom have expressed interest in qi-gathering pills."

As Liu Wei read out the names, Kai listened, his mind already working on strategies. When Liu Wei finished, Kai nodded thoughtfully.

"Good work, Liu Wei. However, we only have twenty pills right now." Kai's brow furrowed slightly as he considered their options. "Our competitors are selling the same pill for thirty spirit stones, and it takes fifteen spirit stones to make one pill. To make a respectable profit, we need to sell them for at least above twenty spirit stones each."

Chen Wei leaned forward. "What price should we aim for, Senior Brother?"

Kai turned to Chen Wei. "Here's what we'll do. Let the thirty potential buyers argue amongst themselves. It's unlikely any of them will pay higher than twenty-seven or twenty-eight spirit stones, so aim for twenty-five spirit stones per pill."

Chen Wei nodded.

"However," Kai added with a sly smile, "if someone is willing to pay more, we have no problem with that. Just don't push too hard and risk losing a sale."

Liu Wei looked slightly nervous. "But what if they try to haggle? Some of these buyers are known for their . . . aggressive negotiation tactics."

Kai's smile widened. "That's where our secret weapon comes in. Chen Wei, if you encounter any issues or resistance, don't hesitate to use my title as Legacy Disciple. It should give our sales pitch some extra weight."

Chen Wei's eyes widened. "Are you sure, Senior Brother? I know you were trying to keep things quiet."

Kai nodded. "I'm sure. Besides, I'm now a novice alchemist. That combined with my status as a Legacy Disciple should be more than enough to smooth over any difficulties you might encounter."

Zhi-Zhi puffed up his small chest. "And I shall act as Chen Wei's protector again! I did a good job last time, did I not?"

Kai couldn't help but smile at the tortoise's enthusiasm. "Yes, you did, Zhi-Zhi. Your presence adds an . . . intimidation factor that can be quite useful in negotiations. Just remember, your primary role is to protect Chen Wei, not to show off."

Zhi-Zhi deflated slightly but nodded. "Of course."

With the plans set, Kai looked at each of his guild members in turn. "Does everyone understand their roles?"

They all nodded.

"Excellent," Kai said. "You're dismissed. Good luck, and remember, your success is the guild's success."

As Chen Wei, Liu Wei, and Zhi-Zhi stood to leave, Kai called out one last time. "Oh, and Chen Wei?"

The young merchant turned back. "Yes, Senior Brother?"

Kai's expression softened slightly. "Your idea about the profit sharing . . . It was a good one. The kind of thinking that will help our guild thrive."

Chen Wei's face broke into a wide smile, and he bowed deeply before following the others out of the pavilion.

Once alone, Kai turned his attention to his cultivation. From within his robes, he produced an ancient-looking scroll: the Heavenly Thunderstorm cultivation method. He carefully unrolled it, his eyes scanning the text until he found the section he was looking for.

Meridian of the Lightning Core
Location: Solar Plexus
Method to Open: Storm's Core—the cultivator consumes a Thundercore elixir, made from Lightning Lotus petals, while concentrating on the solar plexus. The elixir induces a powerful surge of qi, which awakens the core meridian.

Kai's eyes narrowed as he reread the passage. The Storm's Core was different from the typical core that cultivators developed during Core Formation. This core meridian, located at the solar plexus, was opened much earlier in the cultivation process—during the Qi Refining Realm.

Everyone opens a core meridian eventually, Kai mused. *The difference is that mine will have a lightning element infused into its very essence.*

However, as Kai continued reading, he felt a sinking feeling in his stomach. The Thundercore elixir required to open this meridian was far beyond his current alchemical skills. As a novice alchemist, he simply didn't have the expertise to brew such a complex concoction.

Kai sighed, rubbing his temples. *I'll need to buy it with spirit stones. Which, unfortunately, I'm severely lacking at the moment.*

He stood up and began pacing the pavilion as he considered his options. The soft swish of his robes against the floor was the only sound as he thought.

Perhaps . . . An idea began to form in Kai's mind. *Elder Xiao, the Alchemy Master. It shouldn't be too difficult to convince him to give me the elixir on loan. I could always pay the spirit stones back later. For an Elder of his standing, it's hardly a significant amount.*

Kai nodded to himself, his decision made. He would seek out Elder Xiao and present his case. With his status as a Legacy Disciple and his performance in the alchemy exam, surely the Elder would see the wisdom in investing in Kai's progression.

He seems pretty interested in my cultivation anyways. It shouldn't be too hard to convince him.

CHAPTER THIRTY-EIGHT

Kai stood outside Elder Xiao's practice alchemy room, shifting his weight from one foot to the other. The corridor was quiet, with only the occasional muffled sound of bubbling liquids or clinking glassware from behind the closed door.

He'd been waiting for nearly an hour, but patience was a virtue he'd learned to cultivate since arriving in this world. Also, he knew better than to interrupt an Elder during their work.

I hope this isn't a waste of time, Kai thought, glancing at the door. *But if anyone can help me with this elixir, it's Elder Xiao.*

Just as Kai was considering whether to come back later, the door swung open. Elder Xiao stepped out, his eyes widening slightly as he noticed Kai.

"Disciple Kai?" Elder Xiao said. "I didn't expect to see you back so soon. Is everything all right?"

Kai bowed. "Elder Xiao, I apologize for the unexpected visit. I hope I'm not interrupting anything important."

The Elder waved his hand dismissively. "Not at all. I was just finishing up some experiments. What brings you here?"

"Well, Elder, I've been making progress with the Heavenly Thunderstorm cultivation method, and I've reached a point where I need a Thundercore elixir to continue."

Elder Xiao's eyebrows rose. "Ah, so you're trying to awaken the Storm's Core already? Impressive progress, young Kai."

"Thank you, Elder," Kai said. "However, I've run into a small . . . problem."

The Elder's expression turned curious. "Oh? And what might that be?"

Kai felt his face grow warm with embarrassment. "Well, you see, I don't currently have enough spirit stones to purchase the elixir. I was wondering if . . . if perhaps you might be willing to provide one as a loan? I promise I'd pay you back as soon as possible."

Elder Xiao's brow furrowed. "A loan? But, Kai, you should still have plenty of spirit stones left from your stipend. Unless . . ." His eyes narrowed. "You've invested it all in that little trading business of yours, haven't you?"

Kai's silence was answer enough. He managed a sheepish smile. "Hopefully, spirit stones won't be a problem for much longer if this works out."

The Elder sighed, shaking his head. "Ah, you young people. Always chasing after material gains. I wish you'd focus entirely on alchemy, but I suppose that's too much to ask."

Kai opened his mouth to protest, but Elder Xiao held up a hand, his expression growing serious. "Disciple Kai, I don't give out loans like that, no matter how talented the disciple. It sets a bad precedent."

Kai's heart sank. He hadn't expected outright rejection. "I . . . I understand, Elder. I apologize for troubling you."

An awkward silence fell between them. Kai was about to excuse himself when Elder Xiao's stern expression softened into a smile.

"Besides," the Elder said, a glint in his eye, "loans won't help you in the long run. Instead, why don't I coach you to produce the elixir yourself?"

Kai blinked, caught off guard by the offer. "But . . . isn't the Thundercore elixir an intermediate-level concoction? I'm still just a novice alchemist."

Elder Xiao nodded. "Indeed it is. But it's also something that talented novice alchemists can create with proper guidance. In fact, I made my first Thundercore elixir when I was only a novice myself."

"Really?" Kai couldn't hide his surprise.

The Elder chuckled. "Don't look so shocked, young Kai. With my guidance, I believe you're more than capable of creating this elixir."

Kai felt a surge of excitement. Learning to create the elixir himself would be far more valuable in the long run than simply being given one. "Thank you, Elder."

"Excellent," Elder Xiao said, gesturing toward the open door. "Come inside, and we'll get started."

Kai followed the Elder into the alchemy room, his eyes darting around to take in the various apparatuses and ingredients lining the shelves. Elder Xiao moved to a large bookshelf and began rifling through several scrolls and notebooks.

"Now, where did I put that recipe . . . ," he muttered. Seeing Kai's curious look, Elder Xiao explained, "Don't worry, I know the recipe by heart. But you'll need a written version to study. Even though I'll be guiding you, I won't be holding your hand through every step."

Kai nodded, a small smile playing on his lips. "I didn't say anything, Elder."

"No, but I could practically hear you thinking it," Elder Xiao retorted good-naturedly. "Ah, here we are!" He pulled out a slightly yellowed piece of parchment and handed it to Kai. "The recipe for the Thundercore elixir. Read it carefully."

Kai accepted the parchment with both hands and scanned the contents.

Thundercore Elixir

Ingredients:

3 Lightning Lotus petals

1 Thunder Quartz crystal (crushed)

2 drops Storm Serpent venom

1 Azure Cloudberry

5 strands of Skysilk

Method:

1. Begin by infusing the cauldron with lightning-attuned qi.

2. Apply Spiritual Resonance throughout the process to attune the elixir to lightning-based cultivation methods.

3. Crush the Lightning Lotus petals and Thunder Quartz together, using Essence Extraction to draw out their properties.

4. Add the Storm Serpent venom, using Elemental Fusion to combine it with the crushed ingredients.

5. Introduce the Azure Cloudberry, applying Qi Infusion to enhance its spiritual properties.

6. Weave the Skysilk strands through the mixture, using Stability Control to maintain balance.

7. Simmer for one hour, maintaining a constant flow of lightning-attuned qi.

8. Cool and condense into liquid form.

Warning: Extreme caution required. Improper balance may result in volatile reactions.

As Kai finished reading, he nodded to himself. The recipe didn't seem overly complex, but he knew from experience that alchemy was often trickier than it appeared on paper.

"Well?" Elder Xiao asked, watching Kai's expression closely. "What do you think?"

Kai looked up from the parchment. "It doesn't seem too difficult—at least, in theory. And it looks like I won't need to learn any new techniques: the five basic alchemy skills should cover everything."

The Elder nodded. "Good. Now, are you ready to begin?"

Kai rolled up his sleeves, a determined glint in his eye. "Yes, Elder. I'm ready."

Elder Xiao gestured toward a nearby workstation. "Then let's get started. I'll provide the ingredients for your attempts, but I expect to be paid back in full."

I had hoped the situation would be like the qi-gathering pills, but I guess the Elder doesn't want me to take advantage of him. I don't blame him—he's already been more helpful than I deserve.

As Kai moved to the workstation, Elder Xiao gathered the necessary materials. Soon, everything was laid out neatly before him: the Lightning Lotus petals with their faint electric glow, the Thunder Quartz crystal, a small vial of viscous Storm Serpent venom, a plump Azure Cloudberry, and the gossamer-thin strands of Skysilk.

Kai took a deep breath and began by channeling his qi into the cauldron, focusing on the lightning aspect. The cauldron hummed faintly as a few sparks danced along its rim.

"Good start," Elder Xiao commented from where he stood observing. "But be careful not to overdo it. Too much lightning qi at this stage can destabilize the entire process."

Nodding, Kai adjusted his qi flow, tempering it slightly. He then picked up the Lightning Lotus petals and Thunder Quartz and placed them in a mortar. As he began grinding them together, he applied his Essence Extraction technique to draw out the inherent properties of both ingredients.

A fine glittering powder began to form in the mortar, occasionally emitting tiny sparks. Kai carefully transferred this into the cauldron, where it settled into a gently swirling mass.

"Now for the tricky part," Elder Xiao warned as Kai reached for the vial of Storm Serpent venom. "Remember, only two drops. Any more and you risk a violent reaction."

Kai's hand was steady as he uncorked the vial and tilted it over the cauldron. One drop fell, then another. As soon as the second drop hit the mixture, Kai quickly pulled the vial away and recorked it.

Immediately, he began applying his Elemental Fusion technique, working to combine the venom with the powdered ingredients. The mixture in the cauldron began to bubble and spark more vigorously.

"Careful now," Elder Xiao cautioned. "Keep your qi flow steady."

Kai gritted his teeth as he concentrated hard on maintaining the delicate balance. Sweat beaded on his forehead as he reached for the Azure Cloudberry. He dropped it into the cauldron and began applying Qi Infusion to enhance its spiritual properties.

The mixture in the cauldron took on a faint blue glow.

So far, so good.

Next came the Skysilk. Kai carefully picked up the delicate strands and began weaving them through the mixture, using his Stability Control technique to maintain balance. This was perhaps the most challenging part yet—the Skysilk was so fine that it threatened to dissolve instantly in the bubbling concoction.

"Steady hands," Elder Xiao murmured. "Let the Skysilk guide your movements."

Kai tried to relax, allowing his hands to move more fluidly. To his surprise, he found that the Skysilk seemed to almost weave itself as it was drawn by the currents in the mixture.

Throughout the entire process, Kai had been applying Spiritual Resonance to attune the elixir to lightning-based cultivation methods. Now, as the last strand of Skysilk disappeared into the mixture, he increased this resonance, feeling the elixir harmonize with his own qi.

"Excellent work so far," Elder Xiao said, a note of approval in his voice. "Now comes the true test of patience. Maintain a constant flow of lightning-attuned qi for the next hour."

Kai nodded as he settled into a comfortable stance. He regulated his breathing and established a rhythm that would allow him to maintain a steady flow of qi into the cauldron. The mixture continued to bubble and spark, occasionally emitting small flashes of light.

As the minutes ticked by, Kai found his concentration wavering. Maintaining such precise qi control for an extended period was more challenging than he'd anticipated, especially with a qi capacity at the Qi Refining Realm. Sweat dripped down his back, and his arms began to tremble slightly.

"Focus, Kai," Elder Xiao's voice cut through his fatigue.

Kai closed his eyes briefly as he pictured the swirling vortex of lightning qi flow through his meridians and into the mixture.

Finally, after what felt like an eternity, Elder Xiao spoke again. "Time's up. Now, cool and condense the mixture into liquid form."

With a sigh of relief, Kai began to draw back his qi to allow the mixture to cool. As it did so, he used his qi to shape and condense it into a small vial of glowing blue liquid. Occasional sparks danced across its surface.

Kai stepped back from the workstation, his legs wobbling slightly, more from the fatigue than the extended period of standing still. He looked at Elder Xiao expectantly.

The Elder approached and looked closely at the vial. He picked it up, examining it from all angles. After what seemed like an eternity, he set it back down and turned to Kai.

"Well," Elder Xiao began, his face unreadable, "you've certainly produced . . . something."

Kai's heart sank. "It's not right, is it?"

Elder Xiao shook his head. "I'm afraid not. While you've managed to create an elixir, it lacks the proper balance and potency to be a true Thundercore elixir. Consuming this would be . . . unpleasant, to say the least."

Item Created: Thunder Fizzle Elixir
Description: A botched Thundercore Elixir.
Warning: If consumed, it can generate unpredictable lightning in the user's

meridians, potentially disrupting qi flow for weeks. May attract lightning strikes during storms.

Reading the warning, disappointment washed over Kai. He'd been so sure he was doing everything correctly. "What went wrong, Elder?"

The Elder stroked his chin. "Tell me, Disciple Kai, where do you think you made mistakes?"

Kai furrowed his brow, thinking back over the process. "Well . . . I think I might have been too cautious with the Storm Serpent venom. And perhaps I didn't maintain a consistent enough qi flow during the simmering stage?"

"Those are indeed part of the problem." Elder Xiao nodded. "But there's more to it than that. Your Essence Extraction was too aggressive—you drew out too much from the Lightning Lotus petals, which threw off the balance from the very beginning. And your Spiritual Resonance wasn't quite attuned correctly. You were resonating more with your own qi than with the lightning aspect specifically."

Kai listened intently, mentally noting each point of critique. "I see."

The Elder smiled. "Don't be discouraged, Disciple Kai. No one creates a perfect Thundercore elixir on their first try. Even I failed multiple times before succeeding."

This admission made Kai feel slightly better. "How many attempts did it take you, Elder?"

Elder Xiao chuckled. "More than I care to admit. But each failure taught me something valuable. Now, are you ready to try again?"

Kai nodded. "Yes, Elder. I won't give up until I succeed."

"That's the spirit," Elder Xiao said approvingly. He gestured to a fresh set of ingredients he had prepared while Kai was working. "Let's try again. This time, focus on gentler Essence Extraction and more precise Spiritual Resonance."

CHAPTER THIRTY-NINE

Kai stared at the glowing vial in his hand, a tired smile spreading across his face.

Item Created: Thundercore Elixir
Description: An elixir that awakens the Storm's Core Meridian, enhancing lightning-based cultivation.

"Well done, Disciple Kai. It took three days, but you finally did it." Elder Xiao smiled at him.

Kai nodded, his gaze shifting to the System messages that had appeared before him. He watched as each of his five basic alchemy skills leveled up to level four.

You have gained 1000 XP!

Two whole levels from creating an intermediate elixir? Kai's eyes widened. *Not bad at all.*

"Thank you for your guidance, Elder Xiao," he said, bowing his head. "I couldn't have done it without your patience and instruction."

The Elder waved his hand dismissively, but there was a small smile on his face. "You have talent. But talent alone isn't enough. It was your persistence that saw you through."

Kai nodded, remembering the countless failed attempts over the past three days. Each failure had been frustrating but also instructive. He'd learned to fine-tune his Essence Extraction, balancing it delicately to draw out just the right amount of power from each ingredient. His Elemental Fusion had become more precise, allowing him to blend the volatile components without causing unwanted reactions.

"Elder Xiao," Kai began, a question forming in his mind. "Now that I can create an intermediate elixir, does that mean I'm close to becoming an apprentice alchemist?"

"Ah, the impatience of youth." The Elder chuckled. "No, you still have a long way to go. Creating a single intermediate elixir is impressive, but to become an apprentice alchemist, you must master a wide range of elixirs and pills. Not to mention, your foundational skills need to be honed further."

How much further do I need to go? Kai glanced at his skill levels, all now at four. *Maybe I need to get them all to level nine, or even ten, to be considered an apprentice alchemist.*

"I understand, Elder," Kai said. "There's still much for me to learn."

"Indeed." Elder Xiao nodded. "But don't be discouraged. You've made remarkable progress in a short time. Many disciples spend years just to reach where you are now. You can't expect to rush through the ranks overnight."

Kai smiled. With the aid of the System and enough resources, he knew he probably could. He then glanced at his XP bar. *Only eight hundred left before I break through to the next level. I'm so close.*

As if reading his thoughts, Elder Xiao cleared his throat. "Well, what are you waiting for? Off you go to use that elixir. No point in crafting it if you're not going to put it to use."

Kai blinked, snapping out of his thoughts. "Of course, Elder. Thank you again for everything."

He bowed deeply, then turned to leave the alchemy room. As he walked through the door, he heard Elder Xiao call out, "And Kai? Don't forget to come back for more lessons. You may have created one intermediate elixir, but there are many more to master!"

"I won't forget, Elder. I'll be back soon."

When he reached his pavilion, Kai quickly entered and sealed the door behind him. He didn't want any interruptions during this crucial moment. He moved to the center of the room and sat cross-legged on the floor, placing the vial of Thundercore elixir in front of him.

Taking a deep breath, Kai closed his eyes and began to meditate. He needed to prepare his body and mind for the coming transformation. As he sank into a meditative state, he felt his qi circulating through his meridians.

After what felt like hours, but was probably only minutes, Kai opened his eyes. He was ready. Following the instructions from the Heavenly Thunderstorm scroll, he began to close off his core meridian.

It was always a strange sensation, like trying to dam a river with his bare hands, but slowly, ever so slowly, he felt his qi flow diminishing, the warmth in his core fading.

Cultivation reduced to Qi Refining Stage 7

Okay, step one complete. Now for the main event.

He reached for the vial of Thundercore elixir and uncorked it with slightly trembling hands. The liquid inside glowed with a soft blue light. Kai lifted the vial to his lips.

Here goes nothing, he thought, then drank the elixir in one swift gulp.

For a moment, nothing happened. Then, a sensation like liquid lightning coursed through Kai's body. He gasped as his back arched involuntarily. Every nerve felt like it was on fire, every muscle taut with electric energy.

Kai's eyes squeezed shut as he fought to maintain his concentration. He could feel the elixir's power surging through him, seeking out his closed Lightning Core meridian. With monumental effort, Kai directed the energy, guiding it to where he wanted it to go.

In his mind's eye, Kai could see his qi channels lighting up like a network of glowing blue veins. The energy from the elixir flowed along these channels and converged at his solar plexus. There, where his core meridian had been closed off, the energy began to pool.

Kai felt a pressure building in his chest, growing more intense by the second. It was like trying to contain a storm within his body. Just when he thought he couldn't take it anymore, when the pressure threatened to tear him apart from the inside, something shifted.

With a sensation like a dam breaking, the energy burst through the barrier of his closed meridian. Kai's eyes flew open, a gasp escaping his lips. Blue-white light poured from his eyes and mouth, and arcs of electricity danced across his skin.

For a timeless moment, Kai hung suspended between agony and ecstasy, his body a conduit for raw elemental power. Then, as suddenly as it had begun, it was over.

He slumped forward, panting heavily. His whole body tingled, and he could still feel traces of electricity crackling through his veins. But more than that, he felt . . . different. Stronger. More alive.

He looked up, his eyes seeking out the familiar blue rectangle of his status window. A series of messages greeted him:

Congratulations!
You have successfully opened the Storm's Core Meridian!
Cultivation returned to Qi Refining Stage 8
Lightning Affinity increased to 35%

Skill Leveled Up!
Crown of Lightning (Level 5)
Effect: A temporary visible aura of lightning can form around the cultivator's head during meditation, which boosts the cultivator's qi regeneration by 25%.

Skill Leveled Up!
Sky's Favor (Level 5)
Effect: The cultivator's qi-absorption rate increases by 25% whenever they are under an open sky. This increases to 30% during stormy weather.

Skill Leveled Up!
Electric Immunity (Level 5)
Effect: The cultivator gains 25% resistance to lightning-based attacks, reducing the damage taken from electric or lightning-based techniques.

You have gained 300 XP!

Kai let out a long slow breath. He'd done it. He'd successfully opened the Storm's Core meridian. But as he read through the System messages, a small frown creased his brow.

No new techniques? he thought, a twinge of disappointment in his chest. He'd been hoping that opening the Storm's Core would unlock some new lightning-based skills.

Then his eyes caught on the lightning affinity increase. *Wait a minute . . . My lightning affinity went up by five percent? That's . . . that's actually huge.*

Kai's disappointment quickly turned to excitement as he realized the implications. Increasing elemental affinities was notoriously difficult. Most cultivators could only do so with OP cultivation methods like his own or by finding extremely rare treasures like an elemental fruit.

This is worth way more than a new skill. I can always learn new techniques with skill scrolls, but increasing affinities? That's not something you can just buy or learn easily.

As the initial euphoria of his success began to fade, Kai became aware of a bone-deep weariness settling over him. The process of opening the Storm's Core meridian had taken more out of him than he'd realized. He glanced out the window, not the least surprised to see that night had fallen. How long had he been at this?

The others must have already sold the pills. There's no rush—I can meet up them with tomorrow. Right now, I need some well-deserved sleep . . .

With a groan, Kai pushed himself to his feet. His legs felt wobbly, like he'd just run a marathon. He stumbled over to his bed and collapsed onto it, not even bothering to change out of his sweat-soaked robes.

CHAPTER FORTY

After leaving the guild meeting, Chen Wei walked through the bustling grounds of the Outer Sect, his eyes scanning the list of names Liu Wei had given him. As he walked, a few curious glances were cast his way. It had been a while since Chen Wei had ventured into this part of the sect grounds.

"Well, well, look who decided to grace us with his presence!" a voice called out.

Chen Wei turned to see Pan Huo, a fellow Outer Disciple he'd trained with in the past. Pan Huo approached with a grin and slapped Chen Wei on the back.

"We were starting to think you'd forgotten about us little people, now that you're working for a Legacy Disciple," Pan Huo teased.

"How could I forget where I came from?" Chen Wei chuckled, shaking his head. "I've just been busy, that's all."

Another disciple, Li Ling, joined them. "Busy, huh? Must be nice, having important tasks to do. What brings you back to our humble corner of the sect?"

I don't want to attract the attention of our competitors. The first sale needs to go well.

Chen Wei hesitated, not wanting to reveal too much. "Just some errands. Nothing too exciting."

"Come on, Chen Wei," Pan Huo pressed. "You can tell us. We're all friends here, right?"

I can't let them know about the pills, Chen Wei thought. *But I don't want to be rude either.*

"It's sect business," he said finally. "I'm afraid I can't say more than that."

Pan Huo whistled. "Look at you, all mysterious now. Well, don't be a stranger, all right? Come train with us sometime, show us what you've learned from that Legacy Disciple of yours."

Chen Wei nodded. "I'll do that. Take care, both of you."

As he continued on his way, his mind was on the pills. *How should I approach this? Meeting buyers one at a time would take forever, and it wouldn't create the competition Senior Brother Kai wants.* He considered holding a public auction but quickly dismissed the idea. *That would draw too much attention. We don't want to risk conflicts with other groups selling low-grade qi-gathering pills. Even with Zhi-Zhi as backup, I'd rather avoid any confrontations. He's better as a shield than for offense, anyway.*

Lost in thought, Chen Wei almost bumped into a younger disciple hurrying past. As he looked up to apologize, a smile appeared on his face.

It was Li Jun, a scrappy kid who'd do just about any odd job for a few spirit stones. More importantly, Li Jun owed Chen Wei a favor.

Chen Wei's mind flashed back to Li Jun's first days in the sect. The boy had arrived wide-eyed and overwhelmed and had struggled to find his footing in the competitive environment. Chen Wei, remembering his own difficult early days, had taken pity on the newcomer. He'd shown Li Jun around, explaining the unwritten rules of sect life and helping him avoid the pitfalls that often tripped up new disciples. When Li Jun had accidentally offended an older disciple, it was Chen Wei who smoothed things over, saving the boy from a beating—or worse.

Now, seeing Li Jun, Chen Wei realized he might have found the solution to his current dilemma.

"Li Jun!" he called out. "Do you have a moment?"

The younger boy stopped and turned with a mixture of surprise and wariness on his face. "Senior Brother Chen Wei? What can I do for you?"

Chen Wei smiled. "I was hoping you might be able to help me with a small favor."

Li Jun's expression relaxed slightly, but he still looked cautious. "What kind of favor?"

"Nothing too difficult," Chen Wei said, keeping his voice low. "I just need you to deliver some messages for me. Discreetly."

Li Jun's eyes narrowed. "Messages? To who?"

Chen Wei produced the list of names. "To these disciples. I need you to tell each of them to meet me at the old willow grove near the eastern training fields. Today, two hours before sunset."

Li Jun's eyes widened as he scanned the list. "These are all upper-level Outer Disciples. What's this about?"

Chen Wei shook his head. "They already know. It's better if you don't know the details. Can you do that for me?"

Li Jun hesitated, clearly wanting to ask more questions. But after a moment, he nodded. "All right. But . . . you don't owe me for this one, Senior Brother. I haven't forgotten how you helped me when I first got here."

Chen Wei smiled, patting the younger disciple on the shoulder. "I appreciate that, Li Jun. Thank you."

As Li Jun hurried off to complete his task, Chen Wei felt a weight lift from his shoulders.

Now to prepare for the meeting. This could get . . . interesting.

* * *

Two hours before sunset, Chen Wei stood in the shade of the ancient willow tree, its long branches swaying gently in the breeze. The grove was secluded enough to offer privacy, but open enough that no one would feel trapped. Perfect for what he had planned.

A rustle from nearby made him tense, but it was just Zhi-Zhi poking his head out from his hiding spot in a dense patch of undergrowth.

"Are they here yet?" he asked eagerly. "I want to see the look on their faces when—"

"Shh!" Chen Wei hissed, glancing around nervously. "They'll be here soon. You need to stay hidden, remember?"

Zhi-Zhi deflated slightly. "But I wanted to help with the negotiations. I've been practicing my intimidating glare!"

Chen Wei sighed. "I appreciate the offer, but we need to keep this low-key. Just stay out of sight unless there's real trouble, just like last time, okay?"

The tortoise grumbled but retreated back into the bushes. Chen Wei straightened his robes and took a deep breath to calm his nerves.

A few minutes later, the first disciple arrived. It was Feng Yan, a tall, lean young man with sharp features and green eyes. He was at the peak of Qi Refining stage eight and was known for his aggressive demeanor, which probably had something to do with his aggressive cultivation style.

"Chen Wei," Feng Yan said. "Do you have it?"

CHAPTER FORTY-ONE

Before Chen Wei could answer, more disciples began to trickle in. Within minutes, the grove was filled with curious and slightly wary Outer Disciples, their cultivation levels ranging from Qi Refining stage four to stage nine.

Chen Wei recognized most of them. There was round-faced Liu Qian, only at stage four but with an uncanny talent for pill refinement—a shame he had yet to pass the novice alchemy exams. Lin Hui, stage seven, whose sword techniques were the talk of the Outer Sect. Broad-shouldered Wu Cheng, stage nine, rumored to be on the verge of breaking through to Foundation Establishment.

As the group grew, Chen Wei noticed the disciples naturally clustering into their various factions.

The Azure Fang group, known for their brash and confrontational attitudes, gathered near a gnarled tree root. They were the "tough guys" of the Outer Sect, always ready for a fight and quick to assert dominance. Feng Yan was their leader; he was already glaring at the others.

The Misty Palm faction, on the other hand, stood off to one side, eyeing the others warily. They were the intellectuals and strategists, preferring to solve problems with wit rather than brawn. Ling Xiao, their de facto spokesperson, had her arms crossed as she assessed the disciples around her.

Near the center, the Emerald Harmony group chatted animatedly. They were the social butterflies, always organizing events and trying to keep the peace between the other factions. Wu Cheng, ever the mediator, was already moving between groups, trying to ease tensions. Chen Wei knew that Wu Cheng, with his Peak Qi Refining stage nine cultivation, would make sure no conflicts broke out.

Off in a corner, the Shadows of Solitude kept to themselves. These were the loners and outcasts, either by choice or circumstance. Xu Kai, looking nervous as always, kept glancing around as if searching for an escape route.

Once it seemed everyone had arrived, Chen Wei cleared his throat. All eyes turned to him, with a mix of curiosity, impatience, and in some cases, barely concealed hostility.

"Thank you all for coming," Chen Wei began. "I've gathered you here because my friend mentioned that you were interested in some cultivation resources." He reached into his robes and produced a small pouch, then revealed the pills within. "As you can see, I have here twenty low-grade qi-gathering pills. I know many of you have been seeking these to aid in your cultivation."

"Convenient," Ling Xiao muttered. "How do we know these aren't just sugar pills you've cooked up to scam us?"

"A fair question," Chen Wei acknowledged. "But consider this: would I risk my reputation, not to mention potential retaliation from thirty angry disciples, over fake pills? I assure you, these are the real deal."

Feng Yan stepped forward, his eyes fixed on the pills. "But that Inner Disciple was pretty tight-lipped about where these came from. Care to fill us in on that little detail?"

"Wait a moment," Xu Kai said, his voice cutting through the murmurs. "These pills . . . They must be connected to your master, the Legacy Disciple. Am I right?"

A hush fell over the gathering as all eyes turned to Chen Wei, waiting for his response.

Chen Wei nodded slowly. "Yes, these pills are indeed connected to Senior Brother Kai."

Excited whispers broke out among the disciples. Chen Wei raised his voice slightly to be heard over the commotion.

"What's more, I can now reveal that Senior Brother Kai has recently attained the rank of novice alchemist. These pills are some of his first successful creations."

"Novice alchemist?" Liu Qian, the pill refiner, exclaimed. "At his age? That's . . . that's incredible!"

Chen Wei's smile widened. "Indeed it is. Which means you can be assured of the quality of these pills. They're not just any low-grade qi-gathering pills—they're crafted by a Legacy Disciple with exceptional talent."

Zhang Liang spoke up. "But if they're made by a novice alchemist, how do we know they're safe?"

This is my chance to really sell these pills. I need to make Senior Brother Kai look as impressive as possible.

"An understandable concern," Chen Wei acknowledged. "But remember, this is Senior Brother Kai we're talking about. His talent is unprecedented. Even the Alchemy Master, Elder Xiao, was impressed by his skills and wanted to take him as a disciple. These pills have been thoroughly tested and verified by the Alchemy Master himself. They're not only safe but potentially more effective than standard low-grade qi-gathering pills."

The atmosphere in the grove shifted once again. The initial suspicion had given way to a palpable sense of eagerness. Disciples who had been hesitant before now looked at the pills with naked want in their eyes.

"So," Chen Wei said, holding up one of the pills. "Now that you know the true value of what's being offered, let's begin the bidding. Who wants to make the first offer for a pill crafted by the Azure Sky Sect's most promising young alchemist?"

"What's your starting price?" Liu Qian asked.

Chen Wei thought for a moment. "Since Senior Brother Kai cares a lot about customer satisfaction, let's start the bidding at twenty spirit stones per pill."

It was a reasonable starting price, considering that they usually sold for thirty per pill.

"I'll give you twenty-one," called out a voice from the back.

"Twenty-two here," countered another disciple.

Soon, the grove was filled with a cacophony of bids, each disciple trying to outdo the others. Chen Wei watched with satisfaction as the price climbed steadily upward.

This is going even better than I hoped. Senior Brother Kai will be pleased.

As the bidding hit twenty-five spirit stones, tensions began to rise. Some disciples dropped out, unable to afford the increasing price. Others grew more aggressive in their bids, determined to secure a pill at any cost.

"Twenty-six spirit stones!" shouted Ling Xiao.

"Twenty-seven!" countered Feng Yan, glaring at anyone who dared to challenge him.

"Twenty-eight spirit stones!" called out Liu Qian, his round face determined. Studying this pill could be what he needed to break through and become a novice alchemist himself.

The bidding war ended; no one was willing to spend any more spirit stones with it now so close to the standard price.

As the sun began to dip toward the horizon, painting the sky in shades of orange and pink, the rest of the pills were sold off. Most of the disciples had either secured their pills or dropped out of the running, unable to match the increasingly steep prices.

In the end, Wu Cheng claimed five pills at twenty-eight spirit stones each, his resources as a stage-nine disciple allowing him to outbid most of the others. Lin Xiao and Feng Yan each secured three, Liu Qian secured two, while the remaining seven were distributed among various other disciples who had managed to scrape together enough spirit stones.

As Chen Wei carefully handed out the pills in exchange for spirit stones, he couldn't help but smile. He had managed the entire transaction smoothly, without any major incidents.

"Thank you all for your participation," Chen Wei said, bowing slightly. "I hope these pills serve you well in your cultivation."

The disciples nodded, some grudgingly, others eagerly clutching their hard-won pills. As they began to disperse, Chen Wei caught snippets of conversation.

"Can't believe I managed to get one . . ."

"Do you think he'll have more in the future?"

"A Legacy Disciple and an alchemist? No wonder Chen Wei's been moving up so fast."

"But what do you think Senior Brother Su Fang will do when he hears about this . . ."

Once the last disciple had left the grove, Chen Wei allowed himself a moment to relax. He slumped against the old willow tree, letting out a long breath.

"You can come out now, Zhi-Zhi," he called softly.

The spirit tortoise emerged from the bushes, leaves stuck to his shell. "That was amazing!" he exclaimed. "The way you handled them all, it was like watching a master merchant at work!"

Chen Wei chuckled, patting Zhi-Zhi's shell. "I had a good teacher. Now, let's head back. We need to report our success to Senior Brother Kai."

CHAPTER FORTY-TWO

The next day, Zhao Jun stumbled through the Azure Sky Sect grounds, his breaths coming in short gasps. His legs burned from running, but he couldn't slow down. Not when he had such important news to share.

He weaved between groups of disciples, ignoring their startled looks. His eyes were fixed on his destination—the Core Disciple area. More specifically, Sun Jun's quarters.

As he approached the building, Zhao Jun slowed his pace. He took a moment to catch his breath and straighten his robes. It wouldn't do to appear too disheveled in front of a Core Disciple.

With shaky hands, he knocked on the door.

"Enter," a voice called from inside.

Zhao Jun pushed open the door and stepped into Sun Jun's quarters. The room was spacious and well-furnished, unlike the cramped dormitories of the Outer Disciples.

Sun Jun sat at a desk, poring over a scroll. His friend, Lu Chen, lounged on a nearby couch, idly tossing a spirit stone in the air and catching it.

Both young men looked up as Zhao Jun entered. Sun Jun's eyes narrowed.

"What is it?" he asked, his tone sharp. "This had better be important."

Zhao Jun bowed deeply. "Senior Brother Sun Jun, I have news that I believe you'll find very interesting."

Sun Jun leaned back in his chair, raising an eyebrow. "Oh? And what might that be?"

Zhao Jun took a deep breath. "It's about the new Legacy Disciple, Kai. He's . . . he's selling low-grade qi-gathering pills."

The spirit stone Lu Chen had been tossing clattered to the floor. Sun Jun's eyes widened.

"What did you say?" Sun Jun asked, his voice dangerously low.

Zhao Jun swallowed hard. "I . . . I was just at a meeting in the Outer Sect. Chen Wei, who works for Kai, was selling low-grade qi-gathering pills. Twenty of them."

Lu Chen sat up straight. "Twenty? Where did he get so many?"

"He said they were made by Kai himself," Zhao Jun explained. "Apparently, Kai has become a novice alchemist."

Sun Jun's fists clenched. "Impossible. He's only been here for a short time. How could he, a village bumpkin, have advanced so quickly?"

Zhao Jun shrugged. "I don't know, Senior Brother. But Chen Wei was very clear about it. He even said the pills had been verified by Alchemy Master Elder Xiao."

Sun Jun stood up abruptly, his chair scraping against the floor. He began to pace, his face twisted in anger.

"Not only did he steal my Legacy Disciple spot," he spat. "But he is now trying to humiliate me further."

Lu Chen watched his friend. "What does any of this have to do with you?"

Sun Jun whirled to face him. "Don't you see? This Kai, this . . . this nobody from some backwater village, is not only a Legacy Disciple but now a novice alchemist too? And he's using these skills to gain influence among the Outer Disciples? He is trying to take any chance of me becoming the next Sect Master!"

Lu Chen nodded slowly. "I . . . see. But what can we do about it?"

A slow, cruel smile spread across Sun Jun's face. "We don't have to do anything. We just need to make sure the right people know about this."

Zhao Jun, who had been standing silently, spoke up. "What do you mean, Senior Brother?"

Sun Jun turned his gaze to the Outer Disciple. "Tell me, Zhao Jun, how much were these pills being sold for?"

"They started the bidding at twenty spirit stones," Zhao Jun replied. "But by the end, some were going for as much as twenty-eight spirit stones each."

Lu Chen whistled. "That's not bad. Cheaper than the usual price, but still a tidy profit."

Sun Jun's smile widened. "Exactly. And do you know who usually supplies low-grade qi-gathering pills to the Outer Disciples?"

Zhao Jun's eyes widened in realization. "Senior Brother Su Fang!"

"Precisely," Sun Jun said. "I wonder how Senior Brother Su Fang would feel about this new . . . competition."

Lu Chen stood up, a glint in his eye. "Are you suggesting we inform Su Fang about this?"

Sun Jun nodded. "It's our duty as loyal disciples of the Azure Sky Sect to keep our seniors informed of any . . . unusual activities."

Zhao Jun shifted uncomfortably. "But . . . won't that cause trouble for Kai? He is a Legacy Disciple, after all."

Sun Jun's eyes flashed dangerously. "Are you questioning me, Zhao Jun?"

The Outer Disciple quickly shook his head. "No, no, of course not, Senior Brother!"

"Good," Sun Jun said. "Because I think it's time we paid a visit to Senior Brother Su Fang. Don't you agree, Lu Chen?"

Lu Chen nodded. "I think that's an excellent idea, Sun Jun."

Sun Jun turned back to Zhao Jun. "You've done well bringing this information to us. You may go now."

Zhao Jun bowed deeply. "Thank you, Senior Brother Sun Jun."

As he turned to leave, Sun Jun called out, "Oh, and Zhao Jun? Not a word of this to anyone else. Understood?"

Zhao Jun nodded quickly. "Of course, Senior Brother. My lips are sealed."

As the door closed behind Zhao Jun, Lu Chen turned to Sun Jun. "Are you sure about this? Su Fang isn't known for his gentle temperament."

"That's exactly what I'm counting on." Sun Jun smirked. "It's time this village boy learned his place. Legacy Disciple or not, he can't just waltz in here and do as he pleases."

Lu Chen nodded slowly. "And if Su Fang deals with him, our hands stay clean."

"Precisely," Sun Jun said. "Now, let's go pay our respects to Senior Brother Su Fang, shall we?"

The two friends left Sun Jun's quarters and made their way to Su Fang's quarters.

This is perfect, Sun Jun thought. *Su Fang, a Foundation Establishment cultivator, will put that upstart Kai in his place.*

Lu Chen glanced at his friend, noting the satisfied smirk on his face. "You seem pleased with yourself," he observed.

Sun Jun chuckled. "Why shouldn't I be? This Kai has been a thorn in my side since he arrived. It's about time someone did something about him."

"And you're sure Su Fang will react the way you want?" Lu Chen asked.

Sun Jun's smirk widened. "Oh, I'm counting on it. Su Fang's pride won't allow him to let this slide. He'll crush Kai. That village boy will learn that the Azure Sky Sect isn't his personal playground."

As they approached Su Fang's residence, a grand building befitting a senior Core Disciple, Sun Jun paused.

"Remember," he said to Lu Chen, "let me do most of the talking. We're just concerned junior disciples bringing important information to our senior's attention."

Lu Chen nodded. "Of course. I'll follow your lead."

Sun Jun took a deep breath and composed his features into a mask of respectful concern. Then he knocked on the door.

"Enter," came a voice from within.

Sun Jun pushed open the door, Lu Chen close behind him. They stepped into the room. At a large desk sat Su Fang, his sharp eyes fixed on the two young men who had just entered.

"Sun Jun, Lu Chen," Su Fang said. "To what do I owe this . . . pleasure?"

Sun Jun and Lu Chen gave a small bow. "Senior Brother Su Fang," Sun Jun said, his voice dripping with respect. "We apologize for disturbing you, but we have information that we believe you should be aware of."

Su Fang leaned back in his chair, his eyes narrowing slightly. "Oh? And what might that be?"

Sun Jun straightened, meeting Su Fang's gaze. "It's about the new Legacy Disciple, Kai. We've just learned that he's selling low-grade qi-gathering pills to the Outer Disciples."

For a moment, Su Fang's face remained impassive. Then, almost imperceptibly, his left eyebrow twitched.

"Is that so?" he said, his voice carefully neutral. "And where did you hear this?"

"One of the Outer Disciples came to us directly," Sun Jun explained. "Apparently, Kai's assistant held a meeting where he sold twenty of the pills."

Lu Chen chimed in, "They claim the pills were made by Kai himself. That he's become a novice alchemist."

Su Fang's eyes widened slightly at this. He leaned forward, resting his elbows on his desk. "A novice alchemist, you say? That's . . . interesting."

Sun Jun nodded eagerly. "Yes, Senior Brother. And what's more, they were selling the pills for as low as twenty spirit stones each."

This time, Su Fang couldn't hide his reaction. His fist clenched on the desk, and a flash of anger crossed his face.

"Twenty spirit stones?" he repeated, his voice low and dangerous.

Sun Jun fought to keep the satisfaction off his face. *He's taking the bait*, he thought. *Now to reel him in.*

"We were shocked too, Senior Brother," Sun Jun said, his voice full of false concern. "We know you've been supplying the Outer Disciples with pills. We were worried this might . . . interfere with your business."

Su Fang stood up abruptly and turned to look out the window. His back was rigid, his hands clasped tightly behind him.

"Thank you for bringing this to my attention," he said, his voice tightly controlled. "You've done well, both of you."

Sun Jun and Lu Chen exchanged a quick glance. This was going even better than they had hoped.

"We're always happy to help, Senior Brother," Lu Chen said smoothly. "We just want what's best for the sect."

Su Fang turned back to face them, his expression unreadable. "Indeed. Well, if that's all, you may go. I have much to think about."

Sun Jun and Lu Chen bowed again. "Of course, Senior Brother. We'll take our leave."

As they turned to go, Su Fang spoke again. "Oh, and Sun Jun?"

Sun Jun paused, looking back. "Yes, Senior Brother?"

Su Fang's eyes bore into him. "In the future, if you hear anything else about this . . . Kai, I want you to come to me immediately. Understood?"

Sun Jun nodded, suppressing a smile. "Of course, Senior Brother. You can count on us."

As the door closed behind them, Sun Jun and Lu Chen walked quickly away from Su Fang's residence. Once they were out of earshot, Sun Jun let out a low chuckle.

"Did you see his face?" he said, his voice filled with glee. "He was furious!"

Lu Chen nodded, a small smile on his face. "You played it perfectly, Sun Jun. He took the bait hook, line, and sinker."

Sun Jun's eyes gleamed with anticipation. "Just wait. Su Fang won't let this stand. He'll go after Kai, and when he does . . ."

"We'll be there to watch the fireworks," Lu Chen finished.

As they walked back to their own quarters, Sun Jun's mind raced with possibilities. *Soon*, he thought. *Soon that upstart Kai will learn his place. And when he falls, I'll be there to take what should have been mine all along.*

Meanwhile, back in his quarters, Su Fang paced back and forth, his mind whirling with the information he had just received.

A Legacy Disciple selling pills? And not just any pills, but low-grade qi-gathering pills. My pills.

He stopped at the window and looked out over the sect grounds. His eyes narrowed as he considered his options.

On one hand, this Kai was a Legacy Disciple. Going against him directly could be dangerous. But on the other hand, if he let this slide, it could seriously damage his business and his reputation.

I've worked too hard to let some newcomer ruin everything, and it's not like this Kai is another Wang Lin. I'm not defenseless against him. But how to handle this . . .

He turned away from the window, his decision made. He wouldn't confront Kai directly, at least not yet. First, he needed more information.

Su Fang sat back down at his desk and pulled out a blank scroll. He began to write, outlining his plan.

First, verify the information. Then, if it's true, find out more about this Kai. His strengths, his weaknesses, his goals. And most importantly, find out why he's selling these pills. Is he trying to rile me up or is he just looking to make some spirit stones?

As he wrote, a new thought occurred to him. *What if . . . what if I could turn this to my advantage?*

Su Fang leaned back in his chair, a slow smile spreading across his face. Yes, this could work. Instead of seeing Kai as a threat, why not see him as an opportunity?

If he really is a novice alchemist, Su Fang thought, *then he could be incredibly valuable. And if I could bring him into my operation . . .*

With a Legacy Disciple as his alchemist, he could expand his business using the name of a Legacy Disciple. The profits would be astronomical.

Su Fang stood up, his decision made. He would meet this Kai, but not as an enemy. No, he would approach him as a potential business partner.

Let's see what you're made of, Legacy Disciple Kai, Su Fang thought as he headed for the door. *This could be the beginning of a very profitable relationship . . . for both of us.*

CHAPTER FORTY-THREE

Su Fang approached the area demarcating the Legacy Disciple quarters, his steps slowing as he took in the unfamiliar surroundings. He had never ventured this far into the sect's inner sanctum before; a plain Core Disciple like himself had never been important enough to garner Wang Lin's attention.

As he drew near, his eyes widened in surprise. An invisible barrier shimmered into existence, halting his progress. The air in front of him rippled like water—a translucent wall of energy barred his path.

"So, the rumors are true," Su Fang murmured to himself, reaching out a hand to touch the barrier. He felt a gentle resistance, like pressing against a cushion of air. "The Legacy Disciples really do have their own protective wards."

He took a step back, scanning the area with newfound respect. The pavilions beyond the barrier seemed to shimmer slightly, as if viewed through heat haze. Su Fang had always known the Legacy Disciples were afforded special privileges, but seeing it firsthand was another matter entirely.

How am I supposed to get through? he wondered, frowning slightly. *Surely there must be a way for other disciples to visit or at least leave messages.*

Su Fang cleared his throat. "Legacy Disciple Kai? It's Su Fang, a Core Disciple. I was hoping we could talk."

Silence greeted his words. He frowned and strained his ears for any sign of movement within. Nothing. *Is he ignoring me? Or perhaps he's not home?*

Su Fang's frown deepened. He hadn't come all this way to be thwarted by an empty house. With a resigned sigh, he settled himself on a nearby rock, closing his eyes in meditation.

I can be patient. He'll have to return eventually.

Time passed, the sun inching across the sky. Su Fang remained motionless, his breathing slow and even. To any passerby, he might have appeared to be a statue, were it not for the occasional twitch of his eyebrow.

The sound of approaching footsteps roused him from his trance. Su Fang's eyes snapped open, a smile curving his lips. But it wasn't Kai who rounded the corner.

Instead, a young man came into view, accompanied by . . . was that a tortoise? Su Fang blinked, wondering if his eyes were playing tricks on him. But no, there was indeed a spirit beast waddling alongside the boy.

Ah, this must be Kai's servant, Chen Wei, and that tortoise must be Cang Long's disciple, if I recall correctly.

Su Fang stood, brushing off his robes. "Greetings, young Chen Wei. I don't suppose your master is at home?"

Chen Wei froze, his eyes widening as he recognized Su Fang. The tortoise at his side bumped into his leg, letting out a squawk.

"S-Senior Brother Su Fang," Chen Wei stammered. "I . . . I'm afraid Senior Brother Kai isn't here at the moment."

Su Fang's smile didn't waver, but his eyes narrowed slightly. "I see. That's unfortunate. I was hoping to discuss some business with him."

Chen Wei shifted uncomfortably. "Business? What kind of business?"

"Oh, nothing too serious," Su Fang said, waving a hand dismissively. "I just heard some interesting rumors about your master selling low-grade qi-gathering pills. I thought we might have a little chat."

Chen Wei's posture stiffened. "I'm not sure what you mean, Senior Brother. The pill business isn't exclusive. Anyone can sell them if they have the means to produce them."

Su Fang chuckled. "Of course, of course. I'm not here to cause any trouble. Quite the opposite, in fact. I see this as a potential business opportunity. Your master clearly has talent as an alchemist. I thought perhaps we could combine our resources, expand our reach."

Chen Wei's eyes narrowed. He'd seen tactics like this before, back when he worked in the family business. Competitors would come in, all smiles and promises of cooperation, only to try and squeeze them out of business later.

"That's very kind of you to offer, Senior Brother," Chen Wei said carefully. "But I'm afraid I can't speak for Senior Brother Kai on such matters. You'll have to discuss it with him directly."

Su Fang's smile widened. "Of course. I understand completely. I wouldn't expect you to make such decisions. When do you think your master will return? I'd be happy to wait."

Chen Wei's mind raced. He needed to warn Kai about this unexpected development. "I'm not sure, Senior Brother. He didn't say when he'd be back. It could be quite a while."

"That's no problem," Su Fang said, settling back onto his rock. "I can be very patient."

Chen Wei hesitated, then bowed slightly. "If you'll excuse me, Senior Brother, I have some errands to run for Senior Brother Kai. I should get going."

"Of course, of course," Su Fang said, waving him off. "Don't let me keep you."

Chen Wei hurried away, the spirit tortoise scrambling to keep up. As soon as they were out of earshot, the tortoise spoke up.

"I don't trust that guy," Zhi-Zhi said, his tiny eyes narrowed. "He smells like trouble."

Chen Wei nodded. "I agree. We need to warn Senior Brother Kai as soon as possible."

Back at the pavilion, Su Fang remained in his meditative pose, unmoving. Hours passed, the sun slowly sinking toward the horizon.

As night fell, lanterns flickered to life along the paths. Still, Su Fang waited.

One day turned into two. Su Fang maintained the meditative pose, only occasionally shifting his position or taking small sips of water from a flask at his side.

On the second day, as the sun began to set once more, Su Fang finally opened his eyes. His face was a mask of frustration and weariness.

Two whole days, he thought bitterly. *Two days, and still no sign of Kai.*

Su Fang stood up and stretched his stiff muscles. He glared at the still empty pavilion, his patience finally wearing thin.

That Outer Disciple must have warned him, Su Fang realized. *That's why he hasn't returned. He's avoiding me.*

For a moment, anger flared in Su Fang's chest. Was Kai testing him? Trying to see how long he would wait? The thought of being toyed with by some upstart Legacy Disciple made Su Fang's blood boil.

But then, as quickly as it had come, the anger faded. Su Fang took a deep breath and forced himself to think rationally.

Calm down, he told himself. *Think about this logically. If a higher-level cultivator was waiting outside your home for days, how would you feel?*

The answer came to him immediately: Cautious. Wary. Perhaps even a little afraid.

Su Fang took another deep breath and forced himself to relax. He looked at the pavilion with new eyes, a grudging respect growing within him.

Kai is being careful, he realized. *He's not avoiding me out of cowardice but out of prudence. He's assessing the situation before making a move.* A slow smile spread across Su Fang's face. *I can respect that. Caution is a valuable trait in both cultivation and business.*

Decision made, Su Fang straightened his robes and gave a respectful nod toward the pavilion. "Well played, Legacy Disciple Kai," he murmured. "Well played indeed."

As he turned to leave, Su Fang's mind was already formulating a new plan. *I'll do this the right way*, he thought. *Send a formal request for a meeting through proper channels. Show him the respect his position deserves.*

Su Fang walked away from the pavilion, his steps lighter than they had been in days.

This new Legacy Disciple is a cautious man. And I like working with cautious men. This could be the start of a very interesting partnership.

As Su Fang disappeared down the path, the sect grounds fell quiet. The last rays of sunlight faded, leaving the area bathed in the soft glow of lanterns.

For several minutes, all was still. Then, suddenly, a black-robed figure appeared on the path. Without hesitation, the figure approached the barrier. There was no utterance of a pass phrase, no gesture to dispel the protective force. The barrier simply . . . parted, as if recognizing its master's touch.

The black-robed figure slipped inside, the door to the pavilion opening and closing in one smooth motion.

And just like that, Kai was home, Thundercore elixir in hand.

CHAPTER FORTY-FOUR

Kai's eyes fluttered open, sunlight streaming through the window of his pavilion. He groaned, his body still aching from the intense process of opening the Storm's Core meridian.

As he sat up, rubbing the sleep from his eyes, a knock sounded at the door.

"Come in," Kai called out, his voice still rough with sleep.

Chen Wei entered, carrying a tray with a steaming pot of tea and a small pouch.

"Senior Brother Kai, you really are back! How are you feeling?"

Kai stretched, wincing slightly. "Like I've been hit by a lightning bolt. But I'll live. What's that you've got there?"

Chen Wei set the tray down on a nearby table and held up the pouch. "The spirit stones from the pill sale, Senior Brother. We managed to sell all twenty pills for an average of twenty-six spirit stones each."

Kai's eyebrows rose. "That's better than I expected. Well done, Chen Wei."

As Chen Wei poured tea for both of them, Kai's mind raced. *That's 520 spirit stones. Not a bad haul for our first sale. But if word gets out, we'll have competition soon. We need to move fast.*

Congratulations!
Guild members Chen Wei, Liu Wei, and Zhi-Zhi have completed their first task. They have gained 10 contribution points.
Contribution points will now be awarded.

"Senior Brother Kai?" Chen Wei's voice was filled with surprise. "My trident mark . . . It's glowing!"

Kai watched in fascination as 10 percent of the black mark on Chen Wei's right shoulder blade turned a vibrant blue.

"Interesting," Kai murmured. He focused his thoughts, addressing the System directly. *System, when will my guild members be able to use the trident mark to condense qi?*

Once the mark is complete, guild members will be able to use the mark to condense qi at will. Use of the technique will not deplete the mark. However, without continuous compledion of tasks contributing to the guild, they will lose this ability.

And what about the respawn ability? How does that work for guild members?

Guild members can respawn when their mark is complete. However, a respawn will use up the entire mark and their ability to condense qi. They will need to complete the mark once again to regain these abilities.

It would be a waste if condensing qi used up their mark. It makes much more sense for respawning to use up the mark.

Kai turned to Chen Wei, who was still staring at his glowing mark in wonder.

"That's the reward I mentioned, Chen Wei. I'll give you all a qi-gathering pill when I make the next batch. But keep up the good work, and you'll be able to condense qi and even . . . Well, let's just say you'll be much harder to get rid of."

Chen Wei looked up. "Thank you, Senior Brother. I'll work hard to complete this mark!" His expression then shifted, becoming more serious. "There's something else you should know, Senior Brother. Su Fang was waiting outside your pavilion for three days."

Kai frowned as he accepted the cup of tea Chen Wei offered. "Su Fang? I don't know of any Su Fang. What did he want?"

Chen Wei shifted uncomfortably. "He said he wanted to discuss business with you. Specifically, about the low-grade qi-gathering pills we sold."

"I see," Kai murmured, taking a sip of tea. "Tell me everything you know about this Su Fang."

Chen Wei nodded, his brow furrowing in concentration. "Su Fang is a Core Disciple known for his business acumen. He's been selling low-grade qi-gathering pills to Outer Disciples for a while now. From what I've heard, he hires alchemists to make the pills for him."

Kai's eyes narrowed. *So, he sees us as competition. This could be trouble.*

"Is that all?" Kai asked.

Chen Wei hesitated. "Well, there's one more thing. Su Fang's servant arrived about an hour ago. He requested a meeting for Su Fang at a time convenient for you."

Kai leaned back, considering this new information. After a moment, he looked at Chen Wei. "What do you think I should do?"

Chen Wei's eyes widened in surprise. "Me? I . . . I'm not sure, Senior Brother. Su Fang is a Core Disciple. He could be a powerful ally . . . or a dangerous enemy."

"You're right on both counts," Kai said. "But we need to be careful. We can't afford to make enemies this early, but we also can't show weakness."

Kai stood up, pacing the room as he thought. *I can't spend all my time making pills, even if Elder Xiao would love that. We need to make this business sustainable. And for that, we need help.*

An image of Xie Li, the quiet alchemist he'd met earlier, flashed in his mind. *She could be exactly what we need.*

Coming to a decision, Kai turned back to Chen Wei. "All right, here's what we're going to do. Respond to Su Fang's servant. Tell him I'll meet with Su Fang in ten days."

Chen Wei nodded. "And in those ten days, Senior Brother?"

Kai smiled. "In those ten days, we're going to shore up our position. Starting with recruiting some help. I want you to pass a message to Xie Li. Tell her I'm interested in practicing some alchemy with her."

"Xie Li?" Chen Wei asked. "The Inner Disciple who passed the novice alchemy examination?"

"That's the one," Kai confirmed. "She's talented, and we could use her skills."

Chen Wei nodded, a look of understanding dawning on his face. "I see. You want to bring her into our guild?"

"Not yet." Kai shook his head. "We need to vet her first. For now, we'll just see if she's interested in working with us."

"Understood, Senior Brother," Chen Wei said, bowing slightly. "I'll deliver the messages right away."

As Chen Wei turned to leave, Kai called out, "Oh, and Chen Wei?"

The young disciple paused at the door. "Yes, Senior Brother?"

"Good work with the pill sale."

Chen Wei's face lit up. "Thank you, Senior Brother!"

As the door closed behind Chen Wei, Kai sank back onto his bed.

Ten days to prepare for Su Fang. Ten days to set up a sustainable operation. It's going to be a busy week and a half.

With a groan, Kai forced himself to his feet. He had work to do.

Later that day, Kai found himself standing outside the alchemy practice room, waiting for Xie Li to arrive. He'd spent the morning reviewing his alchemy notes and planning his approach.

The sound of footsteps pulled Kai from his thoughts. He looked up to see Xie Li approaching, her steps hesitant and her eyes downcast. As she drew closer, Kai noticed a faint blush on her cheeks.

"Senior Brother Kai," she said softly, bowing. "Thank you for inviting me to practice with you."

Kai smiled, trying to put her at ease. "Thank you for coming, Xie Li. I've been looking forward to working with you."

Xie Li's blush deepened, but she managed a small smile. "What . . . what did you want to practice today?"

"I was thinking we could focus on the Spiritual Resonance technique," Kai said. "It's a crucial skill for creating high-quality pills, and I'd love to get your insights on it."

Xie Li's eyes widened slightly. "Spiritual Resonance? That's quite a difficult technique. Most disciples struggle with it."

Kai nodded. "That's right. But from what I've seen of your skills, I think your understanding of it is quite good. So, shall we go in?"

He gestured toward the practice room door. Xie Li nodded, her earlier nervousness seemingly replaced by excitement at the prospect of practicing alchemy.

As they entered the room, Kai took a moment to observe Xie Li. There was a focus in her eyes that hadn't been there before.

She really comes alive when she's working with alchemy. That's a good sign.

"So," Kai said as they finished setting up, "what's your understanding of the Spiritual Resonance technique?"

Xie Li paused, apparently gathering her thoughts before speaking. "Spiritual Resonance is about attuning the energy of the pill to the spiritual frequency of the cultivator who will use it. It's what allows us to create pills that are tailored to specific individuals or cultivation methods."

"Exactly. And what do you think is the most challenging aspect of the technique?"

Xie Li bit her lip as she considered the question. "I think . . . it's maintaining the resonance throughout the entire pill-making process. It's not enough to just attune the ingredients at the beginning. You have to keep that resonance going as you refine and shape the pill."

"But how do you maintain that resonance? What's your approach?"

Xie Li's eyes lit up as she began to explain her method. Kai listened intently, asking questions and offering his own insights. As they talked, he could see Xie Li becoming more animated, her earlier shyness melting away as she delved into a topic she was clearly passionate about.

She's good. Her understanding is a few levels above my own . . .

After a while, Kai suggested they try putting theory into practice. "Why don't you demonstrate the technique?" he proposed. "I'd love to see your approach in action."

Xie Li nodded, a determined look on her face. She selected a set of ingredients and began the process of creating a simple energy pill. Kai watched closely as she worked, noting the subtle ways she manipulated the qi in the ingredients.

As Xie Li worked, Kai activated his Qi Detection skill, trying to sense the spiritual resonance she was creating. To his surprise, he found he could perceive faint threads of energy connecting Xie Li to the pill she was crafting.

She's not just maintaining the resonance, she's actively shaping it as she works.

When Xie Li finished, she held up a small, perfectly formed pill. It glowed with a soft light, pulsing gently in time with Xie Li's own qi.

"Amazing work," Kai said, genuinely impressed. "The resonance is so clear, I can almost see it."

Xie Li blushed at the praise. "Thank you, Senior Brother. Would you like to try now?"

Kai nodded, stepping up to the alchemy table. He selected his ingredients and began the process, trying to replicate what he'd seen Xie Li do.

As he worked, Kai focused on maintaining a connection between his qi and the forming pill. This was always the technique he found the most challenging—it felt like trying to hold on to a slippery fish. Several times he felt the resonance start to slip away, only to catch it at the last moment.

After ten minutes, Kai completed the pill. It wasn't as perfect as Xie Li's—the glow was a bit uneven and the shape slightly lopsided—but as he held it up, he could feel the resonance humming through it.

A System message popped up in his vision.

Skill Leveled Up!
Spiritual Resonance (Level 5)
You have gained 100 XP!

Kai couldn't help but smile.

"Well done, Senior Brother," Xie Li said, examining the pill. "The resonance is strong, even if the form isn't perfect. With practice, you'll be able to maintain better control over the shape."

Kai nodded. "Thank you, Xie Li. Your demonstration was incredibly helpful. I learned a lot just from watching you work."

Xie Li ducked her head, but Kai could see she was pleased by the compliment.

As they finished cleaning up the alchemy station, Kai decided it was time to make his move.

"Xie Li," he said, his tone casual. "I've really enjoyed working with you today. Your skill in alchemy is truly impressive."

"Thank you, Senior Brother," Xie Li replied, her cheeks pink. "I've enjoyed working with you too."

Kai nodded, then continued. "I have a proposition for you. As you know, I've recently started producing and selling low-grade qi-gathering pills. But as a Legacy Disciple, my time is often limited. I've been thinking of bringing on someone to help with the pill production."

Xie Li's eyes widened as she realized where this was going.

"Would you be interested in making pills for me?" Kai asked. "I'd pay you, of course. Your skill would be invaluable, and it could be a good opportunity for you to gain more practical experience."

Xie Li bit her lip, clearly considering the offer. "It's a generous proposal, Senior Brother. But . . . I'm not sure if I'm ready for such a responsibility. What if I make a mistake? It's not just my reputation at stake but also the reputation of a Legacy Disciple."

Kai shook his head. "Don't sell yourself short, Xie Li. I've seen your work. You're more than capable. And as for mistakes . . . Well, they're part of the learning process. I'm not expecting perfection, just your best effort."

He could see Xie Li was still hesitant, so he decided to sweeten the deal. "Tell you what," he said. "Why don't we start with a trial period? Two weeks. You can see if you enjoy the work, and I can assess how well we work together. After that, if you're not comfortable continuing, we can part ways with no hard feelings. What do you say?"

Xie Li was quiet for a long moment, her gaze fixed on the alchemy equipment around them. Finally, she looked up at Kai, a small smile on her face.

"All right, Senior Brother Kai," she said. "I accept your offer. A two-week trial period sounds fair."

Kai grinned. "Excellent! I look forward to working with you, Xie Li."

"I . . . I do too, Senior Brother."

They then left the practice room together, but Kai was lost in deep thought.

With Xie Li's help, we can increase production and maybe even improve the quality of our pills. Su Fang won't know what hit him.

However, as he glanced at Xie Li, who was still blushing slightly and sneaking shy looks at him, Kai felt a twinge of guilt. *I hope I'm not taking advantage of her. She seems so . . . innocent.* Kai pushed the thought aside. *This is for the good of the guild and for my own survival in this world. I can't afford to be too sentimental. And this will only benefit her—no need to feel guilty.*

As they parted ways, Kai heading back to his pavilion and Xie Li to her quarters, Kai couldn't shake the feeling that things were about to get very interesting.

Su Fang, whoever you are, I hope you're ready for a challenge. Because the Trident Guild is just getting started.

CHAPTER FORTY-FIVE

Kai sat cross-legged on the floor of his pavilion with the Heavenly Thunderstorm cultivation method scroll unfurled before him. He scanned the text once more.

> Meridian of the Thunderclap
> Location: Lower Dantian (Abdomen)
> Method to Open: Thunderclap Meditation—perform a series of physical exercises that simulate the movement of thunderclaps. This vigorous activity helps to channel lightning qi into the lower dantian to gradually open the meridian.

Unlike many of his fellow gamers back on Earth, Kai had never shied away from physical exertion. His mind drifted briefly to memories of university kickboxing sessions.

This should be interesting, he thought, cracking his knuckles in anticipation.

He read through the three exercises outlined in the scroll: Thunderclap Stance, Skyward Reaches, and Electric Dragon Twists.

"All right," Kai muttered to himself, "let's get started."

First, he needed to close his Lower Dantian meridian. He'd done this several times now with other meridians, so the process went smoothly. As he finished, a familiar blue message appeared in his vision:

> Cultivation reduced to Qi Refining Stage 7

"Here goes nothing," Kai said, standing up and shaking out his limbs.

He began with the Thunderclap Stance. Planting his feet firmly on the ground, slightly wider than shoulder-width apart, Kai bent his knees and lowered his center of gravity. He formed fists with both hands, then thrust them downward in a synchronized motion.

Imagine striking the ground with immense force, he reminded himself, visualizing shockwaves of energy traveling up through his legs and into his lower dantian.

Kai held the stance, focusing on deep, rhythmic breathing. He tried to sense the gathering of energy in his abdomen, but . . . nothing happened.

"Hmm." He frowned, straightening up. "Maybe I'm not visualizing it strongly enough?"

He tried again, this time closing his eyes to better focus on the mental image. As he thrust his fists down, Kai pictured bolts of lightning striking the ground and sending ripples of electric energy through the earth and up into his body.

Still nothing.

"Okay," Kai muttered, "let's try the next one. I might have more success with that one."

He moved on to the Skyward Reaches exercise. Standing with his feet shoulder-width apart and arms relaxed at his sides, Kai then slowly raised his arms above his head. He stretched upwards, imagining his fingers grasping at lightning bolts in the sky.

As he reached up, Kai took a deep breath, visualizing himself pulling down energy into his body. On the exhale, he brought his hands down slowly, trying to guide the imagined energy toward his lower dantian.

He repeated this fluid motion several times, focusing intently on the stretch and the imagined flow of energy. But after several minutes, Kai still felt no different.

"Come on," he grumbled. "What am I missing?"

Determined not to give up, Kai moved on to the final exercise: Electric Dragon Twists. He widened his stance, placed his hands on his hips, and began slowly twisting his torso from side to side.

As he reached the peak of each twist, Kai visualized a coiled dragon wrapping around his abdomen, releasing bursts of lightning qi into his lower dantian. He gradually increased the speed and intensity of the twists while maintaining control and focus.

After several minutes of this, Kai stopped, breathing heavily. He waited, hoping to feel some change, some spark of energy in his core. But there was nothing.

"Damn it," he sighed, running a hand through his hair. "What am I doing wrong?"

Kai paced the room, his mind racing. He'd followed the instructions to the letter, hadn't he? Maybe he was missing something obvious. He returned to the scroll and read through the descriptions again more carefully.

As he studied the text, he realized something. "Wait a minute," he murmured. "These exercises are supposed to simulate thunderclaps, right? But I've been too focused on lightning."

He pondered this realization. Thunderclaps weren't just about the flash of lightning—they were about the boom, the vibration, the raw power of nature.

"Let's try this again."

He returned to the Thunderclap Stance. This time, as he thrust his fists downward, Kai didn't just visualize lightning. He imagined the earth-shaking rumble of thunder, the way it could be felt as much as heard.

As his fists connected with an imaginary ground, Kai let out a loud "BOOM!" startling himself with the volume of his own voice.

To his amazement, he felt a slight tremor in his lower abdomen. It was faint, barely perceptible, but definitely there.

"Yes!" Kai grinned. "That's it!"

Encouraged, he moved on to the Skyward Reaches. As he stretched upwards, Kai didn't just picture grasping lightning—he imagined the sky itself rumbling with the promise of an oncoming storm. With each exhale as he brought his arms down, he let out a low rumbling sound from deep in his chest.

The sensation in his lower dantian grew stronger, a buzzing energy slowly building.

Finally, Kai tried the Electric Dragon Twists once more. As he twisted from side to side, he synchronized his movements with imagined claps of thunder. Each twist was punctuated with a sharp exhalation, like the staccato beats of a thunderstorm.

The energy in his core intensified, spreading warmth throughout his body. Kai could feel his qi responding as it swirled and condensed in his lower dantian.

"It's working!" he panted, increasing the speed of his twists.

Sweat beaded on his forehead as Kai pushed himself, repeating the three exercises in sequence. Each time through, he focused on the multisensory experience of a thunderstorm—the flash of lightning, the rumble of thunder, the electric charge in the air.

Hours passed, though Kai barely noticed the passage of time. His world narrowed to the rhythm of the exercises and the growing power in his core. The energy built and built, like a storm gathering strength.

Just when Kai thought he couldn't continue any longer, when his muscles burned and his lungs heaved for air, something shifted. And then, suddenly, the energy in his lower dantian exploded outward.

Kai gasped, his eyes flying open. Blue-white light crackled across his skin, and for a moment, he could have sworn he heard the boom of thunder echoing in the small room.

As quickly as it had come, the surge of power faded. Kai collapsed to his knees, panting heavily. His whole body tingled with residual energy, and he could still feel a new warmth pulsing in his core.

Slowly, a grin spread across Kai's face. "I did it," he whispered, then louder, "I actually did it!"

Congratulations!
You have successfully opened the Meridian of the Thunderclap!
Cultivation returned to Qi Refining Stage 8
Lightning Affinity increased to 40%

Skill Leveled Up!
Crown of Lightning (Level 6)
Effect: A temporary visible aura of lightning can form around the cultivator's head during meditation, which boosts the cultivator's qi regeneration by 30%.

Skill Leveled Up!
Sky's Favor (Level 6)
Effect: The cultivator's qi-absorption rate increases by 30% whenever they are under an open sky. This increases to 35% during stormy weather.

Skill Leveled Up!
Electric Immunity (Level 6)
Effect: The cultivator gains 30% resistance to lightning-based attacks, reducing the damage taken from electric or lightning-based techniques.

You have gained 300 XP!

Kai's smile faltered slightly as he realized that, yet again, he hadn't gained any new skills.

I guess I shouldn't keep expecting new skills every time.

But his disappointment was short-lived as he noticed the increase in his lightning affinity by yet another 5 percent.

Kai's gaze then fell on his XP total, and his excitement returned full force. He was now at 3900 XP, just one hundred away from breaking through to the peak of Qi Refining!

Suddenly, there was a knock on the door.

"Come in," he called out, still catching his breath.

Chen Wei entered, his eyes widening as he took in Kai's disheveled appearance and the faint traces of electricity still crackling in the air.

"Senior Brother Kai," Chen Wei said, bowing slightly. "Sorry, I didn't know you were cultivating."

Kai chuckled, pushing himself to his feet. "It's fine, Chen Wei. If I hadn't finished, I wouldn't have responded."

Chen Wei nodded. "Thank you. I came to inform you that Lin Yue is here to see you."

Kai's eyebrows rose in surprise. "Lin Yue? The Inner Disciple you met in Greenleaf?"

"The very same," Chen Wei confirmed. "He said it's about business. Should I tell him you're available?"

Kai considered for a moment. He was tired from opening the new meridian, but his curiosity was piqued. What could Lin Yue want? Was it related to this Su Fang?

"Yes, tell him I'll see him," Kai said. "But give me a few minutes to clean up first."

As Chen Wei turned to leave, Kai called out, "Oh, and Chen Wei? Could you bring some tea? I have a feeling we might need it."

Chen Wei nodded and left to fetch Lin Yue and prepare the tea.

Alone once more, Kai quickly straightened his robes and smoothed down his hair. He took a few deep breaths, centering himself.

This Lin Yue is a Foundation Establishment cultivator like Su Fang. I can't let my guard down . . .

CHAPTER FORTY-SIX

Kai sat across from Lin Yue, the silence between them broken only by the gentle clink of teacups. After what felt like an eternity, Kai decided to break the silence. He set his cup down with a soft tap and looked directly at Lin Yue.

"So, Lin Yue," Kai began. "What brings you to see me today?"

Lin Yue's lips curved into a polite smile. "Two reasons, actually. First, I wanted to personally apologize for the trouble my associates caused Chen Wei in Greenleaf. It was . . . unfortunate."

Kai nodded. "I appreciate that. Chen Wei mentioned there were some issues."

"Indeed," Lin Yue said, his brow furrowing slightly. "Rest assured, those responsible have been dealt with. It won't happen again."

"Good to hear," Kai replied. He took another sip of tea. "And the second reason?"

Lin Yue's eyes gleamed with a mix of amusement and something sharper. "Ah, yes. I've heard about your . . . situation with Su Fang. It seems many disciples are hoping for some fireworks between you two."

Kai couldn't help but chuckle, though there was little humor in it. "Is that so? Well, they might be disappointed. I've read the sect rules. Disciples can't just fight unofficially. If there's a problem, it has to be settled in the arena." He leaned back. "Besides, I doubt a Foundation Establishment cultivator like Su Fang would challenge a mere Qi Refining cultivator like myself to a battle. It would be embarrassing for him, don't you think?"

Lin Yue nodded slowly, his expression growing more serious. "You're not wrong, Kai. But there are more ways to come to blows than just physical combat." The Inner Disciple leaned forward, his voice dropping to a near whisper. "Su Fang isn't to be trusted. He didn't become the prime seller of qi-gathering pills by playing nice. Rules were bent, competitors were . . . dealt with."

Kai's eyes narrowed slightly. *Not exactly shocking news in the cultivation world,* he mused. Even in a supposedly righteous sect like Azure Sky, business could be cutthroat.

"I see," Kai said aloud. "And what would you suggest I do about that?"

"Well, from what I've observed of your personality, you're not the type to want to spend all your time as an alchemist making pills. Especially not for someone else. Am I right?"

Kai nodded, curious where this was going.

"So, why don't we enter into a partnership?" Lin Yue proposed. "You've already purchased qi-gathering materials from me. Why not make it an official long-term arrangement?"

Kai's eyes narrowed slightly. "Correct me if I'm wrong, but don't you already have someone you supply to? Su Fang, perhaps?"

Lin Yue's smile faltered, replaced by a grimace. "Ah, well . . . Since it's not exactly a secret, I'll be honest. I used to supply Su Fang, yes. But due to certain . . . difficulties and disagreements, we've gone our separate ways."

Sounds like Lin Yue got replaced, Kai thought, studying the Inner Disciple's face.

Lin Yue seemed to read Kai's thoughts. He sighed, running a hand through his hair. "Yes, I suppose you could say I was replaced. But it was because I refused to go along with Su Fang's bullying tactics. There are lines I won't cross, even in business."

Kai remained silent, turning the situation over in his mind. If he partnered with Su Fang, who already had an established business, Kai would be relegated to the role of just another alchemist. He'd have no real ownership or control. Both scenarios went against his reasons for starting his own venture.

On the other hand, not partnering with Su Fang meant they'd be direct competitors. And Su Fang, with his mature business, would likely try to crush Kai's fledgling operation.

No, partnering with Su Fang is out of the question, Kai decided. *It goes against everything I'm trying to build here.*

As for Lin Yue's offer . . . Kai already needed a long-term supplier. Working with Lin Yue couldn't hurt, at least for now. If things didn't pan out, he could always terminate the relationship.

"All right," Kai said, breaking the silence that had fallen between them. "Let's talk specifics. The main ingredients for qi-gathering pills are Spirit Grass, Yin Berries, and Qi Crystals, correct?"

Lin Yue nodded, sitting up straighter. "That's right."

"Now, if bought separately, these materials cost about fifteen spirit stones total per pill," Kai continued. "But I'm planning to buy in bulk. So, let's negotiate."

Lin Yue's eyes lit up with interest. "I'm listening."

"How about nine spirit stones per bundle?" Kai proposed, knowing he was starting too low.

Lin Yue shook his head, a wry smile on his face. "Come now, Senior Brother. You know I can't go that low. How about fourteen spirit stones?"

Kai leaned forward, his voice firm but not aggressive. "Fourteen is barely a discount. Remember, I'm offering you a long-term, stable business relationship. That's worth something. How about eleven spirit stones?"

Lin Yue stroked his chin, considering. "You drive a hard bargain. But eleven is too low for me to make a profit. Let's meet in the middle: twelve and a half spirit stones per bundle."

Kai shook his head. "Close, but not quite there. Twelve spirit stones, and I guarantee you'll be my exclusive supplier for these materials."

Lin Yue's eyebrows rose at that. He paused, clearly weighing the pros and cons. Finally, he nodded. "With that exclusivity guarantee, I'll settle for twelve spirit stones."

They sealed their agreement with a small bow of their heads.

"Now," Kai said, his tone shifting to something more serious. "Tell me about Su Fang's operation. How many alchemists does he have working for him? What's their daily output?"

Lin Yue leaned back, his expression thoughtful. "Su Fang has three novice alchemists under him. Each produces about ten pills per day, which he sells for thirty spirit stones apiece."

Kai's eyebrows shot up in surprise. "Only three alchemists? I would have expected more."

Lin Yue chuckled, shaking his head. "Ah, you'd think so. But alchemists are a prideful bunch. They don't like working under others, especially someone like Su Fang, who's not an alchemist himself."

Kai nodded slowly. *I have Xie Li and myself, though Xie Li is just on a trial basis. And I don't want to spend all my time making pills. But as an alchemist myself, it might be easier for me to hire others—*

His thoughts were interrupted by a knock at the door. Chen Wei's voice called out, "Senior Brother Kai? A servant is here to take you to the Sect Master for your next lesson."

Kai looked at Lin Yue apologetically. "It seems our time is up."

Lin Yue stood, smoothing out his robes. "No worries. We've accomplished much today. My men will be in contact with you regarding the specifics."

With that, he left, leaving Kai alone with his thoughts.

All right, time to plan my next move. My one thousand low-grade spirit stone stipend comes tomorrow. That should be enough to hire two or three alchemists of my own as well as buy a substantial number of materials. I doubt he'll make any moves before our meeting, so if I play this right, I could be a real threat to Su Fang's business before then . . .

CHAPTER FORTY-SEVEN

Kai sat cross-legged on the cushion, facing the Sect Master. To his left, Shen Yu mirrored his position.

The Sect Master's gaze swept over them both. "It's been some time since our last meeting. How has your cultivation progressed?"

Kai straightened his back. "I've made good progress, Sect Master. I opened the next three meridians using the Heavenly Thunderstorm method. Now I only have three left to go."

The Sect Master nodded. "Good. You're moving at a steady pace." He turned to Shen Yu. "And you?"

Shen Yu's face remained blank as he spoke. "I've completed the first layer of the Heavenly Thunderstorm cultivation method."

Kai's eyes widened. He couldn't help but turn to look at his fellow disciple. *Completed the first layer? Already?*

As if triggered by his surprise, Kai's System flashed Shen Yu's stats before his eyes:

Name: Shen Yu
Level: Qi Refining Stage 9 Qi: 500/500 Strength: 80 Agility: 80 Endurance: 80

Holy crap. He really has already surpassed me. But then again, I shouldn't be surprised. Competing with him right now is like a level-one character trying to take on a max-level player who just restarted. My only shot at catching up is to hope his previous cultivation stopped not too far ahead, which is unlikely since he was able to reincarnate or regress . . . For now, I'll focus on my own path and worry about competing with him later . . . much later.

Kai glanced at the Sect Master to see the older man's reaction. The Sect Master's face remained calm, almost as if he'd expected this outcome.

Oh, right. He probably sensed our cultivation levels as soon as we walked in. Or maybe he's been keeping tabs on us this whole time . . .

The Sect Master's lips curved into a slight smile. "Excellent work, Shen Yu. Your progress is truly remarkable."

Shen Yu bowed his head slightly. "Thank you. Now that I've completed the first layer, can I begin learning the sect's legacy wind technique?"

The room fell silent. Kai turned to see how the Sect Master would respond. For a few seconds, the older man said nothing, his eyes studying Shen Yu intently.

Then a smile spread across the Sect Master's face. "Yes, I believe you're ready."

Kai watched as the Sect Master reached into his robes and pulled out a scroll. He handed it to Shen Yu with a nod.

"This," the Sect Master said, "is the Wind God method. Like the Heavenly Thunderstorm cultivation method, it consists of nine layers. The first layer involves opening the same nine meridians you've already worked on, but this time using wind-based qi."

Kai leaned forward. *This is what I've been wondering about. How does someone cultivate two different methods at once?*

As if reading his mind, the Sect Master continued, "Now, you both might be wondering how one cultivates using two different methods. There are a few approaches, but the two most common are as follows."

Kai and Shen Yu listened as the Sect Master explained.

"The first method involves using both techniques in tandem to open each meridian. This approach is more difficult and carries a higher risk of Qi Deviation. The second method is simpler: close the meridian you've already opened, then reopen it using the new technique."

Kai nodded, absorbing the information. He glanced at Shen Yu and noticed that the other disciple didn't seem surprised by any of this.

Of course. He wanted to start both methods from the beginning. He must have been planning to use the first approach all along.

Unable to contain his curiosity, Kai spoke up. "Sect Master, if I may ask . . . Why don't cultivators just keep adding more and more cultivation methods? Wouldn't that make their foundation even more stable and give them greater advantages later on?"

"An excellent question, Kai. The answer isn't as simple as you might think." The Sect Master paused, gathering his thoughts before continuing. "First and foremost, cultivation methods must be compatible with each other. Our sect's legacy methods, the Heavenly Thunderstorm and the Wind God techniques, are designed to work in harmony. But not all methods play well together."

I wonder if my System can tell me which methods are compatible? That could be a huge advantage.

"Let me give you an example," the Sect Master said. "Imagine trying to mix oil and water. No matter how hard you try, they'll always separate. Some cultivation methods are like that—fundamentally incompatible."

"I see," Kai said. "So even if we wanted to, we couldn't just pick up any random method and add it to our cultivation?"

"That is right." The Sect Master nodded. "Which is why I must warn you both: do not attempt to add other cultivation methods to your practice without proper guidance. The consequences could be . . . severe." After a brief pause, the Sect Master continued, "There's another factor to consider as well. While cultivation does increase your lifespan, the higher you climb, the longer it takes to break through to the next level. Cultivators can't afford to spend all their time learning new methods when their lifespans are slowly ticking away."

But with my System, I might be able to learn multiple methods quickly. If I can find compatible techniques, I could have a massive edge.

"Thank you for the explanation, Sect Master," Kai said, bowing his head. "I'll be sure to focus on mastering our sect's methods before considering anything else."

The Sect Master nodded, then his expression shifted to one of mild surprise. "Ah, before I forget, congratulations on becoming a novice alchemist, Kai. Elder Xiao was quite impressed by your performance."

Kai blinked, caught off guard by the sudden change of topic. "Oh, thank you, Sect Master. I'm honored by Elder Xiao's praise."

From the corner of his eye, Kai noticed Shen Yu watching him. The other disciple's face remained neutral, showing no signs of surprise.

Either he already knew I was going to become an alchemist by now, or he heard about it through the sect grapevine. It's not like it was a secret—becoming an alchemist in just three days probably got people talking.

"I must admit," the Sect Master said, "I thought you were more interested in formations than alchemy. What prompted this change?"

Kai shrugged, trying to appear casual. "I'm still interested in formations, Sect Master. But I figured alchemy might be a quicker way to earn spirit stones in the short term."

And to create some useful pills for myself, he added silently.

The Sect Master's eyes narrowed slightly. "A practical approach. Just be sure not to neglect your cultivation, Kai. All the spirit stones in the world won't help if your foundation is weak."

"Of course, Sect Master," Kai said quickly. "I won't let my cultivation suffer, I promise."

The older man nodded, seemingly satisfied. Then his expression grew serious as he looked at both disciples.

"There's something else I need to discuss with you both," the Sect Master said, his voice taking on a graver tone. "Cultivation is about more than just sitting and meditating. You will face trials not only outside the sect but within it as well."

Kai and Shen Yu exchanged a quick glance before returning their attention to the Sect Master.

"I hope you understand," he continued, "that if you have trouble with other cultivators, you should not expect me to intervene. Problems between the younger generation must be resolved by the younger generation."

Kai nodded, keeping his face neutral. *He's talking about my issues with Su Fang. Clearly, he doesn't care that Su Fang's cultivation is higher than mine. He's not going to step in. But that's fine. I never planned on involving him anyway. I'll deal with Su Fang myself.*

"I don't require anyone's help," Shen Yu said bluntly, breaking the momentary silence.

The Sect Master nodded. "Good. That's the attitude I expect from my Legacy Disciples." He paused, looking at them both. "Do you have any questions?"

Kai shook his head. "No, Sect Master. I'll focus on opening the final three meridians."

Shen Yu remained silent.

"Very well," the Sect Master replied. His gaze moved between both disciples. "However, I must caution both of you. Do not attempt a breakthrough to Foundation Establishment without speaking to me first. I can assist you with the necessary preparations."

"We understand, Sect Master," Kai said, bowing his head respectfully. "We'll be sure to seek your guidance before attempting the breakthrough."

Shen Yu nodded once more.

"Good. Unless there's anything else, you're both dismissed."

As Kai and Shen Yu left the pavilion, Kai's mind raced. He needed to talk to Shen Yu privately, but he couldn't be obvious about it. The Sect Master was likely still listening.

Kai stretched casually, then said, "Man, all this cultivation talk has made me hungry. I could really go for some of those spicy dumplings from the dinner hall." He glanced at Shen Yu, hoping the other disciple would catch his hint. "Want to grab a bite?"

Shen Yu's face remained impassive. "No, thank you. I have matters to attend to."

Hmm, I don't know if he is taking me literally or he doesn't want to talk, but I'm not giving up that easily.

As they turned the corner, Kai tried again. "Actually, Shen Yu, I was hoping to ask your advice on something. There's this tricky part of the Heavenly Thunderstorm method I'm struggling with. Maybe we could discuss it on the way to the training grounds?"

Kai held his breath, hoping this approach would work. But Shen Yu's expression didn't change.

"Perhaps another time," Shen Yu replied coolly. "You should speak to the Sect Master. I have my own training to focus on." Before Kai could come up with another excuse, Shen Yu turned to him. His voice was low, lower than even a whisper. "Your cultivation is low. Too low. You need to be faster."

Before he could process what he'd heard, let alone ask for clarification, Shen Yu was gone.

Kai's eyes narrowed as he stood alone.

What the hell was that about? If Shen Yu really is a regressor, is this some kind of warning? Does he know something's coming, something I need to be prepared for? Or maybe I'm reading too much into it. Maybe he's just trying to get under my skin, pointing out how far behind I am.

He shook his head, a determined look settling on his face.

It doesn't matter what his motivation is. He's right. I do need to speed up my cultivation, and it also wouldn't hurt to prepare in case there is some big event coming up.

CHAPTER FORTY-EIGHT

Kai was back in his pavilion. A small pouch rested in his palm. He opened it to look at the thirty-three low-grade qi-gathering pills he'd just finished making.

It had been a full day since his meeting with the Sect Master. Instead of immediately jumping into cultivation, Kai had dedicated his time to crafting pills.

Finally, I can focus on my own cultivation. The guild can handle the sales.

He leaned back and called up his status window.

Name: Kai Thorn
XP: 3900/4000 Level: Qi Refining Stage 8 Qi: 300/300 Strength: 60 Agility: 63 Durability: 67 Intelligence: 30 Wisdom: 29
Titles: Novice Instructor Once in a Hundred Years Talent Legacy Disciple Alchemy Prodigy Novice Alchemist
Elemental Affinities: Lightning: 40% Chaos: 10%
Skills: Qi Condensation (Level 4) Basic Cultivation (Level 3)

Unarmed Combat (Level 2)
Deception (Level 4)
Iron Skin (Level 3)
Swift Wind Step (Level 4)
Flame Palm Strike (Level 3)
Mental Fortitude (Passive)
Spirit Beast Communication (Level 1)
Qi Concealment (Level 1)
Qi Detection (Level 1)
Iron Rebound (Level 1)
Rock Hard (Level 1)
Lightning Step (Level 1)
Static Charge (Level 1)
Crown of Lightning (Level 5) (Passive)
Sky's Favor (Level 5) (Passive)
Storm Eye (Level 1)
Thunder Voice (Level 1)
Heart of Thunder (Level 1)
Essence Extraction (Level 4)
Elemental Fusion (Level 4)
Qi Infusion (Level 4)
Stability Control (Level 4)
Spiritual Resonance (Level 5)

Elemental Resistance:
Lightning (Level 6) (Passive)

Quests:
Active: None

I'm so close to breaking through to the ninth stage of Qi Refining. I've got two options. I could open the next three meridians using the Heavenly Thunderstorm cultivation method, or I could enter the final stage of Qi Refining through the help of the System and then later reopen the last meridian using the Heavenly Thunderstorm cultivation method.

I would have gone with the former method if time wasn't an issue, but I don't know how soon the problem Shen Yu was warning me about will arrive. It's probably best if I break through now. But how should I get that last hundred XP?

Kai scratched his chin, considering his options. Without any active quests from the System, he had limited choices for gaining XP: killing humans or beasts, teaching skills to his followers, or upgrading his own skills through practice.

Kai frowned as he thought about killing humans. *I'm not about to become some murderhobo protagonist, offing people just to level up.* He shook his head. *Maybe if I knew someone who really deserved it, but even then, I can't kill sect members, so I'd have to leave the sect to find someone that met the requirement. And with only two lives left, I'd rather not risk it.*

His mind wandered to teaching skills. *Can't teach sect techniques even to other disciples—that's taboo.* He then pictured Chen Wei learning Swift Wind Step. *Nah, I don't want all my followers using the same moves as me. Defeats the purpose of having a group. And I don't even know what his affinity is. I should probably find out.*

That left upgrading his own skills. *Best way to do that is through combat. Plus, I could use the battle practice.* Kai nodded to himself. *Hunting beasts it is. I can do that without leaving the sect territory. Man, it's been a while since I've seen some action.* He stood up and rolled his shoulders.

"Chen Wei!"

A moment later, the door slid open, and Chen Wei stepped inside. The young man bowed slightly. "Yes, Senior Brother?"

Kai grabbed three pills from his desk and held them out to Chen Wei. "Here," he said. "One each for you, Liu Wei, and Zhi-Zhi."

Chen Wei's eyes widened as he accepted the pills. "Thank you!"

Kai nodded, then picked up the pouch of remaining pills. He tossed it to Chen Wei, who caught it with both hands. "That's the next batch for sale. Xie Li will bring her batch over soon. Once we get the profits, I'll look into hiring another alchemist."

"Understood," Chen Wei said, carefully tucking the pouch into his robes. "Is there anything else you need?"

"Actually, yeah, what's your elemental affinity?"

Chen Wei blinked, surprised by the question. "Oh, it's fire, Senior Brother. Why do you ask?"

Kai nodded, more to himself than to Chen Wei. *Yeah, teaching him a wind technique would be a waste of his and my own time. Better to stick with what suits him naturally.*

"Just curious," Kai said aloud. "It's good to know these things about my team members. Anyways, I'm thinking of getting some battle practice in. What territories and mini-realms does the sect have where I could hunt some beasts?"

"Well, there are several options suitable for disciples in the Qi Refining Realm. Let me think . . ."

Kai leaned against the wall and crossed his arms as he waited for Chen Wei to gather his thoughts.

"All right," Chen Wei said after a moment. "There are five main mini-realms that would be suitable for a Qi Refining disciple like yourself. I'll break them down by difficulty."

Kai nodded, gesturing for him to continue.

"First, there's the Green Forest Realm. It's perfect for lower Qi Refining stages—it's mostly filled with plant-based spirits and small woodland creatures. Then there's the Stone Cavern Realm. It's a bit tougher, good for mid-level Qi Refining cultivators. Lots of rock elementals and cave-dwelling beasts."

Kai nodded, encouraging him to go on.

"The third is the Rainy River Realm. Also mid-level but with water-based creatures. I hear the terrain can be tricky."

Might be fun, but not what I'm looking for right now.

"Fourth is the Windy Plateau Realm. It's on the higher end, good for stages six through eight. Lots of flying beasts and air elementals."

Getting warmer, Kai thought. *But I would rather go against a lightning beast. I could test out my lightning resistance.*

"And finally," Chen Wei said, "there's the Storm Peak Realm. It's the toughest, meant for stages seven through nine. Mostly lightning-based creatures there."

Kai's eyes lit up. "Storm Peak, huh? That sounds perfect."

Chen Wei nodded. "It's a popular choice for lightning cultivators. The beasts there are quite fierce, though."

"Even better." Kai grinned. "Where do I sign up?"

"You'll need to go to the Realm Management Hall," Chen Wei explained. "It's near the center of the sect. You can't miss it—big building with a glowing blue dome."

"Got it," Kai said. "Anything else I should know?"

Chen Wei hesitated. "Well . . . entry to a mini-realm usually costs one hundred spirit stones."

Not cheap, especially if disciples aren't able to earn more than that with the carcasses of beasts they kill. I wonder how these Outer Disciples even survive when everything costs so much here.

"All right, thanks for the info, Chen Wei. I'll head there now."

As Kai walked out of his pavilion, Chen Wei called after him, "Good luck, Senior Brother! Be careful in there!"

"Thanks." Kai waved without looking back.

The walk to the Realm Management Hall took about thirty minutes. Kai found himself wishing he could just fly there on a sword like some of the other cultivators he had seen.

I really need to learn how to fly on a sword. I heard cultivators at Qi Refining Realm stage seven and above can all do it. All it takes is qi manipulation practice. Maybe this hunting trip could be a good time to add that skill to my list. Kill two birds with one stone—or maybe kill some beasts while balancing on a flying sword.

As he approached his destination, Kai couldn't help but smile. True to Chen Wei's word, the building was hard to miss. Its blue dome pulsed with a soft light, like a beacon in the heart of the sect. He noticed other disciples coming and going from there. Some looked excited, others nervous. A few sported minor injuries—scratches, bruises, and the occasional singed eyebrow.

Looks like I'm in for a good time.

He pushed open the heavy doors and stepped inside. The interior was cooler than outside, with a faint smell of ozone in the air. Five large stone arches lined the far wall, each one dark and inactive.

As Kai looked around, he noticed a young brown-haired woman seated at a desk near the entrance. She looked up as he neared, offering a polite smile.

"Welcome, Senior Brother," she greeted him. "How may I assist you today?"

Kai nodded in return. "I'm interested in accessing the Storm Peak Realm."

The disciple's eyes widened slightly. "Ah, Storm Peak. An excellent choice for lightning cultivation. Are you sure you don't want to try one of the safer realms first?"

"I think I'll give this one a try." Kai smiled.

She nodded, reaching into a drawer. "Very well. The entry fee is one hundred spirit stones."

Kai produced the required payment, placing the stones on the desk. The disciple quickly counted them, then handed him a small round token in exchange.

"This token will grant you access to Storm Peak," she explained. "It also serves as your way back. Simply channel your qi into it when you wish to return, and it will teleport you out of the realm immediately."

Kai turned the token over in his hand. "Interesting. What happens if I lose it?"

The disciple's expression grew serious. "Do not lose that token, Senior Brother. Without it, you'll have no way to return unless you can use a communication talisman to call for help or find another disciple within the realm. Most disciples tend to avoid that realm. As for the ones who don't, they don't seem the type to offer any help . . ."

Kai nodded, storing the token securely in his inventory. "Understood. Can you tell me more about what I can expect inside?"

"Storm Peak is . . . intense," the disciple replied. "The moment you enter, you'll feel the charge in the air. Lightning strikes are common, and the beasts there have adapted to harness that power."

"What kind of beasts are we talking about?" Kai asked, his curiosity piqued.

She tapped her chin thoughtfully. "Well, there are the Storm Wolves—they love to hunt in packs. They could probably take down a Foundation Establishment cultivator with their teamwork. Another common type is Lightning Serpents. They are solitary but deadly. Oh, and watch out for the Thunder Birds. They may look small, but they pack quite a punch, and most disciples really struggle to outrun them."

"Anything else?"

"Well, there are rumors of a lightning dragon in the highest peaks, but no one's ever confirmed it. Probably just stories to scare the newbies."

A lightning dragon at Qi Refining Realm? Now that would be worth some serious XP.

"Any particular areas I should be aware of?"

The disciple nodded. "The realm is divided into three main zones. The outer ring is the safest, with weaker beasts and less frequent storms. As you move inward, both the creatures and the weather become more dangerous. At the center is the Eye of the Storm—I wouldn't recommend going there unless you're very confident in your abilities."

"Good to know," Kai said. "Anything else I should be prepared for?"

She thought for a moment. "The lightning there isn't just dangerous—it can also be beneficial. Some cultivators have reported breakthroughs after absorbing the natural energy of the realm. Just be careful not to overdo it."

Kai nodded. "Thanks for the tips. How long can I stay in the realm?"

"Standard time limit is three days. After that, the token will automatically bring you back. You can leave earlier if you want, of course."

"Got it," Kai said. He glanced at the dark portal. "So, how do I activate this thing?"

The disciple pointed to a small pedestal in front of the arch. "Place your token there. It'll open the portal. Step through, and you'll be in Storm Peak. Ready when you are."

Kai took a deep breath, squaring his shoulders. He walked up to the pedestal with the token back in his hand. He placed it on the pedestal. For a moment, nothing happened. Then, suddenly, the arch came to life. The empty space within filled with swirling purplish energy.

Kai could hear the faint rumble of thunder from the other side. The hair on his arms stood up from the static electricity emanating from the portal.

He turned back to the disciple. "Guess I'll see you in three days."

The disciple gave him a smile. "Good luck in there. Try not to die."

"I don't plan to." Kai grinned.

With one last deep breath, he stepped forward into the portal. There was a moment of disorientation, a feeling of being stretched and compressed at the same time. Then, with a flash of light and the crack of thunder, Kai found himself standing on rocky ground.

CHAPTER FORTY-NINE

Kai blinked, adjusting to the new environment. As expected, dark, ominous clouds swirled overhead, occasionally lighting up his surroundings with flashes of lightning.

He looked around and realized that he stood on a wide plateau dotted with jagged rocks and sparse vegetation. In the distance, he could see mountain peaks shrouded in mist, and he could hear the occasional rumble of thunder.

"All right, let's see what we're dealing with here."

Instinctively, Kai focused on the translucent screen showing his current location and the surrounding area. He scanned it carefully, looking for any signs of danger.

Can't be too careful. Even if they say it's just Qi Refining beasts here, you never know. Wouldn't surprise me if one of those Peak Qi Refining beasts broke through to the Foundation Establishment realm . . .

The map showed several clusters of energy signatures scattered throughout the realm. Most were relatively weak, likely lower-level beasts. But as Kai's gaze moved toward the center of the map, he noticed stronger concentrations of energy.

Hmm, the sizes of the red dots are difficult to determine from this distance. I can't tell if these beasts have entered the Foundation Establishment or are a half step away. Guess I'll steer clear of those for now.

Kai took another look at his immediate surroundings. The outer ring of the realm seemed relatively safe, with only a few weak energy signatures nearby.

Perfect. This should be a good spot to work on my skills.

Kai closed the map and focused on his goal. He wanted to improve two particular skills: Qi Concealment and Qi Detection. Both were crucial for survival in this world, especially if the map began to lose its usefulness.

Kai took a deep breath and began to suppress his qi. It was a strange sensation, like trying to hold your breath underwater. He could feel his energy signature dimming, becoming less noticeable to the world around him.

At the same time, he extended his senses as he tried to detect the qi of nearby creatures. It was like straining to hear a whisper in a noisy room. He could sense faint echoes of energy, but nothing concrete.

It's been a while since I've done this. This might take some practice.

Kai realized that to truly improve these skills, he'd need to turn off his map function. The thought made him uneasy. Since unlocking the feature, he'd come to rely on it heavily. It provided a sense of security, even if it couldn't detect the most powerful beings.

Not like Immortal-Rank cultivators would be waiting to ambush small fry like me in this place.

With a mental command, Kai deactivated his map. The world suddenly felt larger, more uncertain. He took another deep breath, steeling himself.

Okay. I can do this. I just have to stay in the outer region and work on my skills. Once I level up one of the skills, I'll automatically break through to the ninth stage of Qi Refining. Then I can worry about working on my battle prowess.

With his plan set, Kai began to move. He picked his way carefully across the rocky terrain, senses alert for any sign of danger. Without the map to rely on, the constant rumble of thunder in the distance kept him on edge, each flash of lightning making him flinch.

As he walked, Kai continued to practice his Qi Concealment. He imagined his energy signature shrinking, becoming as small and unnoticeable as possible. It was hard work and required constant concentration. At the same time, he strained his Qi Detection, trying to sense any nearby presences. Without his map, he felt blind. But slowly, very slowly, he began to pick up faint traces of energy.

There . . . I think I sensed something.

Kai paused to focus on the faint flicker of qi he'd detected. It was weak, probably a low-level beast. He changed course and moved toward it cautiously.

As he drew closer, the energy signature became clearer. Kai could almost picture the creature in his mind—small, quick, with a hint of electrical energy. Probably one of those Thunder Birds the receptionist had mentioned.

Perfect for practice.

Kai crouched behind a large boulder and peered out at the area where he sensed the creature. For a long moment, he saw nothing. Then a flash of movement caught his eye.

A small birdlike creature hopped into view. It was about the size of a crow, with blue feathers. Sparks danced along its wings as it pecked at the ground, searching for food.

Kai watched it intently, focusing on maintaining his Qi Concealment while sharpening his Qi Detection. He could sense the bird's energy more clearly now, a constant buzz of electrical qi.

Okay, this is good practice. Just stay hidden and—

Suddenly, the bird's head snapped up. It looked directly at Kai's hiding spot, eyes glowing with an eerie blue light.

Shit.

Before Kai could react, the bird let out a piercing screech. Electricity arced from its body and struck the ground around it. In a flash, it launched itself into the air and opened its mouth, then shot a lightning bolt through the air toward Kai's head.

He immediately scrambled backward, narrowly avoiding the attack—the lightning bolt struck where he'd been crouching. The Thunder Bird wheeled overhead, screeching in anger.

"So much for staying hidden," Kai muttered, pulling himself to his feet.

He raised his hand and channeled fire qi into his palm. He planned to use Swift Wind Step to appear behind the bird and kill it in one blow using Flame Palm Strike.

Killing the stage-six Qi Refining beast would not be enough for a breakthrough, likely only earning him twenty-five or so points, but the last thing he needed was for it to call for backup. A flying stage-nine Qi Refining beast was not something he was confident in defeating, especially if outnumbered.

However, before he could make his move, the creature let out another screech and flew off, disappearing into the storm clouds.

Well, that could have gone better.

Kai sighed as he lowered his hand and let the fireball dissipate. He dusted himself off, looking around to make sure no other creatures had been drawn by the commotion. The area seemed clear for now. *I need to get out of here quickly before backup arrives . . .*

Kai set off again, moving deeper into the realm but still staying within the relative safety of the outer ring. He found a small ravine, sheltered on both sides by high rock walls. It seemed like a good spot to continue his practice.

Settling into a comfortable position, Kai once again began to suppress his qi. This time, he focused on making his energy signature match the background energy of the realm. It was like trying to camouflage himself, blending in with the constant electrical buzz in the air.

As he worked on his Qi Concealment, Kai also extended his senses. He pictured his Qi Detection as a sort of radar, sweeping out in all directions. Faint blips of energy appeared on his mental map, growing clearer as he concentrated.

Time passed, though Kai wasn't sure how much. The constant storm made it impossible to gauge the time of day. He practiced tirelessly, alternating between hiding his presence and sensing others.

But despite his efforts, his skills didn't seem to be improving. No matter how hard he concentrated, his Qi Concealment and Qi Detection remained stubbornly at level one.

I should have leveled up by now. Kai sighed as he stood up. He'd been sitting in one position for too long, lost in his concentration. As he moved, he noticed a faint ache in his body—a sign that his qi was depleted from constant use.

Maybe I'm going about this the wrong way. Perhaps I should use the skills during battle. It usually helps with the offensive skills. Maybe it'll help with detection and concealment?

With that thought in mind, Kai decided to venture a bit deeper into the realm. He climbed out of the ravine, scanning the area for any signs of life. In the distance, he spotted movement. Something large was prowling among the rocks, its form obscured by the constant flashes of lightning. Kai narrowed his eyes as he focused his Qi Detection on the creature.

Whoa. That's . . . that's a strong one.

The beast's energy signature was powerful, easily matching Kai's own. It was clearly a Qi Refining stage eight creature, just like him.

Perfect. If I can take this one down, even if the skills don't level up during battle, I'll get enough XP to break through to stage nine regardless. I guess I can always focus on the skills later.

Kai crouched low and slowly made his way toward the creature. As he drew closer, he could make out more details. The beast was wolflike in shape but much larger than any normal wolf. As expected of a wolf with a bias toward the lightning element, its fur was a dark blue color.

A Storm Wolf. Just like the receptionist mentioned. If I can get behind it, use Swift Wind Step for a surprise attack . . .

He began to circle around, keeping low and using the rocky terrain for cover. The Storm Wolf seemed unaware of his presence, focused instead on something in the distance.

Kai was just about to make his move when suddenly, his System pinged with a notification. His eyes widened as he read the message.

Skill Leveled Up!
Qi Concealment (Level 2)

Skill Leveled Up!
Qi Detection (Level 2)

You have gained 200 XP!

Oh no, bad timing.

Before Kai could process what was happening, he felt a surge of energy within him. His qi swelled, pushing against the limits of his current stage. In an instant, he knew what was coming.

The breakthrough to Qi Refining stage nine hit him like a thunderbolt. Kai gasped as he felt the rush of qi flowing down to the soles of his feet. The meridians there, previously closed, burst open under the pressure.

Level Up!
You are now Qi Refining Stage 9

Name: Kai Thorn

XP: 0/8000
Level: Qi Refining Stage 9
Qi: 500/500
Strength: 75
Agility: 77
Durability: 79
Intelligence: 32
Wisdom: 30

Titles:
Novice Instructor
Once in a Hundred Years Talent
Legacy Disciple
Alchemy Prodigy
Novice Alchemist

Elemental Affinities:
Lightning: 35%
Chaos: 10%

Skills:
Qi Condensation (Level 4)
Basic Cultivation (Level 3)
Unarmed Combat (Level 2)
Deception (Level 4)
Iron Skin (Level 3)
Swift Wind Step (Level 4)
Flame Palm Strike (Level 3)
Mental Fortitude (Passive)
Spirit Beast Communication (Level 1)
Qi Concealment (Level 2)
Qi Detection (Level 2)
Iron Rebound (Level 1)
Rock Hard (Level 1)

Lightning Step (Level 1)
Static Charge (Level 1)
Crown of Lightning (Level 5) (Passive)
Sky's Favor (Level 5) (Passive)
Storm Eye (Level 1)
Thunder Voice (Level 1)
Heart of Thunder (Level 1)
Essence Extraction (Level 4)
Elemental Fusion (Level 4)
Qi Infusion (Level 4)
Stability Control (Level 4)
Spiritual Resonance (Level 5)

Elemental Resistance:
Lightning (Level 6) (Passive)

The breakthrough had been exhilarating, powerful . . . and incredibly noticeable.

The Storm Wolf's head snapped around, its glowing eyes locking onto him. The beast's lips pulled back in a snarl, revealing razor-sharp teeth. The wolf tilted its head toward the sky and let out a roar that split the air and shook the ground beneath them.

Kai remained still, quickly assessing his situation.

In some cases, a cultivator would fight immediately after a breakthrough, relying on their increased raw power even if it wasn't fully controlled. But that led to a higher chance of Qi Deviation.

Not the best time for a breakthrough, but I can work with this.

A breakthrough using the System allowed Kai to adapt more rapidly. The surge of qi through his meridians was intense but manageable.

As the echoes faded, the wolf slowly lowered its head, its eyes locking onto Kai's own.

For a moment, neither man nor beast moved, locked in a tense standoff.

Wolves are pack animals, Kai thought, eyes narrowing. *So, where's the rest of its pack?*

As if in answer to his thoughts, he heard more howls in the distance. Kai's eyes widened; he turned his head slightly toward the sound while keeping the Storm Wolf in his peripheral vision. The Storm Wolf's pack was coming.

Finally, Kai felt his qi settle within him. A grim smile spread across his face as he moved into a fighting stance.

I'll have to finish this one before the others arrive.

CHAPTER FIFTY

Kai vanished in a blur as he activated Swift Wind Step to appear behind the Storm Wolf. But when he materialized, his eyes widened in surprise. The wolf was gone, leaving only a fading trail of electricity.

Damn, it's faster than I thought.

He scanned the area, muscles tense. A flash of blue caught his eye as the wolf reappeared several meters away.

It's not attacking. Why?

The wolf's eyes met his, and Kai saw intelligence there. It wasn't just a beast—it was a cunning opponent.

It's stalling. Waiting for backup. If the pack didn't have anyone that could challenge me, then it wouldn't be waiting, which means there must be a stage nine in its pack. Maybe more.

Kai knew he had to act fast. He couldn't let the wolf's reinforcements arrive. He opened his mouth and activated Thunder Voice.

The roar that erupted from his throat was deafening. It shook the air, sending shockwaves rippling through the rocky terrain. The retreating wolf, caught mid-leap in another lightning jump, stumbled. Its body flickered into view as it yelped in pain and surprise.

Got you.

Not wasting a second, Kai activated Lightning Step. He became a living bolt of electricity as he streaked across the ground toward the disoriented wolf.

The beast, recovering quickly, snarled. Its eyes flashed with anger and . . . was that fear? It opened its maw.

Oh crap.

The wolf launched the attack and a sphere of pure lightning hurtled toward Kai. There was no time to dodge. In that split second, Kai's Iron Skin skill activated, hardening his body against the incoming blow.

The lightning ball slammed into him. Pain exploded across his chest, but it was duller than he expected. His lightning resistance had kicked in, nullifying almost a third of the attack's power.

Thank goodness for that thirty percent resistance.

Gritting his teeth, Kai pushed through the pain. The wolf's eyes widened as Kai emerged from the dissipating energy, palm blazing with fire.

"Surprise," Kai growled.

The Flame Palm Strike connected with the wolf's neck with a satisfying thud. The wolf let out a pitiful whimper; its body convulsed as fire and lightning danced across its fur. Then it went still, eyes glazing over.

You have gained 50 XP!

Not bad for a quick fight.

Kai sighed, looking down at the smoking corpse. "Sorry, buddy. Nothing personal."

He reached out and focused his qi. The wolf's body shimmered and disappeared into his inventory space. *Might be useful for crafting later.*

Just as the last wisps of smoke cleared, a chorus of howls split the air. Kai's head snapped up, eyes narrowing as he scanned the horizon.

One, two, three . . . twelve? Oh, come on!

But it wasn't just the number that made his stomach drop, it was their cultivation realms. Most were at Qi Refining stages seven and eight—formidable opponents in their own right. But what made him grimace were the larger wolves at the front.

Stage nine. And three of them. Perfect.

Kai began to slowly back away as the wolves fanned out, circling him. Their movements were fluid, coordinated. They were a well-oiled hunting machine.

The largest wolf, its fur as black as night, stepped forward. Its eyes, glowing with an eerie blue light, locked onto Kai. It let out a low, rumbling growl that seemed to vibrate through the ground.

I don't need Spirit Beast Communication to know what that means. "Give back our packmate, or else."

Kai's mind raced. He'd wanted to battle a stage nine beast for the experience, sure. But three at once, plus their underlings? That was suicide.

Sometimes, the best strategy is a tactical retreat.

"Sorry, boys," Kai said, forcing a grin. "Finders keepers."

The black wolf's snarl deepened, lips pulling back to reveal razor-sharp teeth. The circle of wolves began to tighten.

Time to go.

Kai took a deep breath, centering himself. He focused on his heart meridian, feeling the energy building there. With a shout, he activated Heart of Thunder.

The effect was immediate and spectacular. A massive shockwave erupted from Kai's chest, a visible ripple of thunderous energy that expanded outward in all directions. The closest wolves yelped in pain and surprise, and their advance halted as they were pushed back by the force.

Not wasting a second, Kai channeled his qi. His body crackled with electricity, and in a flash, he transformed into a bolt of lightning.

He shot upward, faster than any of the wolves could react. As he ascended, platforms of solidified qi materialized beneath him, providing stepping stones for his lightning form to jump between.

Up, up, and away!

Kai bounded from platform to platform, each one dissipating behind him as soon as he left it. He could hear the frustrated howls of the wolf pack below growing fainter as he put distance between them.

He was careful not to ascend too high—the last thing he needed was to attract the attention of any flying beasts that might be lurking in the storm clouds above. Instead, he kept to a middle altitude as he raced across the landscape in a series of lightning jumps.

Lightning travel is awesome. I need to do this more often.

As he fled, Kai couldn't help but feel a mix of exhilaration and disappointment. On one hand, he'd survived an encounter with a formidable pack of Storm Wolves. On the other . . .

I really wanted to test myself against those stage nine beasts.

An hour later, Kai found himself huddled in a small cave, catching his breath. The relentless pursuit of the wolf pack had driven him deep into the inner region of Storm's Peak before they had finally given up the chase.

Wolves are persistent. Very persistent.

He leaned against the rough cave wall and fished the teleportation token out of his inventory. The small token felt heavy in his hand, a tempting escape route.

I could leave right now. I've already broken through to stage nine. Mission accomplished, right?

But something held him back. A nagging feeling, a mix of ambition and caution.

If Shen Yu's warning was right, I might need more than just raw power. I need experience. Real combat experience.

Kai turned the token over in his hand as he remembered the intense battle with the Storm Wolf. The rush of adrenaline, the split-second decisions, the satisfaction of overcoming a worthy opponent.

When will I get another chance like this? In the sect, everything is controlled, and there's no action. But here, it's raw, unpredictable. With a sigh, he tucked the token back into his inventory. *Besides,* he thought, glancing at the trident mark on his wrist, *I've got a backup plan if things go really south.*

Still, caution was the better part of valor. Kai closed his eyes, concentrating. A moment later, a glowing electric-blue eye materialized in front of him—his Storm Eye skill.

"All right, little spy," Kai muttered. "Let's see what's out there."

The eye zipped out of the cave, and suddenly Kai's vision split. Through the eye, he could see the rocky landscape outside, illuminated by frequent flashes of lightning. The terrain was rougher here in the inner region, with more jagged peaks and deeper ravines.

To double-check, Kai pulled up his map. The area around his position was clear of any hostile signals.

Good. Some breathing room at last. A smile spread across Kai's face as an idea formed. *You know what? Before I jump back into the fray, maybe it's time to learn a new trick.*

He reached into his inventory and pulled out a simple sword. It was a basic model, standard issue for sect disciples. Nothing fancy, but it would do for now.

One day, I'll craft my own. But for now . . . let's see if I can't add "flying" to my resume.

A few seconds later, Kai stood at the mouth of the cave, sword in hand, staring out at the stormy sky.

Okay, I've seen other disciples do this. How hard can it be?

He took a deep breath and channeled his qi into the sword. The blade hummed faintly as it responded to his energy.

"Right," he muttered. "Step one: don't fall and die."

Kai placed the sword horizontally in front of him, then gingerly stepped onto the blade. For a moment, nothing happened. Then, slowly, the sword began to rise, wobbling slightly under his feet.

Holy crap, it's working!

His excitement was short-lived. The sword suddenly tilted, and Kai found himself flailing his arms wildly to keep balance.

"Whoa, whoa, whoa!"

He managed to right himself, but not before nearly face-planting onto the rocky ground. The sword hovered about a foot off the ground, vibrating slightly.

Okay, maybe this is harder than it looks.

Kai took another deep breath and focused on his qi flow. He imagined it as a steady stream flowing from his core, down his legs, and into the sword.

Slowly, steadily, the sword began to rise higher. Kai's legs trembled with the effort of maintaining balance, but he kept his concentration.

Up, up, up. That's it. Nice and easy.

He was about ten feet off the ground when a gust of wind caught him off guard. The sword tilted sharply, and this time Kai couldn't recover. With a yelp, he tumbled off and hit the ground with a thud.

"Ow," he groaned, sitting up and rubbing his backside. The sword clattered to the ground beside him.

Well, that was graceful.

But Kai wasn't one to give up easily. He stood, dusted himself off, and picked up the sword again.

"Round two."

Over the next hour, Kai practiced relentlessly. He fell more times than he could count, each tumble adding new bruises to his collection. But with each attempt, he stayed airborne a little longer, moved a little more smoothly.

It's all about the qi control, he realized. *Like balancing on a tightrope, but the rope is your own energy.*

Finally, after what felt like the hundredth try, something clicked. Kai found himself gliding smoothly through the air, the sword stable beneath his feet. He weaved between rocky outcroppings and even managed a tentative turn.

A wide grin spread across his face. "Now we're talking!"

He waited for the familiar ping of his System, anticipating a new skill notification. But nothing came. Kai sighed, a bit disappointed.

Guess the System doesn't count this as a separate skill. Probably just considers it part of overall qi manipulation.

Despite the lack of a new skill entry, Kai felt proud of his achievement. Feeling bold, he decided to push his limits. He angled the sword upward, ascending higher into the sky. The wind whipped around him, but this time he was ready for it and adjusted his stance to maintain balance.

As he rose above the peaks, the full scale of Storm's Peak revealed itself. Lightning arced between clouds and illuminated the vast treacherous landscape below. Despite the danger, Kai couldn't help but feel a sense of awe.

This is incredible. No wonder cultivators love flying so much.

He was so caught up in the moment that he almost missed the dark shape emerging from a nearby cloud. Almost.

Kai's eyes widened as he recognized the form of a massive bird, easily three times his size. Its feathers crackled with electricity, and its eyes glowed with an intelligence that sent a chill down his spine.

Oh, right. Flying beasts. How could I forget?

Species: Thunder Bird
Level: Qi Refining Stage 9 HP: 898/900 Qi: 400/500 Strength: 70 Agility: 85

Durability: 72

The Thunder Bird let out a screech that seemed to shake the air. Kai winced, his ears ringing.

"Okay, big guy," he said, trying to keep his voice steady. "Let's not do anything hasty."

In response, the bird opened its beak. A ball of lightning qi began to form.

CHAPTER FIFTY-ONE

The Thunder Bird's beak snapped shut, and the ball of lightning it had been forming shot toward Kai.

He tried to maneuver his flying sword out of the way, but Kai wasn't used to aerial combat. The lightning grazed his shoulder, and even with his lightning resistance, it sent a jolt of agonizing pain through his body.

"Okay, not off to a great start," Kai muttered.

He focused on his Qi Condensation skill and rapidly formed a shield of solidified qi in front of himself. Just in time, too, as the Thunder Bird launched another attack.

The lightning bolt splashed against Kai's shield and dissipated harmlessly. But the force of the impact sent him tumbling backward on his sword. He struggled to regain his balance, his feet slipping on the narrow blade.

Aerial battle is much harder than it looks. Maybe I could avoid fighting. I did want to fight a Qi Refining stage nine beast but definitely not in the air.

"Hey there, big guy," Kai said, knowing that with his Spirit Beast Communication skill the beast could understand him. "How about we talk this out?"

The Thunder Bird tilted its head, its glowing eyes fixed on Kai. It opened its beak and let out another ear-splitting screech.

Kai winced. "I guess that's a no on the talking."

It seemed that unlike Zhi-Zhi, this beast's intelligence was very low. It seemed to operate on pure instinct with little room for reason or negotiation.

The Thunder Bird dove toward Kai with its talons extended. Kai managed to dodge, but just barely. He could feel the wind from the creature's wings buffeting him.

I need to get back to the ground, Kai decided. He angled his sword downward, aiming for the rocky terrain below.

But the Thunder Bird wasn't about to let its prey escape. It swooped in front of Kai and blocked his path. Its wings released a stream of electricity, creating a barrier of lightning.

Kai pulled up short, nearly falling off his sword again. "Okay, I guess we're doing this up here."

He took a deep breath and centered himself. He needed to adapt to this new fighting environment quickly if he wanted to survive.

Kai activated his Swift Wind Step skill, hoping it would work in the air as well as it did on the ground. To his relief, he felt his body become lighter, more agile.

When the Thunder Bird lunged at him again, Kai was ready. He sidestepped the attack and landed on a qi platform, then leaped over the beast's back.

As he passed over the Thunder Bird, Kai channeled qi into his palm as he prepared a Flame Palm Strike. He brought his hand down on the creature's back, and a burst of fire erupted on impact.

The Thunder Bird screeched in pain, its feathers singed. It wheeled around, eyes blazing with fury.

"Looks like that got your attention."

The beast retaliated with a barrage of lightning bolts. Kai weaved between them, his improved agility allowing him to dodge more effectively now. But he knew he couldn't keep this up forever. The constant movement was draining his qi reserves. Flying, while exhilarating, was not qi-friendly at all. One misstep could be fatal.

Kai needed a plan. He glanced around, taking in his surroundings. The storm clouds above, the jagged rocks below, the electricity in the air . . .

An idea began to form in his mind. It was risky, but it might just work.

Kai turned to face the Thunder Bird head-on. "All right, big guy. Let's see how you handle this."

He raised his hand, palm out, and activated his Static Charge skill. Sparks danced between his fingers, growing in intensity.

The Thunder Bird, sensing the buildup of electrical energy, responded in kind. It opened its beak wide, and a ball of lightning formed once again.

Kai waited, timing his move carefully. Just as the Thunder Bird was about to release its attack, Kai activated his Thunder Voice skill with a shout. The sound that erupted from his throat was deafening, a perfect mimicry of a thunderclap. The shockwave hit the Thunder Bird just as it released its lightning bolt.

The creature faltered, its aim thrown off. The lightning bolt went wide, missing Kai entirely.

Kai didn't waste the opportunity. He charged forward, his flying sword propelling him at high speed. As he neared the disoriented Thunder Bird, he leaped off his sword, then used Swift Wind Step and a qi platform to close the remaining distance.

His fist, charged with both fire and lightning qi, connected solidly with the Thunder Bird's chest. The impact sent both of them plummeting toward the ground.

Kai gritted his teeth as he fought to maintain his hold on the thrashing creature. The ground was approaching fast, and he knew the landing would be rough. At the last moment, Kai activated his Iron Skin skill, reinforcing his body against the impending impact. They hit the rocky terrain hard, kicking up a cloud of dust and debris.

For a moment, everything was still. Then, slowly, Kai pushed himself up, his body aching but intact. The Thunder Bird lay stunned, but still very much alive, beside him.

Even though he was now on the ground, Kai knew he couldn't let his guard down. He quickly retrieved his sword, which had fallen nearby, and readied himself for the next round.

The Thunder Bird struggled to its feet, shaking off the impact. Its eyes, filled with a mixture of pain and rage, locked onto Kai.

"Round two," Kai said, raising his sword.

The Thunder Bird spread its wings, and it quickly launched into the air and began circling above Kai. He kept his eyes on the beast, tracking its movements. He knew it would be more cautious now, having felt the sting of his attacks.

The Thunder Bird dove, its talons extended. Kai raised his sword to block, the clash of metal and claw sending sparks flying. Kai pushed back, using the sword to create some distance between them. He needed to end this fight soon, before exhaustion set in.

He thought of another idea. Kai focused on his Qi Condensation skill, but instead of forming a shield or weapon, he created a network of thin, nearly invisible qi threads around him.

The Thunder Bird attacked again, this time with a barrage of lightning bolts. Kai dodged and weaved, letting some of the bolts hit his qi threads. The threads caught and held the electrical energy. It was like he had created a web of lightning.

The Thunder Bird, oblivious to the trap, pressed its attack. It swooped in close, aiming to overwhelm Kai with its size and strength.

Kai waited until the last moment, then activated his Heart of Thunder skill. A powerful shockwave erupted from his chest and caught the Thunder Bird mid-dive. The creature screeched in pain and surprise as its momentum carried it forward into Kai's web of electrically charged qi threads.

The effect was immediate and devastating. The Thunder Bird's own lightning combined with the energy from Kai's Heart of Thunder and created a feedback loop. Electricity coursed through the beast's body, amplified by its own conductive feathers.

Kai shielded his eyes from the brilliant display of light. When he looked again, the Thunder Bird lay motionless on the ground, wisps of smoke rising from its singed feathers.

It seems being a lightning beast doesn't come with lightning resistance.

Only high-rank cultivators or more noble beasts typically possessed elemental resistance. Kai's knowledge of beast types was limited, but he knew this Thunder Bird was just a Qi Refining beast and didn't seem particularly special. There were many of its kind in this realm, after all. It was cannon fodder.

The lack of lightning resistance in a lightning beast might seem counterintuitive, but it made sense from a cultivation perspective. These lower-rank creatures hadn't yet reached the level where they could fully internalize and resist their own element. It was a reminder that true mastery and resistance often came at higher levels of cultivation.

Kai approached cautiously, sword at the ready. But there was no need for caution. The Thunder Bird was dead, its once-glowing eyes now dark and lifeless.

You have gained 100 XP!

Kai let out a long breath. He had won, but it had been a close thing.

He knelt beside the fallen creature and placed a hand on its still warm feathers. "You should have taken me up on the offer," he said softly.

The Thunder Bird's body shimmered and disappeared into his inventory space.

As the adrenaline of battle faded, exhaustion hit Kai like a wave. He dragged his body over to his little cave and sat down heavily on a rock. His muscles ached and his qi reserves were nearly depleted, but despite the pain and fatigue, Kai felt a sense of accomplishment. He had faced a formidable opponent and emerged victorious. More importantly, he had gained valuable experience in aerial combat and creative use of his skills.

Kai took a few moments to catch his breath and assess his condition. His clothes were singed in places, and he had a few minor burns and bruises, but nothing serious.

He pulled out a qi-replenishing pill from his inventory, one of many he had prepared for this expedition. He popped the pill into his mouth and felt it dissolve instantly. A cool sensation spread through his body as his qi stores were replenished.

As he rested, Kai reflected on the battle.

That was quite the learning experience, he thought. *Fighting in three dimensions is a whole different game.*

He pondered the ways he had combined his skills, particularly the use of Qi Condensation, to create the lightning web.

That trick worked better than I expected. I need to explore more creative applications of Qi Condensation. There's got to be so much more I can do with it.

His mind then turned to his performance in the air. While he had managed to hold his own, there had been several close calls that made him uneasy. He knew that epic battles between high-level cultivators often took place entirely in the air. Some fights even extended into the upper atmosphere or space itself.

My aerial maneuverability needs work, Kai admitted to himself. *If I had better control of my flying sword, I could have avoided some of those near misses. I can't always count on luck in a fight like that.*

After about an hour of rest and meditation, Kai felt recovered enough to continue his exploration of the Storm Peak Realm. He stood up, stretched his muscles, and retrieved his flying sword.

This time, when he stepped onto the blade, his balance was much steadier. The recent battle had forced him to adapt quickly to aerial movement, and he could already feel the improvement.

Kai pulled out the teleportation token from his inventory, turning it over in his hand. He had accomplished his main objectives—breaking through to Qi Refining stage nine, battling a stage-nine beast, and learning to fly. It seemed like a good time to return to the sect.

Just as he was about to activate the token, a notification popped up in his vision:

> New Quest: Tribulation Challenger
> Objective: Defeat a beast undergoing breakthrough to Foundation Establishment Realm.
> Reward: 2500 XP

Kai's eyes widened at the quest description. It sounded like he would be part of the beast's tribulation. He had heard of humans being part of tribulations for cultivators, but he hadn't considered it might be the same for beasts. It made sense, though—beasts had their own cultivation path, and humans were certainly their enemies.

He hesitated, weighing his options. The safe choice would be to return to the sect now. But the 2500 XP reward made him pause. He still needed almost eight thousand XP for his own breakthrough to Foundation Establishment, and this quest would provide a large chunk of that.

Kai glanced at the mark on his wrist as he reminded himself that he still had two extra lives. The potential reward seemed worth the risk.

With a deep breath, Kai stored the token back in his inventory. He rose into the air on his flying sword and activated his map function, scanning the area for any unusual energy signatures. Almost immediately, a bright marker appeared on the map, pulsing with an intensity that the other markers couldn't compare to.

He focused on the marker, and additional information appeared:

Tribulation Beast
Level: Pseudo Foundation Establishment Status: Preparing for breakthrough

"Pseudo Foundation Establishment," Kai muttered to himself. "That's definitely going to be a much tougher fight than the Thunder Bird."

He understood that a beast at this level would be significantly more powerful than the Qi Refining stage nine Thunder Bird he had just faced. It would likely have more advanced techniques, greater control over its qi, and possibly even some spiritual techniques that weren't just a bolt of lightning.

The thought of facing such a creature made Kai pause. This wouldn't just be a harder battle—it could be downright dangerous, even with his extra lives. The gap between Qi Refining and Foundation Establishment was substantial, and this beast was on the cusp of crossing that threshold.

Still, the potential reward was tempting. Earning 2500 XP would be a significant boost toward his own breakthrough. And the experience of facing such a powerful opponent could be invaluable for whatever was to come next.

"Well, I can't keep playing it safe. I need to take some risks."

With that, Kai angled his flying sword in the direction indicated by the map and set off.

CHAPTER FIFTY-TWO

Kai hovered at the edge of the center of Storm's Peak, known as the Eye of the Storm. The name fit perfectly—winds howled and lightning flashed in a dizzying display of nature's fury. He had flown low and used his Qi Concealment skill to avoid detection by Thunder Birds or other hungry beasts on his way here.

After landing softly on a rocky outcrop, Kai pulled up his map. A large red dot pulsed not far from his position. He pondered what kind of beast it might be.

Lightning affinity, powerful enough to attempt a breakthrough to the Foundation Establishment in a realm designed to hold only Qi Refining beasts . . . What options are there?

Given the lightning-rich environment, several possibilities came to mind—perhaps a Thunder Ox or Lightning Serpent? But then he remembered what that Azure Sky Sect disciple had mentioned before he entered the realm. There were rumors of a dragon.

A dragon makes sense. What better creature to rule over a domain of storms?

Deciding to rest and restore his qi naturally, Kai found a sheltered spot between two large boulders. He didn't want to waste valuable qi pills before a major fight. As he sat down, he noticed new information on his quest log:

Quest: Tribulation Challenger
Time Remaining: 45:00

A time limit? That's new. But it makes sense. The beast won't pause its breakthrough just to wait for me. My life isn't exactly a game . . .

Kai spent the next fifteen minutes in quiet meditation, feeling his qi slowly replenish. When he felt ready, he stood and suppressed his qi even further. He began making his way toward the quest marker, moving cautiously over the rough terrain.

Suddenly, he heard voices approaching. He quickly ducked behind a large rock, peering out carefully.

A group of beasts, ranging from Qi Refining stage seven to stage nine, were making their way up the peak. They were a motley assortment—some furry, some scaled, and ranging in size from that of a large dog to a small horse. Kai's Spirit Beast Communication skill kicked in, allowing him to understand their conversation.

"This tribulation is taking forever," grumbled a creature that looked like a cross between a wolf and a lightning bolt. "How many more offerings does the master need?"

A birdlike beast squawked in response. "As many as it takes! Do you want to volunteer yourself as the next meal?"

The wolf-thing's fur stood on end. "Of course not! I'm just saying, we've been at this for days. My paws are getting sore."

"Stop whining," a third beast, which resembled a gorilla made of storm clouds, grunted. "The master's breakthrough will benefit us all. Now hurry up—I don't want to get eaten for being late with the offerings."

"Do you really think the master will become a true dragon after the breakthrough?" the birdlike beast asked.

"Who knows?" the wolf-beast replied. "But even if not, our master will still be the most powerful creature in Storm's Peak. Now stop yapping and keep moving!"

Kai watched them pass. *So, it's not quite a dragon yet. But it's aiming to become one. Interesting.*

He waited until the group was a safe distance ahead before following, keeping to the shadows and using his Qi Concealment to its fullest. As Kai stalked the group of beasts, his eyes took in the harsh beauty of the Eye of the Storm. Jagged cliffs rose on all sides, their peaks lost in the storm clouds above. Lightning arced between the rocks, creating temporary bridges of pure energy. A constant low rumble of thunder served as nature's background music.

It's incredible. A whole ecosystem built around lightning and storms. But it seems like none of these creatures realize that their entire world is just a mini-realm owned by the Azure Sky Sect.

The realization made Kai pause. He thought back to the realm outside. Could it be possible that the world he was isekaied to was also just a pocket dimension in some greater universe? He'd read plenty of xianxia stories where the protagonist broke through the world's barrier only to discover they were a big fish in a small pond.

No, I need to focus. I can ponder existential questions later. Right now, I have a job to do.

He continued following the beast group, staying well back and using his Qi Detection as well as his map to ensure he wasn't walking into any traps. Eventually, they reached what appeared to be their destination—a massive cave mouth set into the side of the tallest peak.

Kai found a hiding spot with a good view of the cave entrance. He settled in to wait, curious to see what would emerge.

He didn't have to wait long. A massive form slithered out of the cave, and Kai had to stifle a gasp. The creature before him wasn't quite a dragon, but it was certainly on its way there. Its body was long and serpentine, covered in blue scales that seemed to absorb and reflect the lightning around it. A mane of what looked like pure electricity ran down its spine. Its head was more snakelike than draconic, but Kai could see the beginnings of horns forming on its skull.

Most striking, however, was the qi spiraling around the beast. It was dense and powerful, swirling in complex patterns that Kai struggled to follow with his eyes.

So, this is what a breakthrough to Foundation Establishment looks like, Kai thought, awestruck despite himself.

The smaller beasts approached their master and prostrated themselves before offering up the corpses they'd brought. The serpent-dragon's eyes gleamed with hunger. It opened its maw, revealing rows of razor-sharp teeth, and began to devour the offerings.

Kai watched, fascinated and a little horrified, as the creature consumed corpse after corpse. With each one, the qi surrounding it grew denser, more chaotic. Finally, the serpent-dragon finished the last corpse. It raised its head and let out a bone-shaking roar that made Kai want to cover his ears.

"It's not enough!" the beast bellowed, its voice like rolling thunder. "I need more! The breakthrough is almost over. I can feel it!"

The smaller beasts looked at each other nervously. "Master," the wolf-beast said hesitantly, "we've brought all we could find . . ."

The serpent-dragon's eyes narrowed dangerously. Without warning, tendrils of qi shot out from its body and wrapped around the wolf-beast. The creature yelped in terror as it was dragged toward its master's gaping maw.

"No! Please, Master!" the wolf-beast pleaded. But its cries fell on deaf ears. With a single gulp, the serpent-dragon swallowed its own servant.

The other beasts cowered in fear. The serpent-dragon's eyes swept over them, making them shrink back even further.

"Get more," it commanded. "I don't care how. I don't care what. Just bring me more to devour. I NEED MORE!"

The beasts didn't need to be told twice. They scrambled away, practically falling over each other in their haste to escape their master's hunger.

Kai remained in his hiding spot. He checked his map to confirm that the smaller beasts were moving away. When he was sure they were at a far enough distance to not head back, his eyes narrowed. It was time to make his move.

Okay, I need a plan. But first, let's check its stats.

Name: ???

Species: Zhen Lei Shenjiao (Quaking Thunder Divine Flood Dragon)
Level: Pseudo Foundation Establishment
HP: 900/900
Qi: 900/900
Strength: 99
Agility: 96
Durability: 98

Its stats really are just a breadth away from Foundation Establishment Realm. I need to ambush it.

Swift Wind Step would get him close quickly. He could use Qi Condensation to enhance his sword and maybe even combine it with Flame Palm Strike for extra damage. The head seemed like the best target—he wasn't sure about the creature's internal anatomy, and he didn't want to aim for a heart that might not exist or be in an unexpected location.

Just as Kai was about to put his plan into action, the serpent-dragon's massive head swiveled toward his hiding spot. Its blue eyes fixed directly on him.

"Well, well," the beast rumbled, its voice a mix of amusement and resignation. "It seems the heavens truly don't want me to break through. They've sent me a human tribulation."

Kai's eyes widened. His cover was blown, but maybe he could use this to his advantage. He stood slowly and stepped out from behind the rocks with a calm expression on his face.

"The heavens didn't send me. I'm here of my own accord. Killing you will benefit me."

The serpent-dragon's eyes widened slightly. "You speak the tongue of feykin," it said, using an unfamiliar term that Kai's skill translated as a catch-all for magical beasts. The creature shook its massive head. "Ah, but this is how the heavens trick those under the sky. They make you believe you act of your own will when in truth, you dance to their tune."

Kai's calm expression faltered for a moment. The beast's words struck a chord within him. He couldn't help but think of the many xianxia stories he'd read where Heaven's Will manipulated events and people like pieces on a cosmic chessboard. And then there was his own situation—was the System that gave him quests and rewards truly benevolent, or was it manipulating him for its own ends?

No, Kai thought, shaking off the doubt. *Even if that's true, I can't afford to dwell on it now. I need those points.*

"You might be right," he admitted. "But whether it's Heaven's Will or my own choice, the outcome will be the same. One of us won't be walking away from this."

The serpent-dragon regarded Kai with what almost looked like respect. "Brave words, little human. But do you truly think you can stand against me? I stand at the precipice of Foundation Establishment. The power of storms flows through my veins. Whilst you . . . you have only just entered the ninth stage of the Qi Refining Realm. You are walking to your death."

As if to emphasize its point, lightning flared along the beast's spine, illuminating the cave in blue-white flashes.

Kai stood his ground, his hand resting lightly on the hilt of his sword. "I like a challenge, and death hasn't stopped me before."

The serpent-dragon's mouth curved into what might have been a smile, revealing its razor-sharp teeth. "Very well, human. If you wish to be my tribulation, then so be it. Your qi will only benefit my breakthrough."

Just as it seemed Kai was about to reply, he vanished in a blur of wind.

The battle for Storm's Peak had begun.

CHAPTER FIFTY-THREE

Kai appeared behind the Zhen Lei Shenjiao, his hand blazing with fiery qi. He aimed a Flame Palm Strike directly at the beast's head, hoping to catch it off guard.

But the flood dragon was far from helpless. With surprising agility for its size, it suddenly leaped backward in a burst of lightning, and its massive form sailed through the air, easily avoiding Kai's attack.

"Impressive speed, human," the dragon rumbled. "But my Thunderstrike Leap isn't so easily countered."

Kai blinked, momentarily disoriented. His Qi Detection skill was muddled by the residual qi in the air, making it hard to pinpoint the dragon's exact location.

No problem. I've got other tools.

He glanced at the map function floating in the bottom right of his vision and immediately spotted the beast's position. The flood dragon had landed some distance behind him, coiling its serpentine body for another strike.

Without wasting a moment, the Zhen Lei Shenjiao lunged forward, its jaws opening wide. "Taste my Divine Thunder Fang!" it roared.

Kai's eyes widened slightly, but he remained calm. He activated Lightning Step, and his body briefly turned into pure electricity as he zipped to the side. The flood dragon's fangs snapped shut on empty air and sent out a shockwave of thunder that Kai felt in his bones.

That was close. Can't let it get that near again.

As he moved, Kai reached into his inventory and pulled out a set of throwing knives he bought a few days prior. He infused the blades with his qi, hoping to add an extra punch to his attacks. The knives glowed faintly with blue qi as he hurled them at the beast in quick succession.

The Zhen Lei Shenjiao didn't even try to dodge. The knives struck its scales and bounced off harmlessly, clattering to the ground.

Kai's eyes narrowed. *Its durability is off the charts. I need to find a weak spot.*

He studied the beast carefully, looking for any chinks in its armor. The scales seemed to overlap perfectly, leaving no obvious vulnerabilities. But as the flood dragon moved, Kai noticed something. There were small gaps where the scales met at the joints, particularly around the neck and shoulders.

That might be my best shot. But how to exploit it?

For a moment, Kai considered using his Qi Condensation skill to create multiple lightning rods around the battlefield. In theory, these constructs could attract and divert the Zhen Lei Shenjiao's lightning attacks, reducing its offensive power. But he quickly dismissed the idea.

My qi constructs won't last more than a dozen seconds. Not to mention that the beast would easily destroy them. Even with Sky's Favor regenerating my qi, it'd be a waste of energy.

The flood dragon reared up and Kai recognized the signs of a major attack forming. The beast opened its mouth, and a deafening roar filled the air. The sound was more than just noise—it was infused with qi, making it capable of paralyzing enemies and disrupting their energy.

"Behold, the Heaven-Quaking Thunderclap!"

Kai didn't hesitate. He activated his Thunder Voice skill, and his own roar rose to meet the flood dragon's. At the same time, he unleashed Heart of Thunder, sending out a shockwave of his own.

The two thunderous attacks collided in midair. The ground shook, and the air seemed to vibrate. For a moment, it looked like the Zhen Lei Shenjiao's attack might overwhelm Kai's defenses. But slowly, the wave of sound and qi began to dissipate.

When the air cleared, both Kai and the flood dragon stood their ground, seemingly at a stalemate.

A series of notifications popped up in Kai's vision.

Skill leveled up!
Thunder Voice (Level 2)
You have gained 100 XP!

Skill leveled up!
Heart of Thunder (Level 2)
You have gained 100 XP!

Nice, Kai thought, allowing himself a small smile. *Every little bit helps.*

The Zhen Lei Shenjiao regarded Kai with what almost looked like respect. "Impressive, human," it rumbled. "You've managed to counter my Heaven-Quaking Thunderclap. But can you withstand the full fury of a storm?"

The beast's body began to glow, electricity arcing between its scales. The air grew heavy with the scent of ozone.

This is going to be big, Kai thought, bracing himself.

The flood dragon reared back its head and roared, "Witness the Storm Dragon's Wrath!"

Above them, the clouds began to swirl, forming a massive vortex. Lightning crackled within the dark mass, growing more intense by the second. Suddenly, a bolt of electricity in the shape of a colossal dragon shot down from the sky.

Kai's eyes widened. He had no time to dodge—the dragon was too big. He quickly formed a barrier of qi around himself, pouring as much energy as he could into the defense.

The lightning dragon crashed down, engulfing Kai in a sea of electricity. His barrier held for a moment, then shattered under the immense power of the attack. Kai felt the lightning course through his body, every nerve screaming in pain.

When the attack finally subsided, Kai stumbled, his clothes smoking and his hair standing on end. But he was still standing. His lightning resistance buff had protected him from the worst of the damage, though he could feel that he'd taken a significant hit.

Shit, Kai thought, his calm demeanor finally cracking a bit. *I thought I could defeat it. I thought with my higher-level skills, I'd be able to fight a beast half a stage above mine. All the protagonists in those stories were able to do it, but I can't even make it bleed.*

The Zhen Lei Shenjiao looked surprised to see Kai still on his feet. "You're resilient, I'll give you that," it said. "But you must see now that you can't win. Why not surrender? I promise to make your end quick. All you're doing right now is wasting precious qi that I could use to break through!"

Kai's eyes narrowed. He knew he might have to retreat soon, but he had enough left for one more attempt before running became necessary.

"Thanks for the offer," Kai replied. "But I think I'll pass."

Using his Qi Condensation skill, Kai formed a bow out of pure energy. Next, he created an arrow, then infused it with the energy of his Flame Palm Strike.

This is tricky, Kai thought, concentrating hard. *Fire isn't my element. But if I can make this work . . .*

He nocked the flaming arrow and aimed carefully at one of the weak spots he'd identified earlier—a small gap in the scales near the flood dragon's shoulder.

The Zhen Lei Shenjiao's eyes widened as it recognized the threat. "You leave me no choice but to use more qi," it growled. "Storm-Warding Thundercloud!"

Instantly, a thick roiling cloud formed around the beast's body. Lightning crackled within the mist and created a constantly shifting defense that obscured the flood dragon's exact position.

Kai loosed his arrow, but the thundercloud absorbed and dispersed the attack before it could reach its target. He quickly fired several more, but each met the same fate.

Damn it, I can't get a clear shot through that cloud.

He glanced at his map as he tried to keep track of the beast's location within the thundercloud. Suddenly, he felt a change in the air. A massive buildup of energy—not in front of him or behind him but above him. He looked up, his eyes widening as he saw what was coming.

A colossal hammer made of pure lightning was forming in the sky, far above the battlefield. The Zhen Lei Shenjiao's voice boomed from within the thundercloud. "Prepare yourself for the Divine Sky Hammer!"

Oh shit, Kai thought, his calm finally breaking. He tried to form another qi barrier while simultaneously retreating, but he knew it wouldn't be enough. The hammer was simply too big, too powerful.

The Divine Sky Hammer descended with terrifying speed. Kai poured every ounce of his remaining qi into his defenses, but it was like trying to stop an avalanche with a paper fan.

The hammer struck, and the world exploded into light and sound. Kai felt himself being driven into the ground, his body breaking under the immense force. Pain overwhelmed his senses and then . . . darkness.

When the dust settled, all that remained was a crater in the rocky ground. At its center lay Kai's broken body, limbs bent at unnatural angles, his Legacy Disciple robes torn and scorched.

The Zhen Lei Shenjiao slithered to the edge of the crater, looking down at its fallen opponent. "You fought well for a human," it said almost softly. "But in the end, this was inevitable. Your essence will serve me well in my breakthrough. If only you didn't waste so much of that delicious qi . . ."

The flood dragon's serpentine body coiled around Kai's lifeless form. It opened its jaws wide, and in one swift motion, it engulfed the corpse. There was a sickening crunch as bones were crushed between those powerful jaws.

After finishing its meal, the flood dragon made a strange face and muttered, "Strange . . . I sense something unfinished about you, human." It shook its massive head as if trying to clear an odd sensation. Then its eyes narrowed to slits, glowing with intense focus, as it growled, "But no matter. My breakthrough awaits!"

CHAPTER FIFTY-FOUR

The storm clouds gathered above the Zhen Lei Shenjiao as it prepared for its breakthrough.

"At last," the flood dragon rumbled. "The moment I've been waiting for. The barrier between Qi Refining and Foundation Establishment . . . I will shatter it!"

The beast's body began to glow with an intense electric-blue light. Sparks danced across its scales, and the air itself seemed to vibrate with the force of its qi. The Zhen Lei Shenjiao's eyes, normally a deep sapphire, now blazed with white-hot energy.

"Come, heavenly tribulation!" it roared. "I am ready to face your challenge and take my next step toward becoming a true dragon!"

As if in response to its call, the sky split open. A bolt of lightning, far larger and more potent than any natural occurrence, lanced down from the heavens. It struck the flood dragon head-on and enveloped its form in a cocoon of pure electrical energy.

The Zhen Lei Shenjiao's voice rose in a mix of pain and exultation. "Yes! This is the power I seek to become a Jiao Lian Shenjiao—a Quaking Thunder Spirit Serpent!"

Its scales began to shift and change, hardening and taking on a more metallic sheen. The mane of electricity running down its spine grew brighter and more defined. Its small, stubby horns grew longer from its skull, the first signs of its transformation into the next stage of its evolution.

"I can feel it," the beast growled. "The realm of Foundation Establishment . . . It's within my grasp!"

The lightning continued to pour down, relentless in its assault. The flood dragon's body trembled under the onslaught, but it held firm. Its qi swirled and expanded, pushing against the boundaries of the Qi Refining Realm.

As the transformation continued, in its arrogance, the Zhen Lei Shenjiao began to explain its evolutionary path, perhaps to itself or to any who might be listening.

"We flood dragons have a long path to becoming true dragons," it rumbled. "First, we begin as Zhen Lei Shenjiao, apprentices of thunder and lightning. But that is merely the first step." The beast's body continued to change, its form elongating slightly as it spoke. "Upon reaching Foundation Establishment, we evolve into Jiao Lian Shenjiao—Spirit Serpents with a growing understanding of storms. Our lightning becomes infused with spiritual energy, allowing us to start grasping the basics of soul-striking techniques."

A crack of thunder punctuated its words, as if nature itself was confirming the creature's explanation.

"Beyond that lies the Kui Lian Shenjiao—the Thunderclap Spirit Dragon. When we reach that stage, we begin to learn how to influence the weather, calling forth small storms with some effort. Our bodies become more draconic, with longer horns and the beginnings of claws." The flood dragon's eyes gleamed with ambition as it continued its exposition. "After the Kui Lian Shenjiao comes the Pang Lian Shenjiao—the Thunderbolt Divine Dragon. At this stage, we can create and control moderate storms, and our lightning remnants can crack boulders." Despite the pain of its ongoing transformation, the Zhen Lei Shenjiao's voice swelled with pride. "And finally, if we prove worthy, we may become true Lian Long—Thunder Dragons. Masters of the sky, with the power to unleash heaven-shaking storms and lightning that can rewrite the very laws of nature."

The flood dragon's body shuddered as another wave of energy washed over it. "But for now, I focus on the task at hand. To evolve from Zhen Lei Shenjiao to Jiao Lian Shenjiao. To break through to Foundation Establishment and take my first true step on the path to becoming a Lian Long!"

Suddenly, the lightning changed. Instead of striking the Zhen Lei Shenjiao directly, it began to form a sphere around the creature. The sphere pulsed with energy, compressing and intensifying the qi within.

"Ah, I see. The final test." The flood dragon's eyes widened in understanding. "I must break free of this shell to truly advance."

It began to thrash within the sphere, its coils slamming against the barriers of lightning. Each impact sent shockwaves through the air, causing the ground to tremble.

"I will not be denied!" the Zhen Lei Shenjiao roared. "I have come too far, sacrificed too much!"

The sphere began to crack, thin lines of darkness appearing in the blinding light. The flood dragon redoubled its efforts, pouring every ounce of its strength and qi into breaking free.

"Almost . . . almost . . ."

With a final earth-shaking roar, the Zhen Lei Shenjiao shattered the sphere. Lightning exploded outward in all directions, scorching the ground around the beast.

The flood dragon hung suspended in the air, its body still glowing with residual energy. Its transformation was nearly complete—its scales now shimmered with a purple glow, and the horns that adorned its head were larger, more draconic. It was on the very cusp of becoming a Jiao Lian Shenjiao.

"Yes!" it exulted. "I can feel the power of Foundation Establishment flowing through me! I am reborn! I am evolving into a Jiao Lian Shenjiao! I am—"

Suddenly, the glow surrounding the Zhen Lei Shenjiao flickered. Its eyes widened in shock and confusion.

"What? No! This can't be!"

The qi it had absorbed from Kai, which had pushed it to the brink of breakthrough, began to dissipate. The energy that had been fueling its transformation started to fade.

"No! NO!" the flood dragon roared in frustration. "I was so close! How can this be happening?"

Its horns began to shrink, and its scales lost some of their luster. The Zhen Lei Shenjiao thrashed in the air, desperately trying to hold on to the power it had gained.

"I refuse to accept this!" it bellowed. "I will not be denied my destiny!"

But despite its protests, the transformation continued to reverse. The flood dragon's body shrank slightly, returning to its previous size. The mane of electricity along its spine dimmed, and its qi levels began to drop.

"This is impossible," the Zhen Lei Shenjiao muttered, its voice a mix of disbelief and rage. "I had everything I needed. The offerings, the human's qi . . . It should have been enough!"

As the last of the transformative energy faded, the flood dragon slowly descended to the ground. It landed heavily, its massive coils sprawling across the scorched earth. The beast's breathing was labored, exhausted from the failed breakthrough. Its eyes darted around wildly, as if searching for an explanation for its failure.

"How?" it growled. "How could this happen? I was at the very threshold of becoming a Jiao Lian Shenjiao!"

Unbeknownst to the Zhen Lei Shenjiao, a figure was materializing behind it. Kai had respawned with his sword at the ready.

The flood dragon, still lost in its shock and dismay, failed to notice the human's presence. "I must find more qi," it muttered to itself. "Perhaps if I devour more creatures, I can try again. Yes, that's it. I'll—"

Its words were cut short as Kai's sword flashed through the air; he targeted the weak spot he had identified—the gap in the scales near the creature's neck.

The blade struck true, slicing through the vulnerable area with ease. The Zhen Lei Shenjiao's eyes widened in shock and pain, a strangled gasp escaping its throat.

"What . . . How . . . ," it managed to croak out before its massive head separated from its body.

The flood dragon's corpse collapsed to the ground, its coils twitching in their death throes. Kai stood over the fallen beast, his breath coming in quick gasps as the adrenaline of the moment began to fade.

A notification popped up in his vision.

Quest Complete: Tribulation Challenger
Objective: Defeat a beast undergoing breakthrough to Foundation Establishment Realm.
Reward: 2500 XP

Kai let out a long breath as relief washed over him. He had done it. He had defeated the Zhen Lei Shenjiao and completed the quest.

He glanced at his wrist. Where once two red prongs of the trident mark had glowed, now only one remained.

"I don't see any other way I could have killed you," he murmured, his voice barely above a whisper as he stored the massive corpse in his inventory.

Kai took a moment to survey his surroundings. The battlefield was a mess. He knew that in a normal situation, he might have to worry about other beasts in the area taking advantage of the chaos to attack. But he also knew that the flood dragon's followers would understand that anything capable of defeating their master would be far beyond their level. They would be walking to their deaths if they tried to challenge him now.

Still, a nagging thought tugged at his mind. He remembered the Qi Refining stage nine Thunder Bird he had encountered earlier. Beasts like that, which lacked intelligence, might be driven here by their primal need to feed, regardless of the danger. So Kai decided to check his map. He searched for any sign of approaching threats. To his relief, he saw no red dots nearby.

At least something's going right, he thought to himself.

But just as he was about to relax, a new marker appeared on the map. A green dot, moving at high speed, was rapidly approaching his position. Kai's eyes narrowed, and he immediately dropped into a fighting stance.

Green means ally or neutral, but who or what could that be in a place like Storm's Peak?

One of the benefits of his respawn was that he had returned with full health and qi. He wasn't tired from the battle, and he was ready to face whatever it was that was headed his way.

Who is it? Another cultivator from the Azure Sky Sect? Or maybe some kind of neutral beast I haven't encountered before?

The seconds ticked by, feeling like hours as Kai waited. Then, suddenly, a figure appeared on the horizon. It was moving so fast that it seemed to blur, crossing the distance in mere moments.

As the newcomer drew closer, Kai's eyes widened in recognition. The black robes, the familiar stance—it was Shen Yu.

CHAPTER FIFTY-FIVE

The battlefield around them was still smoking from the battle with the Zhen Lei Shenjiao, but Kai stood motionless, his eyes fixed on the black robed figure before him.

I only have one life left; I need to be careful here. Shen Yu is dangerous, and I don't fully understand his motives.

Shen Yu's arrival had been unexpected, and Kai couldn't help but feel a twinge of unease. They may have shared the same master, but Kai knew better than to consider Shen Yu a brother, senior or junior. His previous lives had taught him that the fellow Legacy Disciple was not someone who cared about his well-being.

"What do you want?"

Shen Yu didn't answer right away. He looked around the battlefield, taking in the signs of the battle that had just ended. When he finally spoke, his voice was soft but clear.

"I want to talk. You've been trying to corner me for a conversation for weeks. Now seems like a good time, don't you think?"

Kai didn't lower his guard. *Yes, I did want to have a chat,* he thought. *But I wanted it to be on my terms, in a place where I wouldn't end up going mysteriously missing. If he kills me here, it could easily be explained that I was arrogant and got devoured by beasts.* After all, such things were common.

"How did you find me?" he asked, trying to buy time to think.

"This is a safe place to speak. No one should be listening here. We can talk freely."

Shen Yu's gaze swept across the battlefield, then settled on a particular spot—a deep crater in the rocky ground. It was where Kai had been smashed to bits by the Zhen Lei Shenjiao's Divine Sky Hammer. For the first time, he saw a genuine smile appear on Shen Yu's face. It was small, just a slight upward curve of his lips, but unmistakable.

"You really can come back to life," Shen Yu said. It wasn't a question.

Kai's eyes widened slightly, but he quickly schooled his expression. He couldn't let Shen Yu know how much that statement had rattled him.

"I don't know what you mean," Kai said, keeping his voice steady. Had he been watched during his battle? The thought made his skin crawl.

Shen Yu didn't respond immediately. Instead, he opened his palm and made a gesture. Kai noticed something come down from the sky and land on Shen Yu's hand. It was a small orb made of lightning qi—a Storm Eye.

Kai couldn't hide his surprise this time. He could barely use the Storm Eye skill for surveillance a few hundred meters away from himself, but Shen Yu had to have been at least a mile or more away to be out of Kai's detection range. Worse, Kai couldn't keep relying on his map. It hadn't picked up on the eye's presence, because it wasn't a living being. Unfortunately, his Qi Detection skill was far too weak to notice such a subtle technique, especially in the heat of battle.

I was completely exposed, Kai thought, a cold sweat breaking out on his forehead. *He saw everything.*

Before he could come up with an excuse, Shen Yu spoke again. "Don't try to say it was an illusion. The Storm Eye skill can't be muddled by illusions, especially if you're unaware of its presence."

Kai paused, considering his options. Then he decided to change tactics. He smiled and said, "There's no use in me denying it any longer. It seems like you already knew about it, just like you know other things that you shouldn't."

Shen Yu raised an eyebrow but remained silent, waiting for Kai to continue.

Kai took a deep breath and began to list his observations. "Your cultivation speed could be explained by being a once-in-a-millennium prodigy. But back on the ark, when you broke into the Qi Refining Realm, it was clear you were familiar with cultivation. Your movements were too natural, too instinctive."

Kai paused, gauging Shen Yu's reaction. When the other boy remained impassive, he continued.

"Not to mention your understanding of the sect trials. You knew exactly what trials were appearing and how to complete them to gain the number-one rank. And don't try to say you have inside information. I've asked around, and no one had heard of Shen Yu before you entered the sect." Kai stopped, watching Shen Yu carefully. "There's more. Do you want me to continue?"

Shen Yu stayed silent for a moment, then shook his head. "What are you implying?" he asked quietly.

Kai took a moment to gather his thoughts before responding. "I think you're either a regressor or a reincarnator," he said finally. "More likely a regressor. Not that you did a good job of hiding it."

Shen Yu smiled, but it didn't reach his eyes. "While time manipulation is possible," he said, "time travel is impossible. The heavens wouldn't allow the existence of a technique that allows a cultivator to move backward or forward in time."

Kai stayed silent. He knew that the existence of such an ability was possible—after all, his respawn ability let him rewind time by three seconds and perhaps would allow even more in the future. But he wasn't about to give Shen Yu any more information about himself.

The other Legacy Disciple seemed to take Kai's silence as an invitation to continue. "Let me tell you a story," he said, his voice taking on a tone that Kai hadn't heard from him before. It was almost . . . teacherly. "Long ago, there was a cultivator named Zhu Tianxing. He was known throughout the realms for his incredible talent and swift advancement through the cultivation ranks. Many believed he would become one of the greatest immortals of his age."

Kai listened carefully, wondering why Shen Yu was telling him this story.

"Zhu Tianxing eventually reached the threshold of immortality," Shen Yu continued. "But when he attempted his Immortal Tribulation, he failed. The backlash was severe, damaging his soul foundation to the point where he could never attempt another breakthrough." Shen Yu's eyes seemed to look past Kai, as if seeing something in the distance. "Desperate and bitter, Zhu Tianxing began to research a technique that would allow him to go back in time, to before his failed tribulation. He believed that if he could do so, he could prepare better and succeed."

Kai felt a chill run down his spine. He had a feeling he knew where this story was going.

"For years, Zhu Tianxing worked tirelessly. He delved into forbidden arts, made pacts with dark entities, and even sacrificed parts of his own essence in his quest. And finally, after decades of work, he believed he had succeeded." Shen Yu's voice grew softer, but somehow more intense. "On the night of a full moon, Zhu Tianxing activated his technique. For a moment, it seemed to work. The world around him began to blur and shift. But then . . ."

Kai found himself leaning forward slightly, caught up in the story despite himself.

"The heavens themselves seemed to tear open," Shen Yu said. "A light brighter than a thousand suns engulfed Zhu Tianxing. When it faded, there was nothing left of him. Not his body, not his soul, not even his descendants were spared. His entire bloodline was eliminated."

Shen Yu's eyes refocused on Kai. "That was the punishment of the heavens. And it served as a lesson to all cultivators who came after. Some rules cannot be broken. Some lines cannot be crossed. The flow of time is one of them."

Kai remained silent. The story was likely true—a quick trip to the library would confirm or disprove it, so Shen Yu wouldn't make up such an easily verifiable lie. But something about it felt off. Shen Yu, who rarely spoke more than a few words at a time, had just given a whole monologue. That in itself was suspicious.

Is Shen Yu Zhu Tianxing's reincarnation, or is this a red herring to distract me from my regressor theory?

Before Kai could voice his thoughts, Shen Yu continued speaking. "There's more," he said. "Do you remember the Eye of Veiled Truth during the Trial of Heart?"

Kai nodded slowly. How could he forget? That trial had been one of the most challenging experiences of his life. It had almost made him believe that he had lost access to the System.

"The eye doesn't just test a cultivator's heart. It also examines their soul. Cultivators who reincarnate cannot change the age of their soul. The eye can detect this discrepancy." Shen Yu's eyes bored into Kai's. "There are other signs too. Reincarnated cultivators often have unusual qi patterns, remnants of their previous cultivation methods that linger in their spiritual essence. If I were a reincarnator, it would have exposed me instantly."

That would only be true if Shen Yu was a mortal in his previous life. If he was an immortal . . . he might have ways to trick even an artifact like the Eye of Veiled Truth.

"Your excuses are no better than my illusion excuse," Kai replied.

Shen Yu frowned, but before he could say anything, Kai continued, "As you know, you can't kill me, and I get a strong feeling that I would be a fool to try to kill you. There's no reason for us to fight each other." *At least right now*, he added silently. "So why don't we keep what we know to ourselves? I don't see any reason why anyone else needs to know."

"Just because you can come back to life, it doesn't mean you cannot die," Shen Yu murmured. "True immortality is a lie, no matter what the immortals may preach."

Kai couldn't help but laugh at that. "Don't act like you're here to kill me," he said. "You've been warning me about the Sect Master and whatever else you're worried about is coming next. Your behavior makes me think you want to team up, but I have to admit, you're not doing a good job expressing that."

Shen Yu looked lost in thought for a moment. "Partners," he muttered, almost to himself. Kai noticed something flash in his eyes—was it hurt? Anger? He couldn't tell before the Legacy Disciple's eyes gained clarity again. "Yes," Shen Yu whispered. "I guess we can be that."

Kai nodded, relieved. They had finally made some progress.

"Then tell me, what was the warning you mentioned? What is it that I need to prepare for?"

CHAPTER FIFTY-SIX

Shen Yu's eyes met Kai's, his expression unreadable. "War," he said, his voice barely above a whisper.

Kai blinked, taken aback by the sudden declaration. "War? With who? A demonic sect?"

Shen Yu shook his head, his gaze drifting to the horizon. "Crimson Phoenix Sect," he replied, his voice carrying a weight that Kai couldn't quite decipher.

"Why?"

"There is no why. The war is meaningless. It won't amount to much, except for the death of tens of thousands of disciples."

Kai's brow furrowed as he processed this information. "Maybe we could prevent it?"

Shen Yu turned back to face him, his green eyes piercing through him. "Low-ranked disciples won't be able to prevent the war or change its outcome. All you need to do is stay alive."

Kai raised an eyebrow, surprised by Shen Yu's apparent concern. "And when did you start caring about my life?"

"We're partners now, aren't we?" Shen Yu replied, his tone matter-of-fact.

Kai studied Shen Yu's face, searching for any hint of deception. "Why are you so interested in me? You've kept an eye on me all this time. What makes me so special?"

Shen Yu's expression remained impassive. "Just stay alive," he repeated, avoiding the question.

Kai decided to try a different approach. "How did it end last time, during your previous life?" he asked, probing for more information about the war.

Shen Yu's eyes narrowed slightly. "Before you continue with your time-traveling nonsense, remember that it's possible to get information from sources other than within the sect," he said, then paused for a moment before adding, "There are some techniques in this world that would shock even you."

I don't know what's more shocking than avoiding death over and over again.

"With your title as Legacy Disciple and alchemist, it should keep you off any dangerous battlefields," Shen Yu continued. Then, almost as an afterthought, he added, "This is a good time for you and your little group to make some profit from your pills business. I don't really care as long as you stay alive."

"There's something else I've been meaning to ask you. Why did you tell me not to take the Sect Master as my master?"

For a moment, it was silent. It seemed Shen Yu might ignore the question. But then his eyes hardened. "It would have been better to keep yourself off the Sect Master's radar."

"Is this related to the disappearances? The missing disciples?"

Shen Yu's lips twitched in what might have been a smile, or perhaps a grimace. "Sure."

Kai found that response strange. He could tell there was more to it than Shen Yu was letting on. The casual "sure" seemed at odds with the gravity of the situation. It was as if Shen Yu was confirming Kai's suspicion while simultaneously dismissing its importance.

"What aren't you telling me?" Kai pressed, taking a step closer to Shen Yu. "There's more to this, isn't there? What do you know about the Sect Master?"

Shen Yu's eyes narrowed slightly, the only indication that Kai's questions had struck a nerve. "I've told you what you need to know. Focus on staying alive and preparing for the war. That's all that matters right now."

Kai opened his mouth to ask more questions, but Shen Yu had already begun to walk away.

"What are you going to do?" he called out, trying one last time to get more information.

Shen Yu turned, a glint in his eye. "What I do best," he replied cryptically. Before Kai could ask for clarification, Shen Yu's token activated, and he disappeared.

Left alone, Kai stood in silence, his mind on the news he had just received. The Azure Sky Sect and the Crimson Phoenix Sect were going to war. He needed to prepare. With a deep breath, Kai reached into his inventory and pulled out his own token. He activated it and felt the familiar pull as he was transported back to the sect.

Back in his quarters at the Azure Sky Sect, Kai sat facing Chen Wei, Liu Wei, and Zhi-Zhi. He had been in Storm's Peak for around two days, and it was time to catch up on what had happened in his absence.

"First things first," Kai said, turning to Chen Wei. "How have our sales been going?"

Chen Wei's face lit up. He reached into his robes and pulled out a pouch, which he handed to Kai. "We've sold all the pills, Senior Brother Kai," he said proudly. "This pouch contains over a thousand spirit stones."

Kai nodded, pleased. The money would be useful in the coming days. "Good work," he said. "I think it's time we expand our operation. I'll hire another alchemist to help Xie Li produce more low-grade qi-gathering pills."

The others nodded, looking excited at the prospect of growing their business. But Kai knew he had more important matters to discuss.

"Now," he said, his tone becoming more serious, "I want to know how your cultivation is progressing. Liu Wei, let's start with you."

Liu Wei straightened up, a mix of pride and nervousness on his face. "I've broken through to Qi Refining stage six, Master."

Kai nodded and offered a word of congratulation, but inwardly he couldn't help but think, *That's still too low. We need to push harder.*

"Chen Wei?" Kai asked, turning to the former merchant's son.

"I'm close to breaking through to Qi Refining stage eight, Senior Brother."

Kai nodded, pleased with Chen Wei's progress. Finally, he turned to Zhi-Zhi.

"I'm very close to breaking through to Foundation Establishment." The spirit tortoise shifted slightly. "I'll be training with Master for the next week. He's going to help me with the breakthrough."

Kai didn't know much about the breakthrough process for spirit beasts, but he knew it was very different from humans. The flood dragon's attempted breakthrough at Storm's Peak had demonstrated that clearly enough. It was good that Cang Long would be helping Zhi-Zhi through the process.

"That's excellent news, Zhi-Zhi. Make sure you listen to Master Cang Long's instructions carefully."

Kai reached into his storage ring and pulled out several bottles of low-grade qi-gathering pills. He placed them on the table in front of his followers.

"I'll be preparing more of these for you. Take as many as you need to speed up your cultivation. But be careful," he warned, his voice serious. "Overreliance can lead to a shaky foundation and sometimes even qi toxicity. Use them wisely."

The others nodded.

"From now on, I want you all to prioritize your cultivation," Kai continued, his tone leaving no room for argument. "It's crucial that you advance as quickly as possible while maintaining a solid foundation."

Liu Wei leaned forward slightly, his brow furrowed. "Master, why the sudden urgency? I can tell something has you worried."

Kai took a deep breath. "What I'm about to tell you shouldn't leave this room," he said, then waited for each of them to nod in agreement before continuing, "I've received news that the Azure Sky Sect will likely be going to war soon."

The room erupted with questions.

"War? With who?"

"When?"

"Why?"

Kai held up a hand to quiet them. "The details don't matter right now. All you need to do is focus on your cultivation. I won't be able to protect you on the battlefield." He then looked at each of them in turn. "How are your trident marks coming along?"

They all reported that about a third of their marks were complete.

Kai nodded, his expression thoughtful. "Alongside your current mission of selling pills, your new mission is to break through. We need to finish your marks before the war begins."

Chen Wei couldn't help but ask, "Is the Qi Condensation skill really that powerful, Senior Brother?"

Kai looked at him for a long moment. "Yes, it is," he said simply. But inwardly, he thought, *A complete mark will give you a chance to evade death. And that's what matters most.*

"All right, you're dismissed," Kai said. "Except for you, Chen Wei. I need to speak with you." As the others filed out, Kai turned to his servant. "Do you know of Su Jie?"

"Yes, he's an Outer Disciple. Why do you ask?"

"I need you to tell him to meet me in three hours at the grove," Kai said. The grove was a quiet spot, perfect for a discreet meeting. It would be better than having Su Jie come to the Legacy Disciple quarters.

Chen Wei looked confused but nodded. "Of course, Senior Brother. I'll deliver the message right away."

As Chen Wei left to carry out his task, Kai found himself alone with his thoughts. He began to prioritize his next steps.

His main focus needed to be his own cultivation. He still had three meridians to reopen using the Heavenly Thunderstorm method. His second priority was the pill business, which meant he needed to deal with Su Fang soon. And third . . . Kai's thoughts turned to Su Jie. He had a dangerous mission in mind for the young disciple, one that would take him outside the sect to gather information on the Crimson Phoenix Sect. It was risky, but Kai had a feeling Su Jie was well suited for this type of covert operation.

Kai prepared to take a short nap before his meeting with Su Jie. He closed his eyes, and suddenly, he found himself back on Storm's Peak, the scene as vivid and real as if he were reliving it.

The sky above him darkened. He could feel the electric charge in the air making his hair stand on end. Looking up, he saw it forming—the massive Divine Sky Hammer.

In this vision, time seemed to slow. Kai could see every detail of the technique—how the lightning coalesced, the way the qi flowed and compressed into the hammer's form. He felt the overwhelming power, the sheer destructive force contained within it.

As the hammer descended, Kai's mind kicked into overdrive. He noticed the intricate patterns of energy, the complex weave of lightning and qi. It was beautiful in its terrible power.

Just before impact, his eyes snapped open. The vision faded, but the memory of it burned bright in his mind. He sat up, his heart racing not from fear but from excitement.

That technique . . . I saw how it was formed. The principles behind it. Maybe . . .

As if responding to his thoughts, a notification appeared in his vision:

New Quest: Architect—Create Your First Technique
Objective: Develop an original technique based on your observations and understanding of cultivation principles.
Reward: 3000 XP

Kai couldn't help but smile. It seemed the System approved. Creating his own technique would be challenging, but if he could pull it off, it would be a significant boost to his combat capabilities.

And the three thousand XP that comes with it won't hurt.

With the war looming on the horizon, Kai knew he needed every advantage he could get.

CHAPTER FIFTY-SEVEN

The grove was once part of the Azure Sky Sect's Outer Sect but was now a silent reminder of a devastating battle with demonic cultivators from thousands of years ago.

The ruins of training halls and dormitories lay scattered among overgrown vegetation. Broken stone pillars and crumbling walls peeked out from beneath tangles of vines and roots.

Most disciples avoided this place, finding it unsettling, which made it an ideal location for a secret meeting.

As Kai walked into the grove, he spotted Su Jie leaning against one of the trees, his arms crossed and a scowl on his face. The young disciple straightened as Kai drew closer, his expression a mix of relief and annoyance.

"Senior Brother Kai," Su Jie said, bowing slightly. "I was beginning to think you'd forgotten about me."

Kai raised an eyebrow. "Forgotten? It's only been a few days since our last meeting."

Su Jie's scowl deepened. "A few days? It's been over a week! You said you'd contact me soon, but then nothing. I've been coming here every day, waiting."

Over a week? Kai thought, momentarily surprised. *Has it really been that long? Time flies when you're fighting flood dragons and planning for war, I guess.*

"Ah, I apologize for the delay, Su Jie. Some urgent matters came up that required my immediate attention."

Su Jie's expression softened slightly, but he still looked frustrated. "I understand that you're busy, Senior Brother, but a message would have been nice. I was worried you'd changed your mind about our . . . arrangement."

Kai shook his head. "No, nothing like that. In fact, I have an important mission for you."

Su Jie's eyes widened as curiosity replaced his annoyance. "A mission? What kind of mission?"

Kai glanced around, making sure they were alone. "It's a delicate matter," he said, lowering his voice. "I need you to gather some information for me. Specifically, about the Crimson Phoenix Sect."

"The Crimson Phoenix Sect? Are you crazy?" Su Jie's eyes widened in shock. "They'd kill me if they caught me spying!"

"Calm down," Kai said, holding up a hand. "I'm not asking you to sneak into their sect. That would be suicide, you're right. What I need is for you to visit the towns under Crimson Phoenix territory."

"The towns? What for?"

"To look for signs. Small things that might indicate they're preparing for something big. Increased patrols, stockpiling of resources, that sort of thing. The townspeople might not know exactly what is going on, but they'd pick up on a change. I'm sure there are some whispers floating around."

"But why? What's going on?"

Kai hesitated, then decided a partial truth was necessary. "I have reason to believe there might be conflict between our sects soon. I need to know if the Crimson Phoenix Sect is making any unusual moves."

Su Jie's face paled. "Conflict? You mean . . . war?"

"Potentially." Kai nodded. "That's why this information is so important."

"I don't know, Senior Brother." Su Jie swallowed hard, looking nervous. "This sounds really dangerous. What if I get caught?"

"You won't be doing anything wrong," Kai assured him. "Just visit the towns and keep your eyes and ears open. Act like a regular traveler. You're quick, observant, and most importantly, you know how to stay out of sight when you need to."

Su Jie still looked uncertain. Kai decided it was time for some extra motivation.

"Remember our arrangement, Su Jie," Kai said, his voice taking on a harder edge. "I saved your life and agreed to help you advance. In return, you work for me."

"I know, I know." Su Jie winced at the reminder but nodded reluctantly. "It's just . . . This is big, you know?"

"I'm not asking you to do this for free," Kai continued, his voice softening slightly. "Complete this mission successfully, and I'll give you a low-grade qi-gathering pill as a reward."

Su Jie's head snapped up, his eyes wide. "A low-grade qi-gathering pill? Really?"

Kai nodded. "Really. It should help speed up your cultivation significantly."

Su Jie bit his lip, clearly tempted. After a moment, he said, "Two pills."

"Excuse me?"

"I want two low-grade qi-gathering pills," Su Jie said, a hint of defiance in his voice. "This mission is dangerous. If I'm risking my neck, I want to make sure it's worth it."

He's got guts, I'll give him that. And two pills aren't really that much in the grand scheme of things.

"All right," Kai said finally. "Two pills. But only if the information you bring back is truly valuable. Deal?"

Su Jie grinned and bowed. "Deal!"

Kai bowed back, sealing their agreement. "Good. Now, here's what I need you to do . . ."

For the next half hour, Kai outlined the details of the mission. He explained which areas of the Crimson Phoenix Sect territory Su Jie should focus on, what kind of information to look for, and how to report back safely. Su Jie listened intently, asking questions and making mental notes.

"Remember, Su Jie, discretion is key. Don't take unnecessary risks, and if you feel like you're in danger, abort the mission immediately. Your safety is more important than the information."

"I understand, Senior Brother. I won't let you down."

"Good," Kai said. "You have one week. Meet me back here at the same time next week, and we'll discuss what you've found." As Su Jie turned to leave, Kai called out, "And Su Jie? Be careful."

The young disciple flashed a confident grin. "Always am, Senior Brother. Always am."

Kai watched as Su Jie disappeared into the shadows.

I hope I'm doing the right thing. But we need this information. If war is coming, we need to be prepared.

With a sigh, he turned and made his way back to his quarters. He had his own work to do.

Kai sat cross-legged in his private practice area outside his quarters. The sun warmed his face as a gentle breeze rustled the leaves of nearby trees. It had been a few days since his return from Storm's Peak, and he'd been busy getting things in order, Su Jie's mission being one of them.

Opening his eyes, Kai glanced at a small table nearby. On it sat several bottles of freshly made low-grade qi-gathering pills. A smile spread across his face as he thought about his recent conversation with Xie Li.

"Senior Brother Kai," Xie Li had said, "I've made a decision about your offer."

Kai had raised an eyebrow, trying not to show his eagerness. After her initial reluctance, he'd been unsure of her final decision. "And?" he'd prompted.

Xie Li's face had broken into a shy smile. "I'd like to accept the full-time position, if it's still available."

"Of course it is," Kai had replied, keeping his tone casual despite his relief. "I'm glad you've decided to join us permanently."

"The trial period has really helped me see the benefits of our arrangement," Xie Li had explained. "And I've enjoyed the work more than I expected."

They'd quickly settled on the details—a fixed salary of five spirit stones per pill, with Kai providing all necessary materials.

"Xie Li, there's something else I wanted to discuss," he'd said. "With everything going on, I'm going to be quite busy. I was thinking of bringing on another alchemist to help out. What do you think?"

Xie Li had looked thoughtful for a moment. "That makes sense, Senior Brother. In fact, I might know someone who could help. A friend of mine loves alchemy just as much as me. Would it be all right if I asked her?"

Kai had nodded, pleased that he wouldn't need to waste his time searching. "That would be great. As long as you trust her, I'm happy to offer her the position."

"I do trust her," Xie Li had assured him. "She's reliable and talented. I'll speak with her and let you know what she says."

As Xie Li had left, there was a new spring in her step.

Finally, Kai had thought, watching her go. *One reliable alchemist secured, maybe even two.*

Now, days later, Kai refocused his attention on the task at hand. He closed his eyes again and visualized the Divine Sky Hammer technique. The memory of that colossal lightning construct still sent shivers down his spine. But he'd been struggling to replicate the technique.

He'd decided to prioritize creating this technique over reawakening another meridian. The potential three thousand XP reward was significant, and having a powerful offensive technique would be more immediately useful in the face of the looming conflict with the Crimson Phoenix Sect.

Kai closed his eyes and recalled the moment the Divine Sky Hammer had formed high in the sky above the battlefield. He began breaking down the technique into simpler steps.

Step one: Gather lightning-natured qi in the sky.

Step two: Compress the qi into a dense core.

Step three: Shape the compressed qi into a hammer form.

Step four: Stabilize the construct.

Step five: Direct and release the technique.

"All right, let's try again."

Kai raised his hand and focused on gathering lightning-natured qi not in his palm, as he usually would, but in the air above him. Manipulating elemental qi was already proving more challenging than his usual Qi Condensation skill—creating a construct at a distance was a whole different ball game.

Sparks danced in the air several meters above his head as he pulled qi from his surroundings. It was like trying to manipulate a puppet with very long invisible strings.

So far, so good, but much harder than usual.

Next, he attempted to compress the gathered qi. This proved even more challenging than the gathering phase. The energy sparked and fizzled, resisting his efforts to condense it further. Unlike his usual Qi Condensation, where he could physically cup the qi in his hands, this distant manipulation required much more focus and control.

Kai frowned. *Why isn't this working? Wait . . . Maybe I can apply some alchemy techniques here.*

He considered the Essence Extraction technique he used in pill-making. The process of drawing out the purest essence from materials wasn't so different from what he was trying to do with the lightning qi, even at a distance.

Kai tried again, and this time, he imagined the lightning qi as a raw material floating in the sky. He focused on extracting its purest form and slowly condensing it into a tight ball of energy high above his head. To his surprise, it worked. The qi compressed more easily, forming a pulsing orb of lightning energy.

"Now we're getting somewhere."

The next step was shaping the compressed qi into a hammer form, all while maintaining its position in the air. Kai pondered this for a moment. In alchemy, the Elemental Fusion technique allowed for combining different elemental properties. Perhaps he could use a similar principle here, fusing different "parts" of the lightning qi to form the hammer's shape.

He focused on the compressed ball of energy hovering above, willing it to stretch and form. Slowly, painstakingly, the orb began to elongate and form a rough hammer shape. It was far from perfect, more of a lightning club than a hammer, but it was progress.

Kai's excitement grew. He was onto something here. But as he tried to maintain the shape high in the air, he felt it becoming unstable. The energy crackled dangerously, threatening to disperse.

Stability Control, Kai thought. Another alchemy technique that might help.

He took a deep breath and channeled his qi upwards to stabilize the construct. It was like trying to hold sand together with willpower alone. The lightning hammer flickered, its form wavering in the sky.

"Come on," Kai muttered through gritted teeth. "Hold together."

For a brief moment, the hammer stabilized. Kai's heart leaped with excitement. But then, just as quickly, it collapsed, dissipating in a shower of sparks that rained down around him, singeing the grass.

Kai fell back, panting from the effort. "Damn it," he cursed softly. He was close, so close. But something was still missing.

What am I overlooking? The gathering and compression worked well enough, even at a distance. Shaping was tricky but possible. It's the stability that's the real issue.

He thought back to the Zhen Lei Shenjiao's Divine Sky Hammer. What made it different? It was massive, yes, but it was also . . . cohesive. The lightning that formed it moved as one—not just a collection of electrical charges, but a single unified force.

Kai's eyes widened as realization struck. "Spiritual Resonance," he whispered.

In alchemy, the Spiritual Resonance technique was used to attune creations to specific spiritual frequencies. What if he could apply that principle here? Not just shaping the lightning but attuning it to resonate with itself, thus creating a more stable, unified construct, even when formed high in the sky.

Excited, Kai stood up, ready to try again. He gathered the lightning qi in the air above him, compressing it as he had before. This time, as he shaped it into a hammer form, he focused on more than just the physical shape. He concentrated on the energy itself and willed it to resonate at the same frequency.

There was a humming in the air as the lightning hammer took form high above. It was smaller than the Zhen Lei Shenjiao's version but still significantly larger than anything he could create using Qi Condensation from a distance.

"I . . . I did it," Kai breathed.

But he wasn't done yet. The final step was to direct and release the technique. He looked around and spotted a large boulder at the edge of his practice area. Perfect.

Kai focused on the hammer floating above and established a connection with it that felt different from his usual qi manipulation. With a sharp exhalation, he directed the lightning hammer toward the boulder.

It shot down from the sky with incredible speed and struck the boulder with a thunderous crack. There was a blinding flash, and when his vision cleared, Kai saw a sizable chunk of the boulder had been obliterated, leaving a scorched, smoking crater.

Quest Complete: Architect—Create Your First Technique
Objective: Develop an original technique based on your observations and understanding of cultivation principles.
Reward: 3000 XP

Technique Created: Lightning Hammer Strike
Description: A powerful lightning construct in the shape of a hammer, formed at a distance and directed to strike with devastating effect.

Kai couldn't help but laugh out loud. He'd done it. He'd created his own technique based on the Divine Sky Hammer. It wasn't as powerful as the original, of course, but it was a start. And more importantly, it was his.

CHAPTER FIFTY-EIGHT

Redstone Village was a modest town. The main street wound its way through the center, lined with small shops and homes. At one end stood the town square, a wide-open space where markets and gatherings were held. On the other, a tavern called The Crimson Rooster dominated the view, its painted sign swinging gently in the evening breeze.

As night fell, the tavern doors swung open, and a group of men stumbled out.

"Can't believe I didn't get picked again!" a burly man with a thick beard grumbled, his words slurring slightly. "I'm strong as an ox, I am! What more could them immortals want?"

His companion, a lanky fellow with a receding hairline, nodded vigorously. "It ain't right, Huo. We've been waiting for days, and nothin'! How're we supposed to feed our families if we can't get honest work?"

A third man, shorter than the others but with arms like tree trunks, spat on the ground. "Heard they're paying in gold coins too. Gold! You know what I could do with even one of those shiny beauties?"

Their conversation drew the attention of a figure huddled in a nearby alley. A beggar dressed in tattered rags, his face hidden beneath a wide-brimmed hat, shuffled forward, holding out a trembling hand.

"Spare some coin for a hungry soul?" he croaked, his voice barely above a whisper.

The men barely spared him a glance, too caught up in their own troubles to notice the plea.

Unbeknownst to them, the beggar was far more than he appeared. Beneath the grime and rags was a cultivator. Su Jie had been here for the past three days, and his disguise had been working perfectly. No one gave a second thought to those beneath them; such was human nature.

Su Jie wasn't worried about being detected by other cultivators. Unless they were at the Foundation Establishment Realm or above, it was unlikely they'd realize he was anything more than a common beggar. He'd always had a knack for staying out of sight—it was what made it easy for him to pick pockets.

As he listened to the drunken men's conversation, Su Jie's ears perked up at a snippet of information.

"Hey, did you hear?" the lanky man said. "Word is, the immortal's coming back tomorrow one last time. We might still have a chance!"

"Well, I'll be sure to make a good impression this time." Huo flexed his arms. "They can't ignore these muscles forever!"

"How do you know they're looking for muscle, you lout?" the shorter man scoffed. "Could be they need smarts. In which case, I'd say I have a better shot than you."

This sparked an argument among the men, their voices rising as they debated what the immortals could possibly want with mere mortals.

"Makes no sense, if you ask me," Huo grumbled. "They're immortals! What do they need us for?"

The lanky man shrugged. "Who knows? But I heard they took old Wu the blacksmith last week. And Widow Liu's boy, the one who's good with numbers."

"Don't forget about Ming the carpenter," the short man added. "Seems like they're taking all sorts."

Su Jie shook his head. Mortals had no idea of the complexities involved in running a sect, let alone preparing for war. Even the mightiest cultivator relied on countless mundane tasks performed by ordinary people. But recruiting in such large numbers was uncommon . . .

As the voices faded into the distance, Su Jie sat back, pondering what he'd heard. It seemed the Crimson Phoenix Sect really was preparing for war. They were gathering mortals with various skills in bulk.

Su Jie weighed his options. He had enough information to report back to Kai, but something held him back.

Two pills. I want those two qi-gathering pills. This isn't enough to guarantee that reward.

After some internal debate, he decided to stay another day. If the immortal was truly returning tomorrow, he might learn even more valuable information. It was a risk, but one he felt was worth taking.

Besides, I've always been good at disappearing when things get too hot.

With a sigh, Su Jie settled deeper into his shadowy nook. It was going to be a long night, but if it meant getting closer to his goal, it would be worth it.

The next morning, the townsfolk gathered in the square as they waited for the immortal to arrive.

"Do you think they'll pick me this time?" a weaver asked her friend, fidgeting with her apron.

Her friend, a potter, shrugged. "Who knows? Last time they took blacksmiths and carpenters. Maybe it's our turn now."

Nearby, a group of young men talked in low voices.

"I heard they're looking for strong backs," one said, puffing out his chest.

Another shook his head. "Nah, they've got cultivators for that. We need to offer something special."

As the morning went on, more people arrived. Children played games while their parents talked about what might happen.

"What do immortals need us for, anyway?" an old cobbler wondered out loud.

A seamstress answered, "Maybe they need new clothes. Even immortals must get holes in their robes sometimes."

Suddenly, a child shouted, "Look up there!"

Everyone looked at the sky. A person in red robes was flying down on a shining sword. It was a young man. His face was smooth, and his red robes had golden birds on them. This was Cao Jiayi, from the Crimson Phoenix Sect.

As Cao Jiayi floated down, he frowned. *Why did they send me to do this boring job? I am a breath away from the Foundation Establishment Realm. I should be preparing for my breakthrough, not wasting my time on mortals. This is beneath me.*

His feet touched the ground softly, and he raised his hand for quiet. "Like the previous times, when I call your job, step forward."

The crowd whispered excitedly. Cao Jiayi looked at them, not impressed. "Weavers."

A group of people with callused hands moved to the front. "Potters."

Several men and women, their clothes stained with clay, joined the weavers. "Cobblers."

A few people who made shoes stepped up, looking nervous but hopeful. "Tailors and seamstresses."

A larger group came forward, carrying needles and measuring tapes.

As Cao Jiayi kept listing jobs, those not called started to complain quietly.

"Why aren't they taking farmers?" a man whispered to his wife.

"Maybe immortals don't need food," she joked back.

A group of strong young men stood to the side, looking sad. "I thought for sure they'd need people to carry heavy things."

"Guess they prefer skilled workers over strong ones," another replied, sounding bitter.

Cao Jiayi heard their complaints but didn't care. He was already thinking about going back to his sect. He looked at the ring on his finger, thinking about what it contained.

I hope the letter from the Boundless Earth Sect is good news. If they agree to work with us against the Azure Sky Sect, it could change everything.

He wanted to open the letter and read it, but he knew he couldn't. That information was only for the leader of his sect to see. His job was just to deliver it safely.

But first, I have to deal with these people, he reminded himself, looking back at the villagers.

As he began to address the chosen few, outlining what would be expected of them in service to the Crimson Phoenix Sect, the town leader approached. The man was short and round, with a shiny bald head and an ingratiating smile that made Cao Jiayi's skin crawl.

"Oh, most esteemed cultivator," the town leader began, bowing so low his forehead nearly touched the ground. "We are so grateful for your return. If there's anything I can do to assist you in your noble task—"

Cao Jiayi tuned out the man's fawning words, his senses suddenly alert. Something was wrong. He turned, scanning the crowd, and spotted the source of the disturbance.

A group of cattle, spooked by something, had broken free of their pen. They were charging toward the square, eyes rolling in panic.

Chaos erupted. People screamed and scattered, trying to get out of the way of the stampeding animals.

These mortals and their petty problems. As if mere beasts could threaten a cultivator.

Cao Jiayi watched with detached interest. He made no move to help, seeing no reason to waste his qi on such a trivial matter. Let the mortals sort it out themselves.

The stampede reached a crescendo as people pushed and shoved in their desperation to escape. Just then, a young woman came barreling through the crowd, her eyes wide with fear as she looked over her shoulder at the frightened beasts. Before Cao Jiayi could react, she slammed into him with surprising force.

The impact was nothing to a cultivator of his level, but it did cause him to stumble slightly. Irritation flashed across his face as he caught his balance. He fixed the woman with a withering glare, one that promised pain and suffering for the disrespect shown to him.

The poor woman's eyes went wide with horror as she realized what she'd done. A dark stain spread across her skirts as her bladder gave way in sheer terror.

Cao Jiayi's nose wrinkled in disgust. He turned away from the pitiful mortal and stepped onto his sword. As he rose into the air, a nagging feeling tugged at the back of his mind. Something felt . . . off.

He pushed the thought aside, focusing on the task at hand. From his vantage point, he watched as the cattle thundered through the square, causing chaos everywhere they went. Market stalls lay in splinters, goods scattered across the cobblestones.

Eventually, the cattle were rounded up, and a semblance of order returned to the square. As Cao Jiayi returned to the ground, the town leader scrambled forward once more, his fine silks now torn and muddied.

"M-most honored immortal," the man stammered, "please forgive this . . . this unfortunate incident. I assure you, nothing like this has ever—"

Cao Jiayi silenced him with a look. He had no interest in the man's excuses. All he wanted now was to gather these mortals and be on his way back to the sect.

He reached for his storage ring, intending to summon the flying vessel that would transport the chosen workers. His fingers brushed against bare skin.

Cao Jiayi froze. He looked down at his hand. The ring was gone.

In an instant, his carefully cultivated calm shattered. Rage boiled up inside him, and with it, his qi exploded outward. An invisible wave of pressure slammed into the mortals and drove them to their knees as they cried out in pain and shock.

"You dare?" Cao Jiayi roared, his voice echoing across the square.

Moving faster than regular eyes could see, he appeared in front of the woman who had bumped into him earlier. She cowered before him, shaking uncontrollably.

"Where is it?" he demanded, his voice low and dangerous.

"W-what?" the woman stammered, crying. "I don't know what you're talking about, great immortal. Please, I didn't do anything wrong!"

Cao Jiayi's eyes narrowed. He used his spiritual sense to scan the woman thoroughly. To his frustration, he found nothing. The storage ring wasn't on her.

"You," he growled. "You bumped into me. You must have taken it."

"No, no!" the woman wailed. "I would never steal from an immortal! Please believe me!"

Cao Jiayi gritted his teeth. He could tell she was telling the truth—or at least, she thought she was telling the truth. But if she didn't have the ring, where was it?

The letter—I can't lose the letter!

"Everyone, stay where you are!" he commanded, his voice now sounding a bit panicked. "No one leaves until I find what was stolen from me!"

The townsfolk, still under the pressure of his power, could only nod weakly. They didn't understand what was happening, but they knew better than to disobey an angry immortal.

As Cao Jiayi scanned one mortal after another for the unique spiritual signature that marked the storage ring as his, he failed to notice a figure slipping away from the town.

A beggar, his face hidden under a hat, moved surprisingly quickly for someone who looked so weak. His hand closed around a small object in his pocket—a ring.

Two qi-gathering pills, Su Jie thought to himself. *This should be more than enough to earn them.*

With one last look at the town, he disappeared into the forest, leaving behind a very angry immortal and a group of very confused mortals.

CHAPTER FIFTY-NINE

A crown of lightning danced around Kai's head as he sat cross-legged on his cultivation pillow. He'd been at this for days, pushing himself to the limit. But now, finally, he felt it. With one last push, the last bits of resistance in his body gave way, and his eyes snapped open, a smile spreading across his face.

Congratulations!
You have successfully opened the Charged Wave Meridian!
Cultivation returned to Qi Refining Stage 9
Lightning Affinity increased to 45%

Skill Leveled Up!
Crown of Lightning (Level 7)
Effect: A temporary visible aura of lightning can form around the cultivator's head during meditation, which boosts the cultivator's qi regeneration by 35%.

Skill Leveled Up!
Sky's Favor (Level 7)
Effect: The cultivator's qi-absorption rate increases by 35% whenever they are under an open sky. This increases to 40% during stormy weather.

Skill Leveled Up!
Electric Immunity (Level 7)
Effect: The cultivator gains 35% resistance to lightning-based attacks, reducing the damage taken from electric or lightning-based techniques.

You have gained 300 XP!

Kai let out a satisfied sigh, running a hand through his hair. The progress was welcome, but he couldn't help feeling a twinge of impatience.

"Two meridians left," he muttered, his eyes narrowing slightly. *Two more before I can start preparing for my breakthrough to Foundation Establishment. But with war on the horizon, I don't see myself entering the next realm of cultivation anytime soon . . .*

In this world, those in the Qi Refining Realm were barely considered cultivators at all. They were superhuman, yes, capable of feats that would astound those back on Earth, but their lifespans remained the same as any other mortal.

It was only at the Foundation Establishment Realm that one could begin to call themselves an immortal. Cultivators at that level could live for double or even triple the lifespan of a normal mortal. Kai had even heard stories of the oldest Foundation Establishment cultivator, who was just shy of his three hundredth birthday. Not that anyone in this world celebrated birthdays like they did back on Earth. Here, such celebrations were rare events, reserved only for when one reached a huge milestone like the millennium mark or beyond.

A knock at the door interrupted Kai's thoughts. "Enter."

The door slid open, and Chen Wei stepped in. "Senior Brother, I hope I'm not interrupting. I'm here to remind you that a week has passed since your last meeting with . . . the individual you asked me to keep track of."

"Thank you, Chen Wei. You're not interrupting at all. In fact, your timing is perfect."

"Is there anything else you need?"

"No, that'll be all."

As Chen Wei left, closing the door behind him, Kai stood up. He had promised Su Jie that he would meet him in a week's time, and he didn't want to leave the disciple stranded. Especially since whatever info Su Jie returned with would determine Kai's next steps.

He quickly changed into fresh black robes and made his way out of his quarters.

I really hope Shen Yu is wrong, Kai thought, his jaw clenching. *I hope there is no war. Back on Earth, it always sounded so epic in movies and novels. But living it . . . That's something else entirely. Not that I'm likely to live through it if it comes to that. In a war between sects, what chance does a Qi Refining cultivator really have? Even with my advantages, I'd be nothing more than cannon fodder against Foundation Establishment cultivators, let alone anyone higher. Sure, I've got a few extra lives thanks to this System, but Shen Yu was right. I'm not immortal. Not even close.*

As Kai entered the grove, he noticed something different about Su Jie.

The young disciple leaned against a tree, eyes closed, looking strangely . . . peaceful.

I hope that means he has good news . . .

As if sensing Kai's presence, Su Jie's eyes fluttered open. A smile spread across his face as he bowed. "Senior Brother Kai."

Kai nodded in return. "Su Jie. You look . . . different today."

"Do I?" Su Jie's smile widened. "I guess I'm feeling pretty good about my mission."

"Oh?" Kai raised an eyebrow. "Tell me what you found out. Tell me everything," Kai said, leaning against a broken pillar. "What did you learn about the Crimson Phoenix Sect's movements?"

"They're definitely up to something big, Senior Brother. I visited several towns under their control, and the signs are everywhere."

"Go on."

"First off, they're recruiting mortals in large numbers," Su Jie began. "Craftsmen, mostly. Weavers, potters, cobblers, tailors—anyone with a useful trade. But here's the weird part: they're not taking farmers or laborers."

"That is strange." Kai furrowed his brow. "You'd think they'd need food and manual labor more than anything."

"Exactly! It's like they're preparing for something specific, not just general expansion."

"What else?"

"Well, I overheard some drunk men complaining about not being chosen. They mentioned the recruiters were paying in gold coins. Gold, Senior Brother! That's not normal payment for mortal workers."

"Did you notice any increased military presence?"

"Not really." Su Jie shook his head. "If anything, there seemed to be fewer Crimson Phoenix disciples around than usual. It's like they're pulling back their forces."

Interesting. They're gathering resources but not showing military strength. Are they trying to avoid drawing attention?

"Anything else of note?"

"Well . . . there was one more thing. But it might be nothing."

"Let me be the judge of that," Kai said. "What is it?"

"On my last day there, a Crimson Phoenix disciple came to the town I was in. He was recruiting more workers, but he seemed . . . distracted. Kept fiddling with a ring on his finger and muttering to himself."

"A ring? What kind of ring?"

Su Jie shrugged. "I couldn't get a good look, but it seemed important to him. He kept glancing at it like he was worried about something."

A storage ring, perhaps? Carrying an important message?

Kai nodded slowly. "You've done well, Su Jie. This information is valuable, but . . ." He paused, reaching into his robes. "I'm afraid it's not quite enough for two low-grade qi-gathering pills."

He pulled out a single pill and with a flick of his wrist, he tossed it to Su Jie, who caught it in between his index and middle fingers.

Su Jie looked at the pill, then back at Kai. A sly smile crept across his face. "Oh, I think you might want to reconsider that, Senior Brother."

Before Kai could respond, Su Jie reached into his own robes and pulled out a small object.

"Is that . . ." Kai's eyes widened in surprise.

Su Jie's grin widened as he tossed the object to Kai. "The ring I was talking about, Senior Brother. I got more than a good look. Snatched it right off that Crimson Phoenix disciple's finger."

Kai caught the ring and turned it over in his palm. It was indeed a storage ring, and a decent quality one at that.

"Well, well." Kai chuckled. "I see your fast hands haven't lost their touch."

Su Jie bowed playfully. "I aim to please, Senior Brother."

It seems I was right to choose him.

Kai focused his attention on the ring and called up the System to examine it.

Item: Crimson Phoenix Storage Ring

Quality: High-Grade

Description: A spatial storage device used by disciples of the Crimson Phoenix Sect. Contains unknown items.

Kai closed his eyes and channeled his spiritual sense into the ring. He encountered a barrier: an intricate web of spiritual energy was blocking his probe.

Warning: Access restricted. Spiritual lock detected.

Hmm, as expected. It won't be easy to open.

"I tried to open it myself," Su Jie admitted. "But I didn't have much luck."

Kai nodded, opening his eyes. "These rings are usually locked with the owner's spiritual mark. There are ways around it, but they're not easy."

"Can you break it open?"

"There are two main methods," Kai explained. "One is brute force, but that only works if your cultivation is significantly higher than the owner's. We'd need a Foundation Establishment cultivator for that."

Su Jie's face fell. "Oh. What's the other way?"

"It's like . . . spiritual lockpicking," Kai said. "Using your spiritual sense to manipulate the lock's energy patterns. It's delicate work, but it doesn't require overwhelming power."

"Are you going to try it?" Su Jie leaned forward.

"Why not?" Kai smirked. "It's a good chance to practice."

He closed his eyes again as he focused his spiritual sense on the ring's lock. Carefully, he began to probe the energy patterns, looking for weaknesses or inconsistencies.

It's like a puzzle. Each strand of energy interacts with the others. If I can just find the right sequence . . .

Kai's brow furrowed in concentration as he manipulated the spiritual energies. Suddenly, he felt a sharp backlash, like a mental slap.

"Ow!" His eyes snapped open, and he rubbed his temples.

"What happened?"

"I made a mistake." Kai grimaced. "Triggered some kind of defense mechanism."

"Are you okay?"

"I'm fine," Kai assured him. "Just a bit of a headache. But I learned something from that failure."

The lock doesn't just block access. It actively repels intruders. I need to be more subtle.

Kai took a deep breath and tried again. This time, instead of directly manipulating the energy strands, he gently nudged them, encouraging them to move on their own.

Like coaxing a stubborn animal. Don't force it. Guide it.

Slowly, painstakingly, the spiritual lock began to unravel, and soon the last barrier fell away.

"I did it," he said, opening his eyes with a grin.

Su Jie clapped his hands. "What's inside?"

Kai peered into the ring's spiritual space. "There's . . . quite a bit, actually. A thousand low-grade spirit stones, for one."

"A thousand?" Su Jie's jaw dropped. "That's . . . that's a fortune!"

Kai nodded. "For a Qi Refining disciple, certainly. There are also some cultivation scrolls . . ." He paused, his spiritual sense touching something else. "And a letter."

"A letter?"

Kai reached in and pulled out the scroll. The seal was still intact, bearing the mark of the Boundless Earth Sect.

"Should we open it?" Su Jie asked, eyeing the scroll nervously.

Kai nodded. "We've come this far. Might as well see what's so important."

He broke the seal and unrolled the scroll. The handwriting was elegant, clearly belonging to a well-educated cultivator.

Aloud, Kai read, "My dear old friend, I hope this letter finds you well. It has been far too long since we shared a cup of spirit tea and reminisced about our younger days. How I miss those carefree times! I must say, your proposal caught me quite by surprise. War between the Azure Sky Sect and the Crimson Phoenix Sect? Again? Sometimes I wonder if you youngsters ever learn from history.

"I understand your eagerness, my friend, but I'm afraid the Boundless Earth Sect cannot openly join this conflict at this time. You know as well as I do that these wars between your sects tend to end in stalemate, with both sides licking their wounds for decades afterward. However, I haven't forgotten our friendship or the debts I owe you. While I cannot commit our sect's full strength, I am willing to send some of my personal forces to aid you. We can use this opportunity to weaken some of the Azure Sky Sect's affiliates, which may prove beneficial in the long run.

"That said, if you're truly set on this path, you might consider sweetening the pot, so to speak. The Sect Master is . . . shall we say, practical in his thinking. If the Crimson Phoenix Sect were to offer some additional incentives, I might have a better chance of swaying him to your cause.

"Think it over, old friend. And regardless of what comes, do try to stay alive. I'd hate to lose my favorite drinking partner to another senseless war. May the earth beneath your feet always be stable. Elder Teng."

Kai finished reading and looked up at Su Jie, who seemed overwhelmed by the contents of the letter.

"Senior Brother," Su Jie whispered, "this is . . . big, isn't it?"

"Very big. It confirms that the Crimson Phoenix Sect is indeed planning for war. But more importantly, it gives us insight into the political maneuvering behind the scenes."

"What do you mean?"

"Let's break this down. First, we have the Crimson Phoenix Sect, clearly the aggressors in this situation. They're reaching out to potential allies, trying to build a coalition against the Azure Sky Sect."

"But the Boundless Earth Sect said no, right?" Su Jie interjected.

"Not exactly," Kai corrected. "They're playing a more subtle game. Elder Teng, the author of this letter, is offering limited support through his personal forces. This allows the Boundless Earth Sect to maintain official neutrality while still potentially weakening their rivals."

Su Jie's eyes widened. "So, they get the benefits without the risks?"

"Precisely." Kai nodded. "But there's more. Notice how Elder Teng mentions 'sweetening the pot'? He's angling for more concessions from the Crimson Phoenix Sect. It's a delicate balancing act—he wants to help his friend and gain advantages for his sect but without committing too deeply."

"That's . . . kind of scary," Su Jie admitted. "All this plotting and scheming."

Kai smiled wryly. "Welcome to the world of high-level cultivation politics, Su Jie. It's all about power, influence, and calculated risks. More than the petty theft you're used to."

"So, what do we do with this information?"

Kai fell silent for a moment, considering their options. *This is sensitive information. If I keep it to myself, I could look to see if there is any way for me to use it for personal gain. But both my guild and I are too weak, only Qi Refining cultivators. This Elder Teng's followers are likely above our cultivation and probably by a lot.*

It would be better to see if it can benefit the sect instead of myself. If Shen Yu is right and war is unavoidable, I'd rather see the Azure Sky Sect come out on top. At least then I'd have a chance at survival and future growth. So, my only option is to take it to Master . . .

Kai didn't trust the Azure Sky Sect Master, but the man was the only one with the power to make a real difference in the coming conflict. And Kai had to be realistic—it was unlikely that his own secret intelligence network, which consisted solely of Su Jie at the moment, was better than the sect's. Assuming the Sect Master didn't already know about the impending war would be naive and arrogant.

Also, bringing this to the Sect Master could earn me some favor. He's been trying to play the patient teacher to lower my guard. Well . . . two can play at that game.

"We take it to the Sect Master," Kai said finally. "This is too big for us to handle alone. Besides, it's our duty to report such vital information."

Su Jie's eyes widened. "We're going to see the Sect Master? Together?"

Kai chuckled. "No, not we. I'll handle this part. You've done more than enough already, Su Jie. In fact . . ."

He reached into his robes and pulled out a second low-grade qi-gathering pill. Su Jie's jaw dropped as Kai tossed it to him.

"You've more than earned this," Kai said with a smile. "The information you gathered, combined with this storage ring and letter . . . It's been helpful. Use these pills wisely. We don't want another Qi Deviation situation happening. Oh, and keep training. I have a feeling we'll do great things together."

CHAPTER SIXTY

E nter."

Kai pushed open the doors to the Sect Master's quarters and stepped inside. He found his master standing with his hands clasped behind his back, gazing out of the window.

"Greetings, Master."

As Kai closed the door behind him, Luo Qiang turned around. "Ah, my disciple. What brings you here? Are you struggling with your cultivation?"

Kai shook his head. "No, Master. I've come with important information." He reached into his robes and pulled out the letter he'd obtained from Su Jie. With a bow, he handed it over to the Sect Master.

Luo Qiang's eyebrows rose slightly as he took the scroll. "And where did you acquire this?"

"One of my . . . associates obtained it from a Crimson Phoenix Sect disciple."

"Associates? I wasn't aware you had a network of spies."

Kai kept his face neutral, though inwardly he was skeptical. He doubted any action within the sect went unnoticed by the Sect Master. Still, he chose his words carefully. "Not spies, Master. Just a few resourceful individuals who keep their ears to the ground."

"I see." Luo Qiang unfurled the scroll and began to read. His expression remained impassive, but Kai noticed a slight tightening around his eyes.

For several long moments, there was only silence. Kai stood still, waiting for his master to finish reading. Finally, Luo Qiang set the scroll down and leaned back in his chair.

"You've done well to bring this to my attention," he said at last.

"Thank you, Master. I hope the information proves useful."

Luo Qiang nodded slowly. "Indeed it does. We were already aware of the Crimson Phoenix Sect's preparations for war. However, this information about the Boundless Earth Sect's involvement is new. And potentially very valuable. It could help us prevent significant losses on our side."

The Sect Master reached into his robes and pulled out a small pouch. He tossed it to Kai, who caught it with his right hand. "A reward for your initiative. One thousand low-grade spirit stones."

Kai bowed deeply, hiding his slight disappointment. *I was hoping for some magical artifact, but I suppose this is better than nothing.*

"Thank you, Master. Your generosity is appreciated."

"My men will investigate further to determine which specific areas the Boundless Earth Sect is planning to target," Luo Qiang said. Then his gaze sharpened as he looked directly at Kai. "And once we've confirmed their plans, you will be sent to deal with it."

"Me?" Kai blinked, taken aback. "But, Master, surely this is too high-level for someone of my cultivation. Wouldn't a Nascent Soul Elder be better suited for such a task?"

Luo Qiang waved a hand dismissively. "Don't worry. You won't be going alone. A Nascent Soul Elder will indeed be present, along with a group of Core Formation and Foundation Establishment cultivators. But it would be good for you to gain some experience outside the sect before the war truly begins."

Kai's mind raced, searching for a way out of this unexpected development. "Master, I appreciate the opportunity, but perhaps my time would be better spent focusing on my cultivation? Or my alchemy studies? There's still so much for me to learn here in the sect."

The Sect Master shook his head. "No. It has been decided. You will join this mission."

Kai opened his mouth to protest further, but the look in Luo Qiang's eyes made it clear that arguing would be pointless. With a sigh, he bowed his head. "As you wish, Master."

Inwardly, Kai was far from happy with this turn of events. Leaving the safety of the sect meant there was a real chance he might never return. Some might call him a coward for wanting to avoid the danger, but Kai knew the reality of his situation. He was like an ant compared to these cultivators, and ants got stepped on in wars between giants.

"Your senior brother will lead the mission," Luo Qiang added.

Kai looked up, surprised. "Shen Yu?"

While Shen Yu was chosen by the Sect Master first, making him technically Kai's senior, Kai was older and didn't really see the other disciple as a true senior brother.

"No, not Shen Yu. Wang Lin." The Sect Master smiled.

Kai's eyes widened. He'd been in the sect for months now, but he had yet to meet the mysterious Wang Lin. He'd heard rumors, of course—whispers of a prodigy who had advanced faster than anyone in the sect's recent history. But Wang Lin was rarely seen around the sect; it was said that he was on a secret mission.

"Shen Yu will be joining the mission as well," Luo Qiang continued. "Both of you will be under the protection of your Senior Brother Wang Lin."

Kai nodded. A part of him was curious to finally meet the legendary Wang Lin, but another part was wary. What would this senior brother be like? Would he also be some protagonist-like figure?

"You have about a week to prepare," the Sect Master said, his tone making it clear that the conversation was coming to an end. "I suggest you use that time wisely. And Kai?"

"Yes, Master?"

Luo Qiang's eyes bore into him. "Stay alert. And don't die."

With those cheery parting words, Kai was dismissed.

Back in his own quarters, Kai took stock of his situation. He had about a week before he'd have to leave for the mission. That wasn't much time, but it would have to be enough. He had several things he needed to accomplish before then.

First on his list: learning the new skill scrolls he'd acquired. Kai pulled out the scrolls from his inventory and laid them out on his desk. There were three in total.

The first scroll was titled "Burning Sky Judgment." Kai unrolled it and scanned the description. *"Burning Sky Judgment: Allows the user to summon a fiery sigil in the sky, which releases a rain of fire upon their enemies."*

Kai's lips curved into a smile. This would give him another long-range attack option that was less qi exhaustive than the Lightning Hammer Strike. In a real battle, being able to strike from a distance could mean the difference between life and death.

The second scroll was titled "Fiery Lotus Bloom."

"Creates multiple flaming lotus petals that orbit the user, acting as both offense and defense. The petals can be launched at enemies or used to block incoming attacks."

"Now that's useful," Kai muttered to himself. The ability to attack multiple targets at once would be invaluable in the chaos of war. And the defensive capabilities were an added bonus.

The final scroll was called "Blaze of Renewal."

"The cultivator surrounds their body in a gentle continuous flame that gradually heals wounds and burns away toxins."

Kai let out a low whistle as he finished reading. A healing technique was exactly what he'd been missing. While his System's respawn ability was a powerful safeguard, it would be far better if he could avoid dying in the first place. This technique could help with that.

"All right. Time to get to work."

He picked up the Burning Sky Judgment scroll first. As he focused on it, a System message appeared in his vision:

> Skill Scroll Discovered!
> Name: Burning Sky Judgment
> Would you like to learn this skill?
> Yes/No

Kai nodded, and suddenly, information began flooding into his mind. It was like watching a high-speed tutorial, complete with mental images of the skill in action. He saw the hand signs needed to activate it, felt the way the qi should flow, and understood the intricacies of controlling the falling fire.

When the flood of information stopped, Kai blinked, feeling slightly dizzy. But the knowledge was there, settled into his mind as if he'd spent months practicing it.

> New Skill Unlocked: Burning Sky Judgment (Level 1)
> Description: Summon a fiery sigil in the sky that rains fire upon enemies. Damage and area of effect increase with skill level.

"One down, two to go," Kai murmured, reaching for the next scroll.

He repeated the process with Fiery Lotus Bloom and Blaze of Renewal, each time experiencing the rush of instantaneous learning. When he was done, two more System messages confirmed his new abilities.

> New Skill Unlocked: Fiery Lotus Bloom (Level 1)
> Description: Create flaming lotus petals for offense and defense. Number of petals and damage increase with skill level.
>
> New Skill Unlocked: Blaze of Renewal (Level 1)
> Description: Surrounds the cultivator's body with healing flames. Healing rate and toxin purification increase with skill level.

Kai leaned back in his chair with a smile on his face.

The Crimson Phoenix Sect . . . Using their own skills against them will be deliciously ironic. And knowing their moves gives me an edge in defending against them too.

He'd need to practice them, of course, to get a feel for how they worked in real combat situations. But having them in his arsenal already made him feel more prepared for what lay ahead.

"Now," Kai said, standing up and stretching, "on to the next item on the list."

He turned his thoughts to the matter of a weapon. Up until now, he'd been relying solely on his cultivation techniques, hand-to-hand combat skills, and his basic sword. But in a real war, having a proper weapon could make all the difference.

Kai paced his room, considering his options. The typical xianxia protagonist usually went with a sword or some other kind of blade. They'd bond with their weapon and cultivate together until they became some sort of supreme sword emperor or whatever.

But Kai had never been one to follow the typical path. He wanted something different, something that would suit his style of combat and give him an edge others might not expect.

A bow? Great for long-range attacks, could be useful for sniping enemy cultivators from afar. But it's useless in close combat. And if I run out of arrows, I'm in trouble unless I want to waste qi creating my own. Not to mention that it requires both hands, which limits my ability to use other techniques or items.

Daggers? Quick, easy to conceal. Good for surprise attacks. But they require getting in extremely close. Against higher-level cultivators, that's practically suicide. And I can always condense my own daggers if I'm planning an ambush.

A hammer or mace? Could be devastating, but it is slow. Too slow. Too predictable. I need something that allows for quicker reactions.

A staff . . . No, a spear . . . Wait, why not both? A staff-spear hybrid could work. It'd give me options—keep enemies at a distance or let me get in close if I need to. And with my lightning techniques . . . Yes, I could channel my qi right through it. Turn the whole thing into a giant lightning rod. Now that would catch some cultivators off guard.

Kai nodded to himself, satisfied with the decision. Now he just needed to gather the materials and craft it. He still had the Thunderclaw Tigress corpse and the Roach Carapace, both of which would make excellent components. But for a truly powerful weapon, he'd need more.

"Looks like a trip to the sect marketplace is in order."

The higher the rank of the materials, the more potent the resulting weapon would be. And given the dangers he was about to face, Kai wanted the best weapon he could possibly create.

But before he could do that, there was one more thing he needed to take care of. His meeting with Su Fang.

Kai's expression hardened as he thought about the upcoming confrontation. Su Fang had asked for a meeting under the guise of cooperating, but Kai knew the Core Disciple was looking for ways to pressure him to hand over his alchemy business. But Kai had no intention of surrendering what he'd built.

It was time to make that crystal clear.

The sect may be heading off to war soon, but that's all the more reason to hold on to my alchemy business. Wars aren't just won on the battlefield. They're won in the workshops and laboratories too. Cultivators will need pills, elixirs, and talismans more than ever. If anything, this is when a business truly thrives. And I'm not just talking about alchemy but also formations.

Learning the basics of formations using skill scrolls could be incredibly useful. It would complement my alchemy skills nicely and make it less likely for the Sect Master to throw me on the frontlines to "gain experience." I'm happy playing a supportive role.

Kai took a deep breath as he looked over his appearance, making sure his black Legacy Disciple robes were immaculate. Presentation mattered in these sorts of confrontations.

I should probably bring Lin Yue along with me. Both Lin Yue and Su Fang are Foundation Establishment cultivators. If things get ugly, having Lin Yue there could even the odds. Not that I plan on letting it come to blows, but it never hurts to have a shield . . .

CHAPTER SIXTY-ONE

The Azure Sky Sect's Tea Pavilion was always bustling with activity. It was a place where disciples could unwind after a long day of cultivating, missions, or training. In a secluded corner sat three figures: Kai, Lin Yue, and Su Fang, who sat across from them.

Su Fang's eyes flickered between Kai and Lin Yue. "I see you brought along some protection."

Kai shook his head, a polite smile on his face. "Not at all. Lin Yue is my business partner. It seemed only fitting that he attend our meeting as well."

Su Fang's smile hardened, but he nodded. "Of course. How . . . considerate of you."

Kai took a sip of his tea, savoring the delicate flavor. "Now, Junior Brother Su, you requested this meeting. May I ask why?"

The words felt strange on his tongue. Despite being a Legacy Disciple, addressing someone clearly older and more established in the sect as "junior" felt awkward.

"I have a proposition for you." Su Fang leaned forward. "A partnership, if you will."

"Oh? I'm listening."

"I've been impressed by your recent achievements. Becoming a novice alchemist in such a short time is no small feat. Your low-grade qi-gathering pills have caused quite a stir among the Outer Disciples. I believe," Su Fang continued, his words flowing smoothly like rehearsed lines, "that by combining our resources and expertise, we could dominate the market entirely. With my established distribution network and your alchemy skills, we could be unstoppable." His voice dropped to a whisper. "I'm prepared to offer you a generous deal. For every pill you make for me, you'll receive twenty percent of the profits. With my connections, we could triple your current sales within a month."

As Su Fang outlined his proposal, Kai nodded along, but inwardly, he scoffed. *Twenty percent? This doesn't sound like a partnership at all. It's more like he wants me to work for him.*

He caught Lin Yue's eye and saw the warning there. It was clear the Inner Disciple thought the same.

Su Fang sat back, looking pleased with himself. "What do you say? Shall we join forces and corner the market?"

Kai set down his teacup, the soft clink seeming to echo in the pause that followed. "I appreciate your offer, Junior Brother Su, but I'm afraid I must decline."

"Decline?" Su Fang's smile faltered. "But surely you see the benefits—"

"What I see," Kai interrupted, "is not a partnership, but an attempt to acquire my business. I have no interest in selling."

Su Fang's expression shifted, annoyance flashing across his face, before he schooled it back into a friendly mask. "You misunderstand. I'm only looking out for your interests. Perhaps if I explain the benefits more clearly . . ."

For the next few minutes, Su Fang outlined the supposed advantages of joining forces. Access to higher-quality ingredients, protection from rival sellers, guaranteed buyers for all pills. But with each point, Kai grew more certain that this was a thinly veiled takeover attempt.

This reminds me of those tech giants back on Earth. Google, Amazon—always looking to buy out smaller competitors before they become a threat. Creating their own monopolies. Well, I won't let that happen to me.

When Su Fang finished his pitch, Kai shook his head. "I appreciate the offer, but I'm not interested. My business is doing fine on its own."

Again, Su Fang's smile faltered for a moment before returning, now tinged with something darker. "I understand your hesitation, but consider the consequences of refusing. The cultivation world can be . . . unpredictable. Accidents happen. People go missing. Customers suddenly find other suppliers."

Kai frowned. It was clear Su Fang had no intention of backing down. The veiled threats were becoming less veiled by the second. He glanced at Lin Yue and saw his own thoughts mirrored in his partner's eyes.

"I appreciate your concern," Kai said. "But I believe I can handle any challenges that come my way."

"Are you certain about that, Senior Brother?" Su Fang's smile turned sharp. "You're new to this world of business and cultivation. There's so much you don't know, so many . . . pitfalls you might not see coming."

Kai felt a flicker of anger, but he pushed it down. Getting emotional wouldn't help him here. Instead, he reached into his robes and pulled out a scroll.

"You're right, Junior Brother. There's a lot I don't know," Kai said, his voice level. "Which is why I've made it a point to learn." Kai began to read. "'Su Fang, third son of the Su Clan, one of the top ten clans in the region. Joined the Azure Sky Sect at age twelve. Reached Foundation Establishment by twenty.' Impressive achievements."

Su Fang had a proud smile on his face, but Kai wasn't finished.

"However, your business dealings are less . . . admirable," Kai continued, his eyes fixed on Su Fang. "For instance, three years ago, a promising young alchemist suddenly gave up her craft and left the sect. According to my sources, you threatened to have your friends pay a visit to her village unless she stopped selling her pills."

Su Fang's jaw clenched, but Kai pressed on.

"Then there's the case of a disciple undergoing Qi Deviation during a critical stage of pill refinement. Coincidentally, this happened right after he refused your offer to buy his business. The explosion destroyed his entire stock of spirit herbs and crippled his cultivation." Kai unrolled the scroll further. "Oh, and let's not forget the unfortunate 'accident' that befell the Yun family's pill delivery caravan last spring. Attacked by 'bandits' who somehow knew exactly when and where to strike and precisely which wagons contained the most valuable pills. Strangely, your own shipments were untouched that season."

With each story, Su Fang's face grew paler, his knuckles white as he gripped the edge of the table.

"The scroll goes on," Kai said, his voice level. "Sabotaged spirit herb gardens, mysterious fires in rival workshops, cultivators who dared to compete with you suffering cultivation setbacks or worse. It paints quite a picture, Su Fang. Not of a businessman but of a bully who can't stand fair competition."

One of his men, standing nearby, stepped forward angrily. "How dare you accuse the young master—"

Su Fang held up a hand, silencing his subordinate. His smile had turned ugly, all pretense of friendliness gone. "It's one thing to reject my offer. It's quite another to humiliate me with these . . . accusations."

As he spoke, Su Fang's aura flared, a wave of pressure filling the teahouse. Several nearby tables hurriedly cleared out, not wanting to get dragged in the conflict.

Lin Yue's aura flared in response, pushing back against Su Fang's. But Kai could tell it was mostly for show. Lin Yue, while willing to support Kai, wasn't about to risk himself in a real confrontation with a Core Disciple. At least, not yet. Kai would have to prove he was worth that kind of risk.

It seems I've overestimated the wisdom of cultivators, Kai thought, recalling a phrase he'd often encountered in cultivation novels. *"Courting death." That's what this is called. These cultivators really can't help themselves, can they?*

The concept of a Core Disciple daring to make an enemy of someone clearly favored by the Sect Master and Alchemy Master seemed ludicrous to Kai. It was as if Su Fang's pride had overridden his common sense, blinding him to the potential consequences of his actions.

As the tension in the air thickened, Kai's eyes wandered, taking in the other occupants of the teahouse. His gaze landed on a familiar pair—Sun Jun and Lu Chen were watching them like hawks from the other side.

Ah, so that's how it is. They've set this up, hoping Su Fang would "teach me a lesson."

Kai shook his head. It reminded him of high school drama, petty and short-sighted. But then, young masters in cultivation novels were often portrayed as spoiled and vindictive.

He knew he was in a precarious position. The Sect Master had made it clear he wouldn't intervene in disputes between disciples, but that didn't mean Kai couldn't use his position to his advantage.

"You know, my senior brother is returning soon. Perhaps we should continue this discussion when he arrives? I'm sure Senior Brother Wang Lin would be interested in your business propositions."

Su Fang's face, which had been flushed with anger, suddenly drained of color. "Wang Lin?" he muttered, almost to himself.

Kai watched with fascination as Su Fang visibly struggled to compose himself. It was clear that the mere mention of Wang Lin had stirred some potent memories in the Core Disciple.

Just how scary is this Wang Lin?

He had never met his supposed senior brother, and for all he knew, Wang Lin could be the first to throw Kai to the wolves. But Su Fang didn't know that, and Kai wasn't above using Wang Lin's fearsome reputation to his advantage.

"Yes. Senior Brother Wang Lin," Kai confirmed, watching Su Fang carefully. "I'm sure he'd be very interested to hear about our . . . discussion today."

Su Fang swallowed hard, then forced a smile onto his face. It looked more like a grimace. "No, no, that won't be necessary. There's no need to trouble Senior Brother Wang Lin with such trivial matters."

Seeing Su Fang's discomfort, Kai knew he had an opportunity. "Perhaps we've gotten off on the wrong foot, Junior Brother Su. I may have been hasty in dismissing your proposal entirely. What if we were to . . . adjust the terms?"

Su Fang's eyes narrowed, but there was a glimmer of interest. "I'm listening."

"You mentioned your established distribution network and access to high-quality materials," Kai said, choosing his words carefully. "What if you were to handle all the logistics—providing the materials and managing distribution—while I focus solely on the alchemy side? We could split the profits equally, fifty-fifty."

Su Fang considered this for a moment, and his earlier anger seemed to dissipate as he calculated the potential benefits. It wasn't the complete control he'd initially sought, but it was far better than walking away empty-handed—or worse, with a powerful enemy.

"A partnership of equals," Su Fang murmured, nodding slowly. "It's . . . an interesting proposition."

Kai could see the wheels turning in Su Fang's head. The Core Disciple was likely already planning how he might turn this arrangement to his advantage in the future, but for now, it was a face-saving compromise.

"Very well," Su Fang said at last, giving a slight bow. "I accept your terms, Senior Brother Kai. We have a deal."

"Excellent." Kai bowed back. "I look forward to our cooperation, Junior Brother Su."

With that, Su Fang turned and strode away, his lackeys scrambling to keep up. Kai watched him go, noting the stiffness in Su Fang's shoulders and the way his hands were clenched at his sides.

As the Core Disciple disappeared from view, Kai allowed himself a small sigh of relief. He glanced over at Sun Jun and Lu Chen, noting their disappointed expressions. Clearly, they had been hoping for a different outcome.

"It's risky going into business with Su Fang," Lin Yue said once they were alone. "He won't forget this. He'll be looking for any opportunity to turn the tables."

"I know. But it's a calculated risk."

"What do you mean?" Lin Yue raised an eyebrow.

Kai took a sip of his now cold tea before answering. "It's simple, really. There are two possible outcomes here. Either I'll win Su Fang over, show him the benefits of genuine cooperation, and we'll work together long term . . ."

"Or?" Lin Yue prompted, leaning in closer.

"Or I'll outgrow him," Kai finished, his tone matter-of-fact. "I'll use this opportunity to establish myself, build connections, and become strong enough that Su Fang can't threaten me anymore. Then, I'll end our partnership on my terms."

They left the teahouse and walked in silence for a while before Lin Yue spoke again. "You mentioned Senior Brother Wang Lin. Have you actually met him?"

"No, not yet." Kai shook his head. "But his reputation seems to precede him."

Lin Yue chuckled, but there was a nervous edge to it. "That's an understatement. Senior Brother Wang Lin is . . . Well, let's just say he's not someone you want to cross. Even some of the Elders are terrified of him."

"Is it because he's already reached the Nascent Soul Realm? That kind of power is hard for us to comprehend at our level."

"No, it's not just that." Lin Yue shook his head. "Wang Lin's cultivation speed is unprecedented in our sect's history, true. But it's not his power alone that makes others fear him."

"Oh?" Kai raised an eyebrow. "What is it, then?"

Lin Yue glanced around before lowering his voice. "There are . . . stories about him. Things he's done to those who've crossed him or threatened the sect."

"What kind of stories?" Kai asked, both curious and slightly alarmed.

Lin Yue shook his head, his voice barely above a whisper. "It's best not to repeat them in public. Let's just say that those who've faced Wang Lin's wrath . . . Well, most of them aren't around to talk about it anymore."

"And he's only twenty years old . . ."

"That's right," Lin Yue confirmed. "A true once-in-a-millennium prodigy. Some say he's blessed by the heavens. Others . . . Well, they whisper about darker things."

I really hope Wang Lin isn't as terrifying as everyone makes him out to be. Maybe all those stories are exaggerated, and he's actually someone who looks out for his juniors.

Kai tried to picture a benevolent Wang Lin, but the image kept morphing into something more sinister. He sighed inwardly. *Who am I kidding? With my luck, he's probably every bit the ruthless, power-hungry monster they say he is. I'll be lucky if he doesn't decide to make an example out of me just for breathing wrong. I guess I need to do some research on him. Find out his history, his background. Maybe I can figure out if he fits any of the main character archetypes I know of.*

If Wang Lin's life story followed a recognizable pattern—the orphaned prodigy, the hidden royal, the genius with a broken engagement, or the revenge-driven hero who had his whole clan massacred—it might give Kai some insight into how to deal with him. At the very least, it would be better than going in blind.

Knowledge is power. And when you're dealing with someone who could probably vaporize you with a thought, you need all the power you can get. On that note, it's time to reawaken meridians.

CHAPTER SIXTY-TWO

The next morning, Kai and Chen Wei made their way to the sect marketplace. Unlike the specialized pavilions dedicated to specific crafts, this marketplace was a hodgepodge of everything a cultivator might need—or want.

When they arrived, Kai's eyes darted from stall to stall, taking in the array of goods on display. Colorful banners advertising everything from spirit herbs to magical weapons fluttered in the breeze.

"Senior Brother, if you don't mind me asking, why are we here at the marketplace?" Chen Wei asked. "Wouldn't the Thousand Blades Hall be a better place to get a new weapon?"

"We're here because I want to craft the weapon myself," Kai answered.

"Craft it yourself?" Chen Wei's eyes widened in surprise. "But Senior Brother, I didn't know you were a blacksmith!"

"I'm not—at least, not in the traditional sense." Kai chuckled softly. "But I like to be well-rounded. There's more than one way to craft a weapon, you know."

Kai had another reason for coming to the marketplace—namely, setting up an alchemy stall. But that was for another day. He patted Chen Wei on the shoulder. "You'll see soon enough. Now, let's find the materials we need. We have a weapon to craft."

Chen Wei looked confused but nodded.

As they walked, a message appeared before Kai:

> What would you like to craft?

Kai thought for a moment before mentally responding, *I want to craft a staff with a retractable blade.*

> Staff with Retractable Blade
> Materials needed:

[Empty Slot]—Main Material
[Empty Slot]—Secondary Material
[Empty Slot]—Binding Material
[Empty Slot]—Elemental Crystal
[Empty Slot]—Enhancement Rune
[Empty Slot]—Grip Material

The System then provided explanations for each material.

Main Material: This will form the core of your staff. Choose a sturdy wood with good qi conductivity.
Secondary Material: This will be used for the retractable blade. Select a durable metal that can hold a sharp edge.
Binding Material: This will secure the blade mechanism to the staff. Look for something flexible yet strong.
Elemental Crystal: Optional but recommended. This will imbue your weapon with an elemental affinity, enhancing certain types of techniques.
Enhancement Rune: Optional. This can provide additional effects or boosts to your weapon's capabilities.
Grip Material: This will wrap the handle of your staff. Choose something comfortable that provides a secure grip.

Kai nodded to himself. "All right," he said, turning to Chen Wei. "Let's start with finding some suitable wood for the staff. Any ideas where we might find that?"

"I think I know just the place, Senior Brother. Follow me!"

The young disciple led Kai through the crowded marketplace, weaving between shoppers and ducking under hanging signs. They soon arrived at a stall piled high with various types of wood.

The Outer Disciple manning the stall was a stocky young man with a quick smile and quicker tongue. His eyes lit up as Kai approached.

"Welcome, welcome!" he called out. "Looking for the finest wood in all the Azure Sky Sect? You've come to the right place!"

Kai nodded politely, his eyes scanning the selection. He pointed to a dark, richly grained wood. "What can you tell me about this one?"

The vendor's smile widened. "Ah, excellent eye! That's Thunderstruck Oak, blessed by the heavens themselves! Legend has it that a thousand-year-old tree was struck by divine lightning, imbuing the wood with incredible power. It's said that weapons made from this wood can call down lightning at will!"

Material: Thunderstruck Oak

> Rank: Uncommon
> Description: A sturdy oak wood with slightly enhanced conductivity. May occasionally produce small static discharges when struck.

Kai raised an eyebrow. *"Slightly enhanced conductivity,"* huh? *Quite a gap between that and "calling down lightning at will."*

"Interesting," Kai murmured. "And this one?" He pointed to a pale, almost translucent wood.

The vendor's eyes gleamed. "That, my friend, is Ghost Whisper Willow! It's harvested from trees that grow in haunted forests. Weapons made from this wood are said to be able to strike spirits and incorporeal beings!"

> Material: Ghost Whisper Willow
> Rank: Uncommon
> Description: A lightweight wood with minor spirit-attuned properties. Slightly more effective against spiritual entities.

Kai nodded, hiding his amusement. *"Minor spirit-attuned properties."* This *guy could sell sand in a desert.*

"And what about this blue-tinged wood?" Kai asked, pointing to a stack near the back.

The vendor's smile grew impossibly wider. "Ah, you have a discerning eye indeed! That is Azure Mist Pine, grown in the misty valleys of the Azure Mountains. It's said that weapons made from this wood can control the very air itself, creating mists and fogs to confound your enemies!"

> Material: Azure Mist Pine
> Rank: Rare
> Description: A water-attuned wood with natural moisture retention properties. Can enhance water-based techniques when used in weapon crafting.

Kai's eyes lit up. This was exactly what he was looking for. He turned to Chen Wei, speaking quietly. "I think this is the one."

Chen Wei nodded, then turned to the vendor. "How much for the Azure Mist Pine?"

"Well, it's a rare wood, you know," The vendor stroked his chin. "Very difficult to obtain. I couldn't possibly part with it for less than . . . one thousand low-grade spirit stones."

"One thousand?" Chen Wei spat out. "That's highway robbery!"

The vendor held up his hands. "Now, now. You have to understand the value of what you're getting. This wood is imbued with the very essence of water and mist! Why, I've heard tales of staffs made from Azure Mist Pine that could summon rainstorms with a single wave!"

"Let's not exaggerate." Kai stepped forward. "The Azure Mist Pine has water-attuned properties, yes, but it's not going to be summoning any rainstorms. It enhances water techniques, nothing more."

The vendor's smile faltered for a moment, but he quickly recovered. "Well, of course, the true potential of the wood depends on the skill of the craftsman and the user. But surely you can see why one thousand spirit stones is a fair price for such a rare material?"

Chen Wei opened his mouth to argue further, but Kai held up a hand to stop him. "Six hundred and fifty spirit stones," Kai said. "That's a fair price for a rare, water-attuned wood."

The vendor hesitated, clearly torn between his desire to make a large profit and the fear of losing the sale entirely. "Well . . . I suppose I could go down to 750. But that's my final offer!"

Kai shook his head. "Seven hundred, and we'll throw in a good word to our fellow disciples about your stall."

The vendor sighed dramatically. "You drive a hard bargain. But I can see you know your materials. Seven hundred it is."

As Chen Wei counted out the spirit stones, Kai allowed himself a small smile. *Not a bad start. A little overpriced, but not as bad as it could have been.*

With the Azure Mist Pine secured, Kai turned to Chen Wei. "Next, we need a metal for the retractable blade."

"I know just the place. Old Man Liu's stall is just around the corner."

As they approached the metal stall, Kai was nearly bowled over by the enthusiasm of the vendor. Old Man Liu, despite his name, was a middle-aged man with an energy that belied his years.

"Welcome, welcome!" he practically shouted. "Looking for metal? You've come to the right place! I've got iron that can withstand a thousand blows, steel that can cut through mountain stone, silver that repels evil spirits—"

Kai held up a hand, stemming the tide of words. "Thank you. I'm looking for something specific. A metal suitable for a retractable blade in a staff."

Old Man Liu's eyes lit up. "Ah. Let me show you some options."

As the enthusiastic vendor laid out various metal samples, Kai examined each one carefully, relying on his System messages for accurate information.

Material: Starfall Iron
Rank: Uncommon
Description: A dense, durable iron with trace amounts of celestial ore. Slightly more resilient than standard iron.

Material: Serpent Scale Steel
Rank: Rare
Description: A flexible steel alloy that retains a keen edge. Ideal for weapons that require both strength and flexibility.

Material: Misty River Steel
Rank: Rare
Description: A light and flexible steel with water-attuned properties. Can generate a light mist when swung at high speeds.

Kai's eyes lingered on the Misty River Steel. *Perfect. It matches the water theme of the Azure Mist Pine.*

"I'll take the Misty River Steel," Kai said, interrupting Old Man Liu's ongoing sales pitch.

The vendor blinked in surprise, then grinned. "Excellent choice! This steel is light and flexible, allowing the blade to move as fluidly as a flowing river. And it has an innate ability to generate mist or fog when swung!"

Kai nodded—the vendor's description matched the System message. "It's perfect for what I need. Now, do you have anything that could help make the blade retractable?"

Old Man Liu's eyes widened. "Ah. For that, you'll want something special." He ducked behind his stall and emerged with a small ingot of golden metal. "This is Heavenly Gold. It's highly conductive and incredibly resilient. Perfect for creating springs and gears that won't wear out."

Material: Heavenly Gold
Rank: Rare
Description: A highly conductive and resilient gold alloy. Ideal for crafting intricate mechanisms that channel qi.

"That sounds perfect. How much for both the Misty River Steel and the Heavenly Gold?"

"Well, these are both rare materials . . ." Old Man Liu stroked his beard. "How about eight hundred spirit stones for the pair?"

Chen Wei stepped forward, his eyes narrowing. "Eight hundred? That's a bit steep, isn't it? The Misty River Steel is nice, but it's not that rare. And you're only offering a small amount of the Heavenly Gold."

Kai watched as Chen Wei haggled with the vendor. After several minutes of back-and-forth, they settled on a price of five hundred spirit stones for both materials.

As they turned to leave Old Man Liu's stall, Kai said, "We now need something to bind the core of the staff and secure the blade mechanism."

Chen Wei furrowed his brow. "Bind the core? I'm not sure where we'd find something like that."

"Perhaps I can help," a familiar voice chimed in. They turned to see Old Man Liu leaning over his stall. "For what you're looking for, you'll want some kind of tendon or sinew. Strong, flexible, able to conduct qi. Tan Yifei's stall, two rows over, might have what you need."

Kai bowed slightly. "Thank you for the advice."

When they arrived at the stall, they found Tan Yifei to be a young woman with sharp eyes and a no-nonsense attitude. When Kai explained what he was looking for, she immediately reached under her stall and pulled out a coil of silvery material.

"Silver Serpent Tendon," she said briskly. "Incredibly strong and flexible. Ideal for binding the core of a staff and securing a blade mechanism. It also conducts qi, allowing for smooth energy transfer between the staff and blade."

Material: Silver Serpent Tendon
Rank: Rare
Description: Extremely durable and flexible tendon from a spirit beast. Excellent qi conductor and binding material.

Kai nodded, impressed by the accuracy of her description. "It sounds perfect. How much?"

"One hundred and fifty low-grade spirit stones," Tan Yifei said firmly.

Kai raised an eyebrow. It was a fair price, considering the quality of the material, but he decided to try his luck. "How about one hundred?"

Tan Yifei's eyes narrowed slightly, but then she nodded. "Done. You've got a good eye for materials. Not many would recognize the value of this tendon."

As Kai handed over the spirit stones, he decided to ask about another material he needed. "Do you know where I could find Elemental Crystal shards?"

Tan Yifei pointed down the row. "Third stall on the left. Tell Gramps that Tan Yifei sent you."

"Thank you for your help," Kai said as he bowed slightly.

CHAPTER SIXTY-THREE

As they walked toward the crystal stall, Chen Wei looked at Kai curiously. "Senior Brother, why do you need Elemental Crystal shards?"

"Elemental Crystals are a key component in crafting a weapon with a specific elemental affinity. They help attune the weapon to a particular element, enhancing any techniques of that element used through the weapon."

"Oh! So, you're going to use a lightning shard, right? That would be a strong combination with the water-attuned wood and steel."

Kai shook his head. "Actually, I'm planning to go for a pure water-affinity weapon."

"But . . . why?" Chen Wei asked. "Wouldn't lightning be better, given your cultivation?"

"It's a good question," Kai said. "And you're right, a lightning and water combo would be powerful. But here's the thing: with my lightning element cultivation method, I can always channel my lightning techniques into the water staff for a powerful lightning–water combo when needed. But if I make the staff itself with mixed elements, it will decrease its overall efficiency."

"So, by keeping it pure water, you have more flexibility?"

"Exactly. It gives me more options in battle."

They arrived at the crystal stall, where an elderly man sat surrounded by glittering shards of various colors. Kai approached and bowed.

"Greetings. Tan Yifei sent us."

The old man's wrinkled face creased into a smile. "Ah, any friend of my granddaughter is welcome here. What can I do for you, young cultivator?"

Kai gestured to the crystals. "I need a Water Elemental Crystal shard for weapon crafting."

The old man nodded. "A wise choice. Water is the element of adaptability and flow." He reached into a drawer and pulled out several blue crystals of varying sizes. "The larger the shard, the stronger the elemental attunement. But, of course, the price increases accordingly."

Kai examined the crystals carefully.

Material: Small Water Elemental Crystal Shard
Rank: Uncommon
Description: A crystal infused with water elemental energy. Provides minor enhancement to water-based techniques.

Material: Medium Water Elemental Crystal Shard
Rank: Rare
Description: A crystal with concentrated water elemental energy. Significantly enhances water-based techniques and allows for basic water manipulation.

Material: Large Water Elemental Crystal Shard
Rank: Very Rare
Description: A crystal brimming with water elemental energy. Greatly enhances water-based techniques and allows for advanced water manipulation.

After careful consideration, Kai pointed to the medium-sized shard. "This one, I think. A good balance of power and cost."

"A wise choice indeed." The old man nodded. "For you, five hundred spirit stones."

Chen Wei stepped forward. "Respected Elder, while we greatly appreciate the quality of your crystals, perhaps we could come to a more agreeable price? After all, we were sent by your granddaughter, and we're sure to need more materials in the future . . ."

After several minutes of back-and-forth, they settled on a price of four hundred spirit stones for the medium Water Elemental Crystal shard.

As they left the stall, Kai turned to Chen Wei. "There are two more things we need. Chen Wei, do you know where we could find a rune stall?"

Chen Wei furrowed his brow. "A rune stall? I'm not sure. Why do we need runes?"

"There must be some runes I could apply during the crafting process to give the weapon some extra defense capabilities," Kai explained. "It's always good to have every advantage you can get."

Chen Wei nodded. "Let me ask around."

As Chen Wei darted off to inquire about rune sellers, Kai took a moment to check his crafting menu again.

Materials needed:
[Azure Mist Pine]—Main Material
[Misty River Steel]—Secondary Material
[Silver Serpent Tendon]—Binding Material
[Medium Water Elemental Crystal Shard]—Elemental Crystal

> [Empty Slot]—Enhancement Rune
> [Empty Slot]—Grip Material

Almost there. Just need a rune and something for the grip.

Chen Wei returned a few minutes later, slightly out of breath. "Senior Brother Kai, I found a rune seller. It's this way."

As they made their way through the crowded marketplace, Kai noticed the stalls becoming sparser and less well maintained. Finally, they came to a small rundown stall at the edge of the marketplace. A young Inner Disciple stood behind the counter, his robes slightly frayed at the edges.

"Powerful runes!" the young disciple called out, his voice tinged with desperation. "Strengthen your weapons! Enhance your cultivation! Runes for every need!"

Despite his enthusiastic cries, the area around his stall remained empty of customers. Kai approached, his curiosity piqued.

As soon as the young disciple spotted Kai, his eyes lit up with an almost hungry look. The intensity of his gaze startled Kai for a moment.

He looks . . . desperate, Kai thought. *I've never seen an Inner Disciple in such poor condition before.*

"Welcome, esteemed customer!" the young disciple said, his voice eager. "I have runes of immense power! Runes that can make your sword cut through mountains! Runes that can call down the very lightning from the sky! What kind of rune are you looking for?"

Kai held up a hand to stem the tide of words. "Thank you. I'm looking for something for a new weapon I'm crafting. Do you have any runes that can be applied during the crafting process?"

The young disciple's face fell slightly. "Oh, you don't have the weapon with you? If I could see it, I could give a better recommendation . . ."

Kai smiled awkwardly. "Actually, I haven't made it yet. I'm gathering materials for the crafting process."

The Inner Disciple furrowed his brow, thinking hard for a moment. Then his eyes lit up. "Ah! I think I have just the thing." He ducked behind the counter and rummaged around for a bit before emerging with three small glowing symbols etched onto pieces of parchment.

"These are special runes," he explained. "They're designed to be incorporated into a weapon during the crafting process. I don't have many of these—they're quite difficult to make. Runes that can empower a weapon long term are not easy to come by."

Kai leaned in, intrigued. "Where did you get these?"

"My master made them." The disciple puffed up with pride. "He's a renowned formation master."

If these really were made by a formation master, they could be quite valuable.

"There's a catch, though," the disciple continued. "It's likely that only one rune can be applied to a weapon. These runes . . . They don't work well together. You'd need a higher-level formation master to make them compatible."

Hmmm, maybe I should have learned formations before alchemy. After a moment, Kai shook his head. *No, alchemy is far more valuable, short term and long term.*

"Can you tell me what each rune does?"

The Inner Disciple nodded eagerly. "Of course! This one"—he pointed to a rune that looked like a stylized shield—"is the Rune of Unyielding Fortitude. It increases the durability of a weapon by forty percent." He pointed to the second rune, which resembled a gust of wind. "This is the Rune of Swift Strikes. It increases a weapon's speed by thirty percent." Finally, he indicated the last rune, which looked like a clenched fist. "And this is the Rune of Overwhelming Force. It increases the power of a weapon by thirty percent."

Kai nodded as he checked the System messages for each rune.

Rune of Unyielding Fortitude
Rank: Rare
Effect: Increases weapon durability by 40%.

Rune of Swift Strikes
Rank: Rare
Effect: Increases weapon speed by 30%.

Rune of Overwhelming Force
Rank: Rare
Effect: Increases weapon power by 30%.

Well, at least he's not lying about their effects, Kai thought. He considered his options carefully. *Durability could be useful, but my build focuses on speed. And I don't plan on joining the front lines of a war, so raw power isn't my priority right now.*

"I'll take the Rune of Swift Strikes," Kai said .

The Inner Disciple's face lit up. "Excellent choice! That will be five hundred spirit stones."

Kai's eyes widened at the price. Even Chen Wei, standing beside him, let out a small gasp.

The disciple, noticing their reaction, hurried to explain. "I know it seems high, but you have to understand—these runes are far above my level. I was lucky to get any from my master. They would typically cost more than five hundred spirit stones, but I'm willing to offer a discount."

Chen Wei stepped forward, ready to negotiate, but Kai raised a hand to stop him. Something about this disciple's desperation made Kai pause. He pulled out five hundred spirit stones and handed them over.

"Thank you," Kai said. "May I ask your name?"

The disciple blinked, surprised that the Legacy Disciple even cared to ask. "Yan Fan. My name is Yan Fan."

As soon as Yan Fan spoke his name, a System message appeared in Kai's vision.

<table>
<tr><td>Name: Yan Fan</td></tr>
</table>

<table>
<tr><td>Age: 20
Level: Foundation Establishment Stage 2
Qi: 1200/1200
Strength: 130
Agility: 130
Durability: 128
Special Ability: Inner Eye</td></tr>
</table>

<table>
<tr><td>Inner Eye
Description: Allows the user to perceive qi with unusual clarity.</td></tr>
</table>

Kai's eyes widened slightly as he read the message. *A special ability? And one that's perfect for rune crafting . . . This Yan Fan could be very useful.*

"Yan Fan," Kai said slowly, "I think I'd be interested in working together sometime. Your skills are . . . intriguing."

Yan Fan's eyes widened in surprise, then hope. "Really? I . . . I would be honored, Senior Brother."

Kai nodded, his mind already working on how to incorporate Yan Fan into his plans. "One last thing. Do you have anything I could use for handle wrapping? Something to provide a good grip?"

Yan Fan nodded eagerly, reaching under the counter. He pulled out a roll of silvery fabric. "This is Spirit Silk. It's soft yet incredibly strong. It gives you a comfortable grip while letting you maneuver the weapon with ease. It also has the ability to slightly adjust its texture based on the user's grip, so there'll be no slips in combat."

<table>
<tr><td>Material: Spirit Silk
Rank: Uncommon
Description: A cultivated silk with minor adaptive properties. Provides excellent grip and comfort.</td></tr>
</table>

"How much?" Kai asked, reaching for his spirit stones.

Yan Fan shook his head. "It usually costs twenty spirit stones, but . . . please, take it as a gift."

Kai smiled, accepting the Spirit Silk. "Thank you, Yan Fan. I look forward to working with you in the future."

With that, Kai and Chen Wei made their way back to the Legacy Disciple quarters.

Crafting Menu:
[Azure Mist Pine]—Main Material
[Misty River Steel]—Secondary Material
[Silver Serpent Tendon]—Binding Material
[Medium Water Elemental Crystal Shard]—Elemental Crystal
[Rune of Swift Strikes]—Enhancement Rune
[Spirit Silk]—Grip Material

Time to get crafting!

CHAPTER SIXTY-FOUR

Would you like to craft your weapon?
Yes/No

Kai, who had returned from the marketplace and was now standing alone in his quarters, smiled. *Yes.*

Bring out the materials.

Nodding, Kai reached into his storage ring, and one by one, he pulled out the materials he had gathered from the marketplace. The Azure Mist Pine, Misty River Steel, Silver Serpent Tendon, medium Water Elemental Crystal shard, Rune of Swift Strikes, and Spirit Silk all appeared before him.

The Thunderclaw Tigress corpse and the Roach Carapace . . . I should add those too.

He reached into his storage ring once more and pulled out the remains of the spirit beast he'd defeated what seemed like a lifetime ago and the tough carapace of the monstrous roach. As soon as he placed them with the other materials, a new message appeared.

Analyzing additional materials . . .

Thunderclaw Tigress Corpse breakdown:
Thunder-Infused Bone: Rare material, enhances lightning affinity
Storm Fur: Uncommon material, increases agility
Lightning Heart: Very Rare material, boosts electrical conductivity

Roach Carapace breakdown:
Reinforced Chitin: Rare material, increases durability

These could really take my weapon to the next level.

The following combinations are available to enhance your weapon:
Thunder-Infused Bone + Lightning Heart: 10% chance to stun opponents on hit
Thunder-Infused Bone + Azure Mist Pine: Generates a small thundercloud when swung at high speeds
Lightning Heart + Water Elemental Crystal: Imbues strikes with electrified water and deals 5% damage
Reinforced Chitin + Misty River Steel: Weapon regenerates minor damage over time
Storm Fur + Silver Serpent Tendon: Increases weapon flexibility and allows for unpredictable strikes
Storm Fur + Spirit Silk: Improves grip and increases attack speed by 10%
Reinforced Chitin + Rune of Swift Strikes: Improves overall weapon durability by 10% without sacrificing speed
Please select three desired enhancements.

Kai pondered his options, weighing each combination against his fighting style and needs. *The lightning stun could be a game changer in close combat. The attack speed boost aligns perfectly with my build. And that regeneration . . . That could be incredibly useful in prolonged battles, not to mention in saving me some spirit stones.*

After a few moments, Kai made his choice. *I'll go with options one, four, and six.*

Confirmed. Place the materials in their designated slots.

A new window appeared on the floor that showed empty slots for each component. Kai carefully placed each item into its corresponding slot, making sure everything was aligned correctly. As he inserted the last piece, the window glowed brightly.

All materials in place. Ready to begin crafting. Would you like to proceed? Yes/No

Kai took a deep breath. *Craft,* he commanded.

The window changed to display a progress bar. Kai watched intently as it began to fill and the materials before him started to glow and levitate slightly off the ground. Kai knew there was a chance of failure with rare items like these, and the consequences could be severe. Losing these precious materials would be a waste of spirit stones and a significant setback.

The progress bar crawled forward, seeming to slow down as it neared completion. Kai held his breath. His eyes were fixed on the blue Azure Mist Pine and Misty River Steel as they started moving around each other, like they were mixing together. The Silver Serpent Tendon wrapped around everything, holding it all in place.

The Water Element Crystal shard glowed brightly, making the whole thing look watery. The speed rune lit up with a golden glow before it disappeared into the weapon. The Spirit Silk wrapped itself around the handle, making it look like it would fit Kai's hand perfectly.

As Kai watched, the tigress and roach parts started joining in too. Lightning bolts zapped all over the weapon, and a shimmery look formed around the roach shell.

It's pretty awesome to see it all come together like that.

Finally, with a bright flash of light, the progress bar filled completely.

Crafting successful!

Kai let out a sigh of relief. Then another message appeared.

As this is your first crafted weapon and is intended to be your primary armament, it has been imbued with the unique ability to level up alongside you.

Nice, Kai thought, a grin spreading across his face. *That'll save me from having to replace it anytime soon.*

You have gained 1000 XP for creating your first weapon.

The weapon, still glowing with a soft golden light, floated in the air before Kai. He leaned in, eager to see the fruits of his labor.

Name: Miststrike

Type: Staff-spear hybrid
Rank: Very Rare (Peak Qi Refining)
Durability: 100/100

Special Abilities:
Mist Veil: Creates a shroud of mist that increases evasion by 20% for 30 seconds. (Cooldown: 5 minutes)
Hydro Slash: Releases a pressurized blade of water that deals 150% weapon damage. (Cooldown: 1 minute)

Passive:
Weapon speed increased by 10%
10% chance to stun opponents on hit

Minor damage regenerates over time
Grows in power as the wielder advances in cultivation
Water Affinity: Increases the power of water-based techniques by 15%
Swift Currents: Each successful hit increases attack speed by 2% for 5 seconds
(Max stack: 5)

Kai's eyes widened as he read through the weapon's stats and abilities. *This . . . this is pretty incredible.*

The golden glow faded, and the staff began to fall. Kai's right hand shot out and caught it effortlessly. He twirled it experimentally. The grip molded to his hand as if it had been made for him alone.

Perfectly balanced, as all things should be.

With a thought, Kai activated the blade. The Misty River Steel looked sharp enough to slice through stone. As he channeled a bit of qi into the weapon, a faint blue aura surrounded the blade, and tiny droplets of water began to form along its length.

He gave it a few practice swings, the blade leaving trails of mist in its wake. A wide smile spread across Kai's face as he deactivated the blade and stored the staff in his ring.

Time to test this baby out.

The sun hung low in the sky as Kai stood at the center of his personal training area. Before him, arranged in a loose semicircle, stood the other members of his guild: Chen Wei, Liu Wei, and Zhi-Zhi.

Kai's gaze swept over his companions, assessing their progress since he'd last seen them. Chen Wei stood a little straighter, his qi noticeably stronger—he'd finally broken through to Qi Refining stage eight. Liu Wei's aura wasn't far behind. It seemed he had made another breakthrough and entered stage seven of the Qi Refining Realm.

But it was Zhi-Zhi who truly caught Kai's attention. The spirit tortoise's qi flickered and surged as it danced on the very edge between Peak Qi Refining and Foundation Establishment.

Good. He should enter the Foundation Establishment Realm before the war.

Zhi-Zhi met Kai's gaze. "Why have you called me here? Master Cang is preparing the materials for my breakthrough as we speak."

Kai smiled, a hint of mischief in his eyes. "Don't worry, Zhi-Zhi. This won't take too long. Consider it a warm-up for your breakthrough."

The spirit tortoise's eyes narrowed slightly, but he nodded in acceptance.

Kai addressed the group, his voice taking on a more serious tone. "As you all know, war is coming. We need to be prepared for anything. That's why I've called you here today for some battle training."

As he finished speaking, Miststrike materialized in his hand, and Kai gave it an experimental swing, the blade whistling through the air. "It'll also be a good opportunity for me to try out my new toy."

Chen Wei's eyes widened in surprise. "S-Senior Brother," he sputtered, "how . . . how did you craft it so quickly? We only brought back the materials a few hours ago!"

Kai just gave him a mysterious smile. "A good cultivator never reveals all his secrets," he said with a wink.

Liu Wei leaned forward, his eyes fixed on Miststrike. "It's beautiful," he murmured. "What can it do?"

"Oh, you'll find out soon enough," Kai replied, his grin widening. "Now, here's how this is going to work. It's going to be the three of you against me."

Zhi-Zhi's head retracted slightly into his shell. "Three against one? But even with your new weapon, surely that's not—"

"Fair?" Kai finished for him. "Oh, I think you'll find it's plenty fair. In fact . . ." He paused, letting the tension build. "I want you all to come at me with everything you've got. No holding back."

Chen Wei and Liu Wei exchanged nervous glances. Even Zhi-Zhi, usually so proud, looked uncertain.

"Senior Brother," Chen Wei began hesitantly, "are you sure about this? We don't want to—"

"To what? Hurt me?" Kai laughed, but there was an edge to it. "Chen Wei, Liu Wei, Zhi-Zhi . . . You're my guild members, my companions. But you're also cultivators. And cultivators must be ready for anything." He twirled Miststrike, the blade leaving faint trails of mist in its wake. "Out there, in the real world, our enemies won't hold back. They won't show mercy. If we want to survive, if we want to thrive, we need to push ourselves to the limit and beyond."

Kai's eyes hardened, his voice taking on a tone that none of them had heard before. "So, here's what I want from you. I want you to forget, just for a moment, that I'm your senior, your guild leader, your friend. I want you to look at me and see only an enemy." He spread his arms wide. "Come at me with everything you have. Every technique, every trick, every ounce of power. Work together, coordinate your attacks. Do whatever it takes to bring me down."

The three guild members stared at Kai, a mix of emotions playing across their faces. Uncertainty, fear, but also . . . excitement. The thrill of a true challenge.

"But, Master," Liu Wei spoke up, his voice quavering slightly, "what if we actually hurt you?"

Kai's smile turned predatory. "Oh, I wouldn't worry about that. Worry about yourselves." He settled into a fighting stance, Miststrike held at the ready. "Now, are you ready to begin?"

Chen Wei swallowed hard, then nodded. He dropped into his own stance, the earth around his feet trembling slightly as he called upon his Golem's Stance cultivation method.

Liu Wei took a deep breath, his body seeming to shimmer as he tapped into the Wind Rider's Path. A gentle breeze began to swirl around him.

Zhi-Zhi, after a moment's hesitation, emerged fully from his shell.

Kai nodded approvingly. "Good. You're taking this seriously. But remember . . ." His voice dropped to a near whisper. "Aim to kill."

CHAPTER SIXTY-FIVE

It seemed they had taken his words to heart because as soon as the words left Kai's mouth, Zhi-Zhi tucked himself into his shell and shot forward like a cannonball.

Well, that's a surprise. Zhi-Zhi's never been one to make the first move.

With Zhi-Zhi having the highest cultivation level here, the tortoise was the one he needed to watch out for.

Reacting quickly, Kai swung Miststrike. The weapon connected with Zhi-Zhi's shell and sent the spirit beast flying across the training ground. As Kai lowered his weapon, he noticed his hand trembling from the impact.

Damn, there was some serious force behind that attack. If that had hit me—

Before Kai could finish the thought, movement from both sides grabbed his attention. Chen Wei, to his right, was slamming his foot into the ground.

"Fire Spike Barrage!" Chen Wei shouted.

The air before him rippled, and suddenly, spikes of fire materialized from thin air and raced toward Kai.

Simultaneously, from Kai's left, Liu Wei traced patterns in the air. "Howling Gale Fist!"

The air around his fists condensed, then formed swirling vortexes that shot toward Kai.

Attacking from both sides, eh? Not bad.

Without missing a beat, Kai took a deep breath and roared, "Thunder Voice!"

The sound that left his mouth was less a shout and more a crash of thunder. The shockwave rippled through the air and caused both Chen Wei and Liu Wei to stagger. Their techniques faltered, the earth spikes crumbling and the wind vortexes dissipating harmlessly in the air.

Not wasting a moment, Kai channeled qi into his legs. In a flash of blue light, Kai vanished and reappeared instantly in front of a dazed Chen Wei. Miststrike glowed with a soft blue light as Kai activated one of its special abilities.

"Hydro Slash!"

A blade of pressurized water extended from Miststrike's tip and sliced toward Chen Wei's abdomen. The attack connected, and Chen Wei stumbled backward, clutching his stomach, as blood seeped between his fingers.

He'll be fine, Kai reassured himself. *I made sure to stock up on healing pills before this.*

Just as Kai was about to press his advantage, he felt something wrap around his legs. Looking down, he saw thick roots emerging from the ground, quickly climbing up his body.

Zhi-Zhi! Kai's eyes narrowed. He'd almost forgotten about the spirit tortoise.

Reaching into his sleeve, Kai pulled out a seed, brought it close to his lips, and whispered, "Wake up, little one."

The seed stirred in his hand. Then, in an instant, it grew into a mass of writhing vines that attacked Zhi-Zhi's roots. The two plant-based techniques wrestled for dominance, allowing Kai to break free. No sooner had Kai regained his footing than he sensed an attack from above. Using Lightning Step once more, Kai vanished and narrowly avoided a gust of wind that sliced through the air where he'd been standing.

"Soaring Eagle Strike!" Zhi-Zhi's voice rang out.

Kai reappeared a few meters away, only to be caught off guard by another attack.

"Tempest Palm!" Liu Wei shouted, his hand coated in swirling wind as it struck out at Kai's chest.

At the last second, Kai managed to activate Iron Skin, his body hardening just as the attack landed. Even so, the force sent him skidding backward and left shallow cuts across his chest.

Despite the pain, Kai couldn't help but smile. *Interesting. Liu Wei has the lowest cultivation, but he's the first to actually land a hit on me. Even if it's just a scratch.*

Kai's eyes narrowed as he reassessed the situation. His opponents were starting to work together, timing their attacks. He couldn't beat all three at once without a plan.

Liu Wei I can probably overpower with most of my techniques. For Chen Wei, I'll need Miststrike to keep him down. But Zhi-Zhi . . . That shell is going to be a problem. Kai's gaze fell on the Root Grasping Vines slithering back into his sleeve. *That might be my best bet for Zhi-Zhi.*

As Kai looked up, he noticed Chen Wei had finished speaking to the others. It seemed the young disciple had taken on the role of tactician. Kai's brow furrowed as he watched Zhi-Zhi leap into the air, only to be caught by Liu Wei, who held the spirit tortoise's shell like a shield.

Oh, using my own trick against me.

Deciding to take the initiative, Kai raised his hand to the sky. "Burning Sky Judgment!"

A fiery sigil blazed to life in the air above them and rained down flames upon his opponents. To Kai's surprise, Zhi-Zhi's shell grew large enough to cover all three of them.

"Well, that's new," Kai muttered.

As the flames dissipated, a gust of wind cleared the smoke. Liu Wei burst through, Zhi-Zhi's shell on one arm like a shield, his other hand wreathed in wind qi as he thrust it toward Kai's chest.

Kai smiled as he met the attack with his own. "Flame Palm Strike!"

The two techniques clashed and created a shockwave that kicked up dust around them. Kai's higher cultivation level and more advanced technique gave him the edge, and Liu Wei began to falter. But then Kai's eyes widened as he noticed qi surrounding Zhi-Zhi's shell.

Before Kai could react, a beam of concentrated wind shot from the shell and struck him squarely in the chest. The force sent Kai flying through the air. As he tumbled through the sky, Kai caught sight of Chen Wei above him—the disciple's hand had transformed into a massive fire palm poised to slam Kai into the ground.

Time to turn this around.

"Heart of Thunder!" Kai roared.

A deafening boom echoed across the training ground as a shockwave of thunder erupted from Kai's chest. Chen Wei, caught in midair, was stunned by the attack and fell to the ground. Below, Liu Wei and Zhi-Zhi were similarly affected, momentarily paralyzed by the thunderous assault.

Kai landed on his feet, wincing as his Iron Skin technique shattered, revealing his injuries. Blood trickled from the cuts on his chest, and bruises were already forming where Liu Wei's attack had landed.

> Skill Leveled Up!
> Iron Skin (Level 4)
> You have gained 50 XP!

Ignoring the notification for now, Kai focused on his next move. "Blaze of Renewal!"

Flames erupted around Kai's body, but instead of burning him, they seemed to seep into his skin. His wounds began to close, his bruises to fade, as if they'd never been there.

Another System message popped up:

> Skill Leveled Up!
> Blaze of Renewal (Level 2)
> You have gained 50 XP!

Kai looked at his opponents, who stared back in surprise. All that work, and he'd already healed himself. He couldn't help but smile.

"I have to hand it to you," Kai said. "Your teamwork is impressive. I underestimated you." His smile turned predatory as he continued, "But now, it's time I got serious." Without warning, Kai thrust his hands outward. "Fiery Lotus Bloom!"

Dozens of flaming lotus petals materialized in the air around him, each one as sharp as a blade and burning with intense heat. With a gesture from Kai, the petals shot toward his opponents.

Liu Wei raised Zhi-Zhi's shell, using it as a makeshift shield against the fiery onslaught. Meanwhile, Chen Wei slammed his palms into the ground, and shouted, "Fire Wall!" A thick barrier of stone erupted from the earth to protect Chen Wei from the worst of the attack.

Taking advantage of the distraction, Kai activated Lightning Step once more. He appeared above and behind Chen Wei, Miststrike's blade extended, then plunged downward.

A System message flashed before Kai's eyes:

Skill Leveled Up!
Lightning Step (Level 2)
You have gained 50 XP!

Ignoring the notification, Kai thrust Miststrike into Chen Wei's shoulder, driving the young disciple to the ground. Chen Wei cried out in pain, his free hand grasping at the weapon lodged in his flesh.

"You'll be fine," Kai assured him. "Just don't try to get back up. This will be over soon." Placing his hand on Miststrike's staff, Kai channeled his qi. "Static Charge."

Electricity raced down the length of the weapon and flowed into Chen Wei's body. The young disciple's muscles seized up, effectively immobilizing him. If the young disciple struggled too much, the lightning would zap him again. It would last for a minute, which was all Kai needed.

One down, two to go, Kai thought as he turned to face Liu Wei and Zhi-Zhi.

The pair had managed to clear away the last of the fiery lotus petals. Liu Wei was breathing heavily, while Zhi-Zhi's eyes darted nervously between Kai and the fallen Chen Wei.

Kai raised his hand to the sky and started channeling a massive amount of lightning qi. The air grew heavy with the scent of ozone as dark clouds began to gather overhead.

"Lightning Hammer Strike!"

Slowly, a massive hammer made of pure lightning took shape in the sky.

Liu Wei's eyes widened in alarm. "Master," he called out, his voice tinged with fear, "aren't you going too far?"

Kai shook his head, his expression serious. "Don't worry. It won't be enough to penetrate Zhi-Zhi's shell."

Zhi-Zhi's eyes narrowed at the lightning construct forming in the sky, but he gave a nod.

With a thunderous crash, the lightning hammer plummeted from the heavens and struck Zhi-Zhi's expanded shell. The impact sent a shockwave across the training ground, kicking up a cloud of dust and debris.

As the dust settled, Kai saw Liu Wei standing unharmed with Zhi-Zhi's shell now shrunk to cover only his hand. Before either of them could react, Kai's Root Grasping Vines shot out and wrapped around Liu Wei, separating him from Zhi-Zhi.

The spirit tortoise let out a roar, then summoned his own roots to combat Kai's technique.

Taking advantage of the distraction, Kai appeared behind Liu Wei. "Sleep," he whispered as he delivered a qi-enhanced chop to the back of Liu Wei's neck. The young disciple crumpled to the ground, unconscious.

Turning his attention back to Zhi-Zhi, Kai frowned. The spirit tortoise's wood techniques were overpowering his Root Grasping Vines with surprising ease.

I shouldn't be surprised. He's almost at the Foundation Establishment Realm, after all.

Realizing he needed a new strategy, Kai began to form a bow and arrow using his Qi Condensation skill. As the construct took shape in his hands, he channeled lightning qi into the arrow.

This had better work, Kai thought as he took aim at Zhi-Zhi. Mentally, he commanded his battered Root Grasping Vines to create an opening.

The plant responded by suddenly surging upward and catching Zhi-Zhi off guard. As the spirit tortoise was pushed into the air, his soft underbelly was exposed for a brief moment.

It was all the opening Kai needed.

The lightning arrow flew true and struck Zhi-Zhi in the chest. Electricity coursed through the spirit tortoise's body, causing him to cry out in pain. "I give up! I give up!"

Kai let out a sigh of relief. If that plan hadn't worked, he wasn't sure what else he could have done to beat Zhi-Zhi. In a real fight to the death, Kai wasn't certain he could have killed the tortoise before running out of qi.

Zhi-Zhi gave up too quickly this time. I know he had more fight in him.

Kai reached into his storage ring and pulled out some healing pills. He walked around and handed them out to the others. When he got to Chen Wei, Kai carefully removed Miststrike from the young disciple's shoulder.

"I'm sorry about that, Chen Wei. You took the brunt of my attack," Kai said as he helped him sit up.

Chen Wei shook his head, wincing a little as he swallowed the pill. "No, Senior Brother," he said. "This was a good exercise. I know our enemies won't go easy on us in a real fight."

Kai clapped him on the back, smiling proudly.

As the healing pills did their work, the four cultivators sat in a circle. They began to discuss the battle, talking about what worked and what didn't.

"Liu Wei, that combination attack with your Flowing Wind Palm and Zhi-Zhi's surprise wind beam really caught me off guard," Kai said, rubbing his chest where the attack had landed. "It was clever and effective."

Liu Wei's eyes lit up at the praise. "Thank you, Master. I've been working on incorporating more of my qi into the wind palm technique. And the idea to combine it with Zhi-Zhi's attack just came to me in the moment."

"I surprised even myself with that wind beam." Zhi-Zhi nodded. "I've been practicing it in secret, but I wasn't sure if I could pull it off in actual combat."

"Well, you certainly did." Kai chuckled. "That combination had me flying through the air before I knew what hit me. It's exactly the kind of unexpected teamwork that can turn the tide in a real fight." Kai turned to Chen Wei. "Good job trying to capitalize on that moment. When I was blown into the sky, you immediately tried to take advantage with that fire palm attack. That kind of quick thinking is crucial in battle."

"Thank you, Senior Brother. I saw you airborne and thought it might be my only chance to land a solid hit."

"That's exactly the right instinct," Kai agreed. "Always be ready to seize any opportunity, no matter how brief."

Zhi-Zhi grumbled, his shell shrinking slightly as if trying to hide. "I should not have tried to take you on alone at the beginning. It was foolish and prideful."

"Don't be too hard on yourself," Kai replied. "Sometimes taking the initiative can catch an opponent off guard. Your attack was unexpected, which is valuable in itself."

Liu Wei nodded in agreement. "Plus, your bravery inspired us to act more boldly too. I might not have attempted that wind palm combination if you hadn't set the tone."

"Speaking of which," Chen Wei chimed in, "that trick with your shell was incredible, Zhi-Zhi! I had no idea you could expand it like that. When did you learn to do that?"

Zhi-Zhi's head emerged a bit more from his shell, a hint of pride returning to his voice. "It's a new technique I've been developing in secret. I call it 'Aegis of the Tortoise God.' This was actually the first time I've used it in combat."

"Well, it certainly came in handy," Kai praised. "That expanded shell defense against my Burning Sky Judgment was impressive. If you can teach that technique to other spirit beasts with shells or carapaces, it could be a game changer in large-scale battles."

Zhi-Zhi's eyes widened at the suggestion. "I . . . I hadn't thought of that, Senior Brother. Do you really think it could be that useful?"

"Absolutely. Don't underestimate the value of a good defense, especially one that can protect multiple allies at once."

As the discussion continued, Kai noticed that while the disciples were freely offering each other advice, they seemed hesitant to critique his performance. He smiled as he decided to address the issue directly.

"You know, I'm not infallible. Feel free to give me some feedback too. What could I have done better?"

For a moment, there was silence. Then Zhi-Zhi spoke up, his words coming out in a rush. "Well, for starters, your initial defense against my shell attack was sloppy. If you had angled Miststrike just fifteen degrees to the left, you could have deflected me with thirty percent less effort. And don't even get me started on your use of Burning Sky Judgment. The timing was off by at least . . ."

Kai couldn't help but laugh as Zhi-Zhi continued his critique. Encouraged by Zhi-Zhi's outburst, Chen Wei and Liu Wei began to offer their own observations, albeit more tentatively.

"Your Lightning Step is impressive, Senior Brother," Chen Wei said, "but you tend to reappear in predictable locations. If you varied your positioning more, it would be harder for enemies to counter."

Liu Wei nodded in agreement. "And while your Thunder Voice is powerful, it leaves you open for a moment after you use it. A skilled opponent might be able to exploit that opening."

Kai listened, nodding at each point. "These are all excellent observations," he said. "I'll definitely work on—"

Kai's words cut off, and his eyes widened. On his map, a massive green spot had appeared and was moving toward him from behind at an incredible speed.

That's way too fast for Qi Refining or even Foundation Establishment, Kai thought, his body tensing.

In one fluid motion, Kai spun around, and Miststrike materialized in his hand as he blocked a sword strike aimed at his back. The clash of weapons rang out across the training ground, startling his companions.

Kai found himself face to face with a young man, perhaps no older than twenty. The newcomer had jet-black hair and piercing blue eyes that seemed to bore into Kai's soul.

<table>
<tr><td>Name: ???</td></tr>
<tr><td>Level: Early Nascent Soul Realm
Age: 20 years</td></tr>
</table>

Nascent Soul? At twenty years old? That's . . . that's impossible!

As he stared into those unfamiliar blue eyes, only one name came to mind.

Wang Lin?

CHAPTER SIXTY-SIX

The stranger's eyes widened slightly. He took a step back and sheathed his sword. "Hmm, you have some great senses. I didn't expect you to notice me."

Kai glanced at the black robes the young man wore. "And I guess you're my senior brother."

The stranger nodded. "I'm Wang Lin, the third disciple of the Sect Master."

Behind Kai, his companions reacted with shock.

"T-third disciple?" Chen Wei stammered. "But that means . . ."

"He's a Legacy Disciple too!" Liu Wei exclaimed, his eyes wide with awe.

"A Legacy Disciple?" Zhi-Zhi frowned. "I thought they were meant to be special. Just how many of them are there?"

Kai simply nodded. He'd already known Wang Lin was returning. They had a mission to do, after all.

"I'm Kai," he said with a bow, "the fifth disciple of the Sect Master."

Wang Lin glanced around at the training ground, taking in the signs of the recent battle. "I watched the battle. I must say, I'm impressed."

Kai raised an eyebrow. "Oh?"

"That combination attack you used when you realized that there was no penetrating the tortoise's shell—the Root Grasping Vines to create an opening, followed by the lightning arrow? Brilliant. It showed great tactical thinking and resourcefulness."

"Thank you," Kai said, inclining his head slightly.

"And your use of Burning Sky Judgment was quite clever," Wang Lin continued. "Using such a high-level technique to force your opponents into a defensive position, then capitalizing on that with your Lightning Step? Very well executed."

Kai listened carefully, nodding along. He knew praise from someone of Wang Lin's level was rare and valuable.

But then Wang Lin's tone changed slightly. "However," he said, "there were a few decisions I might have made differently, especially if you hope to survive higher-level conflicts."

Kai's ears perked up. This was the feedback he'd been waiting for.

Wang Lin gestured to the training ground. "First, your qi control is inefficient. You're wasting at least thirty percent of your energy in most techniques. That might not matter in short skirmishes, but in prolonged battles, it could be fatal."

Kai nodded. He didn't have the qi capacity to spam techniques one after another; he would need to work more on his control.

"Second," Wang Lin continued, "your battle awareness is too narrow. You focus too much on immediate threats and lose sight of the bigger picture. A skilled opponent could easily manipulate your attention and trap you."

Kai nodded slowly. He did feel that the other three were manipulating the flow of the battle and that he was reacting more than initiating.

"For example, during your fight with the spirit tortoise and your other two companions, you became too fixated on countering the spirit tortoise's root techniques. While you were occupied with that, you almost missed your friend's wind attack from your left flank."

Kai's eyes widened slightly as he recalled the moment Wang Lin was referring to. He had indeed been so focused on countering Zhi-Zhi's roots that Liu Wei's wind attack had nearly caught him off guard.

"If your friend had been a more experienced cultivator, or if your servant had coordinated a fire attack from your right side simultaneously, you could have been overwhelmed and severely wounded. In war, an injured cultivator is a dead cultivator."

"I see." Kai nodded slowly, he knew this kind of feedback was priceless coming from someone of Wang Lin's caliber.

This is exactly the kind of insight I need to improve. Wang Lin's battle experience is clearly on a whole different level. I wouldn't be surprised if he has killed thousands of cultivators. Being a Nascent Soul cultivator at twenty must require a certain ruthlessness.

"In a real battle, especially against multiple opponents, you can't afford to tunnel vision on a single threat," Wang Lin said. "You need to maintain awareness of the entire battlefield at all times. Track the movements of all opponents, not just the ones directly attacking you."

Kai nodded, already thinking of the map function.

"One technique I find helpful," Wang Lin continued, "is to use your qi sense to maintain a sort of map of the battlefield in your mind. It takes practice, but eventually, you'll be able to track multiple opponents without even looking at them directly."

"That sounds incredibly useful."

The skill would be something to work on in the future when he wasn't going into war. For now, he would need to rely on his real map.

"The final thing I'll mention is that you rely too heavily on your techniques. True mastery comes from understanding the principles behind them. You should be able to adapt and create new applications on the fly."

Making new applications in the middle of a battle was usually something only battle freaks and prodigies could do. Whilst Kai might seem like a genius to his senior brother, he knew he was just a normal guy with a System. He wouldn't classify himself as a genius—at least, not yet.

"Thank you for your insights, Senior Brother." Kai bowed slightly. "I'll work on improving these areas."

"See that you do." Wang Lin smiled, seeming pleased with Kai's openness to criticism. "Before you get the wrong idea, I should explain," he said. "I wasn't spying on you. That's not how I spend my time, just watching juniors train." He chuckled lightly. "But I needed to find out who my new junior brother was and how he fought if he is going to be joining the mission."

Kai nodded. It made sense that Wang Lin would want to assess a new team member before a potentially deadly mission. Kai found himself reevaluating his initial impressions of his senior brother. The rumors he'd heard about Wang Lin's ruthlessness and cold demeanor seemed at odds with the supportive and friendly cultivator standing before him.

Maybe the rumors aren't true after all. Wang Lin seems like a good senior brother. He took the time to observe my techniques, offer detailed feedback, and even explain his actions. That's not the behavior of someone ruthless or uncaring.

Kai felt a wave of relief wash over him. The prospect of working alongside Wang Lin on the upcoming mission suddenly seemed less daunting. Perhaps they could even form a genuine bond of brotherhood through this shared experience.

I shouldn't be so quick to judge based on rumors, Kai chided himself. *Wang Lin has been nothing but helpful and considerate so far. I'm lucky to have such an experienced senior brother looking out for me.*

Just as Kai was about to express his gratitude for Wang Lin's guidance, he noticed a sudden shift in his senior brother's demeanor. The warm smile faded from Wang Lin's face, replaced by an expression Kai couldn't quite read. His eyes took on a distant, almost cold look. "I can see why Master has his eye on you," he said, his voice now carrying an undercurrent that Kai couldn't quite place.

The abrupt change made Kai feel suddenly uncomfortable. There was something in Wang Lin's voice—a mix of emotions that set him on edge. Was it jealousy? Suspicion? Or perhaps . . . pity? The shift was so sudden and complete that Kai felt as if he were talking to a different person entirely.

"I'm honored by the Sect Master's attention," Kai replied carefully, watching Wang Lin's reaction.

Wang Lin's smile widened slightly, but his eyes remained unreadable. "As you should be," he said, his voice low. "It's not every day a Qi Refining cultivator catches Master's interest. I hope you understand what that truly means."

The way Wang Lin said it sent a chill down Kai's spine. It wasn't a threat but a warning.

Kai nodded, trying to shake off the unsettling feeling. "I'll do my best not to disappoint, Senior Brother."

"See that you don't. We leave in five days. The weaknesses I pointed out could be the difference between success and failure. Work on it. For all our sakes, I hope you're a quick learner."

As Wang Lin turned to leave, he muttered something under his breath that caught Kai's attention. "Interesting junior brothers I have . . . Both able to sense a Nascent Soul cultivator while only in the Qi Refining Realm."

Kai's eyes widened slightly at the comment. *It seems Wang Lin paid Shen Yu a visit too. I wonder how that interaction went.*

Once Wang Lin disappeared, Kai's friends exploded with excitement.

"Senior Brother!" Liu Wei exclaimed, his eyes shining. "That was Wang Lin! *The* Wang Lin! Can you believe it?"

Chen Wei nodded eagerly. "I've heard so many stories about him. They say he's the youngest Nascent Soul cultivator in the sect's history and that he will become the next Sect Master!"

"He's pretty cool . . . for a human," Zhi-Zhi muttered, trying to sound unimpressed but failing to hide the awe in his voice.

As their excitement died down, curiosity took over. Liu Wei turned to Kai, his brow furrowed. "Senior Brother, what mission was Wang Lin talking about?"

"Are you going somewhere with him?" Chen Wei chimed in. "Is it dangerous?"

Even Zhi-Zhi leaned forward, clearly interested in Kai's answer.

Kai considered his response carefully. He didn't want to worry his companions, but he also knew they deserved some explanation. "It's related to the Crimson Phoenix Sect and the upcoming war," he said finally. "But that's all I can say. Don't worry about me. You should focus on your own preparations."

He turned to Zhi-Zhi and offered the spirit tortoise a smile. "Good luck with your breakthrough, Zhi-Zhi. I'm sure you'll do great."

With that, Kai dismissed them and made his way back to his quarters. While he walked, his mind was focused on Wang Lin's peculiar behavior. The sudden shifts in mood, the cryptic warnings, the unreadable expressions—it all seemed so . . . bizarre.

Is this what happens when a cultivator reaches the Nascent Soul Realm? Do they all become this . . . strange?

He'd heard rumors, of course. Whispers among the junior disciples about how the truly powerful cultivators were often eccentric, their behavior unpredictable and sometimes unsettling. But he'd always attributed those stories to exaggeration and awe.

Now, having experienced Wang Lin's mercurial temperament firsthand, Kai wasn't so sure. *Maybe it's a side effect of the cultivation process. All that power, the separation of one's soul . . . Perhaps it changes a person in ways we can't understand at lower levels.*

He thought back to other high-level cultivators he'd encountered. The Sect Master, with his enigmatic smiles and piercing gaze. Elder Xiao, with his unhealthy obsession with alchemy. Not to mention the mysterious old man roleplaying as a homeless janitor.

But Wang Lin is only twenty, Kai reminded himself. *He hasn't had decades or centuries for power to warp his mind. Unless . . . unless the process of reaching Nascent Soul so young is what caused this strangeness.*

The thought was both fascinating and terrifying. If this was the price of power, was it worth it? To become so detached, so inscrutable to others?

Kai shook his head, trying to clear his thoughts. *I'm getting ahead of myself. I've only had one conversation with Wang Lin. Maybe he was just having an off day. Maybe I'm reading too much into this.*

But deep down, Kai knew he was grasping at straws. His instincts told him there was more to Wang Lin's behavior than mere eccentricity. Whether it was the result of reaching Nascent Soul or something else entirely, Kai couldn't shake the feeling that he was dealing with a person—or perhaps a being—far more complex and potentially dangerous than he'd initially realized.

I'll need to be on my guard, Kai decided. *Not just against external threats, but against the possible instability of my own allies. If this is what awaits at higher levels of cultivation, I'll need to prepare myself mentally as well as physically.*

With these sobering thoughts, Kai reached his quarters. He had five days to prepare for the mission, and now he had a new aspect to consider in his training. How does one prepare to work alongside a potentially unstable genius?

CHAPTER SIXTY-SEVEN

The sun dipped low on the horizon as Kai made his way to the meeting spot just outside the Azure Sky Sect. Five days had passed since his encounter with Wang Lin, and Kai had spent every waking moment preparing for the mission ahead.

I can't believe I'm actually doing this, Kai thought as he assessed the items in his inventory. It was filled to the brim with pills, talismans, and other supplies he'd either crafted or purchased. *My first time leaving the sect since I became a disciple, and it might be my last.*

He'd focused heavily on improving his qi control, remembering Wang Lin's critique. Hours of meditation and practice had yielded results, but Kai still felt unprepared.

Even with the trident mark, I'm not sure I'll survive if things go wrong. Kai sighed, his hand unconsciously rubbing his wrist where the mark lay hidden. *These high-level cultivators could probably kill me a thousand times over without breaking a sweat.*

As Kai approached the meeting area, he spotted a familiar figure. Shen Yu stood motionless, staring blankly into the distance. Kai raised a hand in greeting as he drew near.

"Shen Yu," Kai said with a nod.

The Legacy Disciple returned the nod but remained silent. As Kai drew closer, his eyes widened. The qi rolling off Shen Yu was . . . different. Stronger.

"You've broken through to Foundation Establishment," Kai said, unable to keep the surprise from his voice. "Congratulations."

Shen Yu's eyes flickered to Kai, narrowing slightly. "I know you'll join me soon."

Kai nodded, thinking of his own progress. *Only seven hundred XP to go before I level up. But that's not the same as a true breakthrough. I'll need to rely on my cultivation method for that.*

An uncomfortable silence fell between them. Kai shifted his weight from foot to foot, then decided to break the ice.

"So, how do you feel about this mission?" Kai asked, trying to keep his tone casual. "Honestly, I'd rather not take the risk. It seems . . . unnecessarily dangerous."

Shen Yu was quiet for a long moment. Just as Kai thought he wouldn't answer, Shen Yu spoke. "I asked the Sect Master for a place on this mission."

Kai blinked in surprise. "You did? Why would you—"

Before he could finish his question, something on his map caught his attention. A large green spot had appeared nearby, seemingly out of nowhere. Kai's head snapped toward it at the exact moment that Shen Yu's did the same.

There was nothing there. At least, nothing visible.

A few seconds passed, and then a young woman's laugh echoed from the empty space. The air shimmered and vibrated, and suddenly, a figure stepped forward as if emerging from an invisible curtain.

The woman who appeared was striking, with long silver hair and eyes that seemed to shift color in the light. She looked between Kai and Shen Yu, a mix of surprise and amusement on her face.

"Well, well," she said, her voice lilting and playful. "Wang Lin said you were both impressive, but I didn't expect you to see through my disguise so quickly. Especially you," she added, nodding toward Kai. "A Qi Refining cultivator shouldn't be able to detect me at all."

Kai and Shen Yu exchanged a quick glance before introducing themselves.

"I'm Yin Mengshuang," the woman said with a slight bow, "a friend of Wang Lin and a member of his team. It's a pleasure to meet you both." Yin Mengshuang's eyes sparkled with curiosity as she looked between Kai and Shen Yu. "So, you're the new Legacy Disciples I've heard so much about. Wang Lin speaks highly of you both."

Shen Yu remained silent, his face an unreadable mask. Kai, for his part, tried to be polite, but his mind was still racing as he tried to think of a way out of this mission.

"It's nice to meet you too, Senior Sister," Kai said, forcing a smile. "I look forward to working with you."

Yin Mengshuang stepped forward, and Kai's eyes narrowed slightly as he took in her status.

Name: Yin Mengshuang
Level: Early Core Formation Realm Age: 27 years

Kai's surprise at her cultivation level must have shown on his face, because Yin Mengshuang's smile widened. "Impressed? Don't worry, you'll get there someday. So, are you two excited for the mission? It's not every day junior disciples get to tag along on something like this!"

Shen Yu turned away, clearly uninterested in conversation.

"It's . . . an honor to be chosen," Kai said carefully. *And a death sentence if things go wrong*, he added silently.

Yin Mengshuang seemed about to say more when a soft voice cut through the air.

"Junior Sister, leave them be. They clearly aren't in the mood for conversation."

All three turned to see a new arrival. A tall man with long dark hair and eyes as deep and calm as the sea approached.

"I am Qi Liaxuan. It's a pleasure to meet you both."

Name: Qi Liaxuan
Level: Late Core Formation Realm Age: 29 years

Two Core Formation cultivators? And Wang Lin at Nascent Soul . . . This is a hit squad! What other kind of mission requires this level of firepower? The knot in Kai's stomach tightened as he gave the new arrival a light bow.

Yin Mengshuang's eyes lit up at Qi Liaxuan's arrival. "Oh, come now, Liaxuan. Don't be such a spoilsport. I was just getting to know our new teammates."

"Your idea of 'getting to know' someone often involves more prying than is polite."

"You wound me," Yin Mengshuang said, placing a hand over her heart in mock offense. "I'll have you know I can be the very soul of discretion when I choose to be."

"And how often do you choose to be?"

As the two bantered, Kai's eyes narrowed slightly. He leaned closer to Shen Yu and whispered, "He's here."

No sooner had the words left Kai's mouth than Wang Lin appeared, seeming to materialize out of thin air. The chatter died instantly as all eyes turned to the Nascent Soul cultivator.

Wang Lin's gaze swept over the group, assessing each of them in turn. When his eyes met Kai's, there was a flicker of . . . something. Approval? Expectation?

"Good, you're all here. It's time we discussed the mission in detail."

Kai nodded; he was overthinking the dangers, surely.

"Our sect has gathered intelligence on the Boundless Earth Sect. A group of their members is heading toward the border between their territory and that of the Crimson Phoenix Sect. They plan to meet in secret with members of the Crimson Phoenix Sect." Wang Lin's eyes hardened as he continued. "The Crimson Phoenix Sect members are bringing offerings to convince the Boundless Earth Sect to ally with them. Our task is to kill the Crimson Phoenix Sect members and then frame the Boundless Earth Sect for their deaths."

Kai felt a chill run down his spine. This wasn't just a simple mission—it was a powder keg waiting to explode. One wrong move could have both the Boundless Earth Sect and Crimson Phoenix Sect attacking the Azure Sky Sect, but being complacent could lead to the same outcome.

Wang Lin turned to Kai and Shen Yu. "You two will primarily be observing. However, if there are any Foundation Establishment cultivators present, it will be your task to deal with them."

Kai frowned, trying to keep his face neutral. *Deal with Foundation Establishment cultivators? Is he serious?* Kai knew Shen Yu, having just broken through, could probably handle most Foundation Establishment cultivators. But Kai himself was still in the Qi Refining Realm. He might be able to keep an early Foundation Establishment cultivator busy for a while. But defeating one? That seemed impossible at this stage.

This has to be some kind of test, Kai thought, biting back the urge to protest. *There's no point in complaining. I'll just have to find a way to make it work.*

"Understood, Senior Brother."

Wang Lin nodded, seemingly satisfied with their acceptance of their roles. He then reached into his storage ring and pulled out what looked like a miniature boat.

"We'll use this to cover most of the distance," Wang Lin explained, holding up the tiny vessel. "It's a high-grade flying artifact that can accommodate all of us. However, when we get closer to our destination, we'll need to rely on our own flight abilities to avoid detection."

As Wang Lin spoke, the miniature boat began to grow until it was large enough for all of them to stand comfortably on its deck.

"Any questions before we depart?" Wang Lin asked, looking at each of them in turn.

Kai had about a thousand questions, but he knew now wasn't the time to voice them. Instead, he shook his head along with the others.

"Very well," Wang Lin said. "Get on. We leave immediately."

As Kai stepped onto the flying boat, he couldn't shake the feeling that things wouldn't be as simple as Wang Lin assumed. He glanced at Shen Yu, expecting to see his usual stoic expression. Instead, Kai caught a fleeting glimmer in Shen Yu's eyes—was that anticipation? It vanished as quickly as it appeared, leaving Kai to wonder if he'd imagined it.

What have I gotten myself into? But more importantly, how am I going to get out of it alive?

CHAPTER SIXTY-EIGHT

The boat glided silently through the air as Kai gripped the railing, his eyes scanning the landscape below. They were a few hundred kilometers away from the border separating the Boundless Earth Sect and the Crimson Phoenix Sect territories.

"You know, this reminds me of my last run-in with those Crimson Phoenix scum," Yin Mengshuang murmured.

Qi Liaxuan sighed, clearly having heard this story before. "Do you really need to tell that tale again, Junior Sister?"

"Oh, come on! It's a good story," Yin Mengshuang protested. She turned to Kai and Shen Yu. "It was about a year ago. I was on a solo scouting mission near the Howling Cliffs. You know the place?"

Kai shook his head, but Shen Yu nodded slightly.

"Well, it's this nasty bit of terrain—all jagged rocks and hidden crevices. Perfect for an ambush, which is exactly what those Crimson Phoenix rats had in mind."

She paused for dramatic effect. "I sensed something was off, but before I could react, they sprang their trap. Three of them: two Core Formation and one late Foundation Establishment. They thought they had me cornered."

"And how did you escape?" Kai asked.

Yin Mengshuang grinned, a mischievous glint in her eye. "Escape? Oh no, little Junior Brother. I didn't escape. I made them regret ever laying eyes on me." She leaned in, "You see, they didn't know about my special technique—the Mirage of a Thousand Dreams. As soon as they attacked, I unleashed it."

"The Mirage of a Thousand Dreams?"

"It's a high-level illusion technique," Qi Liaxuan explained as he let out a sigh. "Yin Mengshuang is quite adept at it."

"Adept?" Yin Mengshuang scoffed. "I'm a master! Anyway, the technique traps the victim in a series of overlapping illusions. Each time they think they've broken free, they find themselves in another layer of the dream." She chuckled, the sound both amused and slightly menacing. "Those Crimson Phoenix fools didn't stand a chance. The two Core Formation cultivators spent the next hour fighting shadows while I picked them apart. And the Foundation Establishment one? He was convinced he'd turned into a spirit beast. Last I saw, he was trying to fly off a cliff, flapping his arms like wings."

She's like Kurenai, a master of illusions. I just hope we don't run into anyone like Itachi out there, Kai thought wryly, remembering how easily the Uchiha prodigy had turned Kurenai's illusions against her.

"What's got you looking so serious, Junior Brother?" Yin Mengshuang's voice broke through Kai's thoughts. "Don't tell me my story scared you?"

Kai shook his head, forcing a smile. "Not at all, Senior Sister. I was just . . . impressed by your skill with illusions. It must have taken a lot of practice to master such techniques."

"Oh, you have no idea!" Yin Mengshuang beamed at him. "But it's worth every moment when you see the look on your enemy's face as they realize they've been trapped in your web."

As Yin Mengshuang launched into her reasons why illusion techniques were the best field to specialize in, Kai found his mind wandering. He looked at the cultivators around him, each ready to risk their lives for the Azure Sky Sect.

Do they really believe in what they're fighting for? Or are they just being used by the higher-ups, like pawns in a game? It's not so different from the wars back on Earth.

The thought left a bitter taste in his mouth. He'd seen firsthand how governments and corporations manipulated people into fighting their battles. Now, in this new world of cultivation and magical sects, it seemed some things hadn't changed.

"This is as far as we can go by boat," Wang Lin said, his voice cutting through Kai's thoughts. "Prepare to disembark."

The boat slowed to a stop, hovering just above the tree line of a dense forest. One by one, they jumped off the deck. As soon as the last person's feet touched the ground, the boat shrank rapidly until it was no bigger than a toy. Wang Lin plucked it out of the air and slipped it into his storage ring.

A loud squawk pierced the air. Kai looked up to see a large raven descending from the sky. It circled once before landing on Wang Lin's outstretched arm. The bird's beady eyes darted between the cultivators before focusing on Wang Lin.

Thanks to his Spirit Beast Communication skill, Kai could understand the raven's message. "Master Wang, the plan was successful. The Boundless Earth Sect members have been delayed as requested."

Wang Lin nodded, gently stroking the raven's feathers. "Well done. Return to your post and keep watch. Alert us if anything changes."

As the raven took flight, Wang Lin turned to the group. "Good news. The

Boundless Earth Sect members have been delayed. This gives us an opportunity to deal with the Crimson Phoenix Sect members without interference."

"Perfect." Yin Mengshuang grinned. "I've been itching for some action."

"Remember," Qi Liaxuan cautioned, "we're here to complete a mission, not satisfy your bloodlust, Junior Sister."

Wang Lin nodded in agreement. "Liaxuan is right. We stick to the plan. We can expect to be up against a team of four or five. We don't have time to play with our food."

He turned to Kai and Shen Yu. "You two, try to keep up. This is your chance to observe and learn."

With that, Wang Lin rose into the air, and his body skimmed low to the ground as he began to fly. Yin Mengshuang and Qi Liaxuan drew their swords to use them as flying mounts. Kai knew that only Nascent Soul cultivators and above could fly without aid from treasures.

Kai and Shen Yu exchanged a glance before drawing their own swords and following the others.

As they flew, Kai's eyes darted between his companions. He could see them clearly with his own eyes, but when he closed them for a moment, relying only on his qi sense, he realized something unsettling. Without his map function or visual confirmation, he wouldn't have been able to detect their presence at all.

This is . . . unnerving, Kai thought, a chill running down his spine. *If I couldn't see them or use my map, I'd have no idea the Core Formation cultivators were even here, let alone Wang Lin at Nascent Soul level.* He opened his eyes, watching Wang Lin's back as they flew. *If someone like that decided to hunt me, I wouldn't even know they were there until it was too late. No wonder cultivators are so paranoid about hidden masters and secret techniques.*

Suddenly, a rustling sound caught Kai's attention. From the bushes below, a small creature emerged. It looked like a cross between a rabbit and a squirrel, with soft brown fur and large intelligent eyes. But despite its cute appearance, Kai could sense an aura of power that dwarfed his own emanating from it.

Core Formation, Kai realized with a start. *That little thing is as powerful as Yin Mengshuang and Qi Liaxuan!*

The creature's nose twitched, and its eyes locked onto their group. Even though the cultivators were suppressing their qi, the beast must have used one of its other senses to detect their presence.

With surprising speed, the creature leaped toward them; it dropped its cute facade to reveal sharp claws and teeth.

Yin Mengshuang scoffed. "How cute. It thinks it can take us on."

Before anyone else could react, Wang Lin lazily waved his sleeve. A burst of invisible force slammed into the creature. In an instant, the Core Formation beast simply . . . ceased to exist. There wasn't even a corpse left behind.

Wang Lin didn't even look back as he spoke. "We don't have time to play. Keep moving."

Kai's eyes lingered on the spot where the beast had been. *What a waste of resources. A Core Formation beast corpse like that could have been useful.* His gaze then shifted to Wang Lin's back. The casual display of power sent another chill through Kai. *The difference between us is too great. There's no trick I could pull, no strategy I could use, that would let me win against someone like him.*

Huang Tao shifted nervously from foot to foot, his eyes darting between the other cultivators gathered in the clearing. At seventeen years old, he was the youngest member of this important mission, a fact that filled him with both pride and anxiety.

I shouldn't be here, he thought, not for the first time. *I'm not ready for this.*

Despite reaching Foundation Establishment at such a young age, a feat that had earned him the title of "genius" within the Crimson Phoenix Sect, Huang Tao couldn't shake the feeling that he was an imposter. That any moment, someone would realize he didn't belong.

His gaze drifted to the Nascent Soul Elder, Master Bu, who sat cross-legged in the air, eyes closed in meditation. The Elder's mere presence was enough to make Huang Tao feel small, insignificant. *With Elder Bu here, we're safe. Nothing can touch a Nascent Soul cultivator.*

"Hey, kid." A gruff voice pulled Huang Tao from his thoughts. It was Li Yuan, one of the Core Formation cultivators. "Stop fidgeting. You'll attract spirit beasts with all that nervous energy."

Huang Tao straightened, trying to still his restless movements. "Sorry, Senior Brother Li. I'm just . . . anxious about the meeting."

Li Yuan's expression softened slightly. "Relax. This isn't your first mission, is it?"

"N-no," Huang Tao admitted. "But it's the first one this important. If we can convince the Boundless Earth Sect to join us against the Azure Sky Sect . . ."

"It would change everything." Li Yuan nodded. "But that's not your concern. Your job is to watch and learn. Let us handle the negotiations."

From across the clearing, the other Core Formation cultivator, Zhao Xiuying, called out, "They're late. Do you think something happened?"

"Who knows with those Boundless Earth types." Li Yuan shrugged. "Probably got distracted by a particularly interesting rock formation."

Zhao Xiuying snorted. "You shouldn't underestimate them. I've heard their earth manipulation techniques are formidable."

"Formidable or not," Li Yuan retorted, "they're still keeping us waiting. It's disrespectful."

As the two Core Formation cultivators bickered, Huang Tao's attention was drawn to the other Foundation Establishment cultivator, a girl named Jin Ling. Unlike Huang Tao, she seemed completely at ease, lounging against a tree with a bored expression.

"Aren't you worried?" Huang Tao asked her in a low voice.

Jin Ling raised an eyebrow. "About what? The Boundless Earth Sect? Please. They're probably just trying to make us sweat a little before they show up."

"But what if it's a trap?" Huang Tao persisted. "What if they're planning to ambush us?"

Jin Ling laughed. "With Elder Bu here? They'd have to be suicidal. Besides, they need this alliance as much as we do. The Azure Sky Sect has been encroaching on their territory for years."

Huang Tao nodded, trying to take comfort in her words. Still, he couldn't shake the feeling that something was off.

As the sun climbed higher in the sky, the mood in the clearing grew tenser. Li Yuan paced back and forth, muttering under his breath about the rudeness of earth cultivators. Zhao Xiuying had given up on conversation and was sharpening her sword with quick, angry strokes.

Even Jin Ling's cool facade had begun to crack. "Okay," she admitted, "this is getting ridiculous. They're nearly an hour late."

Elder Bu's eyes snapped open, startling everyone. "Patience," he commanded. "The Boundless Earth Sect moves at its own pace. We will wait."

No one dared argue with the Nascent Soul Elder, but Huang Tao could see the frustration on his companions' faces.

When more than an hour had passed, Huang Tao's nerves were frayed to the breaking point. Every rustle in the undergrowth made him jump, convinced that something was wrong.

"This is pointless," Li Yuan finally exploded. "They're not coming!"

Just when it seemed like he might actually storm off, Zhao Xiuying spoke up. "Hey, does anyone else feel that?"

Huang Tao frowned, concentrating. Now that Zhao Xiuying mentioned it, there was something . . . off about the air. A faint pressure, barely noticeable but growing stronger by the second.

Suddenly, Elder Bu's eyes snapped open. In a flash, he was on his feet and a green barrier had appeared around the group.

And not a moment too soon. A massive bolt of lightning crashed against the barrier, the sound of the impact like a thunderclap right next to Huang Tao's ears.

"Ambush!" the Elder roared. "Prepare for battle!"

CHAPTER SIXTY-NINE

I should be relaxing in the sect, not risking my life out here, Elder Bu thought bitterly as he floated high into the sky. *A dozen years left to live, and they send me on this mission. If I die, no one will even care.*

His gaze drifted briefly to his companions below. The two Core Formation cultivators were already locked in combat with the Azure Sky Sect members. And young Huang Tao . . .

Poor kid. Talented, but he clearly offended the wrong person to end up here.

Elder Bu pushed those thoughts aside. He had bigger problems. His eyes locked onto the figure floating opposite him—a man in black robes.

So young . . . This can only be Wang Lin.

"I see that the rumors are true," Elder Bu called out. "You've broken through to the Nascent Soul Realm."

A small smile played on Wang Lin's lips. "Indeed. And I must say, Elder Bu, I've taken the heads of many Nascent Soul cultivators in my time. But yours will be the first as a Nascent Soul cultivator myself."

The casual way Wang Lin spoke of killing powerful cultivators sent a chill down Elder Bu's spine. He had heard tales of this young prodigy—not only was he a genius in cultivation, but he was a master of combat as well. If left unchecked, there might come a day when even the Sect Master of the Crimson Phoenix Sect would be no match for him.

If only those assassination attempts on him had succeeded. How many times has the Crimson Phoenix Sect tried to nip this threat in the bud? But each time, this boy has somehow survived, and now he's standing before me as an equal.

Elder Bu knew he had to end this quickly. He couldn't afford to let this fight drag on—it would only give the genius more time to analyze and break down his attacks. He took a step forward, though he stood on nothing but air. His robes began to smolder, then burst into flame. They burned away to reveal his body now covered in crimson fire.

"Crimson Phoenix Flame Body!" It was the name of the technique that had helped Elder Bu slay countless cultivation experts in the past. It was his trump card, and he hoped it would be enough to overwhelm the young upstart before him.

Wang Lin seemed unimpressed. He casually swung the plain black sword that had appeared in his hand. The air around the blade shimmered with an unnatural darkness, and Elder Bu watched in horror as the trees beneath them withered and died from the mere aftereffects of the sword's qi.

"Death qi," Elder Bu muttered. He had heard of Wang Lin's mastery over this rare and dangerous energy, but seeing it in action was something else entirely.

Not wanting to give Wang Lin a chance to attack, Elder Bu vanished in a burst of flame. He reappeared behind the young cultivator with his flaming fist aimed squarely at Wang Lin's head. When he saw no movement from his opponent, Elder Bu's heart soared—Wang Lin wasn't going to be able to dodge!

But at the last second, the young man's form dissolved into black mist. Bu's fist passed harmlessly through the shadows.

"An illusion?" Bu gasped.

"Not quite." Wang Lin's voice came from behind him.

Elder Bu spun around, only to see Wang Lin reforming from wisps of black qi.

"Death Step," Wang Lin explained. "A technique of my own creation. It allows me to temporarily transform my body into death qi."

Elder Bu stared in disbelief. *To create such a technique at his age . . .* He looked down at his fist, still wreathed in flames. But the fire seemed dimmer now, less intense. "What did you do?"

Wang Lin's expression remained neutral. "My death qi doesn't just harm the body, Elder Bu. It corrodes qi itself. Even your Crimson Phoenix Flame Body isn't immune."

I . . . I can't beat him.

They were both beings at the Early Nascent Soul Realm, yet the gap in their abilities was clear. Unlike many other cultivators, Elder Bu still had enough rationality left to know when he was outmatched, so for a brief moment, he considered fleeing. But the importance of this mission held him back. He couldn't abandon his duty, not when so much was at stake.

What has happened to the Boundless Earth Sect members? Has Wang Lin already dealt with them?

But no, Elder Bu realized, shaking his head. Wang Lin had said this would be his first Nascent Soul kill as a Nascent Soul cultivator. That meant the Boundless Earth Sect cultivators were still alive, perhaps delayed by some means.

A plan began to form in Elder Bu's mind. If he could hold out long enough, surely the qi disturbances from their battle would draw the attention of the Boundless Earth Sect members. With their help, he might stand a chance against this monstrous young cultivator.

"What's the matter, Elder?" Wang Lin called out, his voice tinged with amusement. "Having second thoughts about our little dance?"

Elder Bu gritted his teeth. "You're skilled, boy, I'll give you that. But don't think for a moment that your youth and talent will be enough to overcome centuries of experience!"

With that, he charged forward once more, his body a comet of crimson flame. The Elder knew he couldn't win in a direct confrontation, but perhaps he could buy enough time for help to arrive.

As the two Nascent Soul cultivators clashed high above the forest, a very different battle was unfolding below.

Yin Mengshuang stood face to face with Li Yuan, both Core Formation cultivators sizing each other up.

"Well, well." Li Yuan smirked. "What do we have here? A little girl playing at being a cultivator?"

Yin Mengshuang's eyes flashed dangerously. "This 'little girl' is about to teach you a lesson in respect, old man."

Li Yuan laughed. "Big words. Let's see if you can back them up!"

He lunged forward, his fist glowing with fiery qi. Yin Mengshuang didn't move, a small smile playing on her lips. Just as Li Yuan's fist was about to connect, Yin Mengshuang's form shimmered and vanished.

"What?" Li Yuan stumbled, his momentum carrying him forward.

"Over here, old timer," Yin Mengshuang said from behind him.

Li Yuan spun around, only to find himself face to face with . . . himself?

"Like what you see?" his doppelganger asked, wearing Yin Mengshuang's mischievous grin.

"An illusion?" Li Yuan growled. "You'll have to do better than that!"

He lashed out with a kick, but his foot passed right through the illusion. Laughter echoed around him. Suddenly, he was surrounded by copies of himself, each wearing that same irritating grin.

"What's wrong?" they all asked in unison. "Can't tell reality from illusion?"

Li Yuan gritted his teeth. "Enough of these games!"

He closed his eyes and focused on his qi sense. There! A flicker of real qi among the illusions. With a roar, he charged forward, his fist aimed at the real Yin Mengshuang. But just as he was about to strike, the ground beneath his feet turned to quicksand. Li Yuan sank up to his knees, thrown off balance.

"Too slow," Yin Mengshuang taunted, appearing a few feet away. "Maybe if you spent less time talking and more time training, you wouldn't be so easily fooled."

Li Yuan's face turned red with anger. "You little brat! I'll show you the power of a true Core Formation expert!"

He gathered his qi, preparing to break free of the illusory quicksand. But before he could, silver threads shot out from Yin Mengshuang's sleeves, wrapping around his arms and legs.

"What is this?" Li Yuan said as he struggled against the bindings.

Yin Mengshuang smirked. "Dream Binding Threads. A little technique I picked up. They're quite useful for dealing with overconfident fools."

Li Yuan roared in frustration, his qi flaring as he tried to break free. But the more he struggled, the tighter the threads became.

"Now, then," Yin Mengshuang said, her voice suddenly serious. "Let's have a real fight, shall we?"

Meanwhile, on the other side of the clearing, Qi Liaxuan faced off against Zhao Xiuying. Unlike the heated exchange between Yin Mengshuang and Li Yuan, these two Core Formation experts regarded each other with cold calculation.

"I've heard of you," Zhao Xiuying said. "Qi Liaxuan, master of the Dao of the Flowing Abyss."

Qi Liaxuan inclined his head slightly. "And I've heard of you, Zhao Xiuying. Your fire techniques are said to be quite impressive."

"Flattery won't save you," Zhao Xiuying snapped. She raised her hands, flames dancing between her fingers. "Prepare yourself!"

She unleashed a barrage of fireballs, each one hissing through the air toward Qi Liaxuan. But the Azure Sky Sect cultivator remained calm. With a wave of his hand, a wall of water rose up before him and extinguished the flames in a cloud of steam.

"Fire against water," Qi Liaxuan mused. "A classic confrontation, wouldn't you agree? Like the eternal dance of yin and yang."

Zhao Xiuying's eyes narrowed. "Save your philosophizing for someone who cares. I'm here to fight, not chat."

She charged forward, her body wreathed in flames. But as she neared Qi Liaxuan, she found herself slowing. It was as if she were trying to run through thick syrup.

"What . . . what is this?" she gasped.

"The Dao of the Flowing Abyss is not just about water, you see." Qi Liaxuan smiled. "It's about flow itself. Time, space . . . All can be manipulated if you understand the true nature of flow."

With a gesture, he sent a wave of water crashing toward Zhao Xiuying. But this was no ordinary water. It moved in impossible ways, splitting and reforming, defying gravity.

Zhao Xiuying tried to dodge, but in the warped space around her, her movements were sluggish and uncoordinated. The water struck her, not with physical force, but with something far stranger. She felt time itself wash over her, years passing in seconds.

When the wave receded, Zhao Xiuying found herself gasping for breath. Her hair had streaks of gray in it now, and her skin felt looser, older.

"What . . . what did you do to me?" she demanded, her voice shaking.

Qi Liaxuan's expression was almost pitying. "I simply showed you a glimpse of the Abyss. Time flows differently there. But don't worry—the effects are temporary. Probably."

"How can you do this to me? This is power beyond the Core Formation Realm!" Zhao Xiuying snarled as she gathered her qi, preparing for a massive attack. But before she could release it, Qi Liaxuan spoke again.

"Tell me, Zhao Xiuying. Have you ever considered the transient nature of our existence? How we are but ripples on the surface of a vast, uncaring universe?"

Despite herself, Zhao Xiuying found her concentration wavering. "What are you talking about?"

"Life, death, victory, defeat . . . In the grand scheme of things, do they truly matter? We fight, we struggle, but to what end?"

Zhao Xiuying shook her head, trying to clear it. But Qi Liaxuan's words seemed to echo in her mind, mixing with the lingering effects of the time distortion.

"I . . . I don't . . ."

"Perhaps," Qi Liaxuan continued, his voice soft and hypnotic, "it would be better to simply . . . let go. To allow yourself to be carried by the current of fate, rather than fighting against it."

Zhao Xiuying felt her will to fight draining away. A part of her knew this was wrong, that she was falling into some kind of trap. But another part . . . another part just wanted to rest.

Qi Liaxuan watched as confusion and doubt played across Zhao Xiuying's face. He knew his words were having an effect, burrowing into her mind, weakening her resolve.

The Dao of the Flowing Abyss is as much about the mind as it is about physical techniques, he thought. *Break the enemy's will and victory is assured.*

But he knew better than to let his guard down. Zhao Xiuying was still a dangerous opponent, and if she broke free from his mental assault, her anger would make her even more formidable.

So he prepared himself, gathering his qi for his next move. Whatever happened, he would be ready.

As these intense battles raged on, Kai and Shen Yu found themselves facing off against the two Foundation Establishment cultivators, Huang Tao and Jin Ling.

Kai eyed them warily. Being in the Qi Refining Realm, he knew he couldn't underestimate them. Foundation Establishment was a significant leap in power.

"Shen Yu," he said softly, "how do you want to play this?"

Shen Yu's face remained impassive. "Take the girl. I'll handle the boy."

Without another word, Shen Yu dashed forward, his movement so fast it left afterimages. Huang Tao's eyes widened in surprise, but he quickly recovered and raised his hands to defend himself.

Kai turned his attention to Jin Ling, who stood ready with a short sword in her hand. Her eyes narrowed as she assessed Kai.

"A Qi Refining cultivator?" Jin Ling scoffed. "They must be desperate to send someone like you."

Yes, underestimate me. That's the only way I survive this. He knew his only chance against a Foundation Establishment cultivator was to catch her off guard. The more she looked down on him, the better his odds.

Outwardly, Kai allowed a flicker of uncertainty to cross his face, as if Jin Ling's words had shaken his confidence. "I . . . I'm stronger than I look," he said, his voice deliberately wavering slightly.

Jin Ling's smirk widened. "Oh, I'm sure you are," she mocked, twirling her sword in the air. "This will be over quickly, little Qi Refiner. Try not to embarrass yourself too much."

That's it. Keep thinking I'm no threat. You have no idea what's coming.

CHAPTER SEVENTY

Without warning, Jin Ling dashed forward. Her sword became a blur as she aimed for Kai's neck. Time seemed to slow as Kai's survival instincts kicked in.

"Swift Wind Step!" he gasped.

Kai's body blurred as he narrowly avoided decapitation, leaving afterimages. The sword passed so close that he felt the wind brush against his skin.

"Oh? Not bad for a Qi Refiner." Jin Ling's eyebrows rose slightly. "You might last a whole minute at this rate."

Kai didn't respond, instead focusing on maintaining his defensive stance. *I can't let her dictate the pace of this fight. I need to find an opening.*

Jin Ling didn't give him much time to think. She lunged forward again, this time with a technique of her own. "Crimson Flame Strike!"

Her sword erupted in brilliant red flames, the heat intense even from a distance. Kai knew he couldn't dodge this one. Instead, he activated another skill.

"Iron Skin!" he shouted. A faint metallic sheen covered his body just as Jin Ling's flaming sword made contact.

The impact sent Kai skidding backward, his feet leaving furrows in the ground. He gritted his teeth against the pain. The Iron Skin had reduced the damage, but he could still feel the burn where the sword had struck.

"Interesting," Jin Ling murmured as she raised an eyebrow. "You're full of surprises, aren't you?"

Kai managed a grin, despite the pain. "I try to keep things exciting."

This isn't good. One hit, and I'm already feeling it. I need to turn this around somehow.

He decided to go on the offensive. Gathering his qi, Kai activated another skill. "Flame Palm Strike!"

He dashed forward, his palm wreathed in fire. Jin Ling's eyes widened slightly, clearly not expecting a fire-based attack. She didn't even try to dodge. As Kai's flaming palm struck her chest, she didn't so much as flinch. Instead, she grinned as the flames seemed to be absorbed into her body.

"Cute," she said as she grabbed Kai's wrist. Her touch was scorching hot. "But fire is my domain, little cultivator."

With a casual flick of her wrist, she sent Kai flying across the clearing. He slammed into a tree with bone-crushing force, then slid to the ground in a crumpled heap.

Get up, Kai commanded his battered body. *Get up or you're dead.*

Slowly, agonizingly, he pushed himself to his feet. Blood trickled from the corner of his mouth, and he was pretty sure he had several broken ribs.

Jin Ling watched with a mix of amusement and grudging respect. "I'm impressed you can still stand. Ready to give up yet? I promise I'll make it quick."

"Not a chance." Kai spat out a mouthful of blood.

Jin Ling shrugged. "Your funeral." She raised her hand, and suddenly, the air around them became unbearably hot. "Crimson Inferno Cage."

Walls of flame sprang up around Kai in a tight circle. The heat was suffocating, making it hard to breathe. Sweat poured down his face as he looked for a way out. Kai closed his eyes as he focused on the flames, searching for any openings.

"Lightning Step!"

Kai eyes shot open as electricity crackled around his feet, and in a flash, he burst through the wall of flames; his clothes were smoking, but his body was largely unharmed thanks to Iron Skin.

"Wind, fire, and now lightning? But . . . how?" Jin Ling's eyes widened.

Kai disappeared once more and reappeared behind her, his hand covered with electricity. "Static Charge!"

His palm struck Jin Ling's back . . . and she didn't even flinch.

"Interesting," she mused, turning to face him. "I can tell you have the potential to be a powerful cultivator."

Before Kai could react, Jin Ling's hand shot out and grabbed his throat. She lifted him effortlessly, Kai's feet dangling above the ground.

"But potential isn't enough," she continued, her grip tightening. "You lack the time to grow."

Kai clawed at her hand, gasping for air. Black spots danced in his vision. *Can't . . . breathe . . .*

Just as Kai was about to lose consciousness, Jin Ling tossed him aside like a rag doll. He hit the ground hard, coughing and gulping in air.

"Get up," Jin Ling commanded. "I'm not done playing yet."

Kai pushed himself to his hands and knees, every movement agony. *I can't win. She's too strong, too fast. I need . . . I need a miracle.*

As if in answer to his desperate thought, a bolt of lightning split the sky overhead. The battle between the Nascent Soul cultivators was intensifying, their clash sending ripples of power through the air.

An idea began to form in Kai's mind. It was insane, probably suicidal, but it was all he had left. *I need more time to make this work . . .*

Slowly, painfully, Kai rose to his feet. Jin Ling watched with mild interest.

"Oh? Still have some fight left in you?" she asked, amused.

Kai didn't respond. Instead, he closed his eyes and focused on his remaining qi. Subtly, he began drawing in the ambient lightning energy from the air and channeling it high above them, where the chaos of the Nascent Soul battle would mask its presence.

"What are you planning now, little cultivator?" Jin Ling's eyes narrowed. "Another futile attack?"

Kai opened his eyes, a glint of determination shining through the pain. "Why don't you find out?"

"Bold words for someone barely standing. Fine, let's see what you've got," She dashed forward, her speed blurring her form. "Crimson Flame Whip!"

A long fiery whip materialized in her hand and lashed out toward Kai. He activated his Swift Wind Step, narrowly avoiding the scorching attack. The whip struck the ground where he had been standing, leaving a deep smoldering gash in the earth.

Kai reappeared a few meters away, panting heavily. *Just a little longer . . .*

"Flame Serpent Strike!"

She thrust her palm forward, and a massive snakelike stream of fire shot toward him.

A faint shimmering barrier of pure qi formed around Kai as the fiery serpent slammed into him. He gritted his teeth and poured more energy into the shield. When the attack finally dissipated, Kai's barrier was barely holding, but he was still standing.

Jin Ling looked genuinely surprised.

"You're more resilient than I thought," she admitted. "But how long can you keep this up?"

Not long enough, Kai thought grimly. He could feel his qi reserves depleting rapidly. His final attack was nearly ready, but he needed to buy just a bit more time.

"My turn," Kai said, trying to sound more confident than he felt. He reached into his storage ring and pulled out seven slender daggers.

"Nice toys you have there, little cultivator."

Kai didn't respond. Instead, he closed his eyes, concentrating intensely, and infused lightning qi into them. With a series of rapid gestures, Kai sent the daggers flying toward Jin Ling. Each blade moved in a complex, unpredictable pattern.

Jin Ling's eyebrows rose slightly, genuinely intrigued. She dodged gracefully, her body weaving between the daggers with inhuman speed.

"Not bad," she admitted as she easily evaded the attacks. "But you'll have to do better than that."

Suddenly, the daggers changed direction mid-flight. Instead of striking at Jin Ling directly, they embedded themselves in the ground around her, forming a perfect heptagon.

Before Jin Ling could react, arcs of lightning sprang between the daggers and formed a field of electricity. The air sizzled as the lightning cage closed in around her.

"Thunderbolt Prison," Kai gasped, sweat beading on his forehead from the effort of maintaining the technique.

For a moment, Jin Ling stood motionless within the lightning field, her expression unreadable. Then, a small smile played across her lips.

"Clever," she admitted. "Using real weapons as conduits . . . You're more resourceful than I gave you credit for." She reached out and touched one of the lightning arcs with her fingertip. The electricity sparked and flared but seemed unable to harm her. "But still," Jin Ling continued, her smile turning predatory, "far too weak."

With a casual wave of her hand, crimson flames erupted around her. The fire expanded outward, pushing against the lightning field. For a brief second, fire and lightning clashed in a spectacular display of light and energy. Then, with a sound like shattering glass, the lightning field broke. The daggers, overwhelmed by the intense heat, began to melt where they stood.

Jin Ling stepped out of the fading lightning cage, brushing an imaginary speck of dust from her shoulder. She looked almost bored.

"A valiant effort, little cultivator," she said, her voice dripping with condescension. "But now, let me show you true power. Crimson Phoenix Talons!"

Her hands became engulfed in intense flames shaped like the talons of a massive bird. She swooped down and raked fiery claws across Kai's qi barrier. The barrier shattered like glass, and Kai screamed as the flames seared his flesh. He was sent flying, crashing through several trees before coming to a stop.

Kai struggled to his feet, his body a mass of pain. Blood trickled from numerous cuts, and angry red burns covered his arms and chest.

Jin Ling landed gracefully, flames still dancing around her hands. "Had enough yet?"

Kai spat out another mouthful of blood. "Not . . . not even close," he gasped.

Jin Ling's eyes flashed with anger. "You're either incredibly brave or incredibly stupid. Let's find out which. Crimson Inferno!"

The air around them suddenly became unbearably hot. Flames erupted from the ground and formed a swirling vortex around Jin Ling. Trees caught fire, and the clearing became a raging inferno.

Kai felt the heat searing his skin, his clothes beginning to smolder. *Almost there . . . Just need to hold on a little longer . . .*

As the wall of flames rushed toward him, Kai's body took on a metallic sheen. The fire struck him with tremendous force, but instead of incinerating him, it rebounded.

Jin Ling's eyes widened in shock as her own flames rushed back at her. She raised her arms to defend herself, but the unexpected reversal caught her off guard. The rebounded fire struck her, sending her stumbling backward with a cry of pain and rage.

"You . . . you dare?" she snarled, her perfect composure finally cracking. Angry red burns marred her skin where her own flames had struck her.

The air around Jin Ling shimmered with heat. Her body began to glow, and suddenly, she was engulfed in flames shaped like a phoenix. The fiery bird screeched, the sound painfully loud.

"Crimson Phoenix Flames!"

The massive firebird spread its wings, the heat so intense that the very ground began to melt. The sheer power emanating from Jin Ling was overwhelming, scorching the air around them.

Kai stumbled back, but even as fear gripped his heart, a smile tugged at his lips. *It's ready.*

"Any last words, little cultivator?" Jin Ling asked, her voice echoing with power and fury.

Kai looked up, meeting her fiery gaze. "Just five," he said. "Thunder Voice: Lightning Hammer Strike!"

His voice, amplified and charged with lightning qi, boomed across the clearing. The sudden burst of sound caught Jin Ling off guard, making her flinch for just a crucial second.

In that moment of distraction, the massive hammer of pure lightning that Kai had been quietly forming throughout the battle came to life. It streaked down from the sky, moving faster than Jin Ling could react.

The hammer of lightning struck with devastating force. There was a blinding flash and a deafening boom that shook the entire clearing. For a moment, everything was obscured by a brilliant light and billowing smoke.

When the air cleared, there was nothing left of Jin Ling but a scorched crater in the ground where she had been standing.

Cultivator Jin Ling eliminated

+150 XP

+150 XP for eliminating a cultivator a realm higher

Kai collapsed to his knees as he stared at the smoking crater. He felt a burning sensation on his wrist and looked down to see the a second prong on his trident mark glowing brightly.

I did it, he thought, his mind struggling to process what had just happened. *I actually did it. I killed a Foundation Establishment cultivator.*

But there was no time for celebration. The sounds of battle still raged around him, reminding Kai that the fight was far from over.

With a groan, Kai turned to survey the battlefield. His body screamed in protest, every muscle aching, his qi reserves almost completely depleted. But he couldn't rest yet. His eyes found Shen Yu, who was kneeling beside the body of his fallen opponent.

Kai watched, curious, as Shen Yu's hand moved swiftly and retrieved something from the corpse. From this distance, Kai couldn't make out what it was, but he saw Shen Yu quickly tuck it away into his storage ring. Then, to Kai's surprise, Shen Yu gently closed the dead cultivator's eyes, his movements almost respectful.

As Shen Yu stood and turned, his eyes met Kai's. For a moment, Kai thought he saw a flicker of . . . something in Shen Yu's eyes. Surprise? Respect? Guilt? But before he could be sure, Shen Yu's face returned to its usual impassive mask.

"Well fought," Shen Yu said. "But the battle isn't over yet."

Kai nodded weakly, his vision blurring at the edges. The thought of facing another opponent, especially a Core Formation cultivator, made his stomach churn. He could barely stand, let alone fight.

"I . . . I can't fight anymore," Kai admitted, his voice hoarse. "I'm completely drained."

Shen Yu's eyes narrowed slightly, but there was a hint of understanding in his gaze. "Those Core Formation cultivators are beyond our current abilities. Even a glancing blow from one of them could be fatal."

Kai felt a mixture of relief and surprise at Shen Yu's admission. It was rare for the usually stoic disciple to acknowledge any weakness.

"What should we do?" Kai asked as he fought to stay conscious.

Shen Yu was silent for a moment, his eyes scanning the battlefield. Finally, he spoke. "There's a hill to the east. We should go there and keep watch. If we see any reinforcements coming, we can signal the others. That's how we can help without risking our lives needlessly."

Kai nodded. It wasn't much, but it was something they could actually do in their current state. "Let's . . . let's head there now."

When they reached the top of the hill, Kai turned to see how the others were faring.

Yin Mengshuang was still locked in combat, but her illusions were keeping the Crimson Phoenix cultivator off-balance. She seemed to be playing around with him. It wouldn't be long before he was killed. Qi Liaxuan also seemed to have the upper hand against his opponent, his strange time-altering techniques slowly wearing her down.

And high above it all, Wang Lin and the Nascent Soul Elder continued their titanic clash. The sky itself seemed to tremble with each exchange of blows.

As Kai watched, he couldn't help but feel a sense of awe. This was the power of true cultivators, the kind of strength he would one day have.

CHAPTER SEVENTY-ONE

Kai watched from the hilltop as the battles below reached their climax. His body ached from his own fight, but he couldn't look away from the scenes unfolding before him.

This is no battle, Kai thought as he watched the fight between Yin Mengshuang and Li Yuan. *It's a one-sided slaughter.*

As the silver threads tightened around Li Yuan's body, his struggles became more frantic. The Dream Binding Threads glowed ominously as they fed on his deepest fears and insecurities.

"No . . . Please . . ." Li Yuan gasped, his earlier bravado completely shattered.

Yin Mengshuang's smile was cruel, her eyes glittering with malicious glee. "What's this? A mighty Crimson Phoenix expert begging for mercy? How pathetic."

She made a sharp gesture with her hand, and the threads suddenly constricted. There was a sickening crunch of bones, and Li Yuan's body went limp, his life extinguished in an instant.

Yin Mengshuang looked down at her fallen opponent, a mix of satisfaction and disappointment on her face. "Well, that was fun while it lasted," she mused, casually brushing a strand of silver hair from her face. "Though, I expected more of a challenge from a Core Formation cultivator of the Crimson Phoenix Sect."

Kai felt himself grow pale. The casual cruelty of Yin Mengshuang's actions was chilling. It was something he would have only expected from a demonic cultivator.

"She's . . . terrifying," he muttered.

Beside him, Shen Yu nodded, his expression unreadable. "Yin Mengshuang is known for her sadistic streak. It's why many in the sect avoid her."

Kai turned his attention to the other battle, where Qi Liaxuan stood staring down Zhao Xiuying.

"This is where your journey ends," Qi Liaxuan said.

Zhao Xiuying struggled against the mental fog clouding her thoughts. Her eyes, once filled with purpose, now reflected only confusion and weariness.

"No . . . I can't . . . I won't give up," she muttered, her voice barely above a whisper. With tremendous effort, she began to gather her qi once more, flames flickering weakly around her hands.

Qi Liaxuan's eyes narrowed slightly. "I see you still cling to your defiance. Very well. Let me show you the true nature of the Flowing Abyss."

With a fluid motion, he extended his hand toward Zhao Xiuying. The air between them seemed to ripple and distort, as if reality itself was bending to his will.

"Eternal Flow Convergence."

Suddenly, Zhao Xiuying found herself unable to move. It wasn't that she was paralyzed—rather, time itself seemed to have stopped for her. She could see Qi Liaxuan approaching; his movements blurred as if he were existing in multiple moments simultaneously.

"What you experienced before was but a taste," Qi Liaxuan explained, his voice echoing strangely in the distorted space. "Now, you will truly understand the transient nature of existence."

He placed his palm on Zhao Xiuying's forehead. In that instant, she felt an overwhelming rush of sensations. She experienced a lifetime—no, multiple lifetimes—in the span of a heartbeat. Birth, growth, decay, death, rebirth—the endless cycle played out in her mind at dizzying speed.

"What's he doing?" Kai whispered, more to himself than to Shen Yu.

Shen Yu's eyes narrowed slightly. "He's using a Domain."

"A Domain?" Kai's eyes widened in surprise. "But I thought only cultivators above the Nascent Soul Realm could use those!"

Shen Yu shook his head slightly. "Normally, yes. But Qi Liaxuan's understanding of the Dao surpasses many Nascent Soul cultivators. He's managed to form a rudimentary Domain even at the Core Formation stage."

Zhao Xiuying's body began to change rapidly. Her hair cycled through black, gray, and white. Her skin smoothed and wrinkled, over and over. She aged and rejuvenated countless times in mere seconds.

Finally, as the technique reached its peak, Zhao Xiuying let out a final, agonized gasp. Her body, unable to withstand the strain of countless lifetimes compressed into a moment, simply . . . ceased to be. There was no explosion, no dramatic disintegration. One moment she was there, and the next, she was gone, leaving behind nothing but a faint shimmer in the air.

Qi Liaxuan lowered his hand, his face impassive. "And so, the cycle continues," he said, almost to himself. "May you find wisdom in your next incarnation, Zhao Xiuying."

Kai felt his stomach lurch. He'd seen death before, had even caused it himself, but this . . . this was something else entirely.

"She's . . . gone," Kai said, his voice barely above a whisper. "Just like that. No body, no ashes. Nothing."

He turned to Shen Yu, seeking some kind of reassurance or explanation. "Is this normal? For Core Formation cultivators to just . . . erase someone from existence?"

"Normal? No." Shen Yu shook his head. "But for someone who has truly grasped the Dao of the Flowing Abyss like Qi Liaxuan, it's possible. Within his Domain, he didn't just kill her body. He erased her very existence from this cycle of reincarnation."

"I knew cultivators were powerful, but this . . ." Kai shook his head, still struggling to find words. "It's like he rewrote reality itself."

Shen Yu's gaze drifted to the horizon, his eyes taking on a distant, almost wistful look. When he spoke, his voice was soft, as if he was speaking more to himself than to Kai.

"Qi Liaxuan is . . . special, even among Core Formation cultivators. His understanding of the Dao surpasses many Nascent Soul Realm experts, perhaps even Wang Lin himself. To form even a rudimentary Domain at his level . . . It's almost unheard of."

There was something in Shen Yu's tone that caught Kai's attention—a mix of admiration and what almost sounded like longing. He turned to look at his fellow disciple and was struck by the faraway expression on Shen Yu's face.

"The way he manipulates the flow of time and space," Shen Yu continued, his eyes still fixed on some distant point, "it's a glimpse of what true mastery of the Dao looks like. In time, he may reshape the very foundations of reality itself."

As Kai listened, he couldn't shake the feeling that Shen Yu wasn't just making assumptions.

Is Shen Yu describing Qi Liaxuan from . . . the future?

Shen Yu blinked as he seemed to come back to the present moment. He turned to Kai, his usual impassive mask sliding back into place. "You should focus on the battle above. You can learn a lot from the way Nascent Soul cultivators battle."

But before Kai could do that, he had a question he needed to ask. A question that had been nagging at him since their own fights ended.

"Hey, Shen Yu . . . What did you take from that cultivator you killed? I saw you grab something from the body."

Shen Yu's expression didn't change, but there was a slight pause before he answered. "Just some resources. It's standard practice to loot the bodies of fallen enemies. Don't tell me you've never done it?"

Kai didn't buy the excuse. There was something off about Shen Yu's response, a hint of evasiveness that set off alarm bells in his mind.

"Well, my Lightning Hammer Strike kind of . . . disintegrated her." Kai smiled wryly, thinking of his battle with Jin Ling. "Didn't leave much behind to loot."

"Ah," Shen Yu said. "That's . . . unfortunate. You should be more careful in the future. A cultivator's storage ring often contains valuable treasures and resources."

"I'll keep that in mind for next time."

Kai couldn't shake the feeling that his fellow disciple was hiding something. The way Shen Yu had carefully removed the item from the corpse, the slight hesitation before answering Kai's question . . . It all pointed to something more than simple looting.

Could Shen Yu have some connection to the Crimson Phoenix Sect? The idea seemed absurd at first—Shen Yu was a disciple of the Azure Sky Sect, after all. But then again, if Kai's suspicions about Shen Yu being a reincarnator or regressor were true, who knew what connections he might have had in a past life?

Could Shen Yu have been friendly with the Crimson Phoenix Sect in his previous existence? Was he trying to preserve some memento or information from his past? Or was it something even more sinister? Was Shen Yu playing both sides somehow?

He wanted to press further, to demand a more detailed explanation from Shen Yu. But he held back; he knew that if his suspicions were correct, confronting Shen Yu directly would lead nowhere and could even be dangerous.

Their conversation was cut short as a massive surge of qi rippled through the air. Both Kai and Shen Yu turned their attention back to the sky, where Wang Lin and Elder Bu were still locked in their titanic clash.

The elderly cultivator floated high in the air, his face contorted with rage and desperation. The bodies of his fallen comrades lay scattered across the battlefield below.

"You . . . you monsters!" he roared, his voice echoing across the clearing. "You'll pay for this! The Crimson Phoenix Sect will burn your precious Azure Sky Sect to the ground!"

Wang Lin faced him calmly, seeming unperturbed by the Elder's outburst. A small smile played on his lips.

"I think I'm done playing around, Elder Bu," Wang Lin said. "It's time to end this."

Elder Bu's eyes widened as Wang Lin raised his sword. The blade began to glow with an eerie black light.

"What . . . what are you doing?" Elder Bu demanded, a note of fear creeping into his voice.

Wang Lin didn't answer. Instead, his body began to shimmer and distort. To

Elder Bu's astonishment, Wang Lin's form seemed to merge with his sword as he became a being of pure shadow.

"Impossible," Elder Bu whispered. "What kind of technique is this?"

The shadow that was Wang Lin spoke, its voice echoing strangely. "This, Elder Bu, is the Shadow Sword Merge. A technique that can only be mastered by one who has achieved perfect unity with both their sword and their elemental affinity."

Elder Bu's mind raced. He'd never heard of such a technique before. How could someone so young have mastered something so advanced?

"You're bluffing," he said, trying to sound confident. "This is just some illusion, like that silver dream witch uses!"

The shadow chuckled, the sound sending chills down Elder Bu's spine. "Oh, I assure you, this is very real."

Suddenly, the shadow vanished. Elder Bu blinked, confused. Where had Wang Lin gone?

Then he felt a presence beside him. He turned and came face to face with the young Nascent Soul expert, who had reappeared out of thin air.

"How did you—" Elder Bu began, but his words cut off abruptly.

He felt . . . strange. Disconnected. He looked down and saw his own body standing there—without a head.

With growing horror, Elder Bu realized what had happened. His consciousness, somehow still intact, watched as his headless body toppled from the sky.

No! This can't be happening!

In a desperate attempt to survive, Elder Bu's consciousness retreated to his Nascent Soul. The glowing miniature version of himself emerged from his falling body, trying to flee. But Wang Lin was faster. His hand made a slashing motion, too quick for the eye to follow. The Nascent Soul split into a thousand glowing fragments, each one fading away like sparks from a dying fire.

As the last fragments of his existence faded away, Elder Bu's final thought was one of bitter regret. *I should have stayed home today . . .*

Wang Lin floated back down to the ground, his sword returning to its normal state.

"Well done, everyone. Now we need to make this look like the work of the Boundless Earth Sect."

"Ooh, a frame job!" Yin Mengshuang's eyes lit up. "This should be fun."

Qi Liaxuan merely nodded. "It will be done, Senior Brother. But won't they be able to sense our qi signatures?"

Wang Lin smiled as he reached into his storage ring. He pulled out a small, unassuming stone. "Not with this," he said. "It's a Qi Distortion Stone. It will mask our presence and make it appear as though Earth-attributed qi was used here."

He activated the stone, and a subtle ripple spread across the clearing. Kai watched in fascination as the very feel of the air seemed to change.

"This will also interfere with any scrying attempts by other sects," Wang Lin explained. "They'll see only what we want them to see."

The Core Formation cultivators nodded, impressed. They set about arranging the bodies and planting false evidence, working quickly and efficiently.

As they worked, Wang Lin turned to Kai and Shen Yu. "You two did well," he said, a note of approval in his voice. "Master wasn't wrong to choose you."

Kai felt a surge of pride at the praise, mixed with a healthy dose of relief. They'd survived—and, apparently, impressed Wang Lin in the process.

"Thank you, Senior Brother," Kai said, bowing slightly.

Wang Lin nodded. "We need to leave soon. The Boundless Earth Sect members will be arriving shortly, and we don't want to be here when they do."

As they prepared to depart, Kai couldn't help but feel a mix of emotions. Relief at having survived, pride at their success, but also a nagging unease. This mission had been far more intense and morally ambiguous than he'd expected.

The casual display of power he'd just witnessed had shaken him to his core. This, he realized, was the true face of cultivation. Beautiful, terrible, and utterly beyond his current comprehension.

He glanced at Shen Yu, wondering if his fellow disciple felt the same way. But Shen Yu's face was as unreadable as ever.

I really hope this is the end of it, Kai thought as he followed Wang Lin away from the battlefield. His eyes darted around nervously, half expecting another ambush or challenge to appear. *No more surprises, please. No secret cultivators waiting in the shadows, no last-minute twists. I've had enough excitement for one day . . .*

CHAPTER SEVENTY-TWO

As the sun began to peek over the horizon, a group of cultivators from the Boundless Earth Sect were still a few hundred kilometers away from the clearing. A tall man with a long gray beard, Elder Song, led the group.

"We should have been here hours ago," he grumbled. "This delay is unacceptable."

Beside him, a younger cultivator named Dong Xin nodded wearily. "That spatial tear was unlike anything I've ever seen, Elder. Do you think we should send word back to the sect about it?"

Elder Song's frown deepened. "Once we've concluded our business here, yes. Such anomalies are rare and dangerous. The Sect Master will want to know."

As they walked, the cultivators behind them muttered among themselves.

"I still can't believe we made it out," one whispered. "When that tear started pulling at us, I thought for sure we were done for."

Another nodded vigorously. "If it weren't for Elder Song's quick thinking with that earth barrier technique, we might all be lost in some twisted dimension right now."

Elder Song glanced back at them, his expression softening slightly. "You all performed admirably in the face of an unprecedented threat. Take pride in that. But now we must focus on the task at hand. Our delay may have already complicated matters with the Crimson Phoenix Sect."

The group fell silent at that. Sobered by the reminder of their mission, they pressed on.

As they neared their destination, a clearing in the heart of the forest, Elder Song suddenly held up a hand, signaling the group to stop. His eyes narrowed as he scanned the area ahead.

"Something's not right," he muttered. "Be on your guard."

Cautiously, they entered the clearing. What they saw made them freeze in their tracks.

The ground was littered with bodies, the unmistakable robes of the Crimson Phoenix Sect stained dark with blood.

"By the heavens," whispered one of the Core Formation cultivators, her hand flying to her mouth. "They're all dead!"

Elder Song nodded grimly. "Take a closer look at the ground around them."

Dong Xin looked more closely and gasped. The earth was torn and twisted, great furrows carved into the soil. In some places, jagged spikes of stone jutted out at odd angles.

"These . . . these are earth techniques," Dong Xin said, his voice shaking. "Our techniques."

"But that's impossible!" The female Core Formation cultivator's face paled. "We were delayed. We only just arrived!"

Elder Song's expression darkened. "This is bad. Very bad. We need to—"

His words were cut off by a sudden surge of powerful qi. The air shimmered as three figures materialized in the clearing. Their robes proudly showed off the emblem of the Crimson Phoenix Sect. The one in the center, an elderly man with a short white goatee, radiated an aura at the Peak Nascent Soul Realm.

"Song Huai!" the Crimson Phoenix Elder bellowed, his eyes blazing with fury. "What in the name of the heavens have you done?"

Elder Song stepped forward, his hands raised in a placating gesture. "Elder Hu, please, this isn't what it looks like—"

"Isn't what it looks like?" Elder Hu scoffed. "We rushed here the moment Elder Bu's soul lamp was extinguished, and what do we find? You and your Boundless Earth Sect disciples standing over the bodies of our fallen brothers and sisters!"

A scarred man, one of the other Nascent Soul cultivators flanking Elder Hu spoke up, his voice dripping with disdain. "Look at them, Elder Hu. They didn't even have the decency to flee the scene. Such arrogance!"

Elder Song's face paled. "No, you don't understand. We only just arrived ourselves. We were delayed by—"

"Delayed?" Elder Hu's qi flared. "Do you take us for fools, Song Huai? The evidence of your earth techniques is written all over this battlefield!"

Elder Song took a deep breath, trying to maintain his composure. "Elder Hu, please listen. We're being set up. Someone is trying to pit our sects against each other. If you'd just let me explain—"

His words were cut off by a rumbling from beneath their feet. The ground between the two groups suddenly burst upward, showering them with dirt and stones. As the dust settled, a figure emerged from the newly formed hole.

It was a young man, no more than twenty years old, with wild black hair and piercing violet eyes. Despite his youth, he radiated the unmistakable aura of a Nascent Soul cultivator. But there was something . . . off about him. His gaze was unfocused and darted around as if reading something only he could see.

"Another dead end," the young man muttered to himself, frowning at the empty air. "Are you sure the trail leads here? I'm not sensing any other System users."

The cultivators from both sects stared at the newcomer in bewilderment. The young man seemed oblivious to their presence as he continued his one-sided conversation.

"What do you mean, 'keep looking'? I've been searching for days! If your detection abilities are so great, why can't you pinpoint the exact location?"

Finally, Elder Hu cleared his throat loudly. "Young man, who are you? And what are you talking about?"

The youth's head snapped up, and his eyes focused on the group for the first time. A slow smile spread across his face, but it didn't reach his eyes. "Oh, hello there. I didn't see you. Tell me, does anyone here have a System?"

The cultivators exchanged confused glances. Dong Xin was the first to speak up. "A . . . system? What do you mean?"

The young man's smile widened. "You know, a System! A magical interface that shows you your stats, skills, and quests. Surely one of you must have one?"

Elder Song stepped forward, his brow furrowed. "Young man, I'm afraid we don't understand what you're talking about. Perhaps you could explain?"

The youth sighed dramatically. "It's simple, really. A System is like . . . a personal cultivation assistant. It helps you track your progress, gives you quests, and even provides rewards for completing tasks. Some are more advanced than others, of course. Mine is quite impressive, if I do say so myself."

He paused and cocked his head to the side as if listening to something. "What? No, I'm not bragging. I'm just explaining . . . Fine, fine, I'll ask them directly."

The young man turned back to the group, his violet eyes scanning each face intently. "So, none of you have experienced anything like that? No mysterious voices in your head? No floating screens showing your cultivation progress?"

The cultivators looked at each other, their expressions a mix of confusion and concern. The scarred man leaned close to his peers and whispered, "The poor boy has clearly lost his mind. It happens sometimes when one reaches the Nascent Soul Realm too young."

The other Nascent Soul cultivator accompanying Elder Hu, a flame-haired woman, nodded solemnly. "Such a waste. He must have been a prodigy to reach this level at his age."

The young man's eyes narrowed, having clearly heard their whispered conversation. "I assure you, I'm perfectly sane. But I can see you don't believe me. It doesn't matter, really. System or no System, it seems you all need to die now."

Before anyone could react, purple qi began to leak from the young man's body. It swirled around him and grew denser and more opaque until it completely engulfed him. Then it continued to expand, taking on a massive human-oid shape.

When the transformation was complete, the young man stood encased in a colossal purple construct easily twenty meters tall. It resembled an ancient warrior, complete with armor and a helm that obscured the youth's face.

"What . . . what is this?" gasped Dong Xin, stumbling backward.

Elder Hu gritted his teeth. "I've never seen anything like it. Even at my level, I've never encountered such a technique."

The young man's voice boomed from within the construct, tinged with amusement. "Oh, this? Just a little something my System cooked up for me. It's inspired by my favorite anime. Neat, isn't it?"

The Elders from both sects exchanged glances. Without a word, they seemed to come to an agreement. Whatever their differences, this new threat took precedence.

Elder Hu stepped forward, his qi flaring around him. "Young man, I don't know who you are or what your quarrel is with us, but I suggest you stand down. You may be powerful, but you face four Nascent Soul cultivators. You cannot hope to win, let alone survive."

The purple construct's head tilted slightly.

"Hmm, you might have a point there," the young man murmured. "But you know what I see when I look at you guys? Walking XP banks. Bags of loot just waiting to be cashed in." He chuckled, the sound disturbingly lighthearted. "And I can't have my payday running off, now, can I?"

Elder Song's brow furrowed in confusion. "XP banks? Loot? Payday? What in the name of the Heavenly Dao are you babbling about, boy?"

The young man ignored him and raised one massive purple hand. "So, let's set up the arena, shall we? Can't have a proper boss fight without walls! Domain Expansion!"

A wave of qi exploded outward from the construct, far more potent than should have been possible for an early Nascent Soul cultivator. It spread rapidly to form a rectangular prison of purple energy that enclosed the entire clearing.

"There," the young man said. "Now we can have some real fun. I'll even let you make the first move. Come on, show me what you've got!"

Elder Song glanced skyward, as if seeking answers from the heavens themselves. "What kind of dog-shit luck," he muttered under his breath, "do you need to have to run into a lunatic like this?" He shook his head. "If I survive this, I'm retiring to a nice quiet mountain. Far, far away from any of this nonsense."

CHAPTER SEVENTY-THREE

Formation Alpha!" Elder Hu barked to his fellow Crimson Phoenix cultivators. To the Boundless Earth Sect members, he called, "Support us however you can. We must work together to survive this!"

The three Crimson Phoenix cultivators took up positions around the purple construct. Elder Hu stood directly in front of it, while the flame-haired woman and the scarred man flanked it on either side.

"Crimson Phoenix Triad Formation!" Elder Hu roared.

Immediately, all three Nascent Soul cultivators burst into flames. The fires surrounding them grew and took the shape of three massive fiery birds. Elder Hu's phoenix was the largest, its wingspan easily matching the purple construct in size.

The young man's voice echoed from within his qi armor, sounding almost bored. "Oh, is that all? I expected something more impressive from a Peak Nascent Soul cultivator."

Elder Hu's eyes narrowed. "You'll soon learn not to underestimate the Crimson Phoenix Sect, boy. Now!"

At his command, all three phoenixes screeched and dive-bombed the purple construct. The heat they generated was so intense that the very air seemed to waver and distort.

Meanwhile, Elder Song saw an opportunity. "Quick!" he shouted to his disciples. "While he's distracted!"

The Boundless Earth cultivators began a series of complex hand signs. The ground beneath the purple construct suddenly liquefied, turning into a deep pit of quicksand. For a moment, it seemed their combined strategy might work. The construct sank up to its knees in the quicksand, while the phoenixes battered it from all sides.

But then, a chilling laugh emanated from within the purple armor. "Is that really the best you can do? I'm disappointed."

With a casual swipe of its massive hand, the construct batted away two of the phoenixes as if they were nothing more than annoying insects. As they crashed into the walls of the purple Domain, their fires sputtered out.

As for the quicksand, the construct simply stepped out of it. With each step, the earth hardened beneath its feet, leaving perfect footprints in the once-liquid ground. "A valiant effort," the young man's voice mocked, "but ultimately futile."

Elder Hu, still in his phoenix form, circled warily. "Who are you?" he demanded. "What do you want from us?"

The construct's helmet retracted to reveal the young man's face. He was smiling, but his eyes were cold. "Who am I? Just another cultivator seeking power. As for what I want . . ." He paused, cocking his head as if listening to something. "Ah, yes. I need to kill you all to gain points. Nothing personal, you understand. It's just business."

With that, the helmet snapped back into place, and the construct charged forward with frightening speed. Its fist, larger than a man, swung toward Elder Hu.

The Crimson Phoenix Elder barely managed to dodge the massive fist—it passed so close that he felt the rush of air. "Impossible," he muttered. "Such speed at that size . . ."

The other cultivators weren't idle. The Boundless Earth Sect members had recovered from their earlier shock and were now fully in the fight. Elder Song slammed his palm into the ground and caused sharp stone spikes, each as tall as a person, to erupt beneath the construct's feet. At the same time, Dong Xin wove a complex pattern in the air and created a swirling vortex of sand that engulfed the purple giant.

For a moment, it seemed their attacks might have an effect. The construct stumbled, its movements slowed by the sand and stone. But then a pulse of purple energy burst outward that shattered the stone spikes and dispersed the sandstorm.

"I'm afraid you'll have to do better than that," the young man's voice boomed.

The construct's arms suddenly elongated, stretching to impossible lengths. They shot toward Elder Song and Dong Xin with terrifying speed.

Elder Song's eyes widened, but his centuries of cultivation didn't fail him. He quickly slammed his palm into the ground. A thick wall of solid rock erupted from the earth and rose between him and the approaching hands. Simultaneously, he shouted, "Dong Xin, move!"

But Dong Xin was only a Core Formation cultivator—he wasn't fast enough. A massive hand wrapped around him and lifted him high into the air. The other hand smashed through Elder Song's hastily erected barrier. Chunks of rock flew in all directions as the wall crumbled. Elder Song leaped back, narrowly avoiding the grasping fingers.

"Impressive reflexes, old man," the young man's voice echoed. "But how long can you keep it up?"

Elder Song's hands flashed through a series of complex seals. The ground beneath the construct began to churn and rise, then formed into a giant stone fist that matched the construct's own in size. It swung upward, aiming for the construct's chin. But the purple giant simply caught the stone fist with its free hand and crushed it effortlessly.

Meanwhile, Dong Xin screamed in agony as purple energy flowed down the construct's arm and enveloped him. His qi was being forcibly extracted from his body.

"Dong Xin!" Elder Song cried out, his face contorted with anguish. He flew forward, but before he could reach his disciple, the construct's other hand finally caught him midair, wrapping around his torso.

Elder Song struggled fiercely; his Nascent Soul cultivation allowed him to resist the draining effect far longer than Dong Xin. He managed to free one arm and slammed his palm against the construct's fingers. Cracks appeared in the purple armor, spreading rapidly.

For a moment, it seemed he might break free. But then the young man's voice rang out, "Enough of this!"

The purple energy intensified, becoming almost blinding. Elder Song's struggles weakened, his face paling as his life force was rapidly drained.

"Stop this madness!" Elder Hu roared as he dove toward the construct in his phoenix form.

But he was too late. By the time he reached them, Elder Song and Dong Xin were nothing more than withered husks, all of their life force drained away. The construct casually tossed their remains aside, where they landed with dull thuds among the debris of the battle.

"Ah, much better," the young man sighed. "The Nascent Soul cultivator's qi was particularly . . . invigorating."

The female Boundless Earth member fell to her knees in shock. "You . . . you monster!"

The construct turned toward her, its featureless helm somehow managing to convey amusement. "Monster? I prefer to think of myself as efficient."

The remaining cultivators regrouped, their faces dark. They knew now that they faced no ordinary opponent. This was a battle for survival.

Elder Hu addressed the other elders. "We must use our trump cards. It's our only hope."

The flame-haired woman nodded. "Agreed, though it may cut off any chance of advancement."

The scarred man cracked his knuckles. "Better to burn out in a blaze of glory than be drained like those poor fools."

Their only option was to use a forbidden technique that would burn up their very essence for a moment of ultimate power.

As one, the three Crimson Phoenix cultivators began to chant. The air around them started to shimmer with heat and their bodies to glow with an inner fire.

The young man in the construct seemed to realize what they were planning. For the first time, a note of concern entered his voice. "Oh? What's this, now? System, analyze their technique!"

But before he could react further, the three completed their chant. Their bodies erupted into pillars of white-hot flame, so bright that it was painful to look at directly. The light faded, and where they had stood now hovered a single massive phoenix. Its feathers were made of living flame, and its eyes burned with the combined will of the three cultivators.

The phoenix opened its beak and spoke with their blended voices. "Now, abomination, face the true power of the Crimson Phoenix Sect!"

The massive firebird dive-bombed the purple construct, its talons extended. This time when they clashed, the construct was actually forced back, its feet leaving deep furrows in the earth.

"Impressive!" the young man's voice called out, sounding genuinely excited for the first time. "Now this is more like it! Show me what you've got!"

The battle that followed was nothing short of cataclysmic. The phoenix and the construct traded blows that shook the very foundations of the earth. Each impact sent shockwaves of qi rippling through the air that scorched the ground and uprooted trees. Without the purple Domain surrounding them, the collateral damage would have leveled mountains.

For a while, it seemed that the phoenix might actually win. Its relentless assault pushed the construct back, step by step. Cracks began to appear in the purple qi armor, and the young man's voice grew strained.

"System!" he shouted. "I need more power! Divert all non-essential functions!"

Whatever response he received seemed to satisfy him. The construct's eyes flared with a brighter purple light, and its movements became even faster, more fluid.

The tide of the battle slowly began to turn. The construct's blows landed more frequently, each one chipping away at the phoenix's fiery form. The great firebird's attacks, while still devastatingly powerful, began to slow.

Finally, with a mighty two-handed swing, the construct smashed the phoenix into the ground. The impact was so great that the female Core Formation cultivator observing the battle was thrown off her feet, despite being at the edge of the clearing.

When the dust settled, the phoenix was gone. In its place lay the three Crimson Phoenix cultivators, their bodies broken and burnt almost beyond recognition. They still lived, but only barely, their chests rising and falling with shallow, labored breaths.

The construct stood over the fallen Crimson Phoenix Sect members, its purple glow dimmed but still intimidating. The helmet retracted once more to reveal the young man's face. He was breathing heavily, and a thin trickle of blood ran from his nose.

"Well," he panted, "that was certainly exciting. You actually made me work for it. I'm impressed."

He looked down at the fallen cultivators, a hint of respect in his eyes. "It's almost a shame to finish you off. You'd make excellent training dummies." He paused and tilted his head as if listening to something. "What? No, I'm not getting sentimental. I'm just saying . . . Fine, fine. I'll end it quickly."

The construct's massive foot rose and hovered over the helpless cultivators before it came crashing down. There was a sickening crunch, and the once-mighty Crimson Phoenix Sect members were no more.

The young man turned his attention to the female Boundless Earth Sect member, who stood frozen in terror. Her robes, once a pristine brown with green trim, were now stained with dirt and the blood of her fallen comrades. "Your turn, lady. Any last words?"

The woman's eyes darted around frantically as she searched for an escape that didn't exist. Her mouth opened and closed, but no sound came out. Her gaze was fixed on the purple giant looming over her, its power beyond anything she had ever encountered.

"No?" the young man said with a malicious grin. "Well, that makes this easier."

The construct's hand shot out faster than the cultivator could blink. In an instant, she found herself engulfed in a sickly purple glow. A scream caught in her throat as her qi, her very life force, was drained away. She tried to struggle, to summon her qi, but it slipped through her control like sand.

In a few moments, all that remained of the once-proud Core Formation expert was a withered husk, her face frozen in an expression of horror and disbelief. The construct casually tossed her remains aside, where they landed with a dull thud among the bodies of her fallen sect mates.

With all the cultivators defeated, the young man dispelled his construct. The purple qi receded, leaving him standing alone in the devastated clearing. He surveyed the carnage around him, a satisfied smile on his face.

"Mission complete," he announced to the empty air. "Now, let's see about those rewards." His smile quickly faded, replaced by a frown. "What do you mean, the rewards are lower than expected? I just took out multiple Nascent Soul cultivators! That should be worth a fortune in XP!" The young man began to pace, gesticulating wildly. "This is ridiculous! Do you know how much effort I put into this mission? And you're telling me the payoff is subpar? Yes, yes, I know you promised there'd be a lot more rewards if you got an upgrade," he said, rolling his eyes. "But how am I meant to find this other System user? I already used up the Resonance Compass, and that was my last one!"

He kicked at a pebble, sending it skittering across the blood-stained ground. "If you want me to find System users, why are you so stingy with giving me items that find them? It doesn't make any sense!" The young man's voice rose in frustration. "And what's with all these rules you have to follow? These arbitrary limitations? They just hold us back! We could be so much more efficient if you'd just . . . What? No, I'm not questioning your superiority. I'm just saying there's room for improvement!"

He continued his rant, gesticulating wildly at the empty air. To any observer, it would have appeared as if he was arguing with an invisible entity. His behavior was erratic, almost manic.

"It's strange, you know," he mused, his tone suddenly contemplative. "These rules you have to follow . . . They seem like they were designed to create conflict, to drive the plot of some cosmic story." He shook his head, chuckling darkly. "But that would be absurd, wouldn't it?"

Finally, the young man seemed to deflate, his shoulders sagging in defeat. "Fine," he sighed. "I'll save up more credits and buy another Resonance Compass soon. But this upgrade better be worth it, System. I'm getting tired of these wild goose chases."

He cast one last look around the clearing, his eyes devoid of any emotion as they swept over the bodies of those he had so casually slaughtered. "What a waste," he muttered. "All this power, and not a single System user among them."

The ground beneath his feet began to liquefy. The young man sank into the earth as if it were water.

"This upgrade better be worth it."

And with that, he was gone. The soil sealed seamlessly behind him, leaving no trace of his passage.

CHAPTER SEVENTY-FOUR

Zhi-Zhi stood outside Cang Long's cave, his tiny shell quivering as he gazed up at the darkening sky. He knew what was coming—his Foundation Establishment tribulation.

What if my shell isn't strong enough? What if the lightning cracks it open like an egg? Zhi-Zhi's thoughts raced, each more terrifying than the last.

He took a deep breath, trying to calm down. "Okay," he muttered to himself, "I can do this. I'm not fighting anyone. It's not a battle. It's just . . . standing still while the sky tries to kill me."

He paused, realizing his pep talk wasn't very encouraging.

"No, no, that's not right," he said, shaking his head. "It's a test. A test of my defenses. And defense is what I do best, right? I'm a tortoise! The most defensive creature in the world!"

As if in response to his words, a deafening roar echoed from inside the cave. Zhi-Zhi jumped, his shell clattering against the ground.

"Master?" he squeaked, peering into the darkness of the cave.

"It's time, my disciple! Show the heavens what you're made of!" Cang Long's voice boomed out.

Zhi-Zhi gulped. There was no turning back now. He closed his eyes and focused on the qi flowing through his body. He could feel it—the barrier between the Qi Refining Realm and the Foundation Establishment Realm. He was already teetering on the edge, halfway there. This tribulation would push him over, helping him build his first Foundation pillar.

Here goes nothing.

With a mental push, Zhi-Zhi released the restraint on his qi. It surged forward and broke past the barrier as it rushed into the Foundation Establishment Realm. The moment it did, thunder roared from the heavens so loudly that it shook the ground beneath him.

Zhi-Zhi's eyes snapped open, and he gasped at the sight above him. The clouds were swirling and merging together into a shape. Not just any shape—a tortoise. A massive tortoise made entirely of clouds.

It was similar to Zhi-Zhi in many ways, but the differences were striking. Its shell was more defined with intricate patterns etched into the cloudy surface. Its limbs were longer and ended in sharp, dangerous-looking claws. The head was larger with a more pronounced beak.

Is that . . . is that what I'll look like if I succeed?

The thought filled Zhi-Zhi with a mix of excitement and terror. He wanted to grow stronger, to become more impressive. But the idea of changing so much . . . It was scary.

Inside the cave, Cang Long watched the proceedings with keen interest. His massive form shifted as he nodded approvingly at the sight of the cloud tortoise.

Ah, the tribulation of a spirit beast. So different from that of human cultivators, yet no less challenging.

For spirit beasts like Zhi-Zhi and himself, breakthroughs were less about comprehending the Dao and more about refining their bloodline. With each realm they conquered, their blood became purer, closer to that of their immortal ancestors. It was a process of transformation, of becoming more like the legendary creatures they descended from.

Zhi-Zhi is fortunate. As a Spirit Shell Tortoise, he already possesses a noble lineage. It will make him stronger than other tortoises at the same cultivation level, and his journey should be smoother.

A flicker of movement caught Cang Long's eye. The cloud tortoise was moving, its massive head turning toward Zhi-Zhi. Cang Long's eyes narrowed. The tribulation was beginning.

Outside, Zhi-Zhi watched in terror as the cloud tortoise's eyes fixed on him. There was a moment of stillness, a calm before the storm. Then, without warning, a bolt of lightning shot from the tortoise's mouth.

Zhi-Zhi didn't think. He acted on pure instinct and retreated into his shell as fast as he could. The lightning struck a heartbeat later.

The world exploded into light and sound. The ground shook violently, and for a terrible moment, Zhi-Zhi thought his shell would crack. But it held.

As the light faded and the rumbling subsided, Zhi-Zhi cautiously poked his head out. He was still in one piece.

"I . . . I did it? I survived the first strike!"

Before he could celebrate further, he felt a strange sensation. Some of the energy from the tribulation was seeping into his body, changing him ever so slightly. His shell felt a bit heavier, his limbs a bit stronger. When he looked at his claws, he noticed they were just a tiny bit longer and sharper.

I'm changing. Becoming more like that tortoise in the sky . . .

But there was no time to dwell on these changes. The sky rumbled again, and Zhi-Zhi looked up to see the cloud tortoise preparing another attack.

This time, instead of lightning, a stream of fire poured from its mouth. Zhi-Zhi yelped and ducked back into his shell, bracing for impact. The heat was intense as it washed over his shell in waves. Zhi-Zhi could feel his shell heating up, but it didn't burn. As the flames died down, he emerged. Smoke rose from his shell, but otherwise he was unharmed.

"Zhi-Zhi!" Cang Long's voice boomed from the cave. "Remember your training! Use the Shell Reinforcement technique!"

Zhi-Zhi nodded and gathered his qi. He focused on channeling it into his shell and creating a protective layer. Just in time too—the next attack came in the form of sharp stone spikes raining down from the sky. They clattered against his reinforced shell, unable to penetrate. Zhi-Zhi allowed himself a small smile. *Maybe I can do this after all.*

But the tribulation was far from over. The attacks came one after another, each testing a different aspect of Zhi-Zhi's defenses.

Next came a massive gust of wind so powerful that it threatened to lift Zhi-Zhi off the ground. He dug his claws into the earth, desperately trying to anchor himself.

"Stone Stance!" Cang Long instructed. "Make yourself as heavy as a mountain!"

Zhi-Zhi focused on this other technique he had learned during his training. He channeled his qi downward as he imagined roots growing from his body into the earth. Gradually, he felt himself becoming heavier, more stable. The wind howled around him, but Zhi-Zhi held his ground.

A torrent of water then tried to sweep him off the mountain. Zhi-Zhi used his newly strengthened limbs to stand firm against the current.

With each attack, Zhi-Zhi felt himself changing, growing stronger. His shell became harder, his claws sharper, his mind clearer. The energy of the tribulation was refining him, purifying his bloodline.

Through it all, Cang Long's voice guided him, reminding him of techniques they'd practiced.

As the eighth attack faded—a barrage of icy spears that shattered against his shell—Zhi-Zhi felt a sense of accomplishment. *I've almost done it. Just one more to go!*

But when he looked up at the cloud tortoise, his newfound confidence wavered. The massive creature was moving, no longer content to attack from afar. It was diving straight toward him, its cloudy form growing larger by the second.

Zhi-Zhi's eyes widened in terror. "M-Master?" he called out, his voice shaking. "What do I do?"

Cang Long's reply was calm, filled with confidence in his disciple. "Stand your ground, little one. Your shell is your greatest weapon and your strongest defense. Trust in it. Trust in yourself."

Zhi-Zhi wanted to run, to hide, to do anything but stand there as the giant tortoise descended upon him. But he forced himself to stay put, drawing on every ounce of courage he possessed.

He closed his eyes and focused all his qi into his shell. *I am a Spirit Shell Tortoise*, he told himself. *My shell is impenetrable. I am strong. I can do this.*

The cloud tortoise crashed into him like a meteor. For a moment, Zhi-Zhi thought he would be crushed. But then, to his amazement, the cloudy form enveloped him instead. It was like being swallowed whole; everything went dark, and he felt as if he was floating in a vast empty space.

Then, suddenly, pure unfiltered energy poured into him from all sides and filled every part of his being. It was overwhelming, almost painful in its intensity. But beneath the discomfort, Zhi-Zhi could feel himself changing, evolving.

His shell hardened and expanded. His limbs grew stronger. He could feel his very essence being refined and purified by the tribulation energy.

Cang Long watched as the cloud tortoise swallowed his disciple. The massive creature looked satisfied, even smug. It let out a loud burp, cloudy wisps escaping its mouth.

For a moment, nothing happened. Then, the cloud tortoise began to bulge oddly. Its form shimmered and wavered like a mirage in the desert. Suddenly, with a sound like thunder, the cloud tortoise exploded outward. As the cloudy fragments dissipated, they revealed Zhi-Zhi standing tall and proud.

But this wasn't the Zhi-Zhi who had started the tribulation. This Zhi-Zhi was larger, his shell more defined and patterned. His limbs were longer and ended in sharper claws. His head was slightly bigger, and an aura of power rolled off him—the unmistakable aura of Early Foundation Establishment.

As Zhi-Zhi stood there, the wind around him started to move strangely. It swirled gently, as if drawn to him. Small pebbles and bits of dirt near his feet trembled and shifted slightly. He could feel the wind and earth responding to him in a way they never had before. It was like they were saying hello to their new friend.

"Well done, little one! You've successfully entered the Foundation Establishment Realm!" Cang Long's face split into a wide grin. He lumbered out of the cave, each step causing mini earthquakes. When he reached Zhi-Zhi, he extended one massive claw and gently patted his disciple on the shell. "How do you feel?"

Zhi-Zhi looked up at his master, his eyes wide with wonder. "I feel . . . different. Stronger. Like I could move a mountain if I wanted to."

Cang Long chuckled. "That's the power of Foundation Establishment. But don't get too ahead of yourself. Moving mountains comes much later."

Zhi-Zhi nodded, still in awe at his new form. He flexed his claws, feeling the increased strength in them. "Master, was your Foundation Establishment tribulation like this too?"

A gleam entered Cang Long's eye, one that Zhi-Zhi had come to recognize. It meant a story was coming.

"Oh, my tribulation?" Cang Long said, puffing up his massive chest. "Well, let me tell you, it was quite the spectacle. The sky turned completely black, and not just any black—it was so dark it seemed to swallow light itself!"

Zhi-Zhi settled in, knowing this could take a while. But for once, he didn't mind. He was too excited about his breakthrough to be annoyed by his master's boasting.

"Lightning rained down like never before. Each bolt was as thick as a mountain and hot enough to melt stone! The ground shook so much, it created new valleys and mountains!"

"Really?" Zhi-Zhi asked, his eyes wide. "That sounds . . . intense."

"Oh, it was." Cang Long nodded sagely. "But that wasn't even the hardest part. No, the real challenge came when the tribulation took the form of a dragon. It was so large, its body wrapped around the entire mountain range three times!"

"A dragon?" Zhi-Zhi's jaw dropped. "But . . . but I thought tribulations took the form of your own species?"

Cang Long winked. "Normally, yes. But I'm no ordinary tortoise, am I? I'm a Dragonback Tortoise. The dragon in my bloodline recognized its kin and manifested accordingly."

"Wow," Zhi-Zhi breathed. "So, what happened next?"

"Well," Cang Long said, settling into his storytelling groove, "the dragon attacked with all five elements at once. Fire hot enough to vaporize oceans, water pressure that could crush mountains, wind sharp enough to cut through the hardest materials, lightning that could split the sky, and earth that could reshape continents."

Zhi-Zhi listened. Part of him wondered if his master was exaggerating. But another part, the part that had just experienced the awesome power of a tribulation, couldn't help but believe every word.

"And you survived all that?" Zhi-Zhi asked.

Cang Long nodded proudly. "Not only survived but thrived! I absorbed the energy of each attack and grew stronger with every moment. By the end, I had grown to twice my original size!" He leaned in close, his voice dropping to a whisper. "Want to know the secret of how I did it?"

Zhi-Zhi nodded eagerly.

"The key," Cang Long said, tapping his shell, "is to never doubt yourself. Believe in your strength, in your bloodline, in your destiny. The tribulation isn't just a test of your body, but of your spirit. If you waver, you fail. But if you stand firm, nothing can break you."

Zhi-Zhi absorbed these words, feeling their truth resonate within him. Hadn't he done exactly that during his own tribulation? When he stopped doubting and started believing in himself, he had succeeded.

"Thank you, Master. I'll remember that."

"Good. Now, tell me about your experience. What did it feel like inside the cloud tortoise?"

The two tortoises, master and disciple, spent the rest of the day discussing cultivation, tribulations, and the path that lay ahead.

CHAPTER SEVENTY-FIVE

Kai breathed a sigh of relief as he stepped through the gates of the Azure Sky Sect. *No ambushes, no last-minute twists. Maybe I was worried for nothing.*

As they walked through the sect grounds, Kai noticed some curious glances from other disciples. He realized he must look tense and on edge compared to the others.

"You okay there, Kai?" Yin Mengshuang asked, raising an eyebrow. "You look like you're expecting an attack at any moment."

Kai forced himself to relax. "Just leftover adrenaline from the mission, I guess."

Yin Mengshuang laughed. "Relax, we're home now. Save that energy for training."

Wang Lin, who had been walking ahead of them, turned back. "Speaking of which, we need to report to the Sect Master. Follow me."

As they made their way to the Sect Master's quarters, Kai couldn't help but feel a mix of pride and nervousness. They had completed their mission successfully, but facing the Sect Master always made him a bit uneasy.

The group arrived at a grand building near the peak of the highest mountain. Two guards stood at attention outside.

Wang Lin nodded to the guards, who bowed respectfully and opened the doors.

Sect Master Luo Qiang sat behind a massive desk; his eyes held a hint of something Kai couldn't quite place. Anticipation? Worry?

"Welcome back," the Sect Master said. "I trust your mission was successful?"

Wang Lin stepped forward and bowed. "Yes, Master. We completed our objectives as planned."

"Excellent. Give me a full report."

Kai listened as Wang Lin recounted the events of their mission. He described the ambush, the battles with the Crimson Phoenix cultivators, and how they set up the scene to frame the Boundless Earth Sect.

"The two junior disciples performed better than expected," Wang Lin said.

"Shen Yu defeated his opponent with ease. But Kai . . ." Wang Lin paused, a hint of surprise in his voice. "Kai managed to defeat a Foundation Establishment cultivator despite being at the Qi Refining stage."

Kai saw the Sect Master's eyes widen slightly at this. There was a flash of something in Luo Qiang's gaze, but it disappeared before Kai could identify it.

"Is that so?" Luo Qiang said, his gaze fixed on Kai. "That's quite an accomplishment. Well done."

"Thank you, Sect Master." Kai bowed. "I was merely fortunate to find a weakness in my opponent's defense."

The Sect Master nodded, then turned his attention back to Wang Lin. "And there were no complications? No witnesses or unexpected arrivals?"

"None, Sect Master," Wang Lin replied confidently. "We left the scene exactly as planned. By now, the Boundless Earth Sect should have discovered the bodies, and tensions between them and the Crimson Phoenix Sect should be rising."

"Excellent work, all of you." Luo Qiang smiled, clearly satisfied. "This will give us the advantage we need in the coming conflict. I'll keep you updated on the situation and let you know when we're ready to make our next move. For now, rest and prepare yourselves. War is coming, and we must be ready."

Just as they were turning to leave, a sharp beeping sound filled the air. Everyone froze, then turned to look at the Sect Master. Luo Qiang frowned as he reached into his robes to pull out a glowing communication token.

"What is it?" he asked sharply after activating the token.

A panicked voice came through, loud enough for everyone to hear. "Sect Master! We have a problem! The Boundless Earth Sect members and the cultivators sent by the Crimson Phoenix Sect to investigate their missing members—they're all dead!"

Kai felt his blood run cold. *What? How is that possible?*

The voice continued, growing more frantic. "They were killed by a young Early Nascent Soul cultivator. Witnesses describe him as being in his early twenties. The only known cultivator fitting that description is—"

"Wang Lin," Luo Qiang finished, his voice tight with anger.

Kai glanced at Wang Lin and saw shock and confusion on his face. *He didn't do it. We left before the others arrived. But who could have . . . ?*

The voice on the communication token confirmed their fears. "Both sects are blaming us, Sect Master. They've . . . they've officially declared war on the Azure Sky Sect."

The room fell silent as the weight of those words crushed down on all present. Kai felt his heart racing. This was far worse than he had imagined.

Luo Qiang's face hardened. "Understood. Activate our defensive arrays immediately. Alert all sect Elders and have them report to me at once. Recall any disciples on outside missions. Send word to all our allies—we'll need every bit of support we can get. We move to a war footing as of now."

"Yes, Sect Master!" the voice replied before the communication cut off.

Luo Qiang turned to face them. "It seems our plans have been complicated by an unknown party. Wang Lin, I sent you to ensure there were no issues. It appears that was my mistake."

Kai watched as Wang Lin's face darkened. It was clear he had never experienced failure before, and the sting of the Sect Master's disappointment was palpable.

"I . . . I apologize, Sect Master," Wang Lin said, his voice tight with barely contained fury. "I take full responsibility for this failure. Please, allow me to lead the counterattack. I'll make sure that those responsible pay for their actions."

Luo Qiang shook his head. "No, Wang Lin. Your skills will be needed here. The Crimson Phoenix and Boundless Earth Sects will likely bring the fight to our doorstep. If we go on the offensive now, we'll leave ourselves vulnerable to attack."

The Sect Master stood, his presence seeming to fill the entire room. "Everyone, prepare for battle. We have less than twenty-four hours before the first wave of attacks begins. Wang Lin, gather the other Nascent Soul cultivators and begin strengthening our defensive formations. Yin Mengshuang, Qi Liaxuan, I want you to organize the Core Formation and Foundation Establishment disciples. Make sure they're ready to support our main forces or evacuate if necessary."

As the others bowed and turned to leave, Luo Qiang's gaze fell on Kai and Shen Yu. "You two have shown great potential. Kai, your defeat of a Foundation Establishment cultivator proves you're ready for more responsibility."

Kai straightened, expecting to be assigned to the alchemy department. It would be a safe role away from the front lines. He could contribute without putting himself in too much danger. But the Sect Master's next words shattered that hope.

"Kai, I want you to form your own team. You'll be one of the groups targeting key Qi Refining and Foundation Establishment weaknesses in the enemy's defenses."

Kai's eyes widened in shock. "Sect Master, I . . . I don't understand. Wouldn't I be more useful in the alchemy department? My skills—"

Luo Qiang shook his head, cutting off Kai's protest. "Any alchemist can brew potions, Kai. But your skills will be best put to use during battle. You've proven you can handle yourself against stronger opponents. We need that on the front lines."

This wasn't what Kai had expected at all. He had thought he'd found a safe niche for himself, a way to contribute without risking his life directly. Now he was being thrown right into the thick of the fighting.

"But, Sect Master," Kai tried again, his voice wavering slightly, "I'm still only at the Qi Refining stage. Surely there are others more qualified—"

"Others who haven't defeated a Foundation Establishment cultivator," Luo Qiang interrupted, his voice firm. "You have a unique perspective, Kai. You see weaknesses others might miss. That's what we need out there."

Kai swallowed hard as he realized there was no way out of this. He bowed deeply, trying to hide the fear in his eyes. "I . . . I understand, Sect Master."

"Shen Yu," Luo Qiang continued, "you're in charge of organizing the Qi Refining cultivators. Report to Wang Lin. He'll be there to mentor you."

"Understood, Sect Master," Shen Yu replied.

As they all filed out of the Sect Master's quarters, Kai couldn't help but feel overwhelmed. Everything had changed so quickly. What should have been a successful mission had turned into the prelude to all-out war.

He glanced at Shen Yu, hoping to see some reaction from his usually stoic fellow disciple. To his surprise, he caught a fleeting look of excitement in Shen Yu's eyes before it vanished behind his usual mask of indifference.

What was that about? Is he actually looking forward to this war?

As they walked down the mountain path, the sect was already a flurry of activity. Disciples rushed back and forth carrying messages and supplies. It seemed that word about the war had already spread.

Yin Mengshuang broke the silence. "Well, this is going to be fun," she said, her voice dripping with sarcasm. "Nothing like a good old-fashioned sect war to liven things up."

Qi Liaxuan shook his head. "War is never something to be taken lightly, Mengshuang. Many lives will be lost in the coming days."

"I know that," she snapped back. "But what else can we do but face it head-on? I'd rather laugh than cry about it."

Wang Lin, who had been silent since leaving the Sect Master's quarters, suddenly spoke up. "We need to focus on our tasks. There's no time for idle chatter. Yin Mengshuang, Qi Liaxuan, gather the disciples as the Sect Master ordered. Shen Yu, come with me. We need to start planning our defensive strategies immediately."

As the others dispersed, Kai found himself alone, his mind reeling from the sudden change in his role. He knew he needed to start forming his team, but the weight of the responsibility was crushing.

A war. We're actually going to war. And I'm supposed to lead a team into battle. What are my chances of surviving this?

Just then, a hand clapped down on his shoulder, making him jump. He turned to see Elder Xiao, the head of the alchemy department, standing behind him.

"There you are, Disciple Kai," Elder Xiao said, his usually jovial face serious. "I heard about your assignment. It's not what any of us expected, but if anyone can do it, it's you. Come with me. Let's discuss what kind of supplies your team will need. You may not be working in the alchemy department, but we'll make sure you're well equipped for what's ahead. I can't have you die anytime soon, boy."

Kai nodded, grateful for the Elder's support. If he was going to lead his guild into battle, he'd make damn sure they were as prepared as possible.

I might not have wanted this role, but I'm going to do everything in my power to keep my team alive.

ABOUT THE AUTHOR

Kalzara is the author of the Demonic Sect Elder series, originally released on Royal Road. He is an avid reader of LitRPG and cultivation novels so it was only a matter of time before he decided to write one of his own.

RESPAWN YOUR CURIOSITY

follow us on our socials

 podiumentertainment.com

 @podiumentertainment

 /podiumentertainment

 @podium_ent

 @podiumentertainment